HOUSECAT TROUBLE

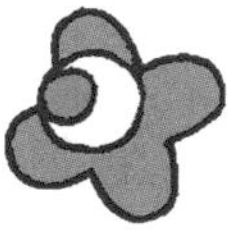

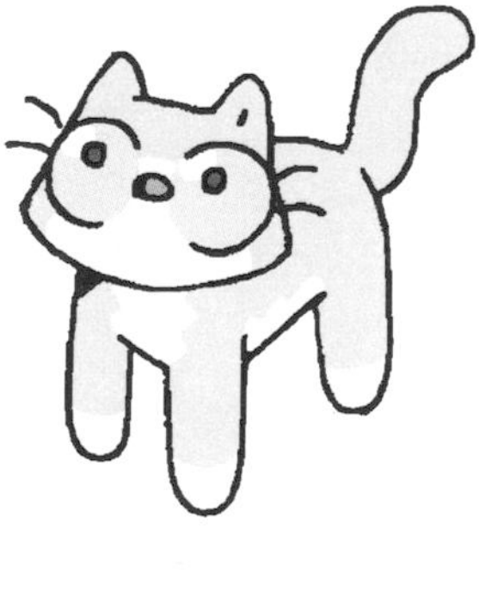

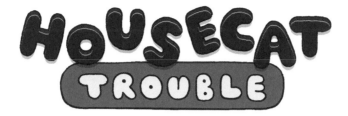

HOUSECAT TROUBLE WAS DRAWN ON
8.5" × 14" 110LB INDEX PAPER WITH
SAKURA PIGMA MICRON PENS AND
THEN COLORED DIGITALLY WITH
CLIP STUDIO PAINT.

Text, cover art, and interior illustrations copyright © 2022 by Mason Dickerson

All rights reserved. Published in the United States by RH Graphic, an imprint of Random House Children's Books, a division of Penguin Random House LLC, New York.

RH Graphic with the book design is a trademark of Penguin Random House LLC.

Visit us on the web! RHKidsGraphic.com • @RHKidsGraphic

Educators and librarians, for a variety of teaching tools, visit us at RHTeachersLibrarians.com

Library of Congress Cataloging-in-Publication Data is available upon request.
ISBN 978-0-593-17345-9 (hardcover) — ISBN 978-0-593-17346-6 (lib. bdg.)
ISBN 978-0-593-17347-3 (ebook)

Designed by Patrick Crotty

PRINTED IN THE UNITED STATES
10 9 8 7 6 5 4 3
First Edition

A comic on every bookshelf.

HOUSECAT TROUBLE

MASON DICKERSON

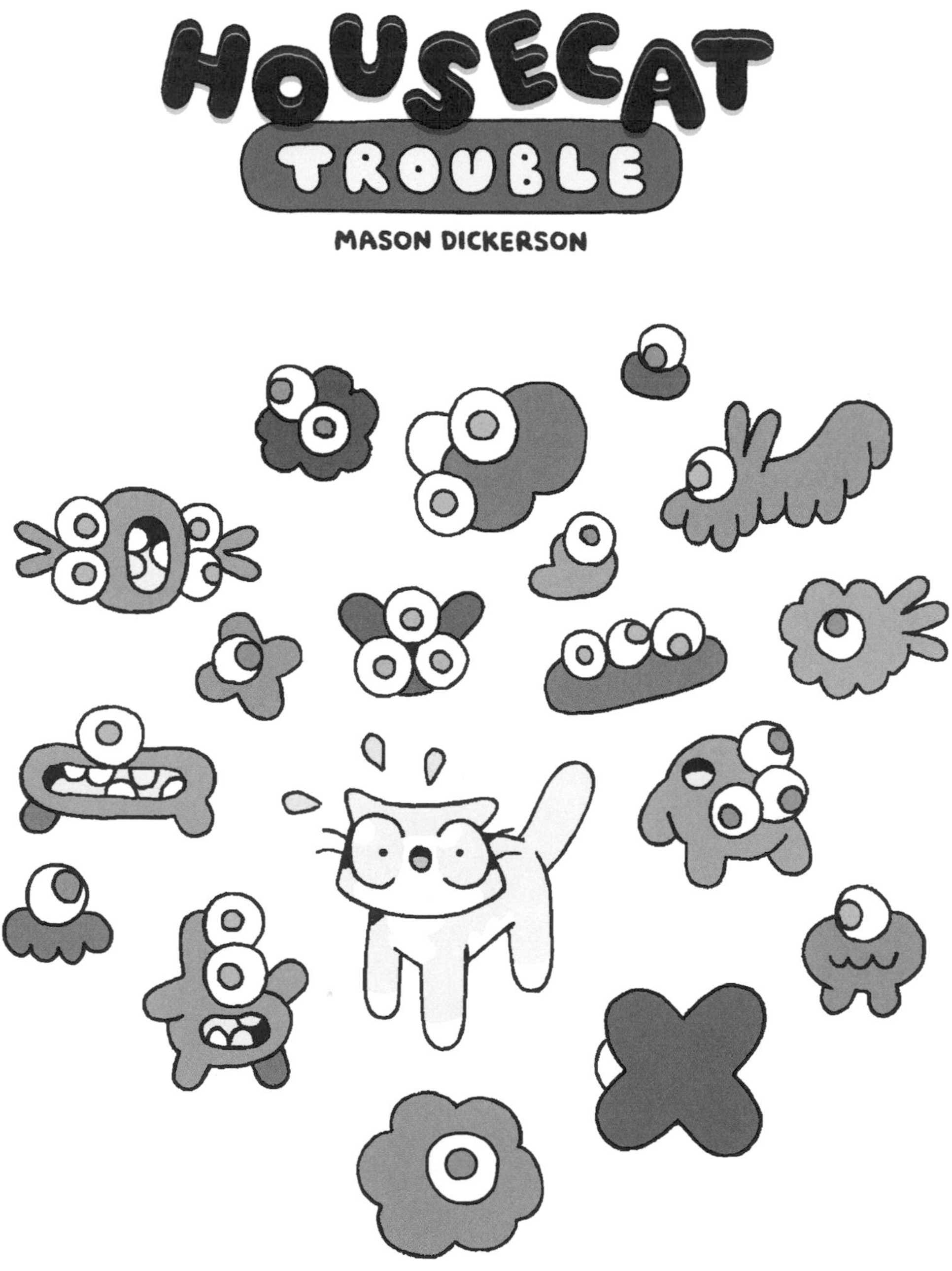

CHAPTER 1

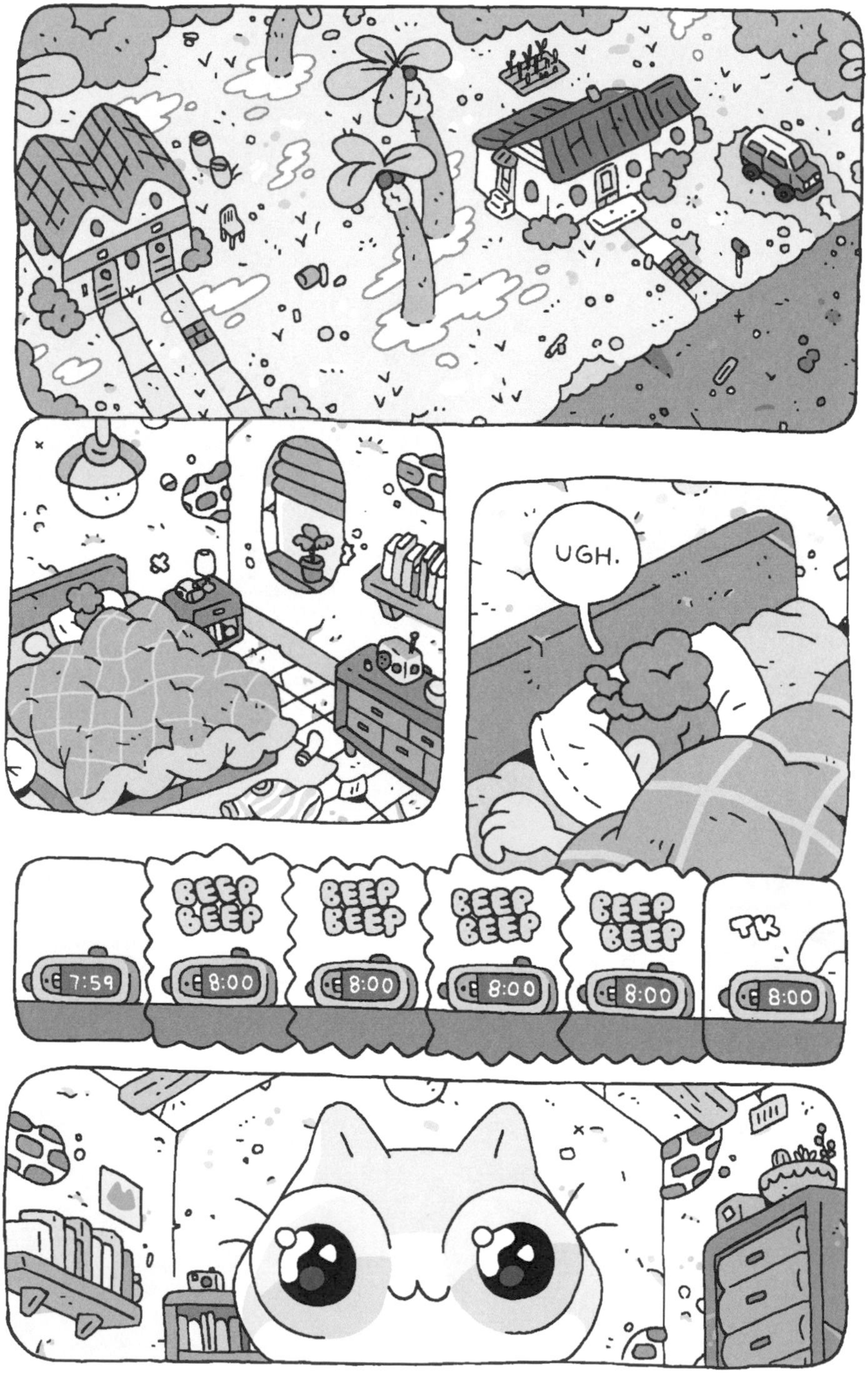
UGH.
7:59
BEEP BEEP
8:00
BEEP BEEP
8:00
BEEP BEEP
8:00
BEEP BEEP
8:00
TK
8:00

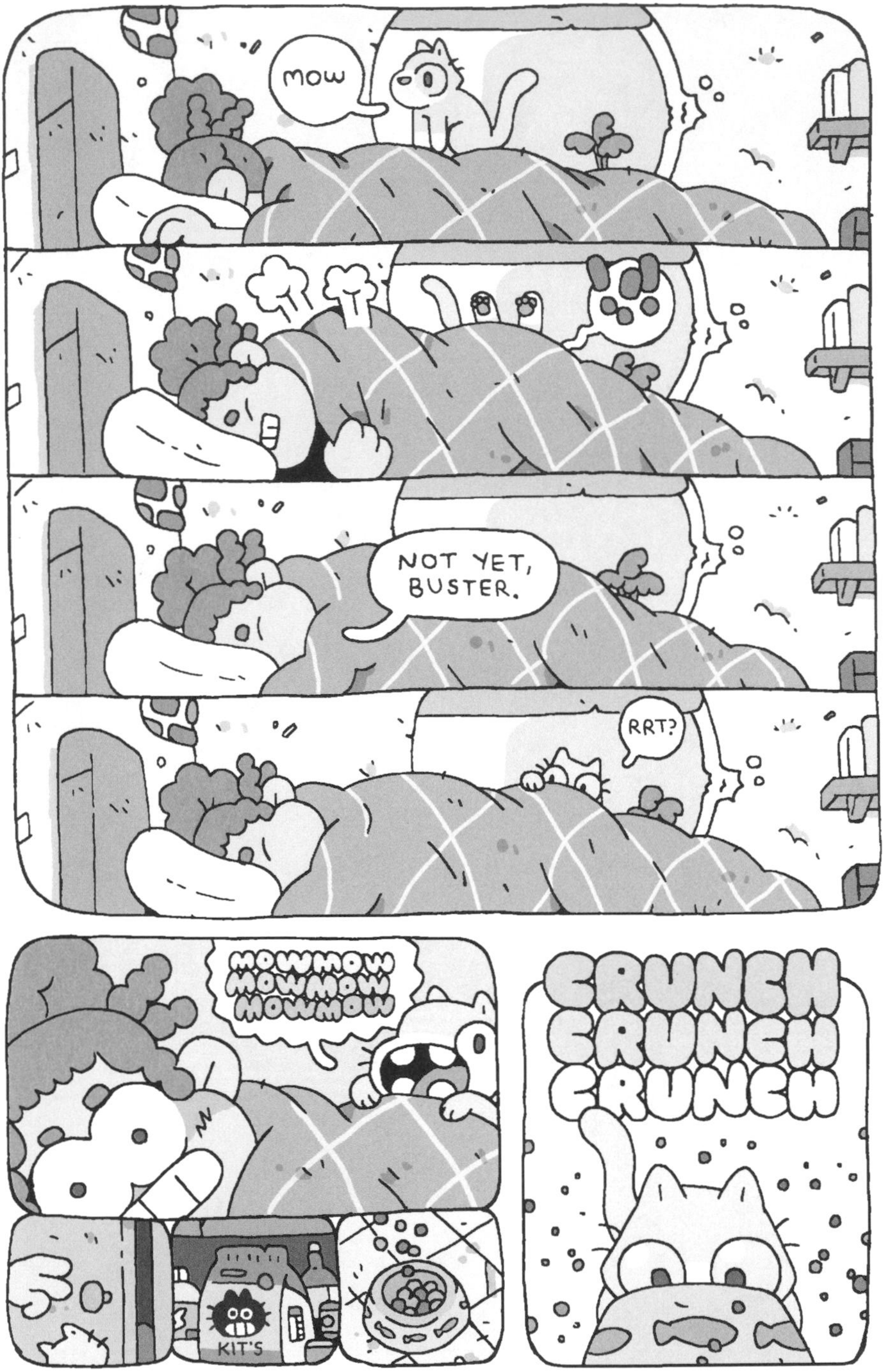
MOW
NOT YET, BUSTER.
RRT?
MOWMOW MOWMOW MOWMOW
CRUNCH CRUNCH CRUNCH
KIT'S

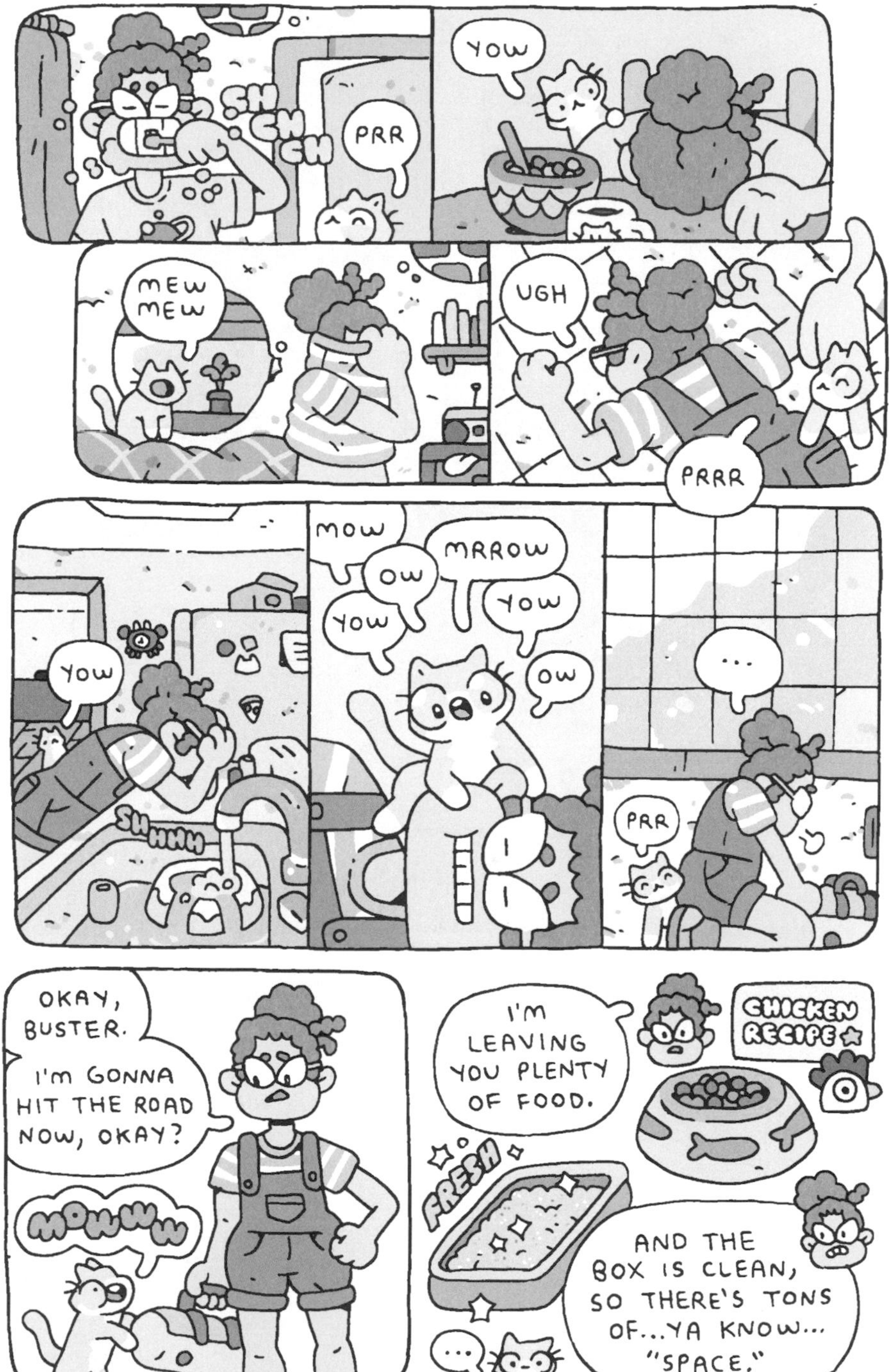
SH
CH
CH
PRR
YOW
MEW MEW
UGH
PRRR
YOW
SHHHH
MOW
OW
MRROW
YOW
YOW
OW
...
PRR
OKAY, BUSTER.
I'M GONNA HIT THE ROAD NOW, OKAY?
MOWWW
I'M LEAVING YOU PLENTY OF FOOD.
CHICKEN RECIPE
FRESH
AND THE BOX IS CLEAN, SO THERE'S TONS OF...YA KNOW... "SPACE."
...

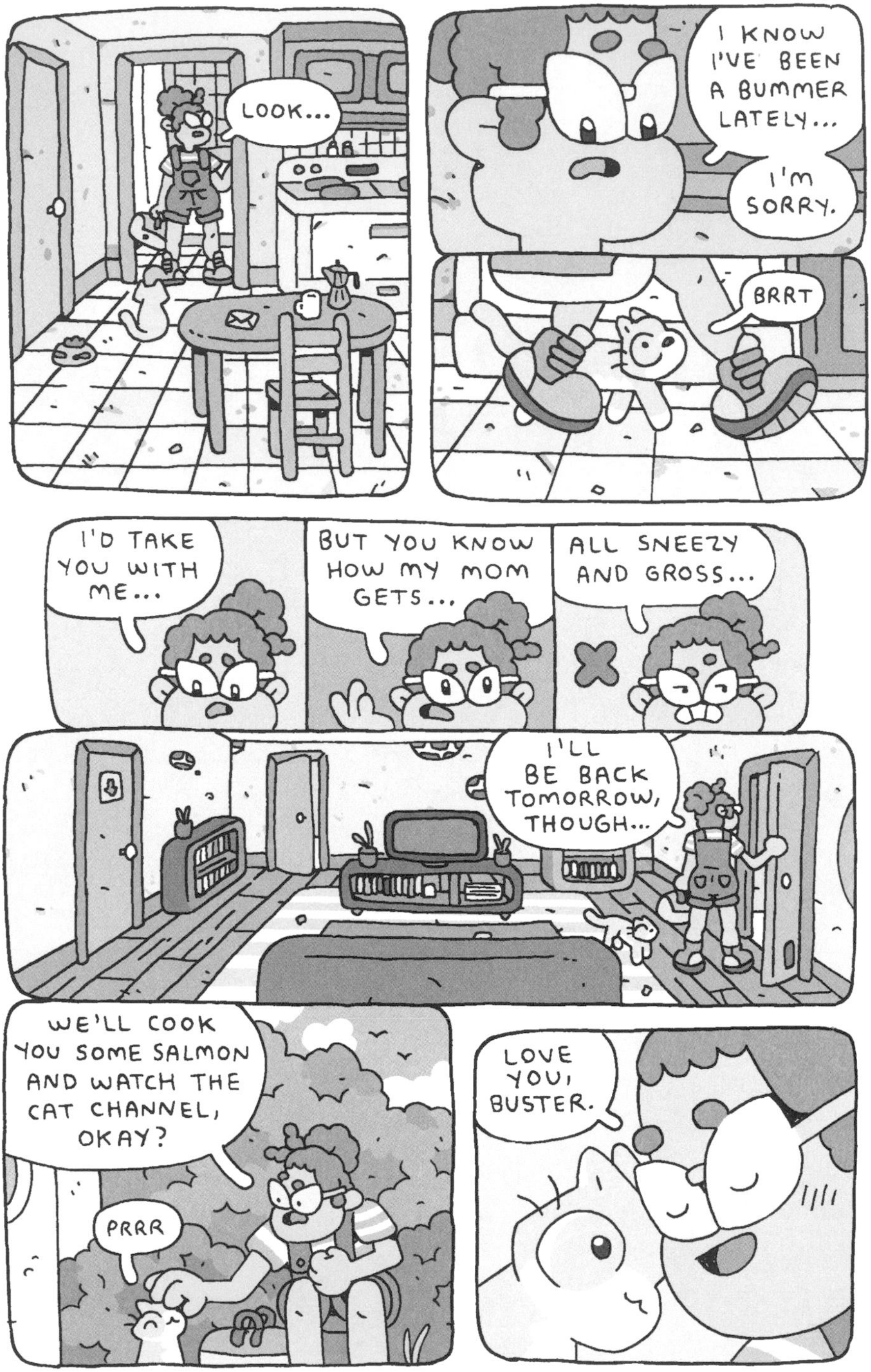
LOOK...
I KNOW I'VE BEEN A BUMMER LATELY...
I'M SORRY.
BRRT
I'D TAKE YOU WITH ME...
BUT YOU KNOW HOW MY MOM GETS...
ALL SNEEZY AND GROSS...
I'LL BE BACK TOMORROW, THOUGH...
WE'LL COOK YOU SOME SALMON AND WATCH THE CAT CHANNEL, OKAY?
PRRR
LOVE YOU, BUSTER.

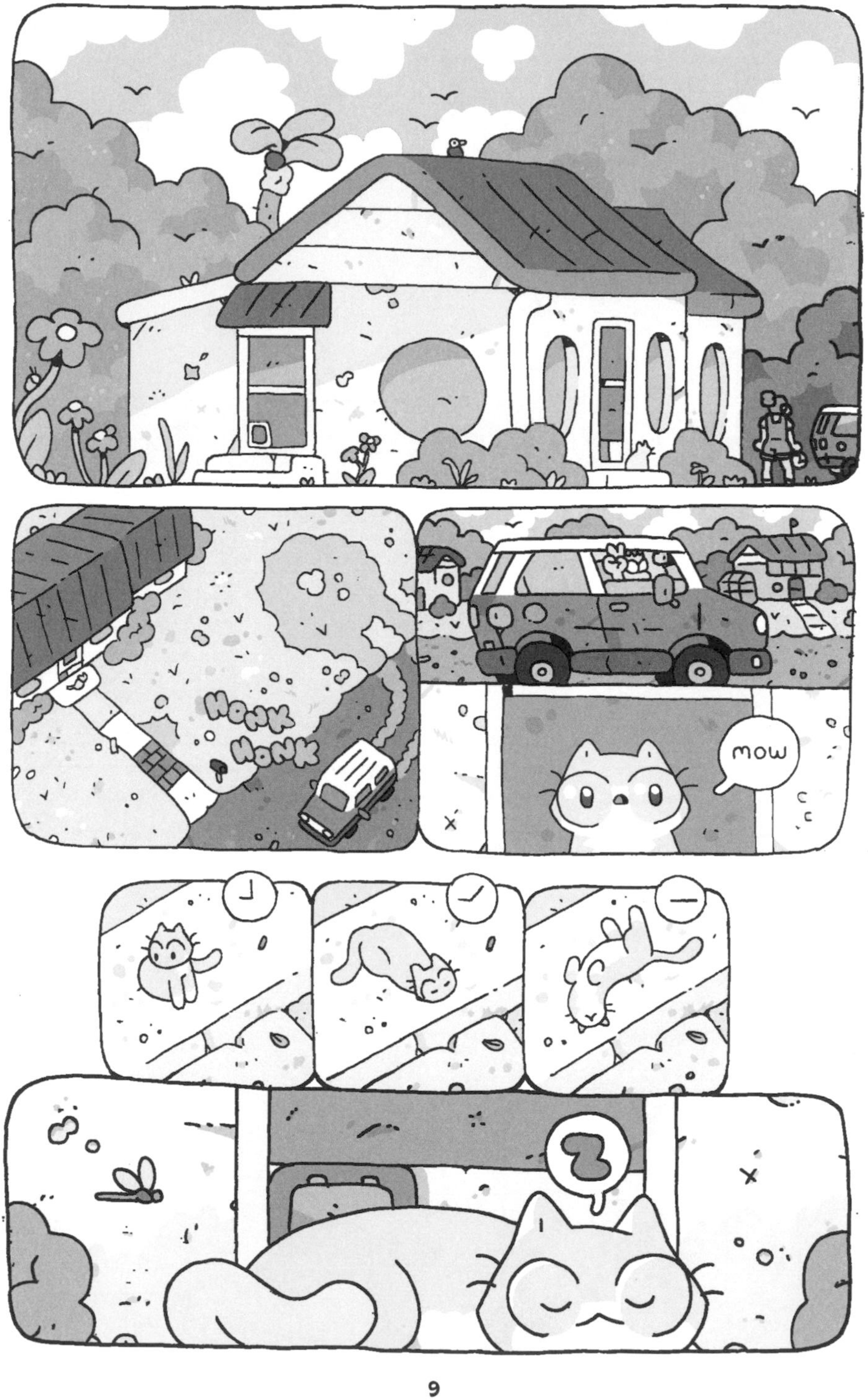
HONK
HONK
mow

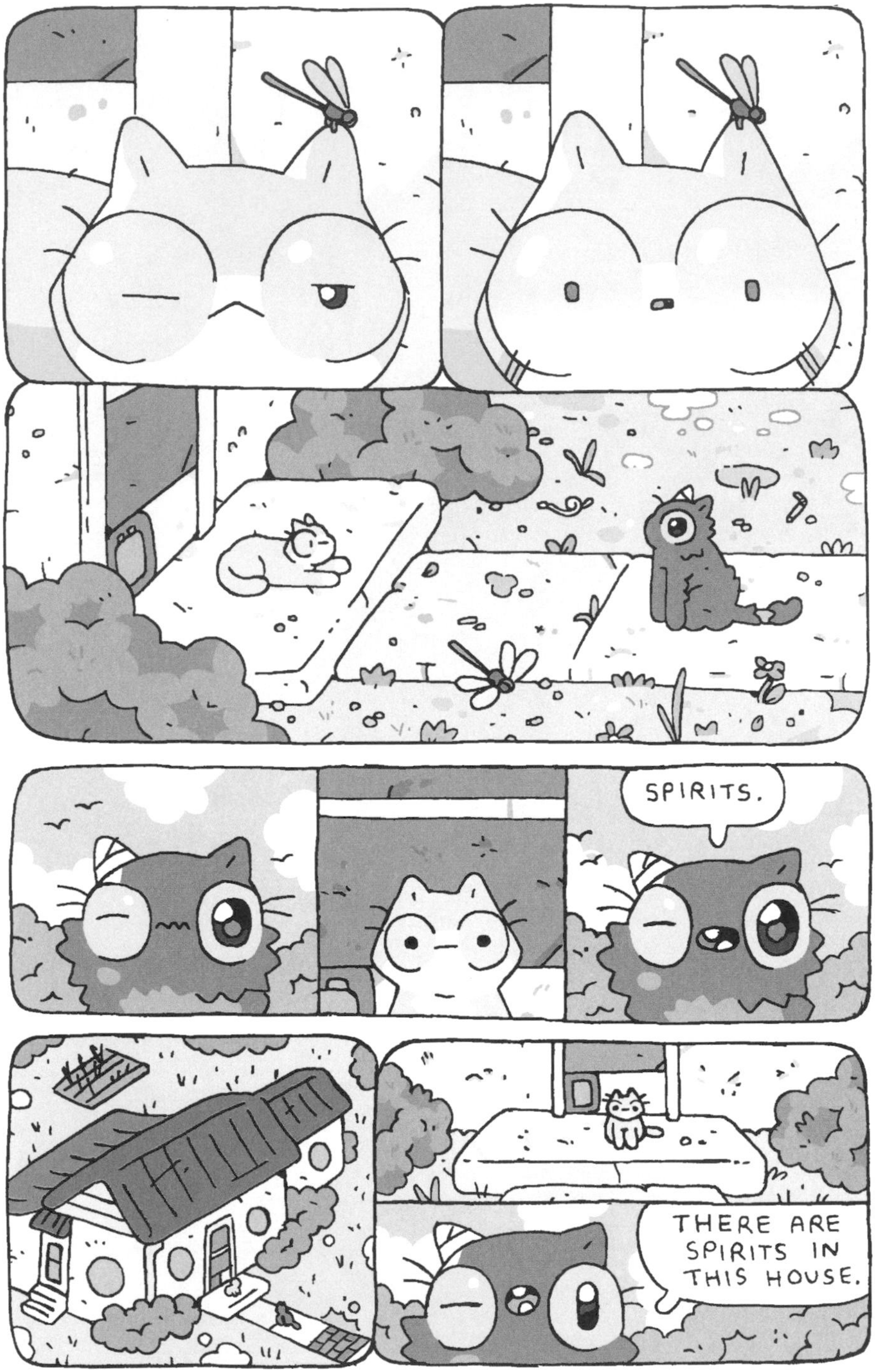
SPIRITS.
THERE ARE SPIRITS IN THIS HOUSE.

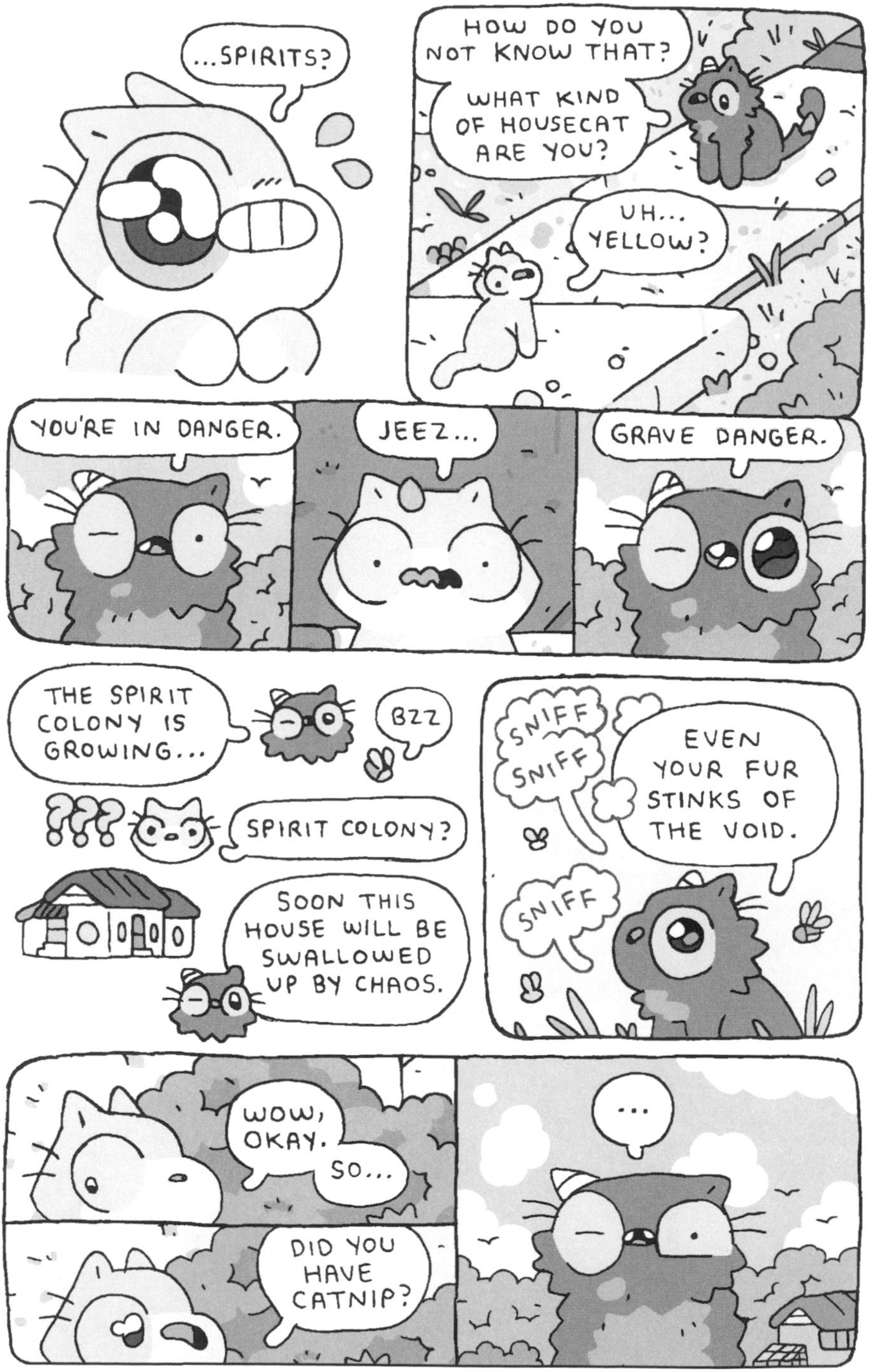
...SPIRITS?
HOW DO YOU NOT KNOW THAT?
WHAT KIND OF HOUSECAT ARE YOU?
UH... YELLOW?
YOU'RE IN DANGER.
JEEZ...
GRAVE DANGER.
THE SPIRIT COLONY IS GROWING...
BZZ
SPIRIT COLONY?
SOON THIS HOUSE WILL BE SWALLOWED UP BY CHAOS.
SNIFF
SNIFF
EVEN YOUR FUR STINKS OF THE VOID.
SNIFF
WOW, OKAY.
SO...
DID YOU HAVE CATNIP?
...

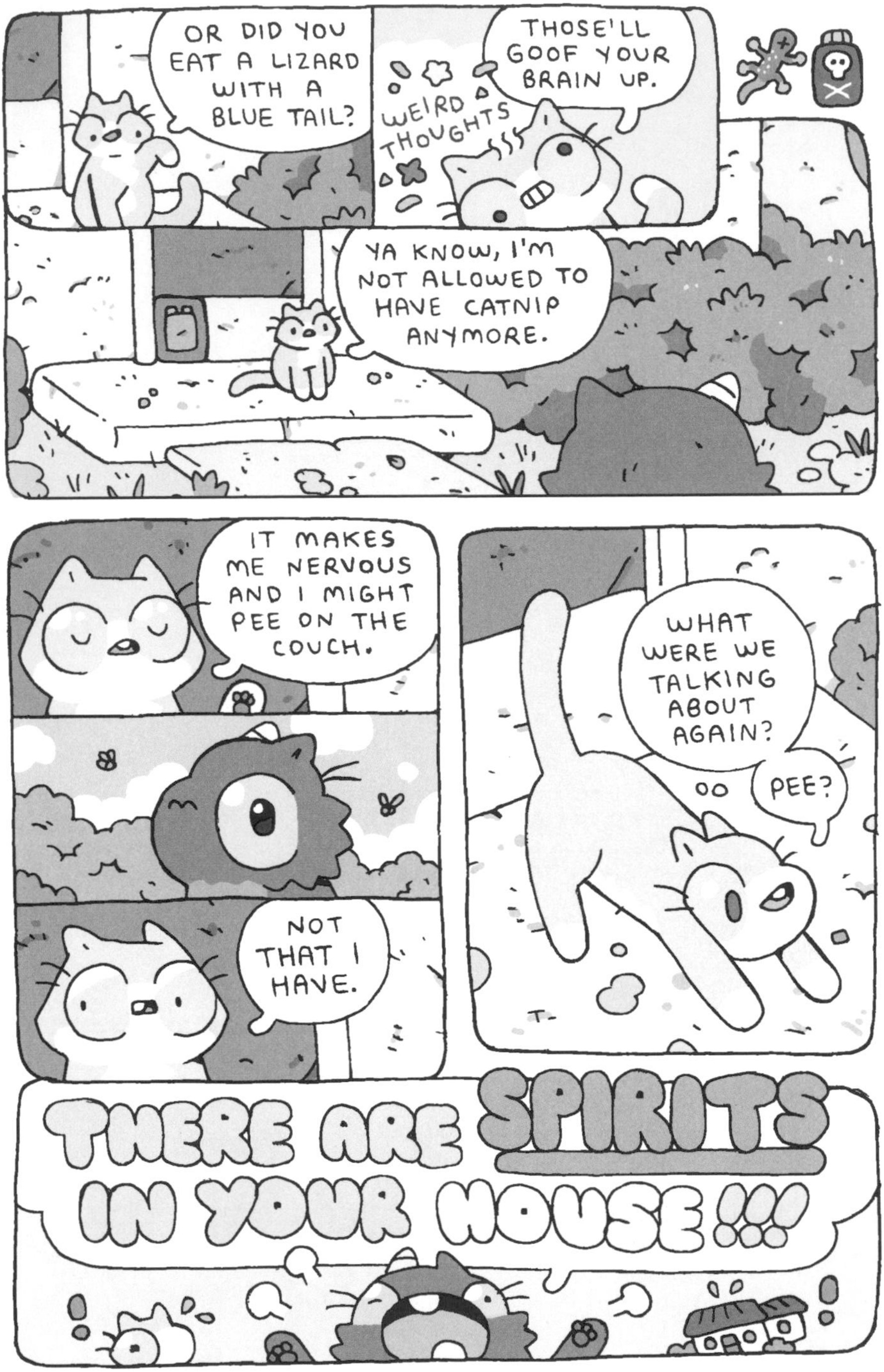
OR DID YOU EAT A LIZARD WITH A BLUE TAIL?
THOSE'LL GOOF YOUR BRAIN UP.
WEIRD THOUGHTS
YA KNOW, I'M NOT ALLOWED TO HAVE CATNIP ANYMORE.
IT MAKES ME NERVOUS AND I MIGHT PEE ON THE COUCH.
NOT THAT I HAVE.
WHAT WERE WE TALKING ABOUT AGAIN?
PEE?
THERE ARE SPIRITS IN YOUR HOUSE!!!

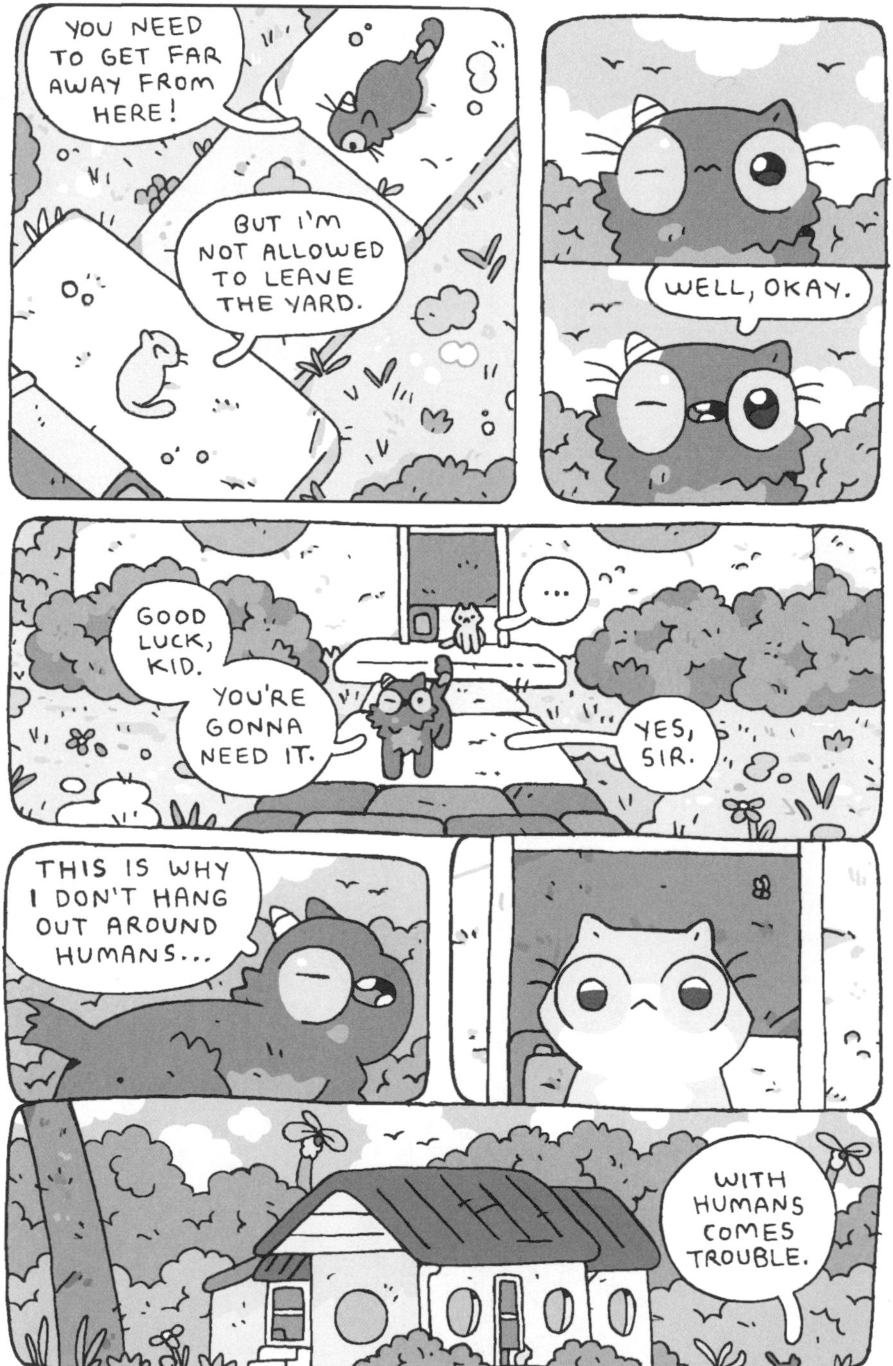
YOU NEED TO GET FAR AWAY FROM HERE!
BUT I'M NOT ALLOWED TO LEAVE THE YARD.
WELL, OKAY.
...
GOOD LUCK, KID.
YOU'RE GONNA NEED IT.
YES, SIR.
THIS IS WHY I DON'T HANG OUT AROUND HUMANS...
WITH HUMANS COMES TROUBLE.

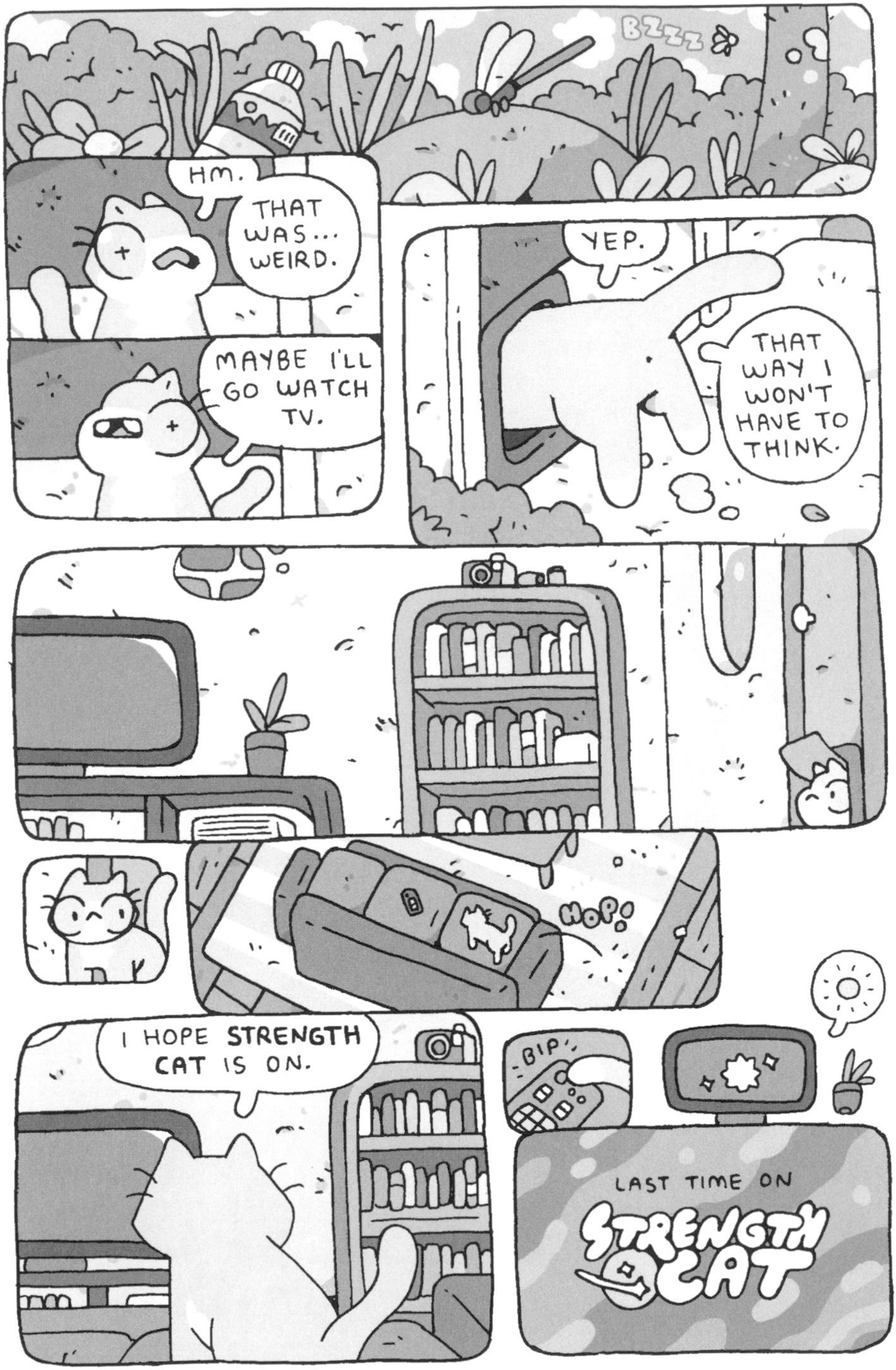
BZZZ
HM.
THAT WAS... WEIRD.
MAYBE I'LL GO WATCH TV.
YEP.
THAT WAY I WON'T HAVE TO THINK.
HOP!
I HOPE **STRENGTH CAT** IS ON.
BIP
LAST TIME ON
STRENGTH CAT

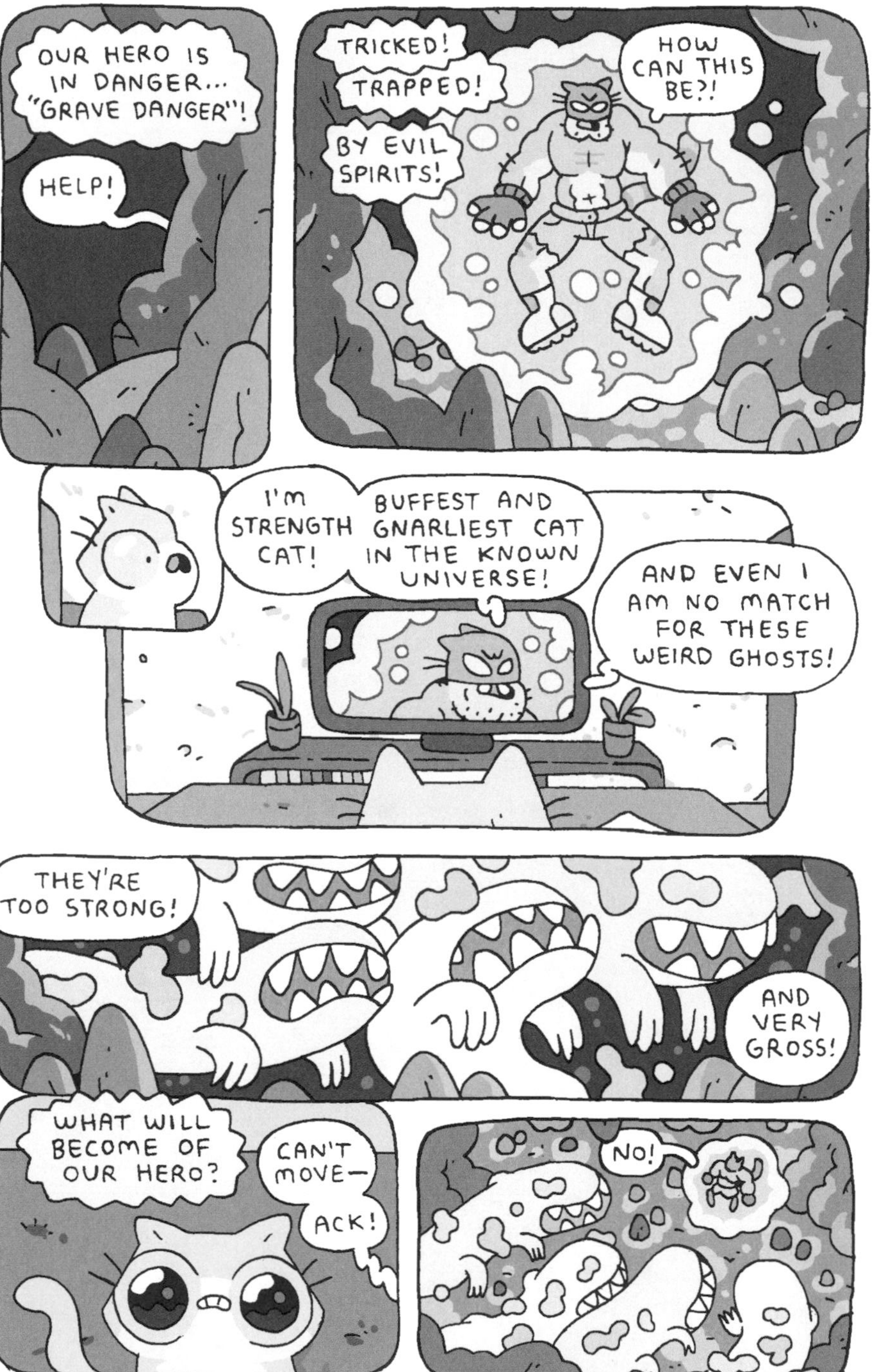
OUR HERO IS IN DANGER... "GRAVE DANGER"!
HELP!
TRICKED!
TRAPPED!
BY EVIL SPIRITS!
HOW CAN THIS BE?!
I'M STRENGTH CAT!
BUFFEST AND GNARLIEST CAT IN THE KNOWN UNIVERSE!
AND EVEN I AM NO MATCH FOR THESE WEIRD GHOSTS!
THEY'RE TOO STRONG!
AND VERY GROSS!
WHAT WILL BECOME OF OUR HERO?
CAN'T MOVE—
ACK!
NO!

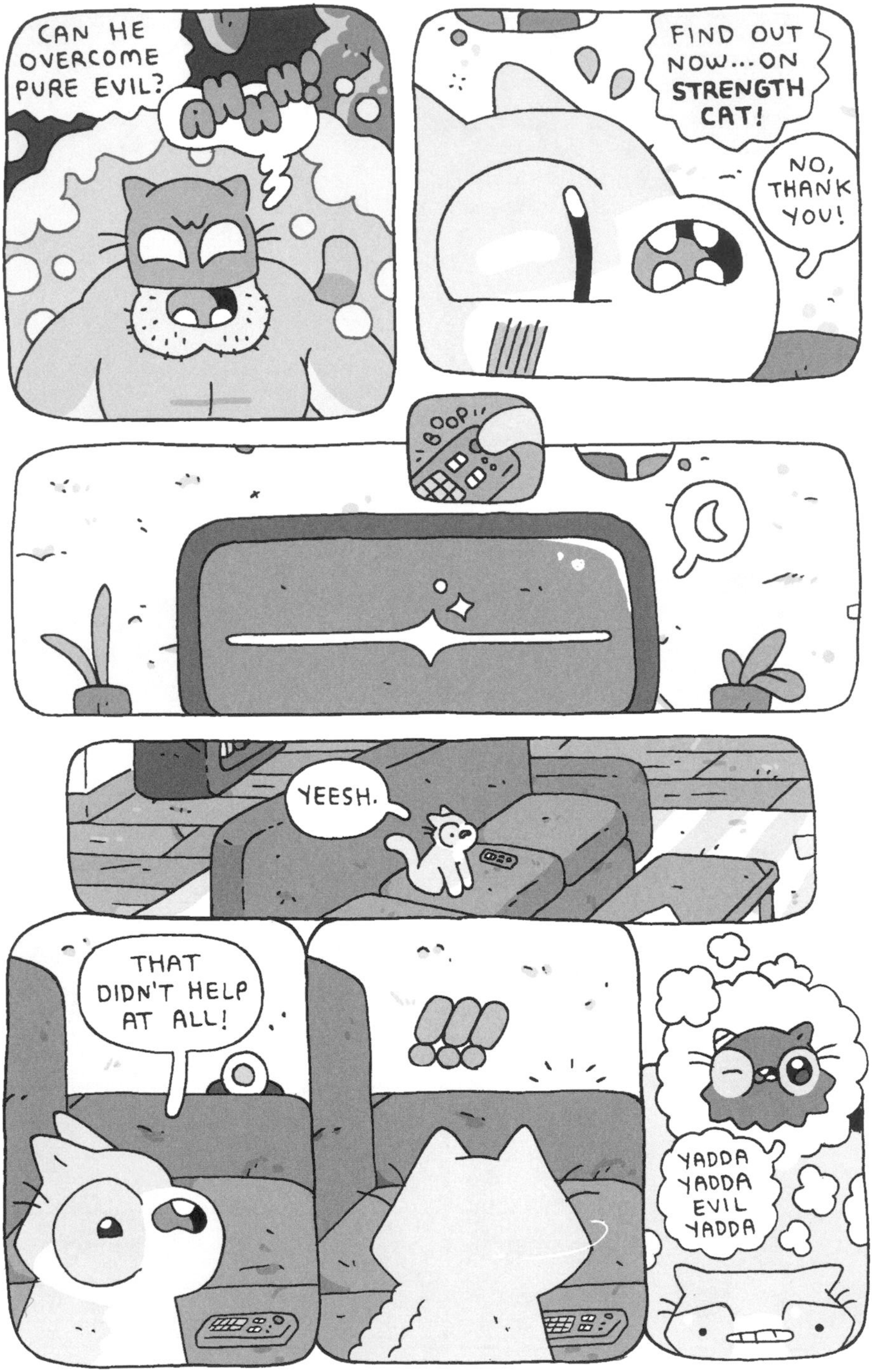
CAN HE OVERCOME PURE EVIL?
AHHH!
FIND OUT NOW...ON STRENGTH CAT!
NO, THANK YOU!
BOOP
YEESH.
THAT DIDN'T HELP AT ALL!
YADDA YADDA EVIL YADDA

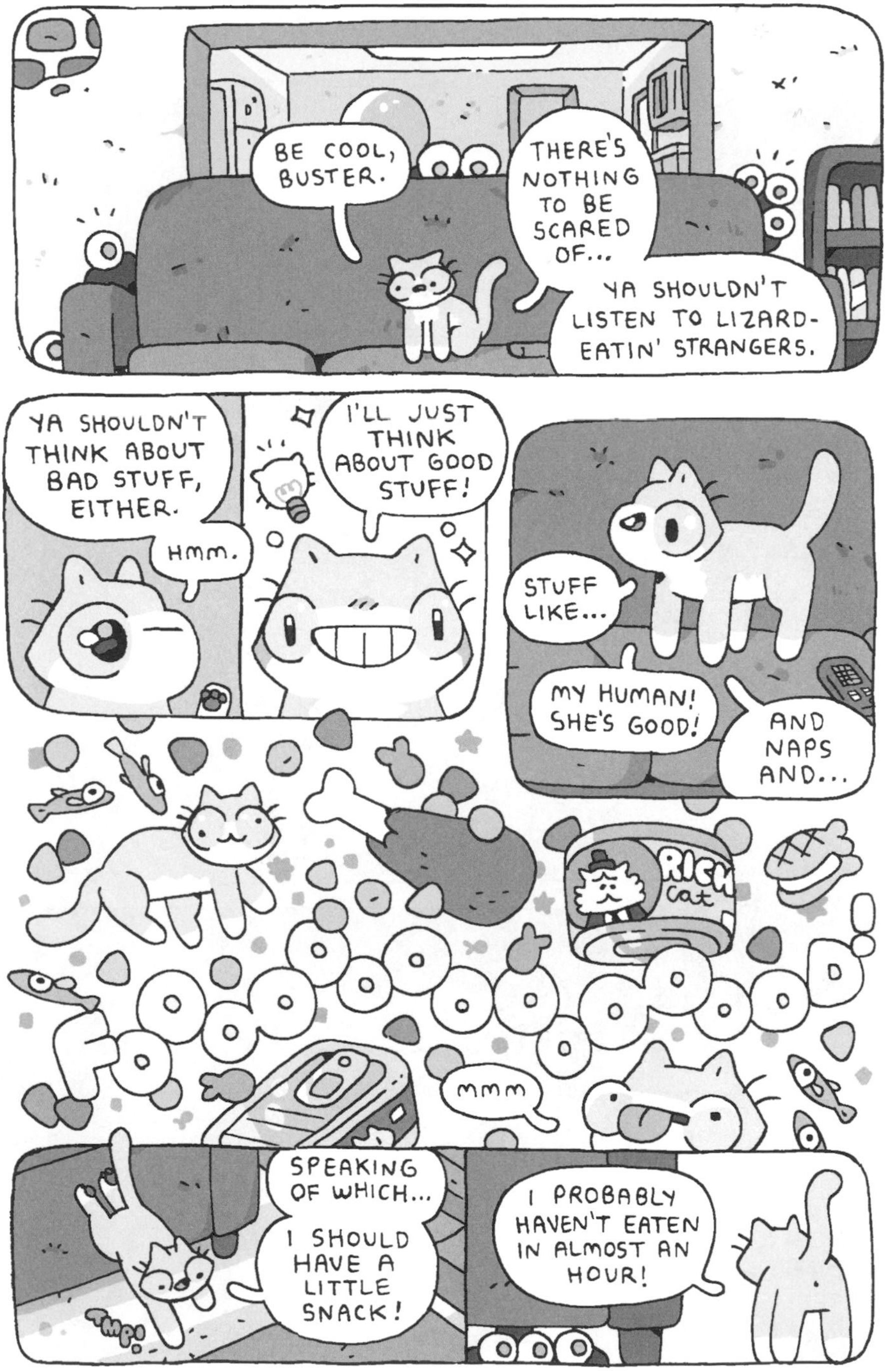
BE COOL, BUSTER.
THERE'S NOTHING TO BE SCARED OF...
YA SHOULDN'T LISTEN TO LIZARD-EATIN' STRANGERS.
YA SHOULDN'T THINK ABOUT BAD STUFF, EITHER.
HMM.
I'LL JUST THINK ABOUT GOOD STUFF!
STUFF LIKE...
MY HUMAN! SHE'S GOOD!
AND NAPS AND...
RICH Cat
FOOOOOOOOOOOOOD!
mmm
SPEAKING OF WHICH...
I SHOULD HAVE A LITTLE SNACK!
TMP!
I PROBABLY HAVEN'T EATEN IN ALMOST AN HOUR!

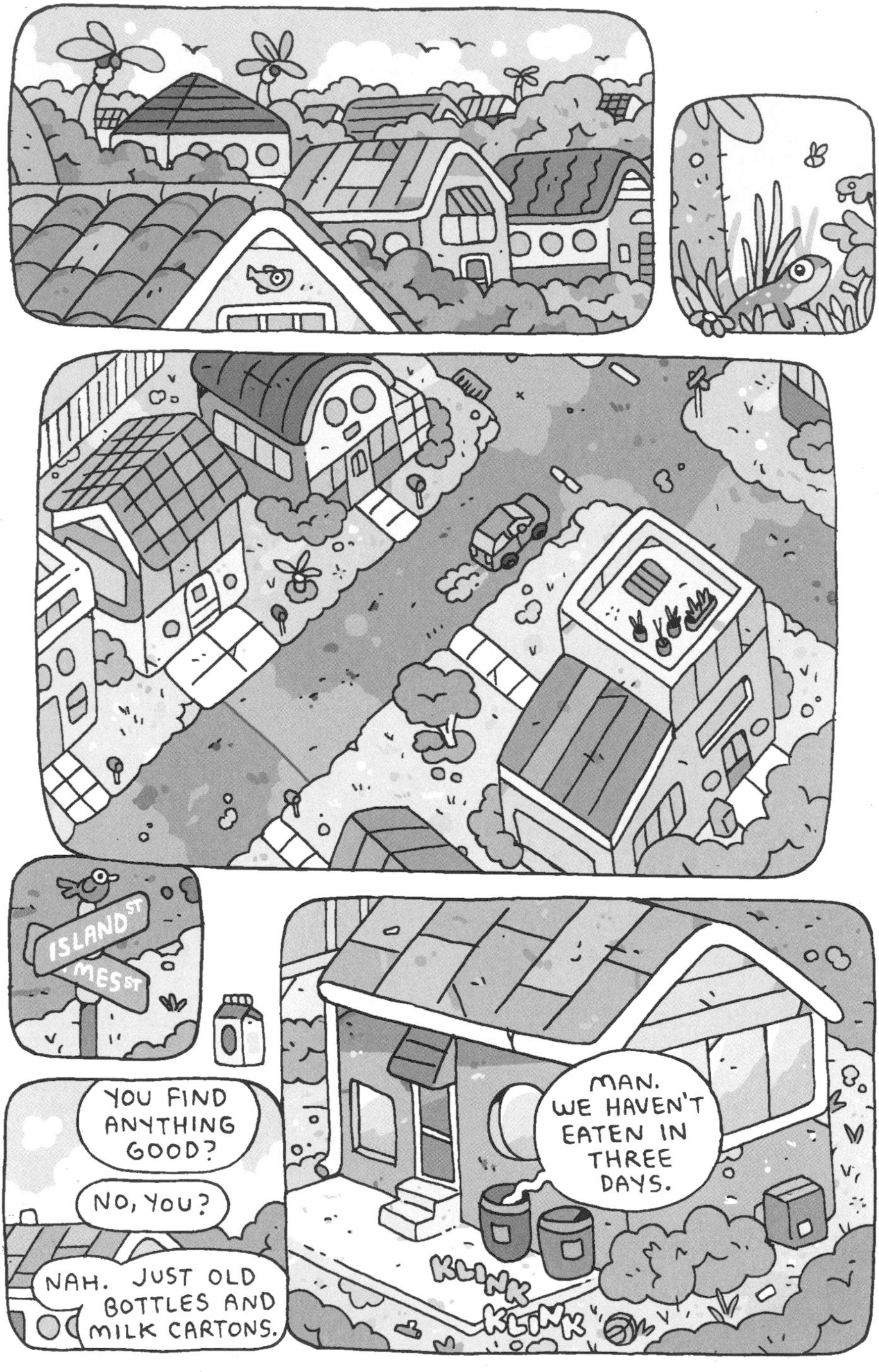
ISLAND ST
MES ST
YOU FIND ANYTHING GOOD?
NO, YOU?
NAH. JUST OLD BOTTLES AND MILK CARTONS.
MAN. WE HAVEN'T EATEN IN THREE DAYS.
KLINK
KLINK

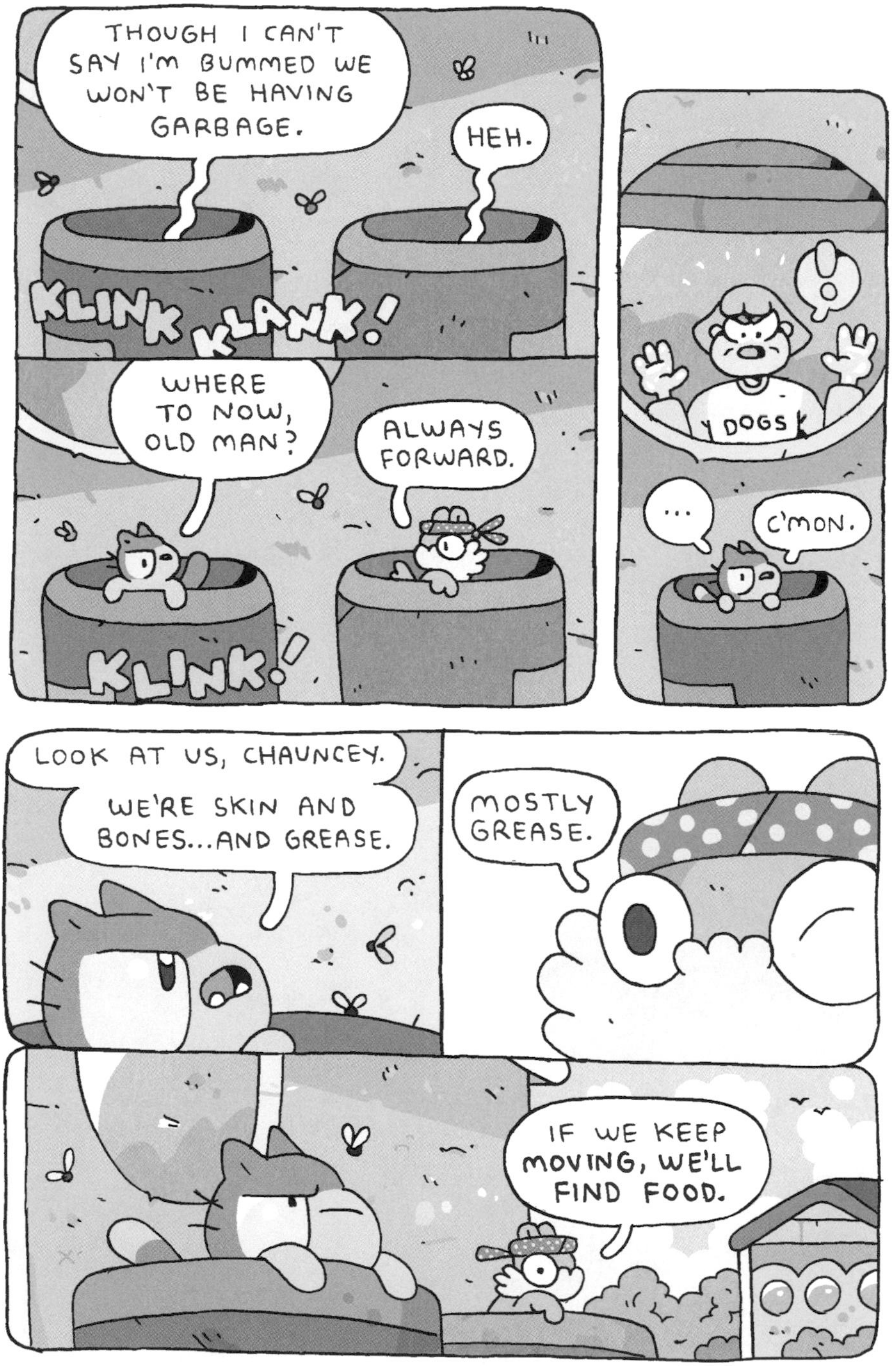
THOUGH I CAN'T SAY I'M BUMMED WE WON'T BE HAVING GARBAGE.
HEH.
KLINK KLANK!
!
WHERE TO NOW, OLD MAN?
ALWAYS FORWARD.
KLINK!
DOGS
...
C'MON.
LOOK AT US, CHAUNCEY.
WE'RE SKIN AND BONES...AND GREASE.
MOSTLY GREASE.
IF WE KEEP MOVING, WE'LL FIND FOOD.

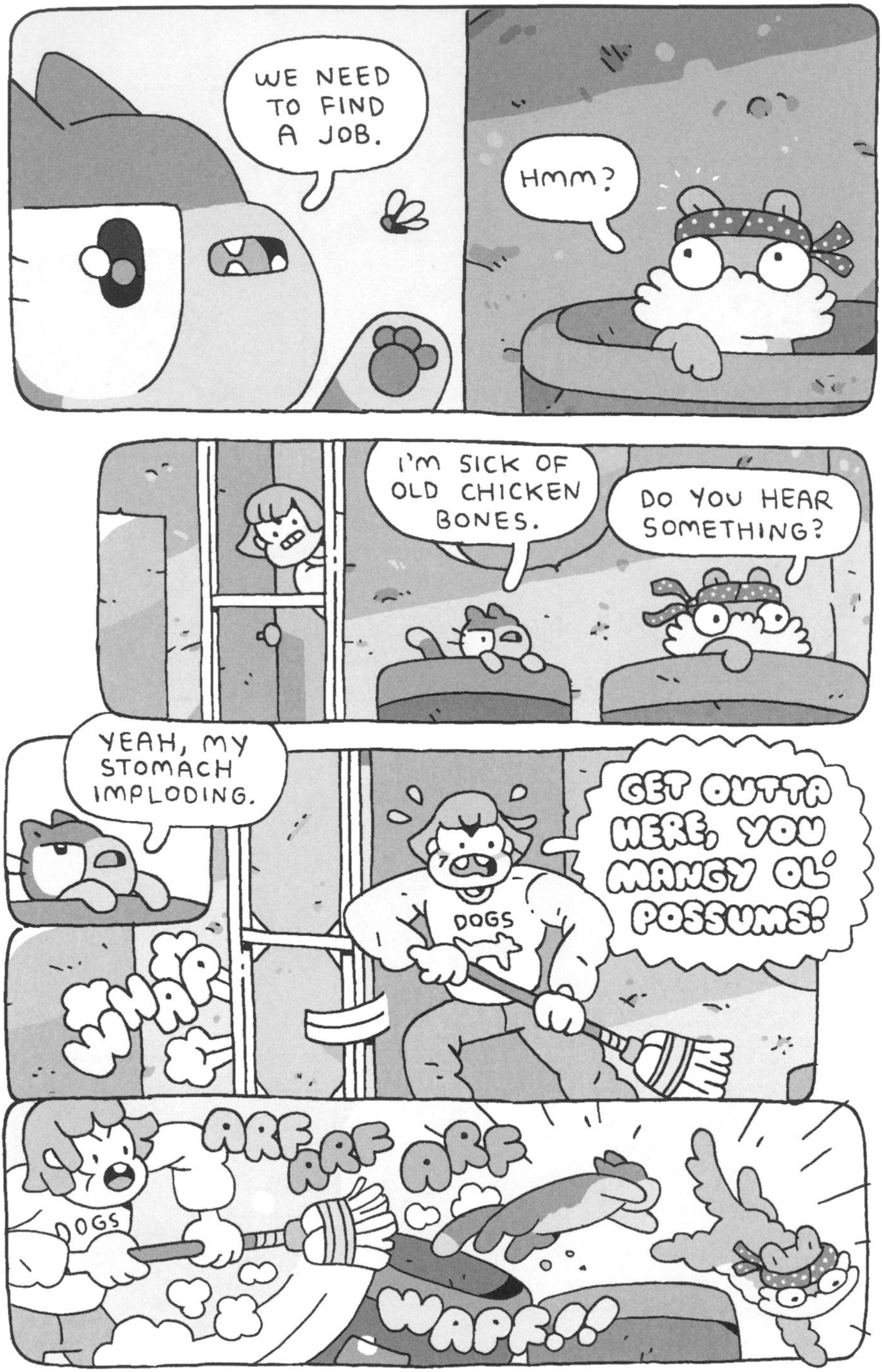

WE NEED TO FIND A JOB.
Hmm?
I'M SICK OF OLD CHICKEN BONES.
DO YOU HEAR SOMETHING?
YEAH, MY STOMACH IMPLODING.
GET OUTTA HERE, YOU MANGY OL' POSSUMS!
DOGS
WHAP
ARF ARF ARF
DOGS
WAPF!!

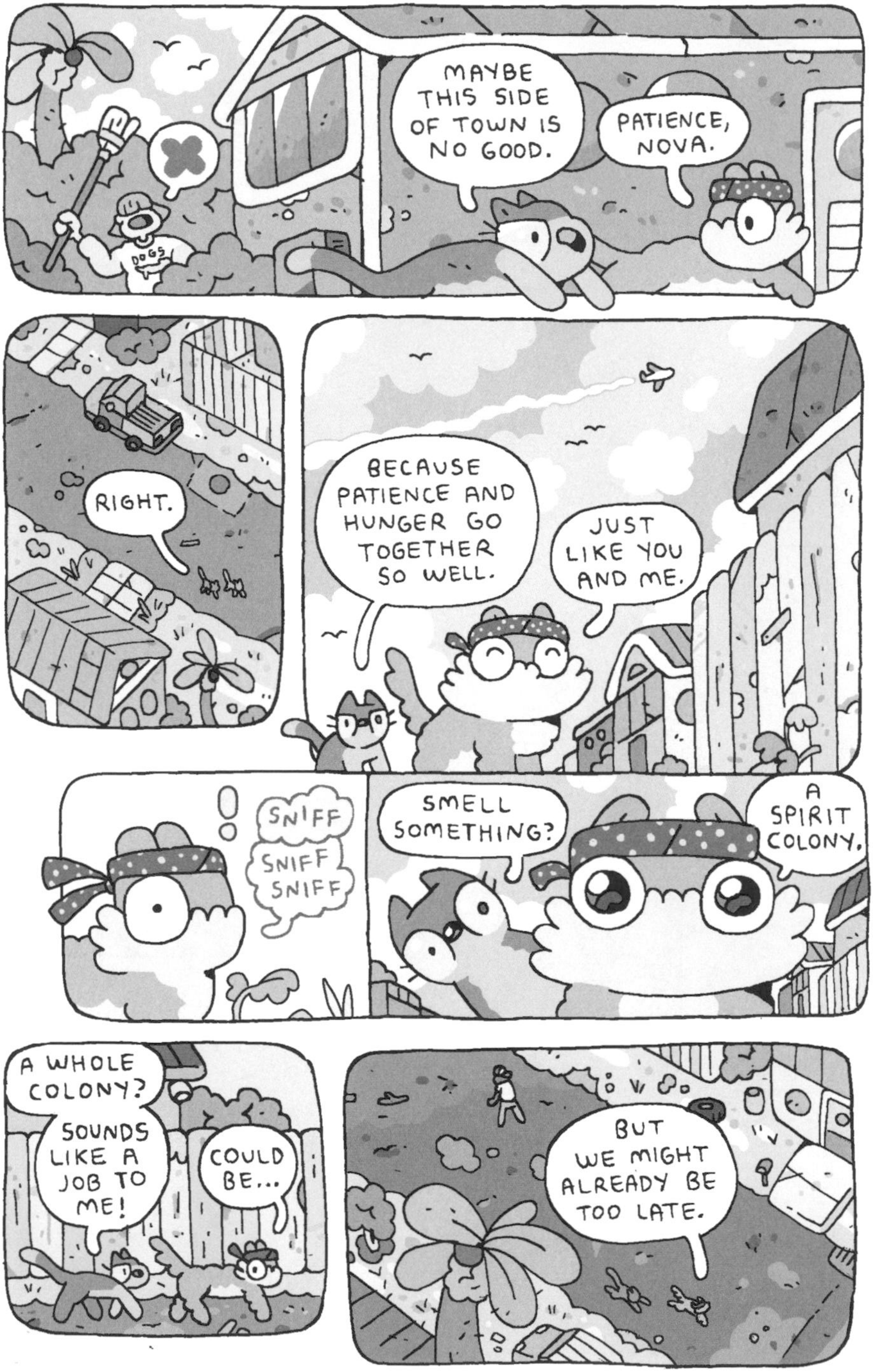
DOGS
MAYBE THIS SIDE OF TOWN IS NO GOOD.
PATIENCE, NOVA.
RIGHT.
BECAUSE PATIENCE AND HUNGER GO TOGETHER SO WELL.
JUST LIKE YOU AND ME.
SNIFF
SNIFF SNIFF
SMELL SOMETHING?
A SPIRIT COLONY.
A WHOLE COLONY?
SOUNDS LIKE A JOB TO ME!
COULD BE...
BUT WE MIGHT ALREADY BE TOO LATE.

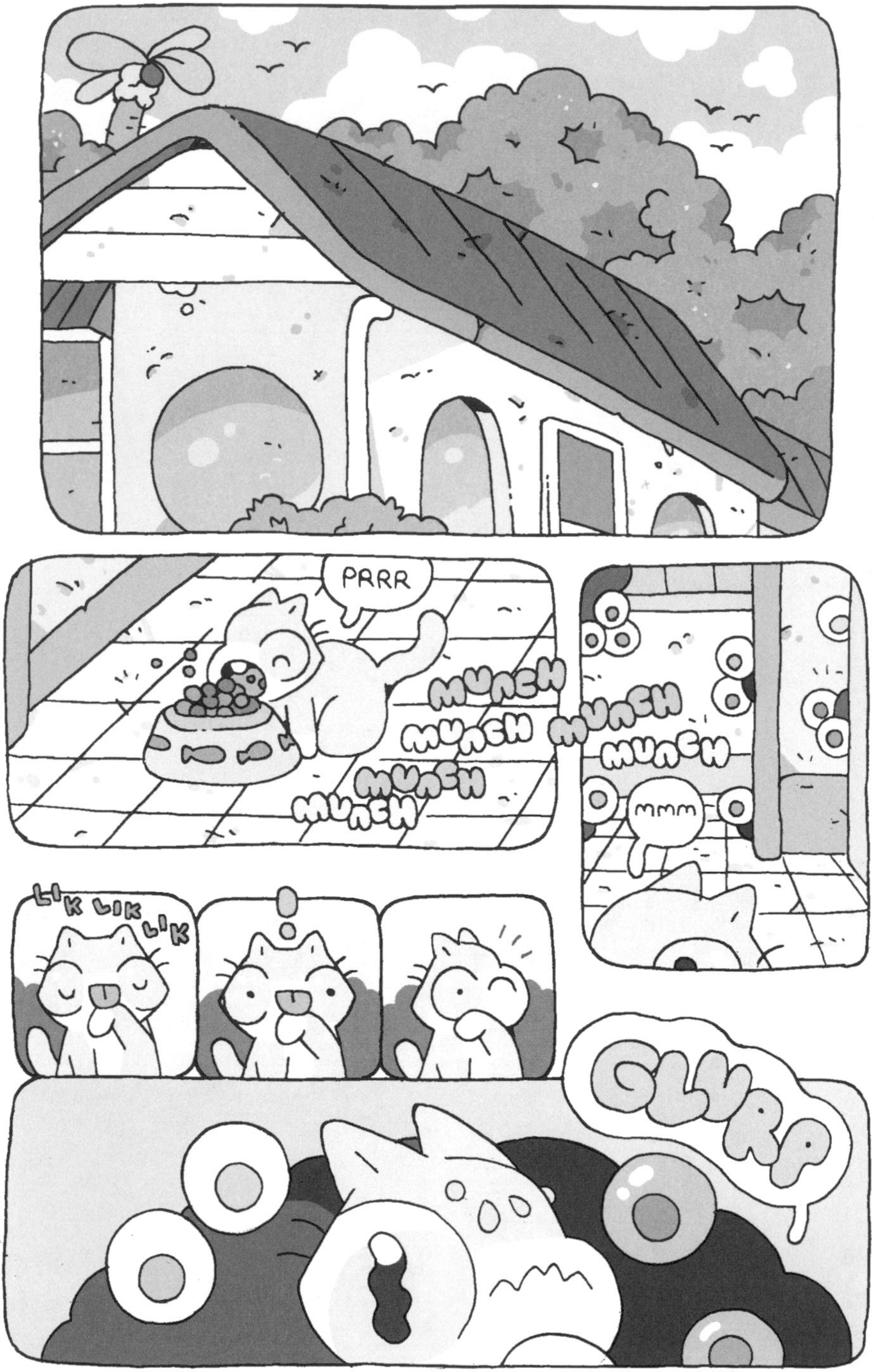
PRRR
MUNCH
MUNCH
MUNCH
MUNCH
MUNCH
MUNCH
MMM
LIK LIK LIK
GLURP

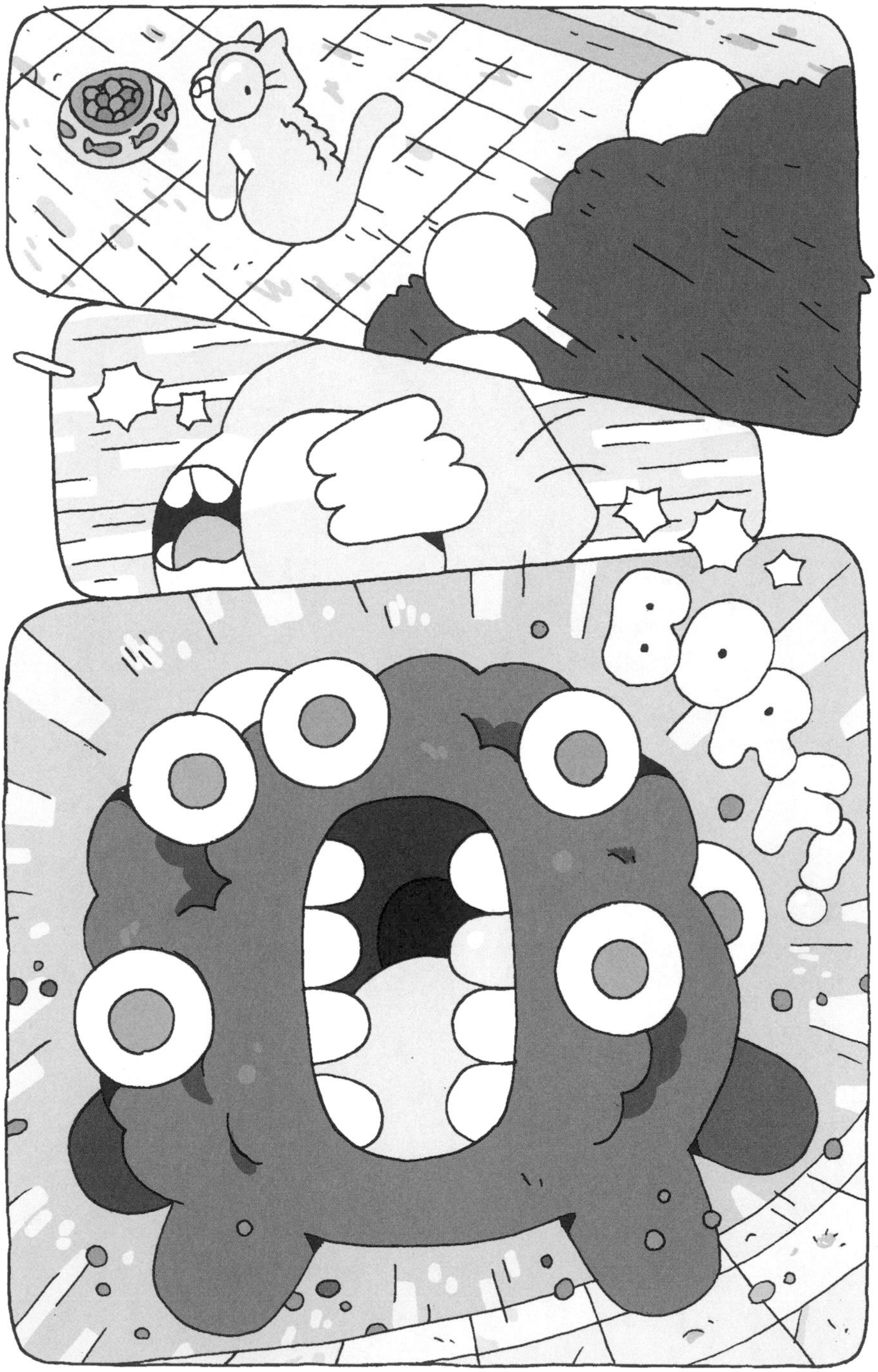
BORF!

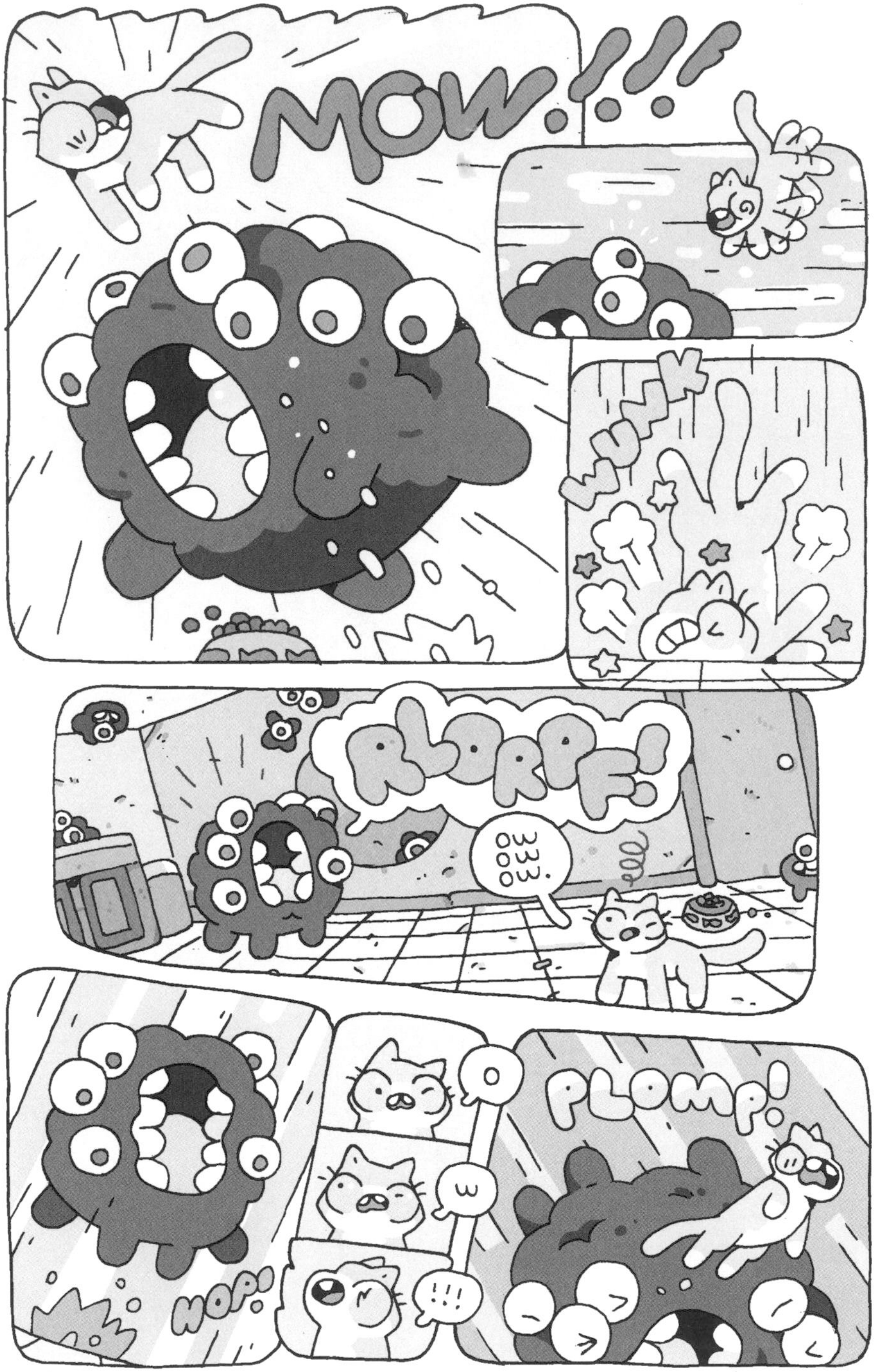
MOW!!!!
WUNK
RLORPF!
OW OW OW OW OW.
O
W
!!!
HOP!
PLOMP!

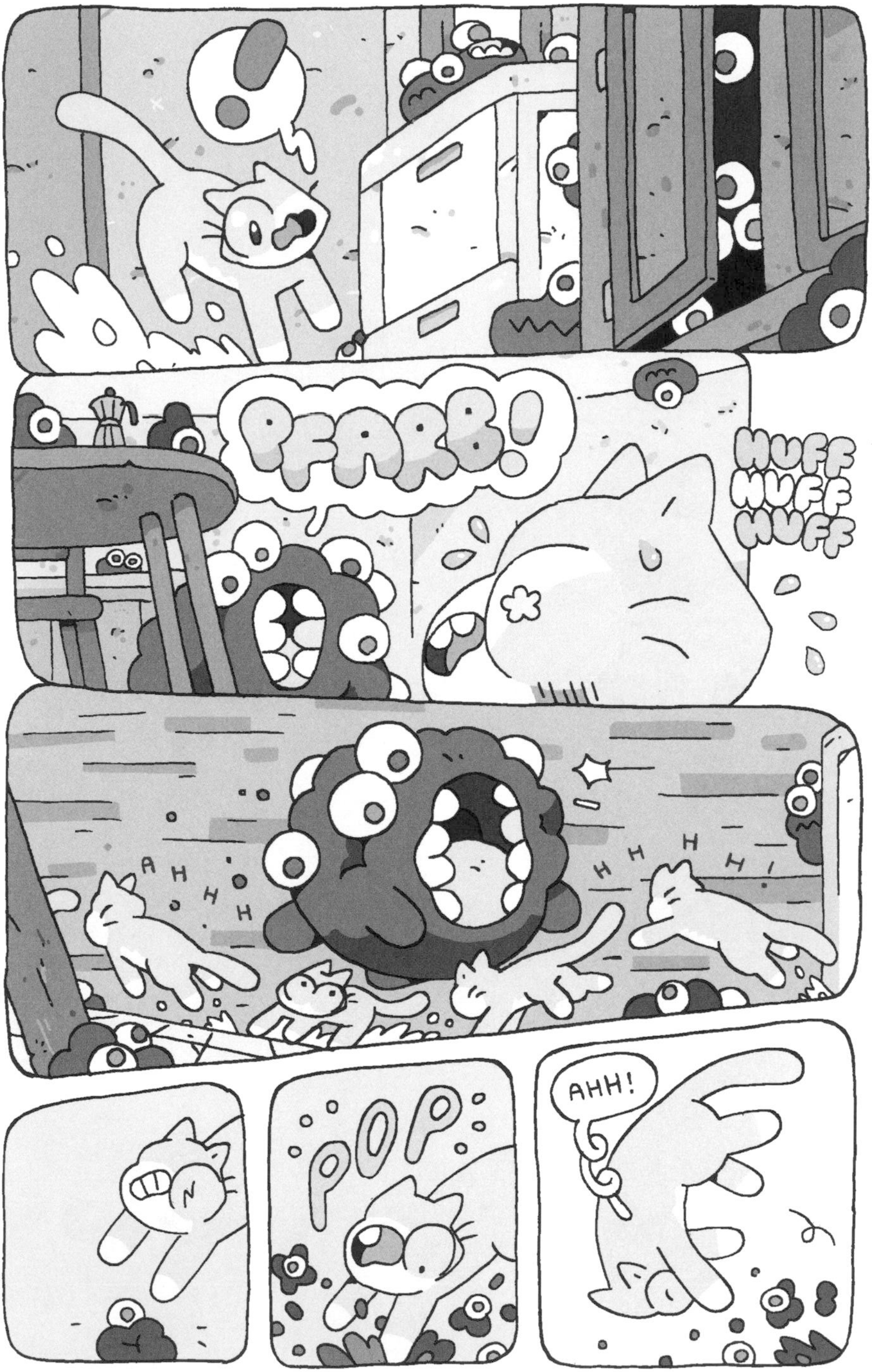
PFARB!
HUFF HUFF HUFF
AHHH
HHHH!
POP
AHH!

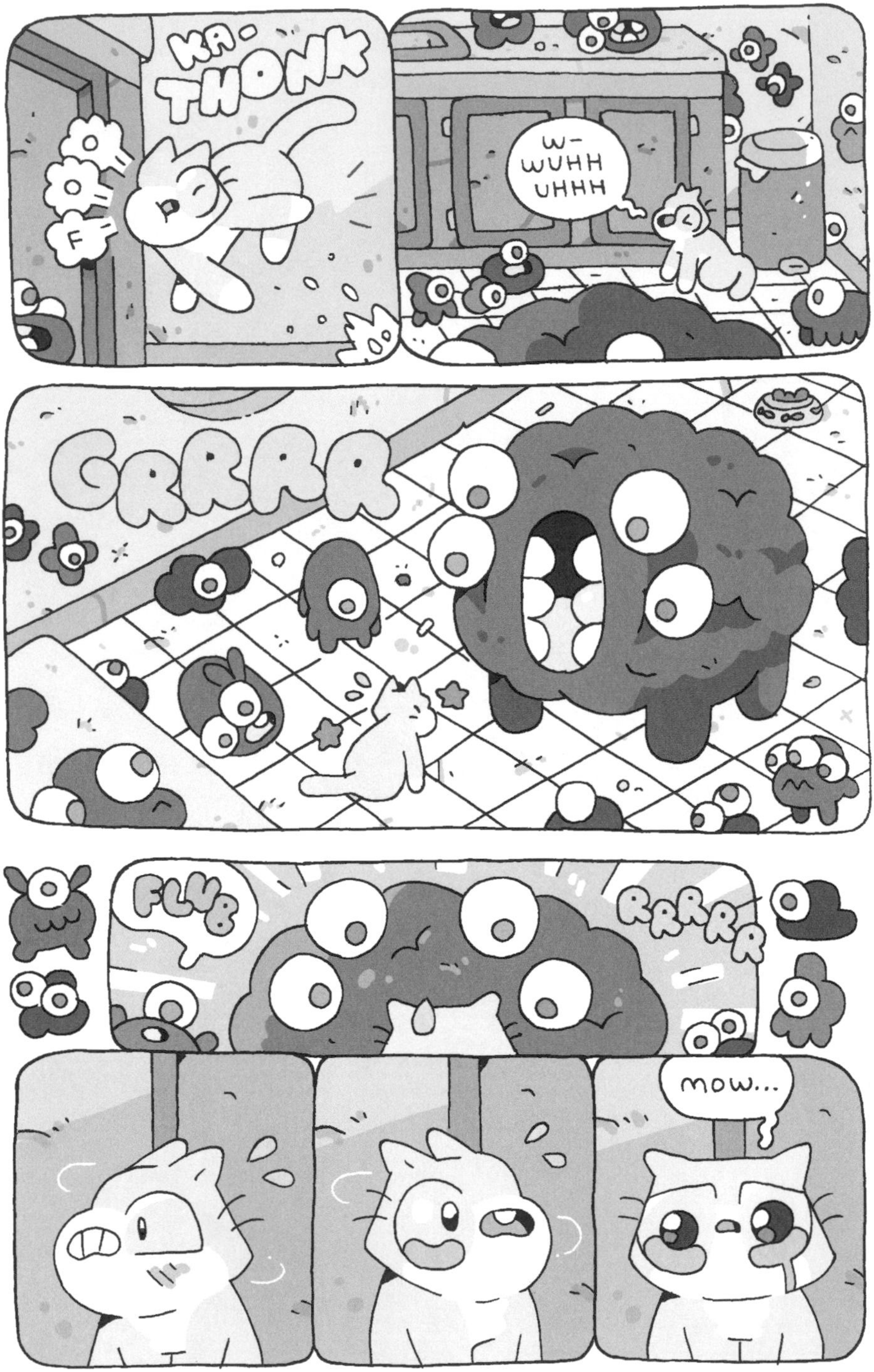
KA-THONK
W-WUHH UHHH
GRRRR
FLUB
RRRRR
mow...

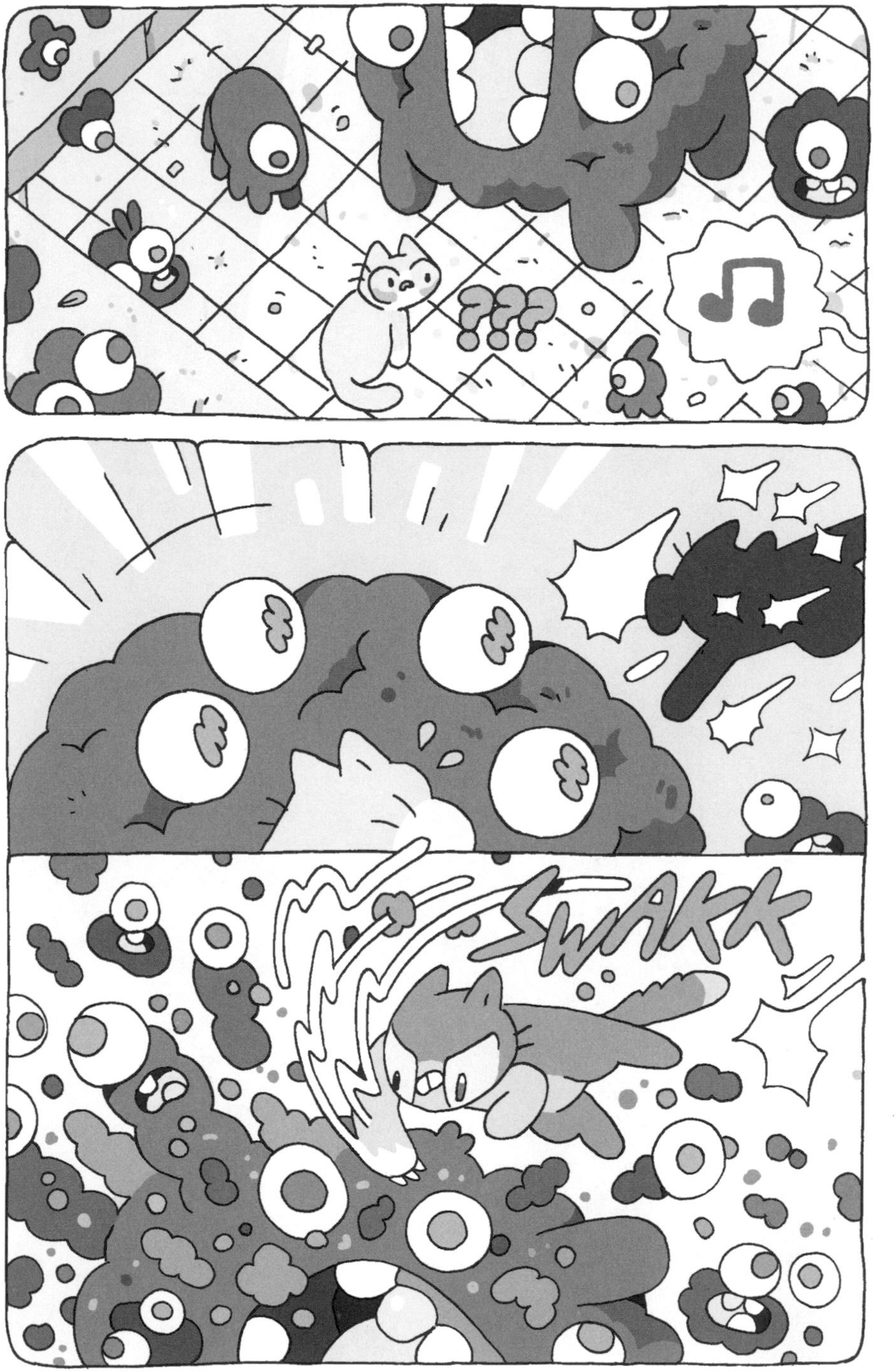
???
SWAKK

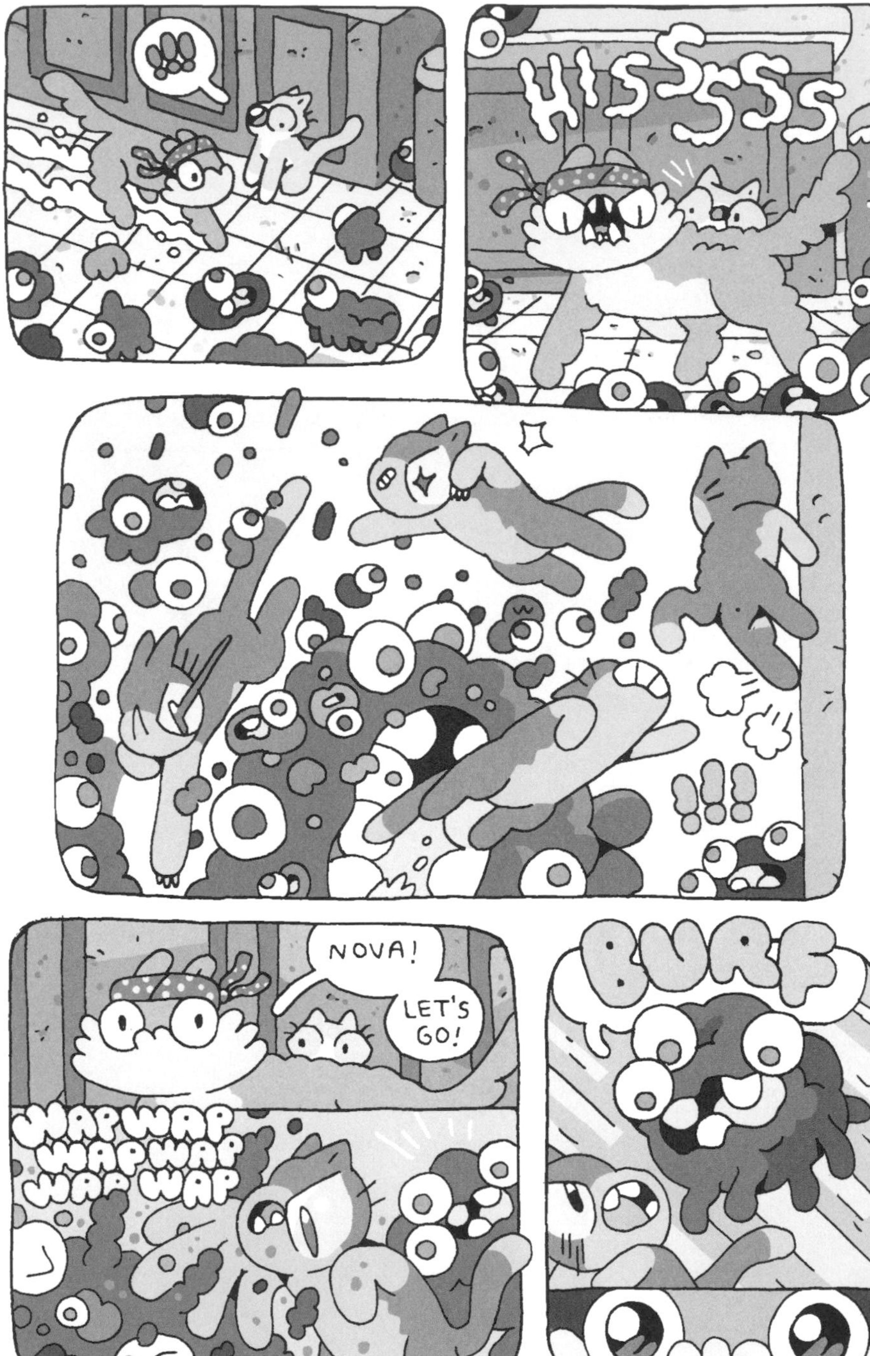
HISSSSSS
!!!
NOVA!
LET'S GO!
WAPWAP WAPWAP WAP WAP
BURF

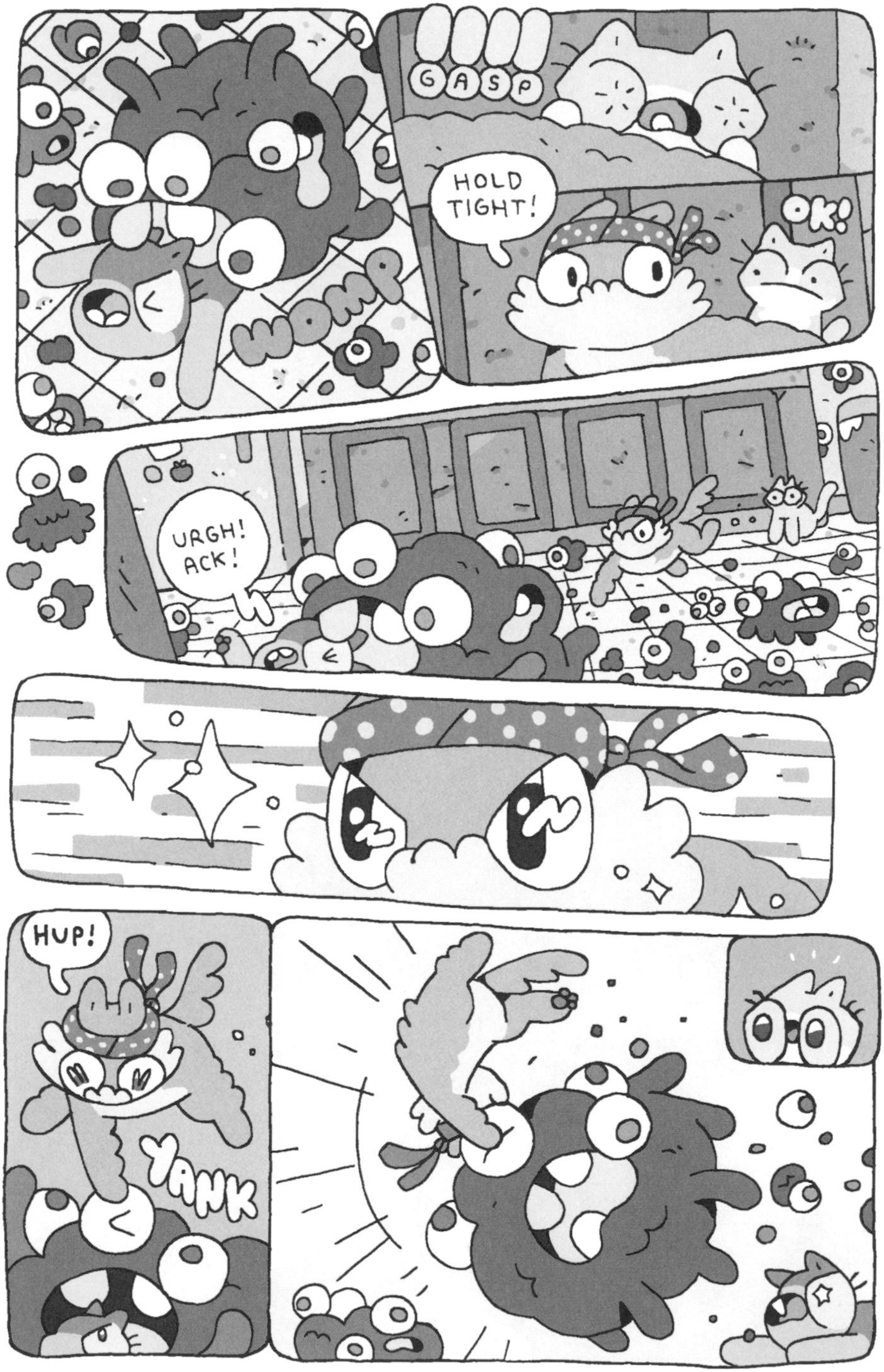
WOMP
GASP
HOLD TIGHT!
OK!
URGH! ACK!
HUP!
YANK

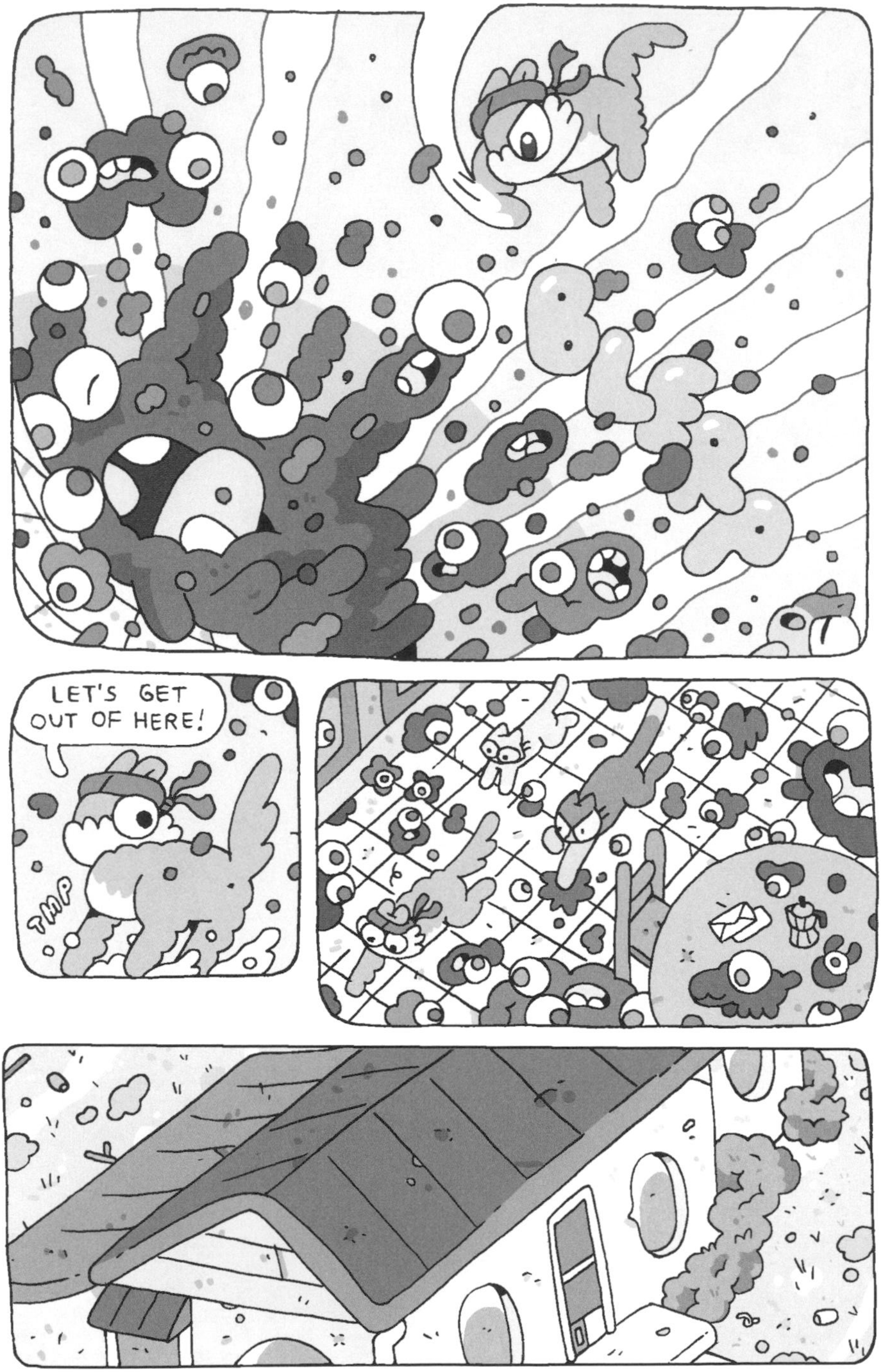
BLERP
LET'S GET OUT OF HERE!
TMP

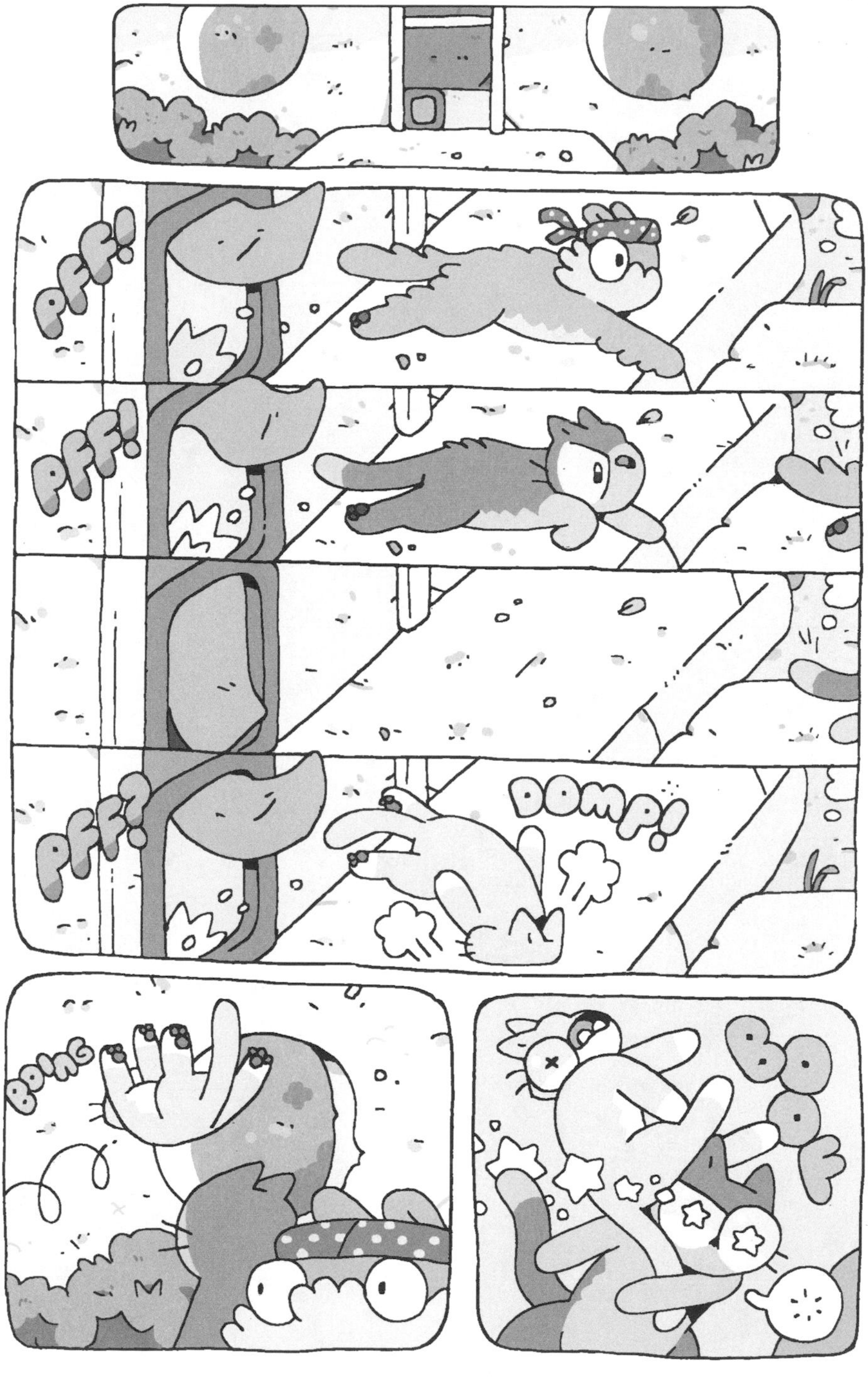
PFF!
PFF!
PFF?
DOMP!
BOING
BOOF

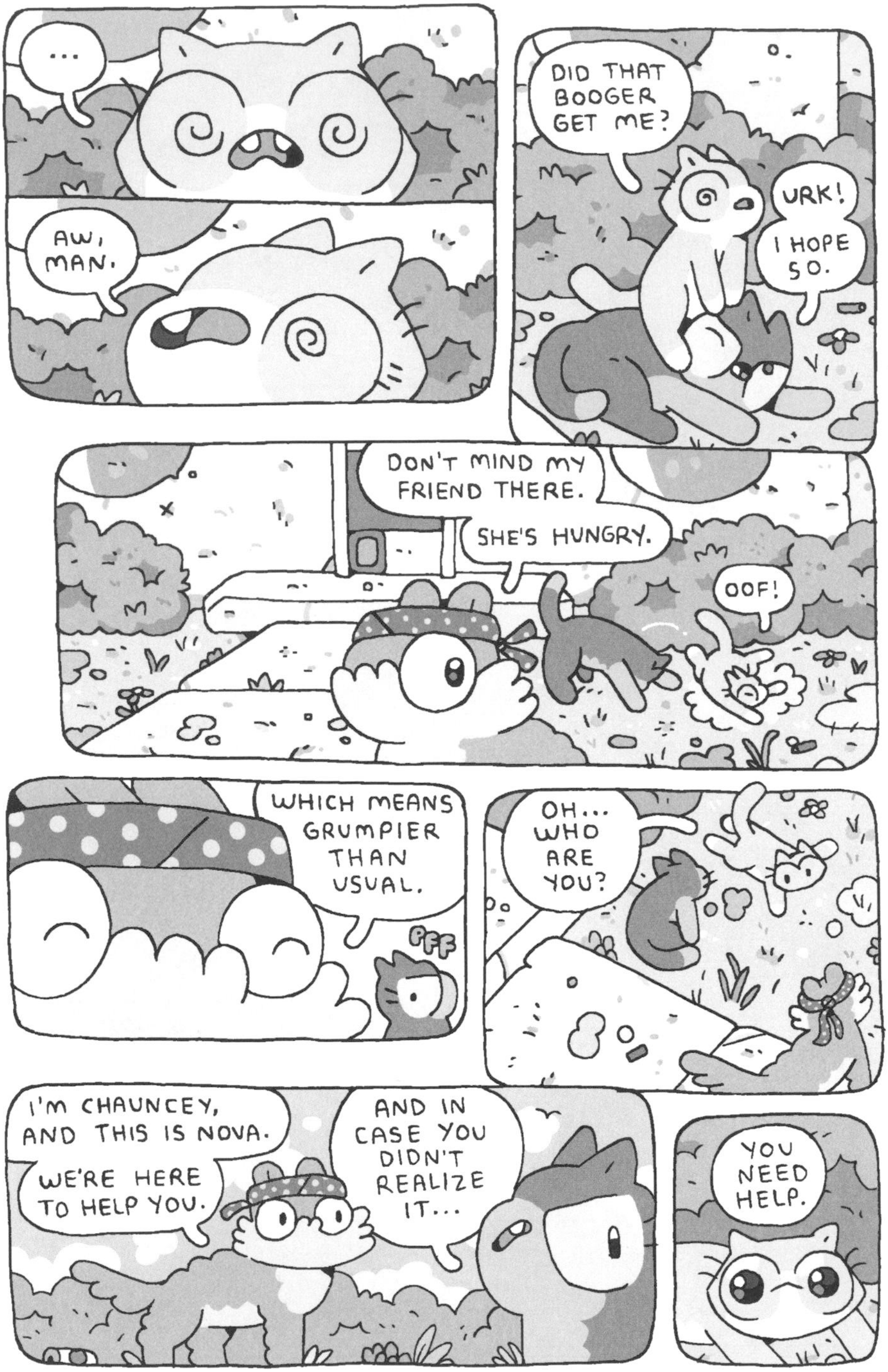
...
AW, MAN.
DID THAT BOOGER GET ME?
URK!
I HOPE SO.
DON'T MIND MY FRIEND THERE.
SHE'S HUNGRY.
OOF!
WHICH MEANS GRUMPIER THAN USUAL.
PFF
OH... WHO ARE YOU?
I'M CHAUNCEY, AND THIS IS NOVA.
WE'RE HERE TO HELP YOU.
AND IN CASE YOU DIDN'T REALIZE IT...
YOU NEED HELP.

CHAPTER 2

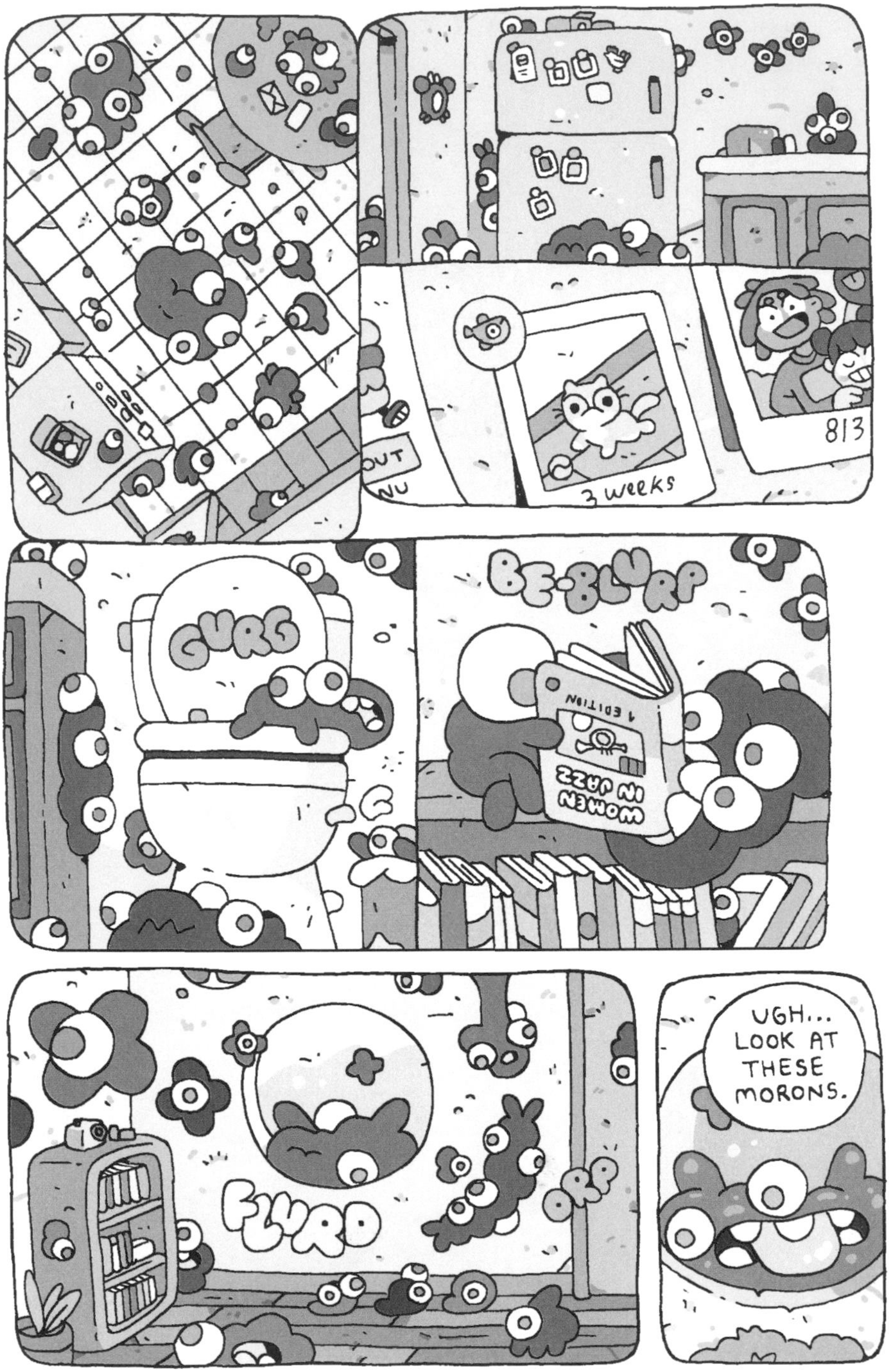
OUT
NU
3 weeks
813
GURG
BE-BLURP
1 EDITION
WOMEN IN JAZZ
FLURD
ORP
UGH... LOOK AT THESE MORONS.

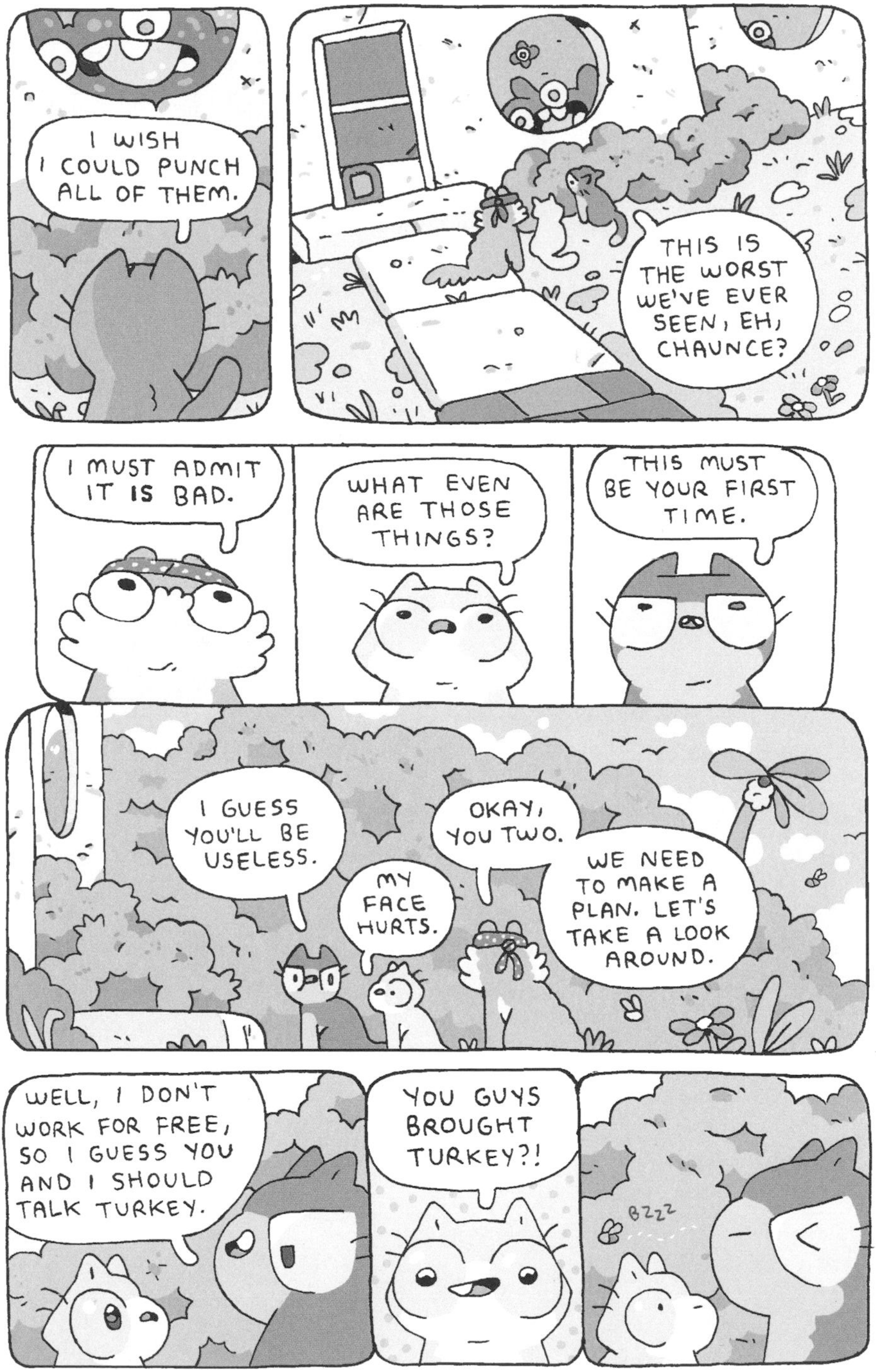
I WISH I COULD PUNCH ALL OF THEM.
THIS IS THE WORST WE'VE EVER SEEN, EH, CHAUNCE?
I MUST ADMIT IT IS BAD.
WHAT EVEN ARE THOSE THINGS?
THIS MUST BE YOUR FIRST TIME.
I GUESS YOU'LL BE USELESS.
MY FACE HURTS.
OKAY, YOU TWO.
WE NEED TO MAKE A PLAN. LET'S TAKE A LOOK AROUND.
WELL, I DON'T WORK FOR FREE, SO I GUESS YOU AND I SHOULD TALK TURKEY.
YOU GUYS BROUGHT TURKEY?!
BZZZ

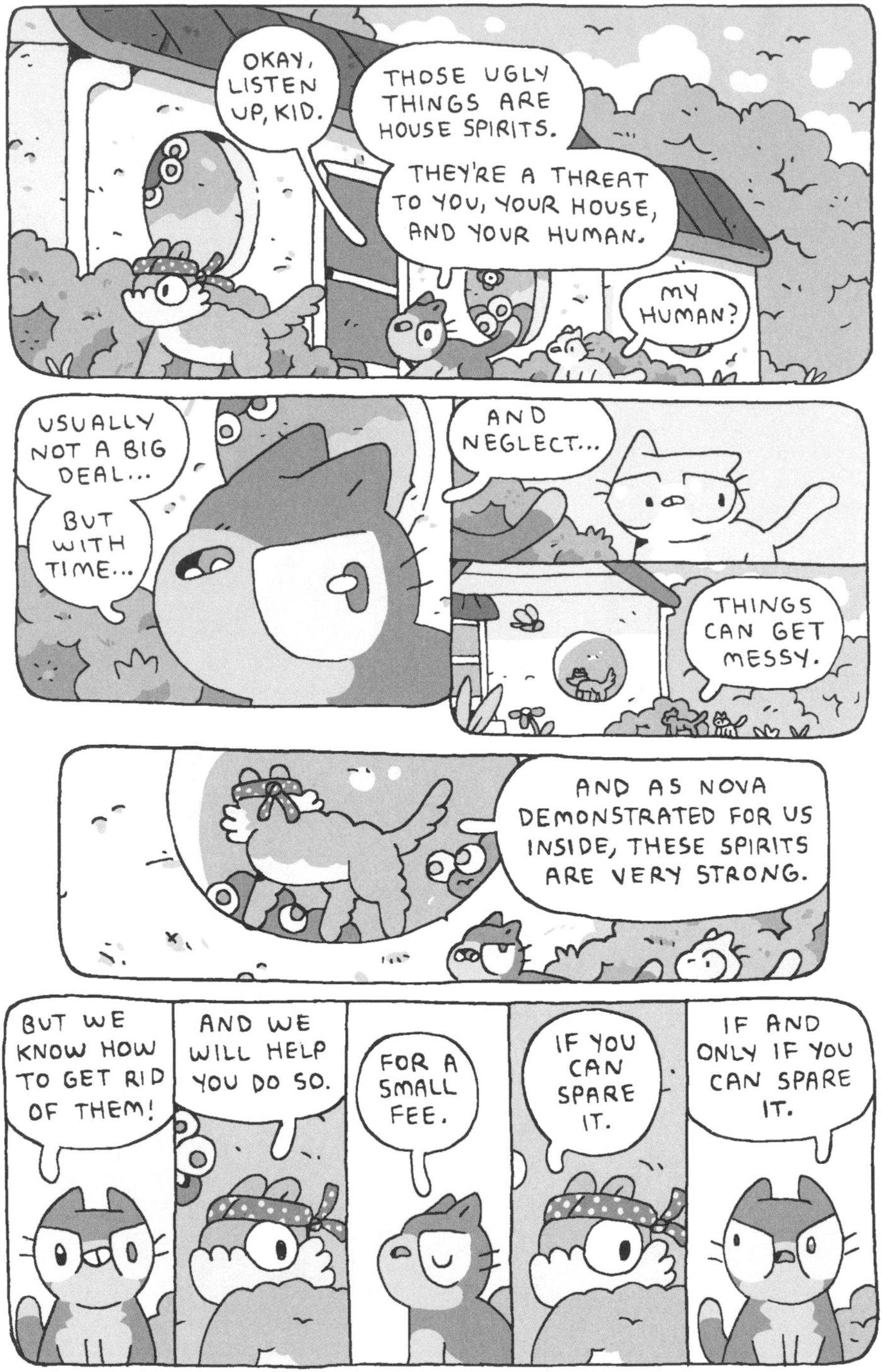
OKAY, LISTEN UP, KID.
THOSE UGLY THINGS ARE HOUSE SPIRITS.
THEY'RE A THREAT TO YOU, YOUR HOUSE, AND YOUR HUMAN.
MY HUMAN?
USUALLY NOT A BIG DEAL...
BUT WITH TIME...
AND NEGLECT...
THINGS CAN GET MESSY.
AND AS NOVA DEMONSTRATED FOR US INSIDE, THESE SPIRITS ARE VERY STRONG.
BUT WE KNOW HOW TO GET RID OF THEM!
AND WE WILL HELP YOU DO SO.
FOR A SMALL FEE.
IF YOU CAN SPARE IT.
IF AND ONLY IF YOU CAN SPARE IT.

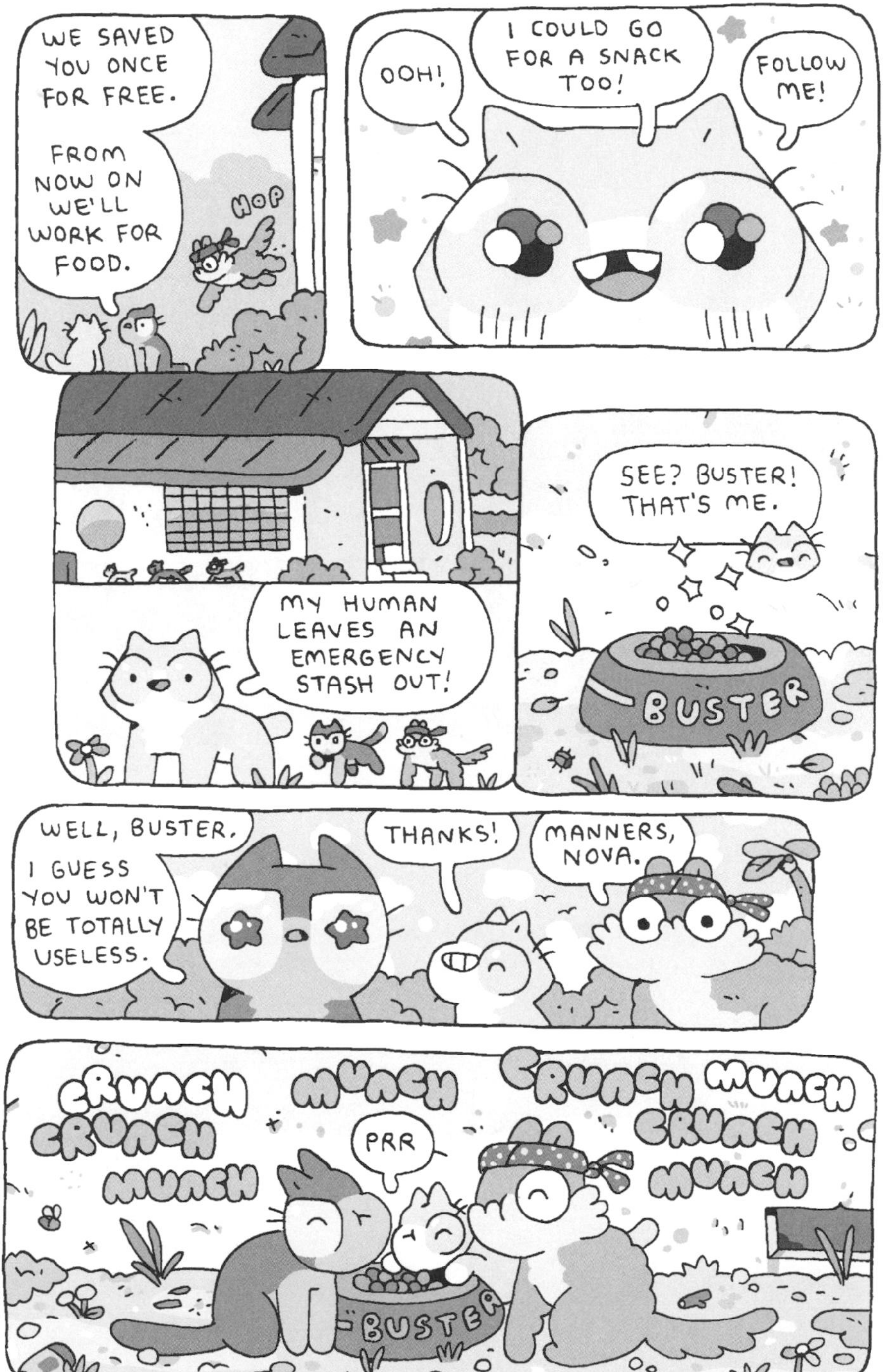
WE SAVED YOU ONCE FOR FREE.
FROM NOW ON WE'LL WORK FOR FOOD.
HOP
OOH!
I COULD GO FOR A SNACK TOO!
FOLLOW ME!
MY HUMAN LEAVES AN EMERGENCY STASH OUT!
SEE? BUSTER! THAT'S ME.
BUSTER
WELL, BUSTER.
I GUESS YOU WON'T BE TOTALLY USELESS.
THANKS!
MANNERS, NOVA.
CRUNCH MUNCH CRUNCH MUNCH
CRUNCH MUNCH CRUNCH MUNCH
PRR
BUSTER

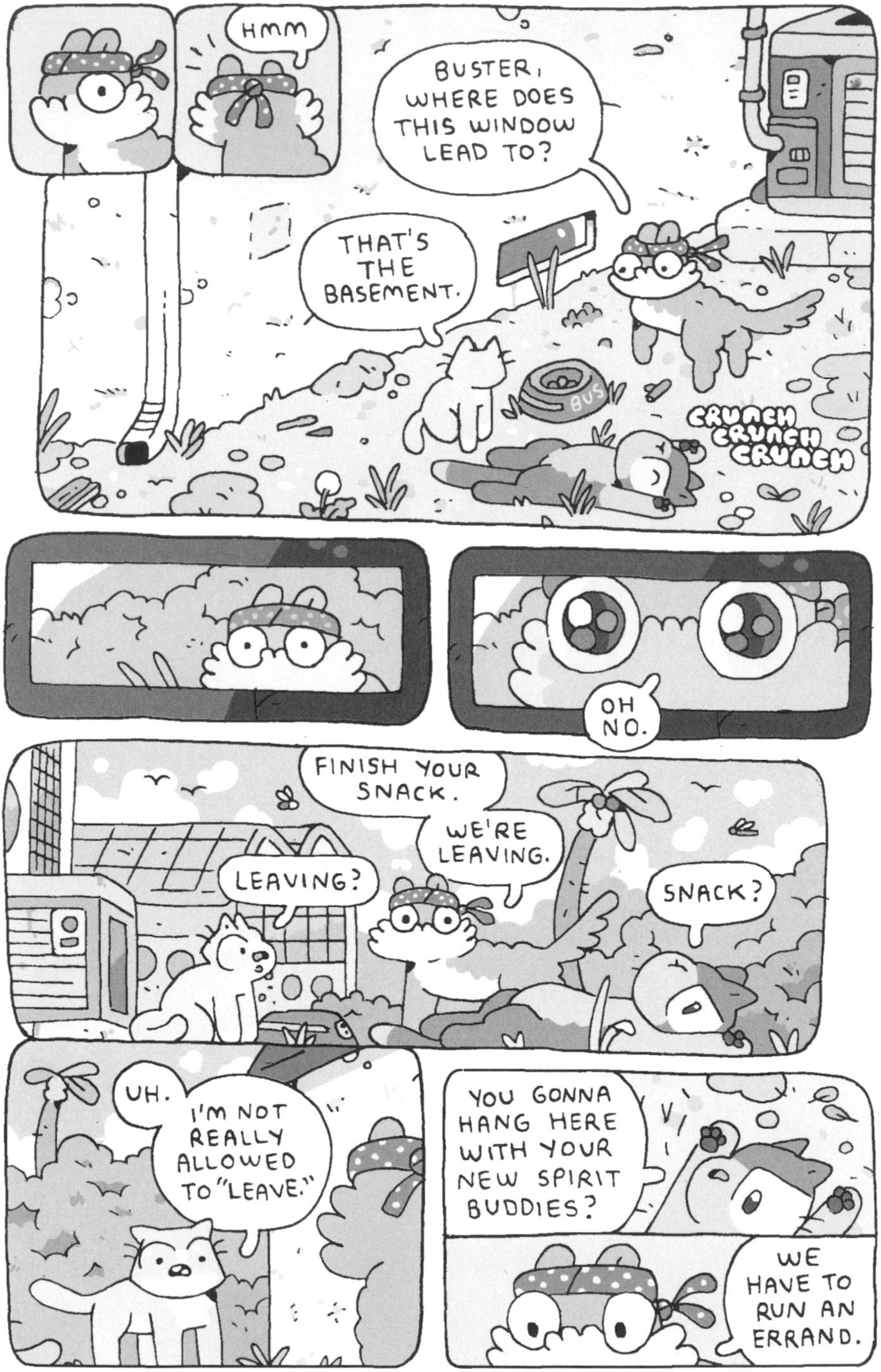
HMM
BUSTER, WHERE DOES THIS WINDOW LEAD TO?
THAT'S THE BASEMENT.
BUS
CRUNCH CRUNCH CRUNCH
OH NO.
FINISH YOUR SNACK.
WE'RE LEAVING.
LEAVING?
SNACK?
UH.
I'M NOT REALLY ALLOWED TO "LEAVE."
YOU GONNA HANG HERE WITH YOUR NEW SPIRIT BUDDIES?
WE HAVE TO RUN AN ERRAND.

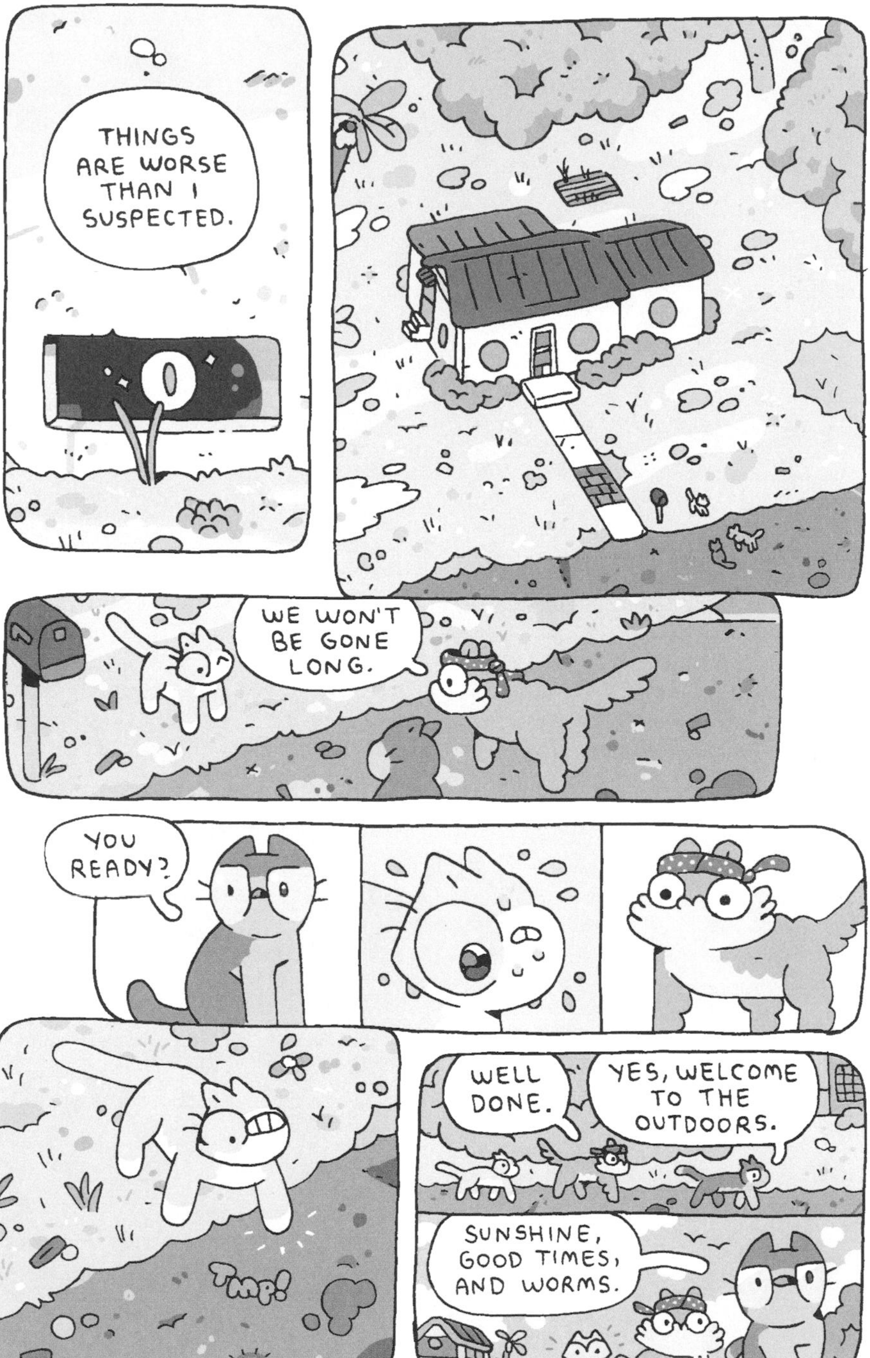
THINGS ARE WORSE THAN I SUSPECTED.
0
WE WON'T BE GONE LONG.
YOU READY?
TMP!
WELL DONE.
YES, WELCOME TO THE OUTDOORS.
SUNSHINE, GOOD TIMES, AND WORMS.

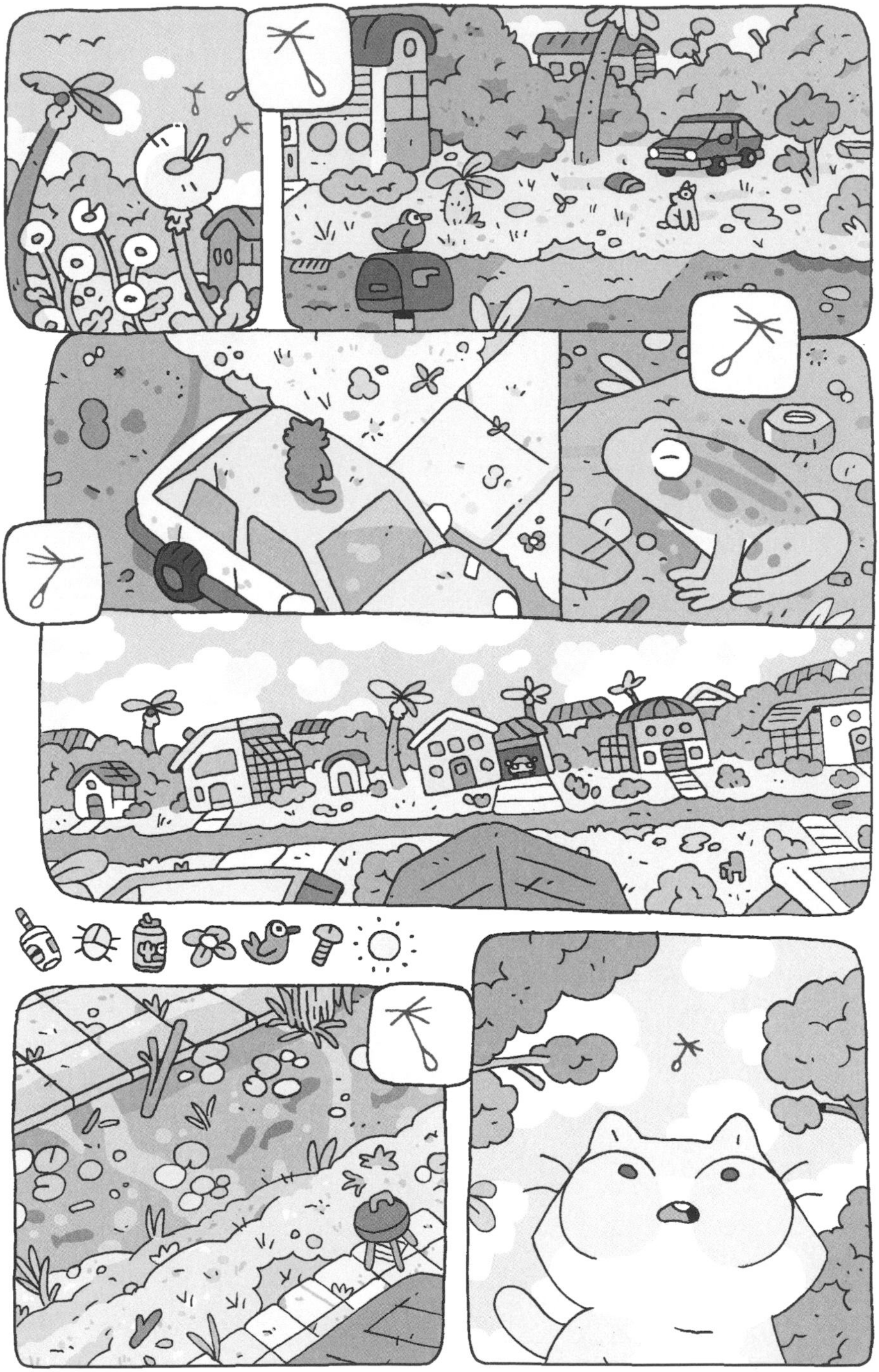

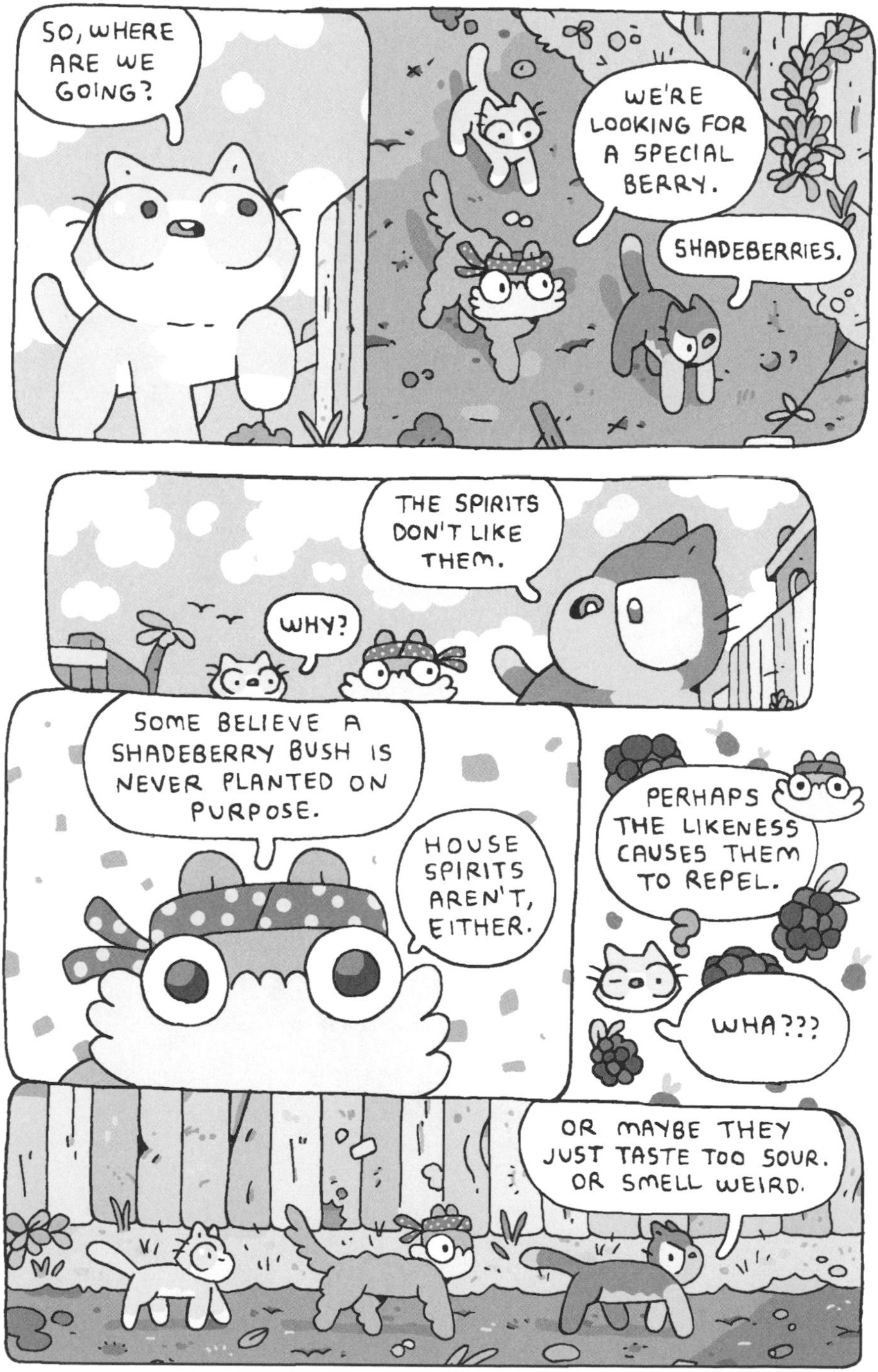
SO, WHERE ARE WE GOING?
WE'RE LOOKING FOR A SPECIAL BERRY.
SHADEBERRIES.
THE SPIRITS DON'T LIKE THEM.
WHY?
SOME BELIEVE A SHADEBERRY BUSH IS NEVER PLANTED ON PURPOSE.
HOUSE SPIRITS AREN'T, EITHER.
PERHAPS THE LIKENESS CAUSES THEM TO REPEL.
WHA???
OR MAYBE THEY JUST TASTE TOO SOUR. OR SMELL WEIRD.

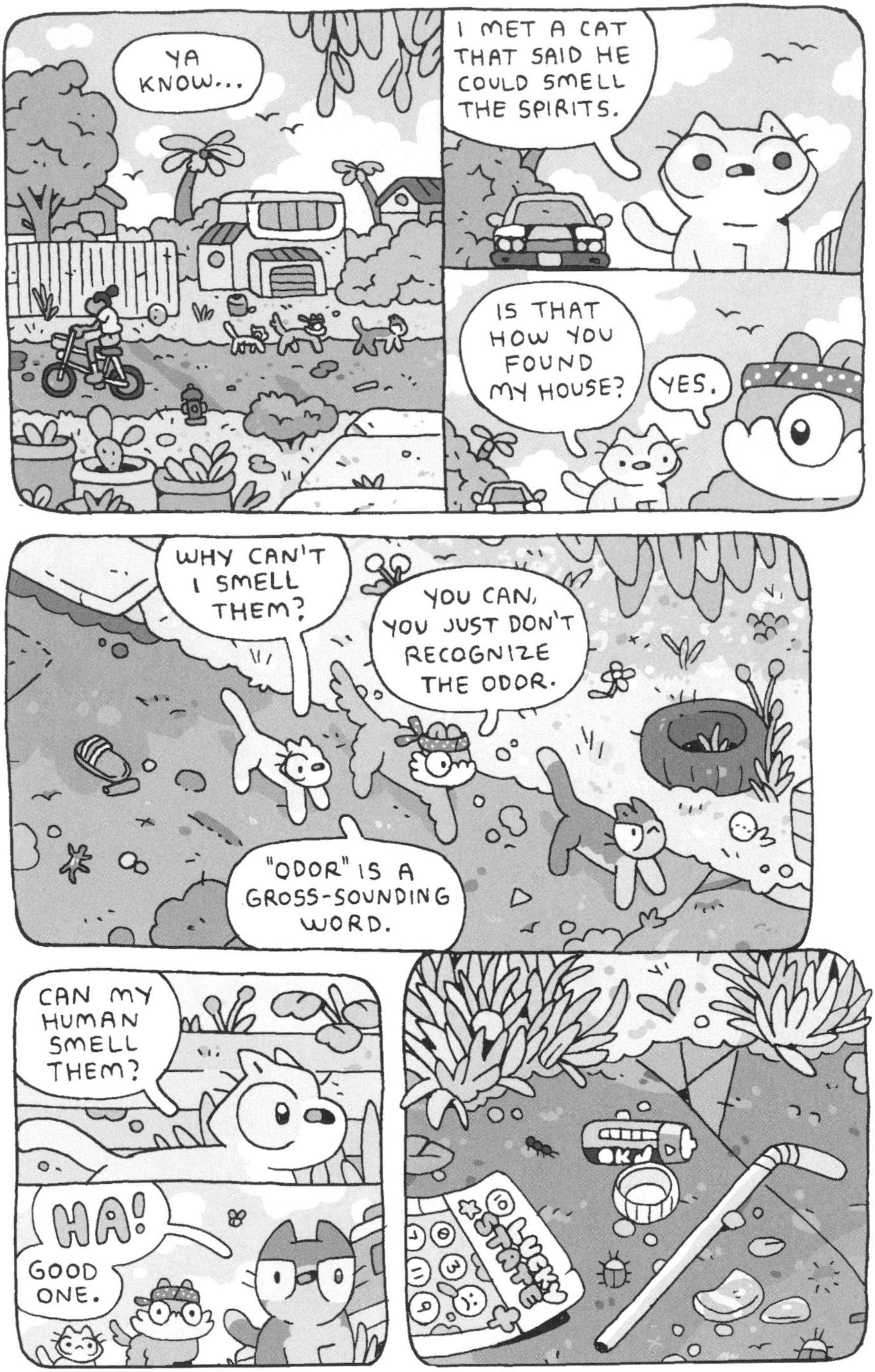
YA KNOW...
I MET A CAT THAT SAID HE COULD SMELL THE SPIRITS.
IS THAT HOW YOU FOUND MY HOUSE?
YES.
WHY CAN'T I SMELL THEM?
YOU CAN, YOU JUST DON'T RECOGNIZE THE ODOR.
"ODOR" IS A GROSS-SOUNDING WORD.
CAN MY HUMAN SMELL THEM?
HA! GOOD ONE.
LUCKY STAFF

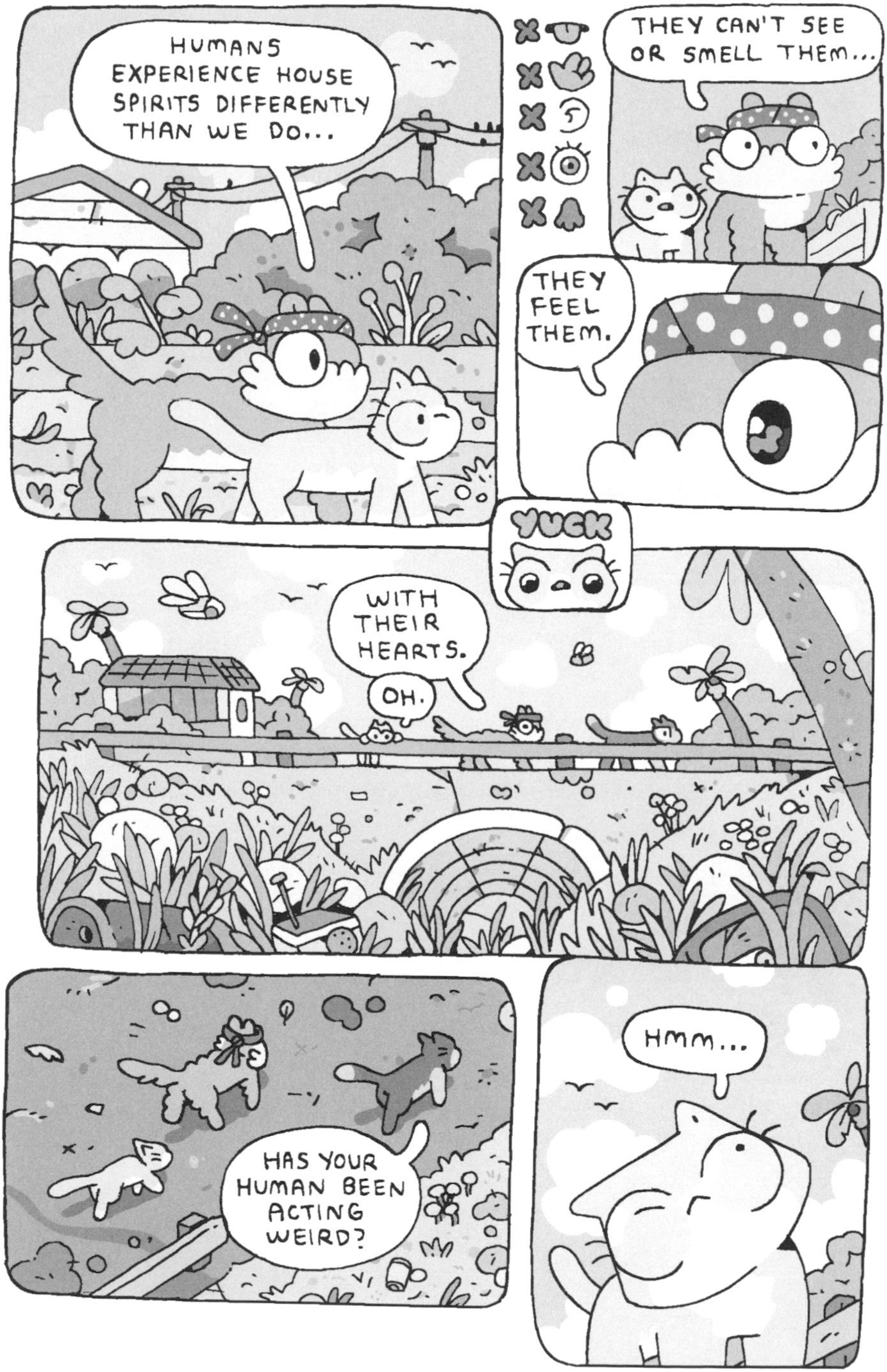
HUMANS EXPERIENCE HOUSE SPIRITS DIFFERENTLY THAN WE DO...
THEY CAN'T SEE OR SMELL THEM...
THEY FEEL THEM.
YUCK
WITH THEIR HEARTS.
OH.
HAS YOUR HUMAN BEEN ACTING WEIRD?
HMM...

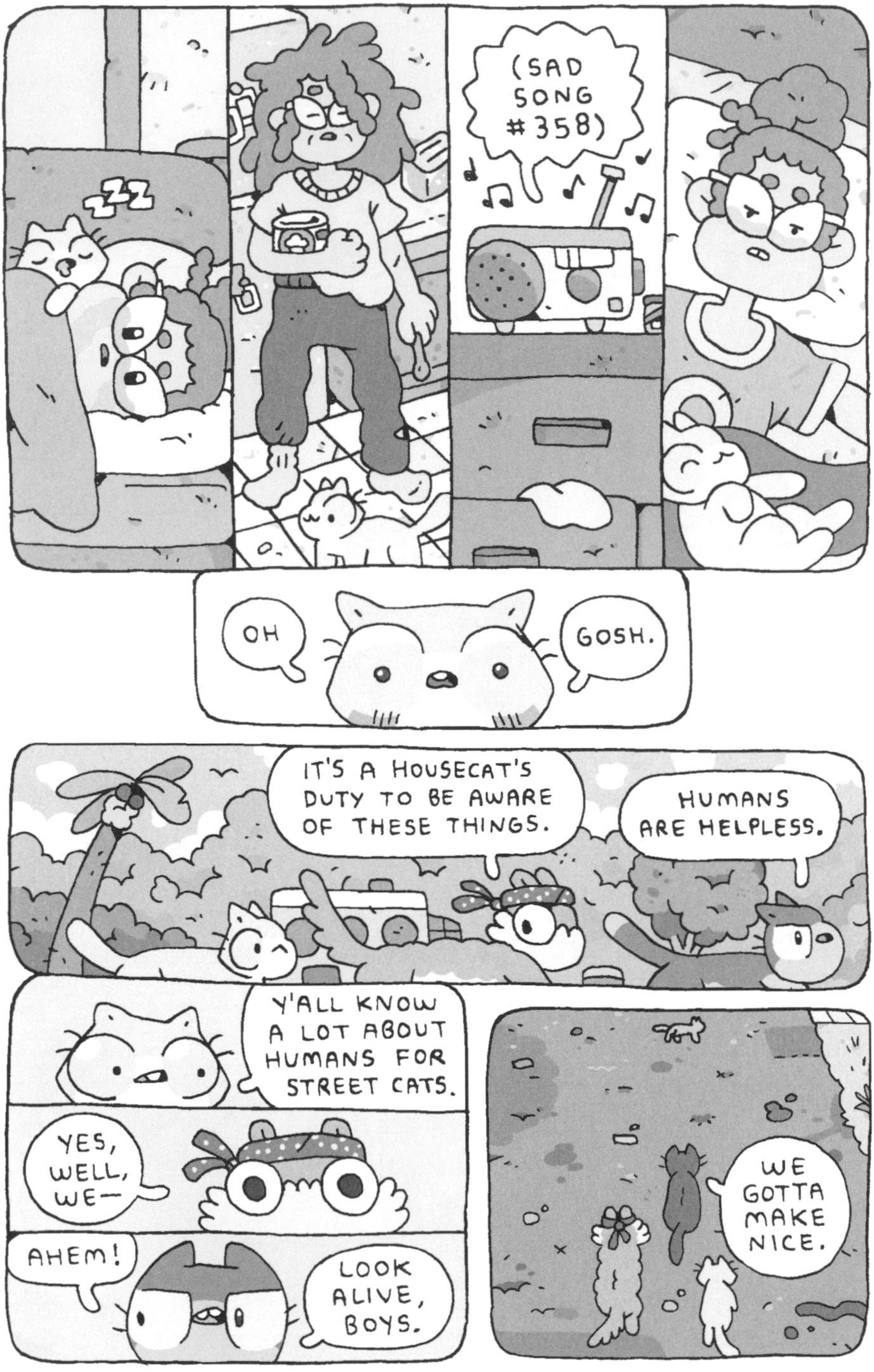
(SAD SONG #358)
OH
GOSH.
IT'S A HOUSECAT'S DUTY TO BE AWARE OF THESE THINGS.
HUMANS ARE HELPLESS.
Y'ALL KNOW A LOT ABOUT HUMANS FOR STREET CATS.
YES, WELL, WE—
AHEM!
LOOK ALIVE, BOYS.
WE GOTTA MAKE NICE.

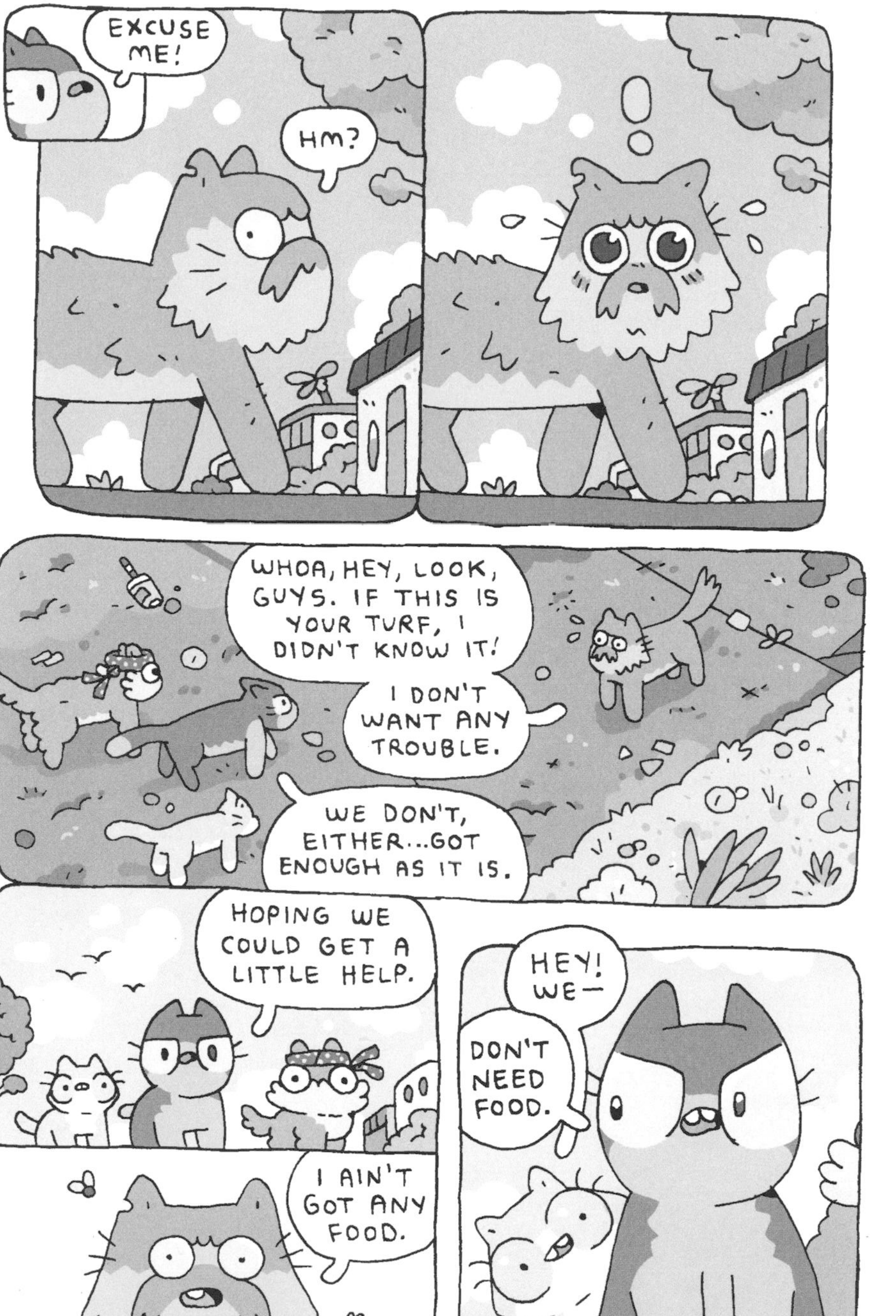
EXCUSE ME!
HM?
!
WHOA, HEY, LOOK, GUYS. IF THIS IS YOUR TURF, I DIDN'T KNOW IT!
I DON'T WANT ANY TROUBLE.
WE DON'T, EITHER...GOT ENOUGH AS IT IS.
HOPING WE COULD GET A LITTLE HELP.
I AIN'T GOT ANY FOOD.
HEY! WE—
DON'T NEED FOOD.

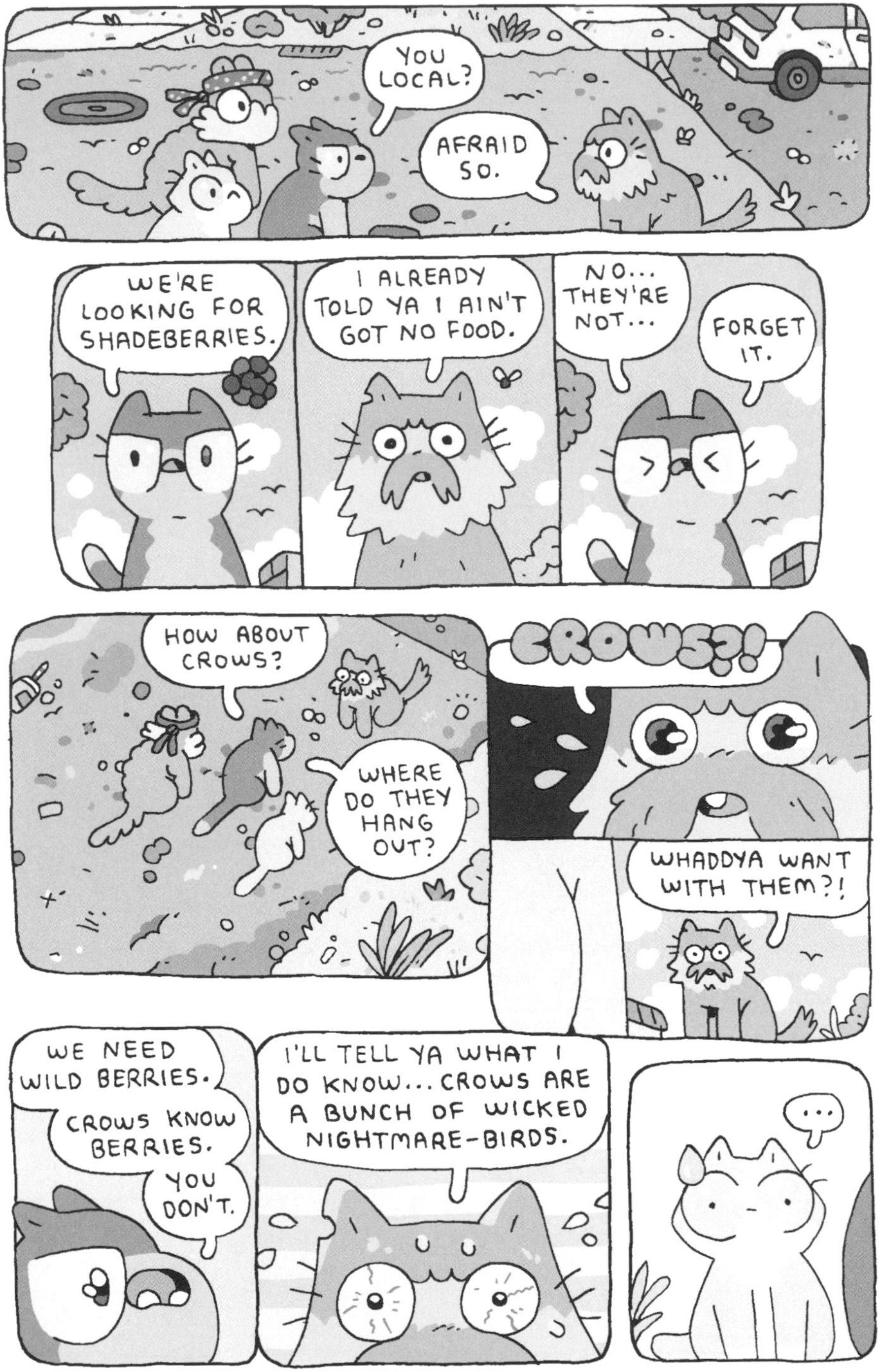
YOU LOCAL?
AFRAID SO.
WE'RE LOOKING FOR SHADEBERRIES.
I ALREADY TOLD YA I AIN'T GOT NO FOOD.
NO... THEY'RE NOT...
FORGET IT.
HOW ABOUT CROWS?
WHERE DO THEY HANG OUT?
CROWS?!
WHADDYA WANT WITH THEM?!
WE NEED WILD BERRIES.
CROWS KNOW BERRIES.
YOU DON'T.
I'LL TELL YA WHAT I DO KNOW... CROWS ARE A BUNCH OF WICKED NIGHTMARE-BIRDS.
...

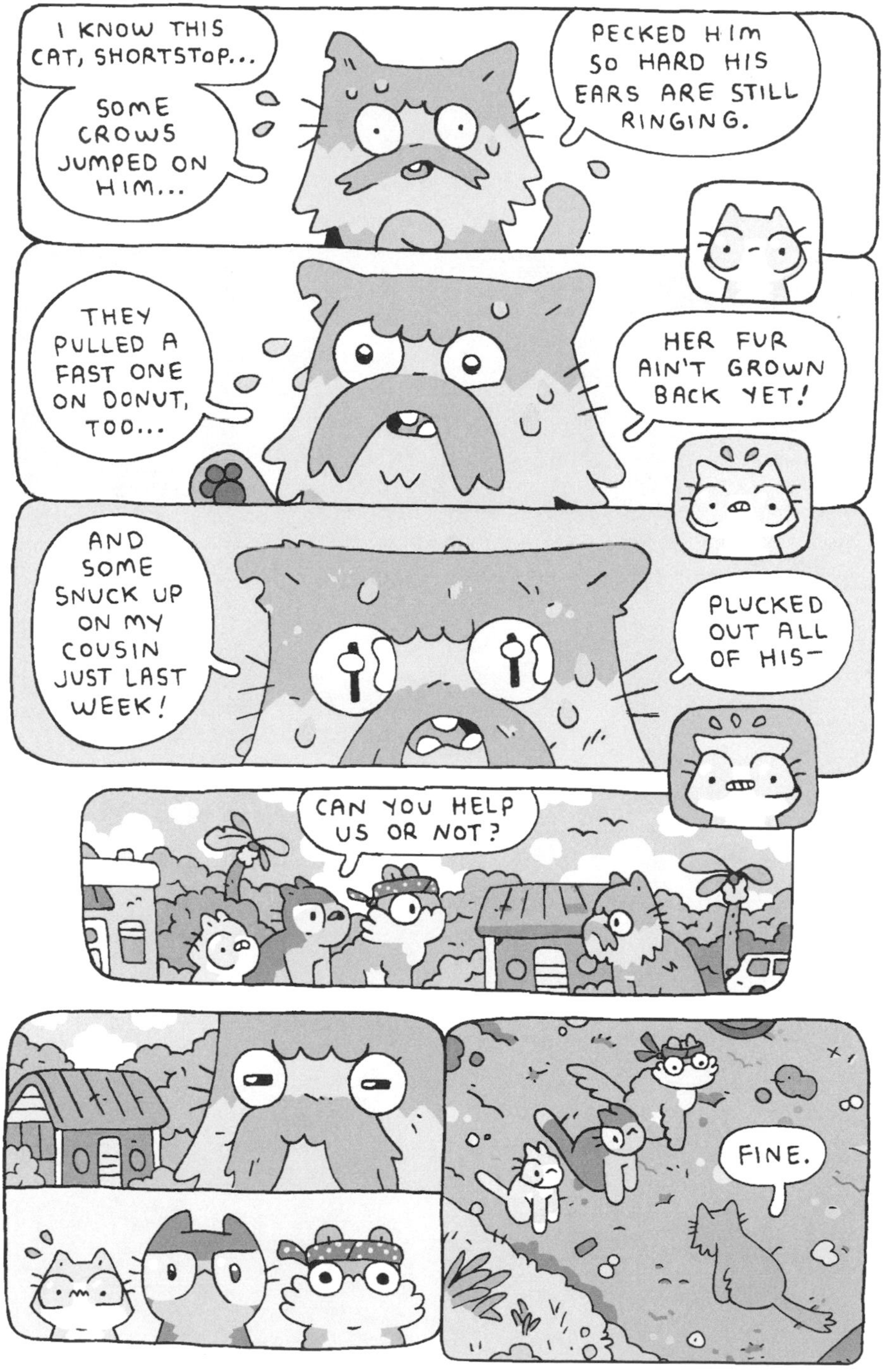

I KNOW THIS CAT, SHORTSTOP...
SOME CROWS JUMPED ON HIM...
PECKED HIM SO HARD HIS EARS ARE STILL RINGING.
THEY PULLED A FAST ONE ON DONUT, TOO...
HER FUR AIN'T GROWN BACK YET!
AND SOME SNUCK UP ON MY COUSIN JUST LAST WEEK!
PLUCKED OUT ALL OF HIS—
CAN YOU HELP US OR NOT?
FINE.

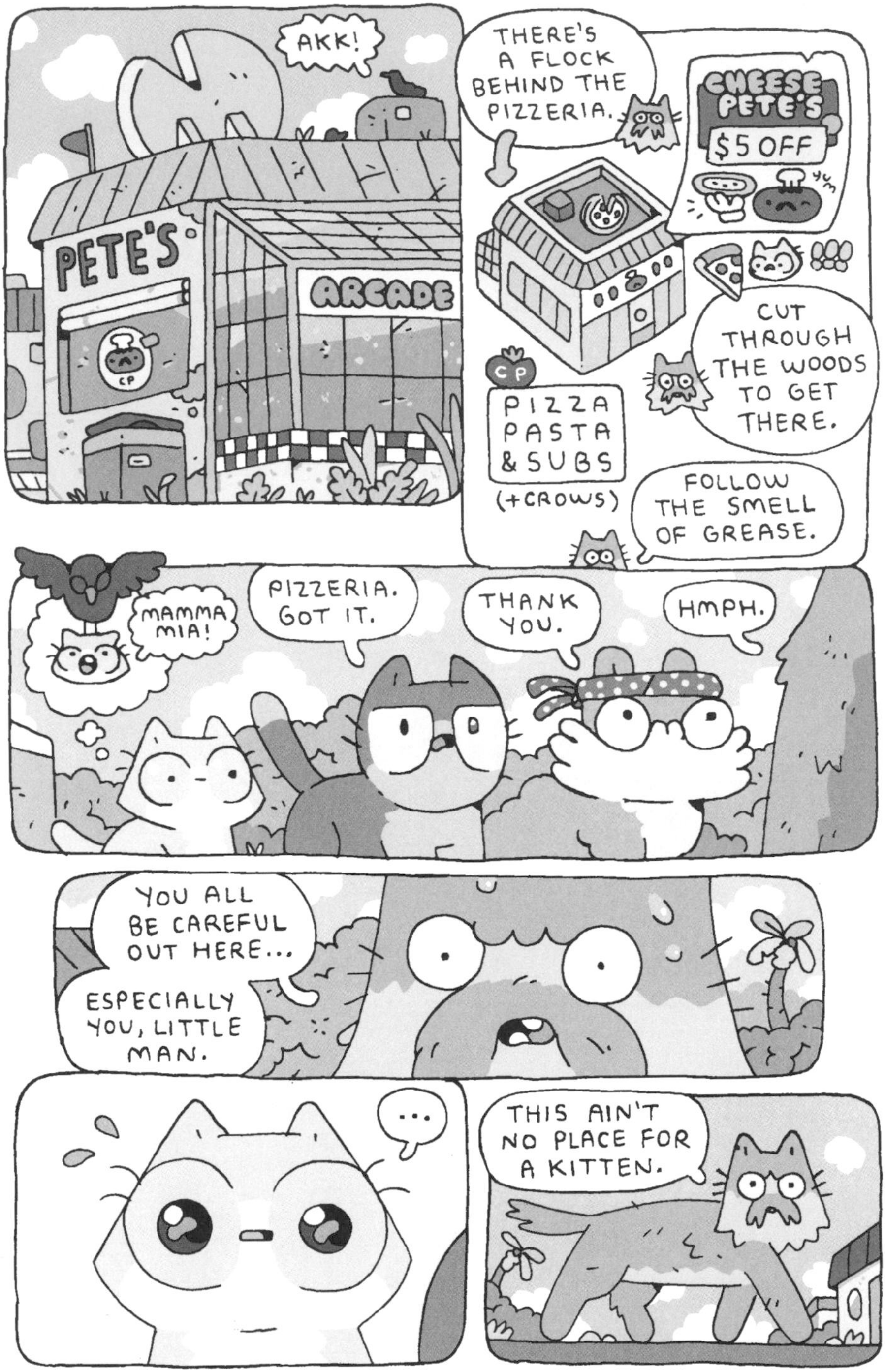
AKK!
PETE'S
ARCADE
CP
THERE'S A FLOCK BEHIND THE PIZZERIA.
CHEESE PETE'S
$5 OFF
yum
CUT THROUGH THE WOODS TO GET THERE.
CP
PIZZA PASTA & SUBS
(+CROWS)
FOLLOW THE SMELL OF GREASE.
MAMMA MIA!
PIZZERIA. GOT IT.
THANK YOU.
HMPH.
YOU ALL BE CAREFUL OUT HERE...
ESPECIALLY YOU, LITTLE MAN.
...
THIS AIN'T NO PLACE FOR A KITTEN.

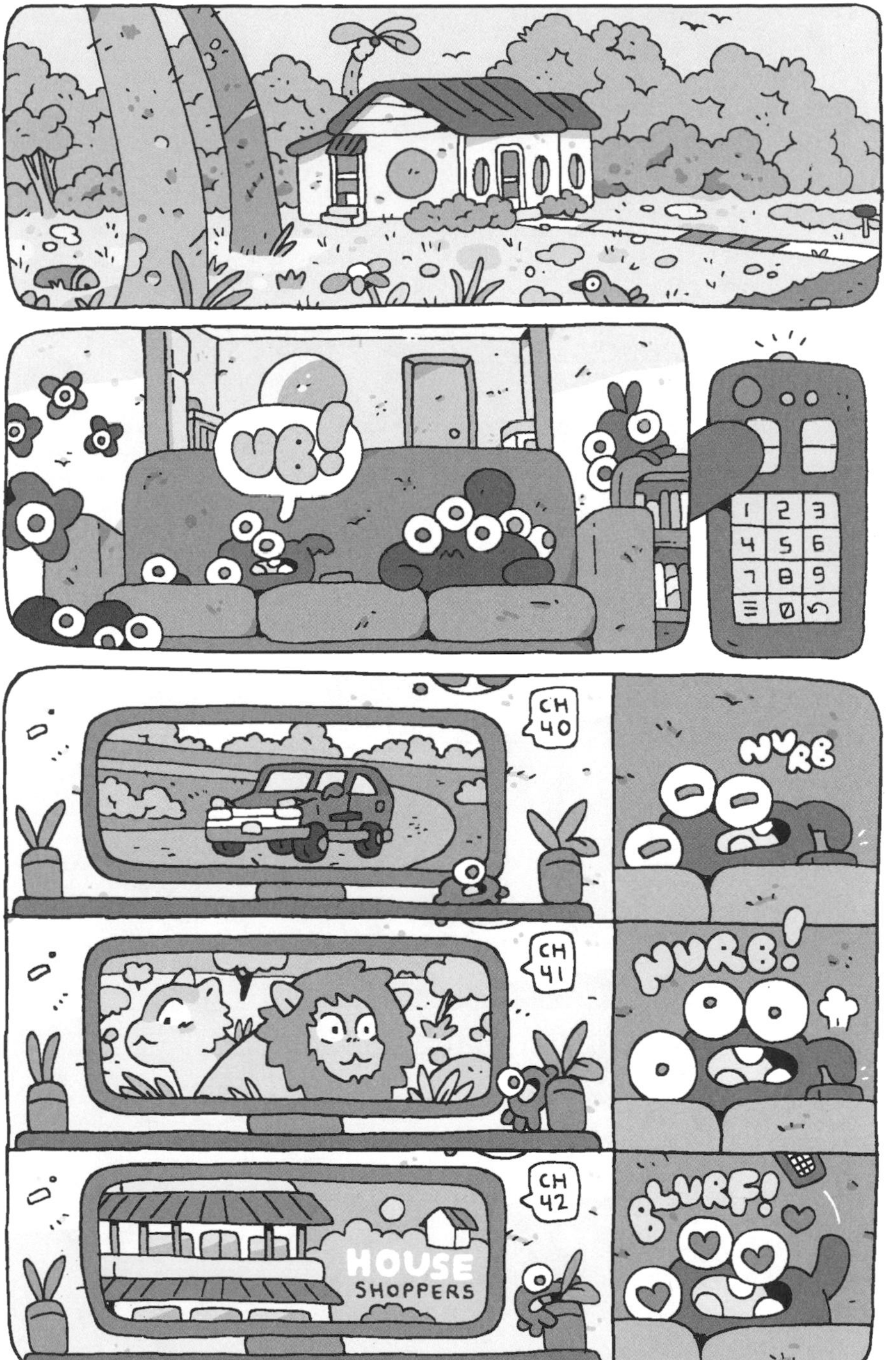
UB!
CH 40
NURB
CH 41
NURB!
CH 42
HOUSE
SHOPPERS
BLURF!

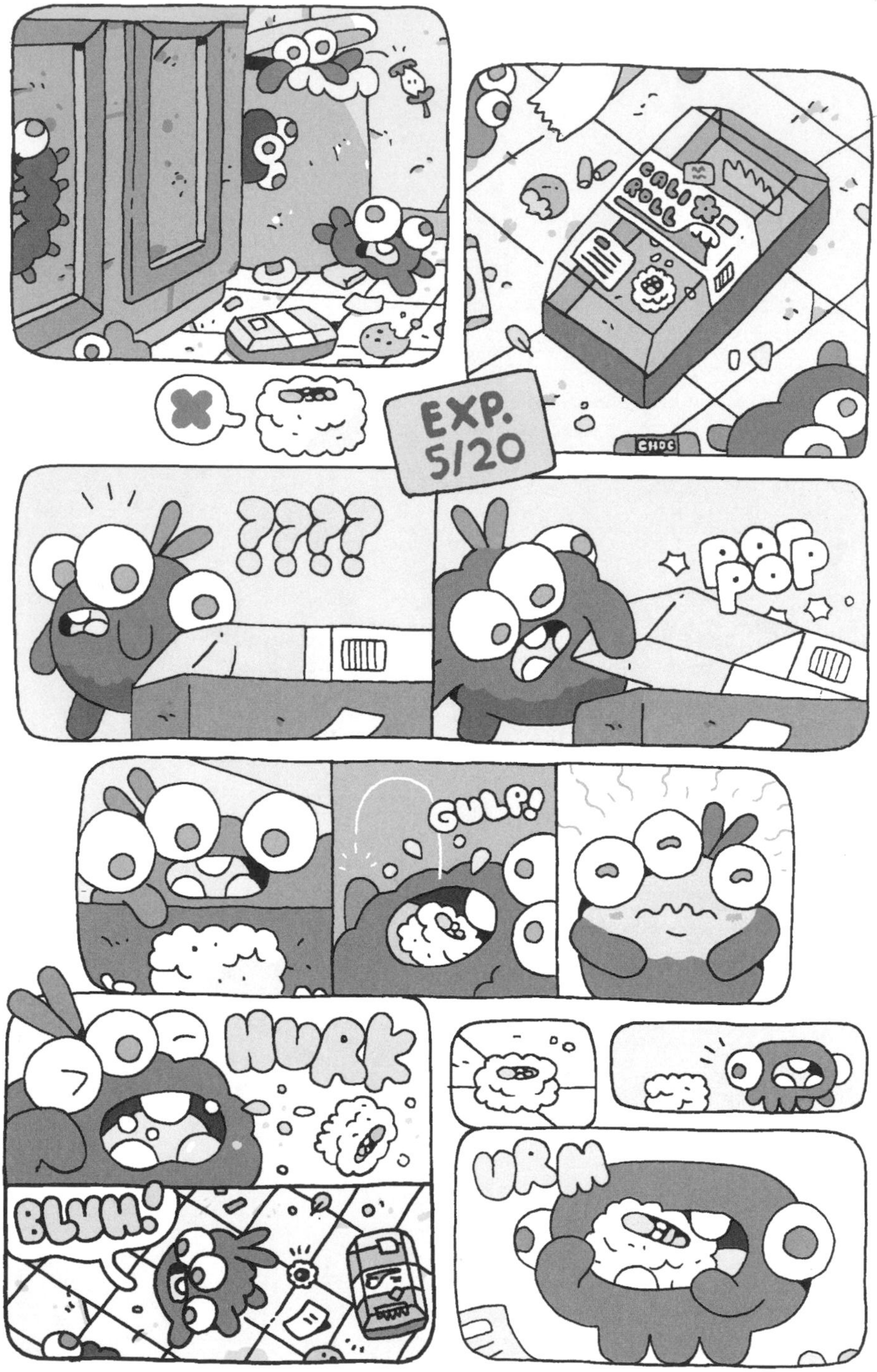

CALI ROLL
EXP. 5/20
CHOC
????
POP POP
GULP!
HURK
BLUH!
URM

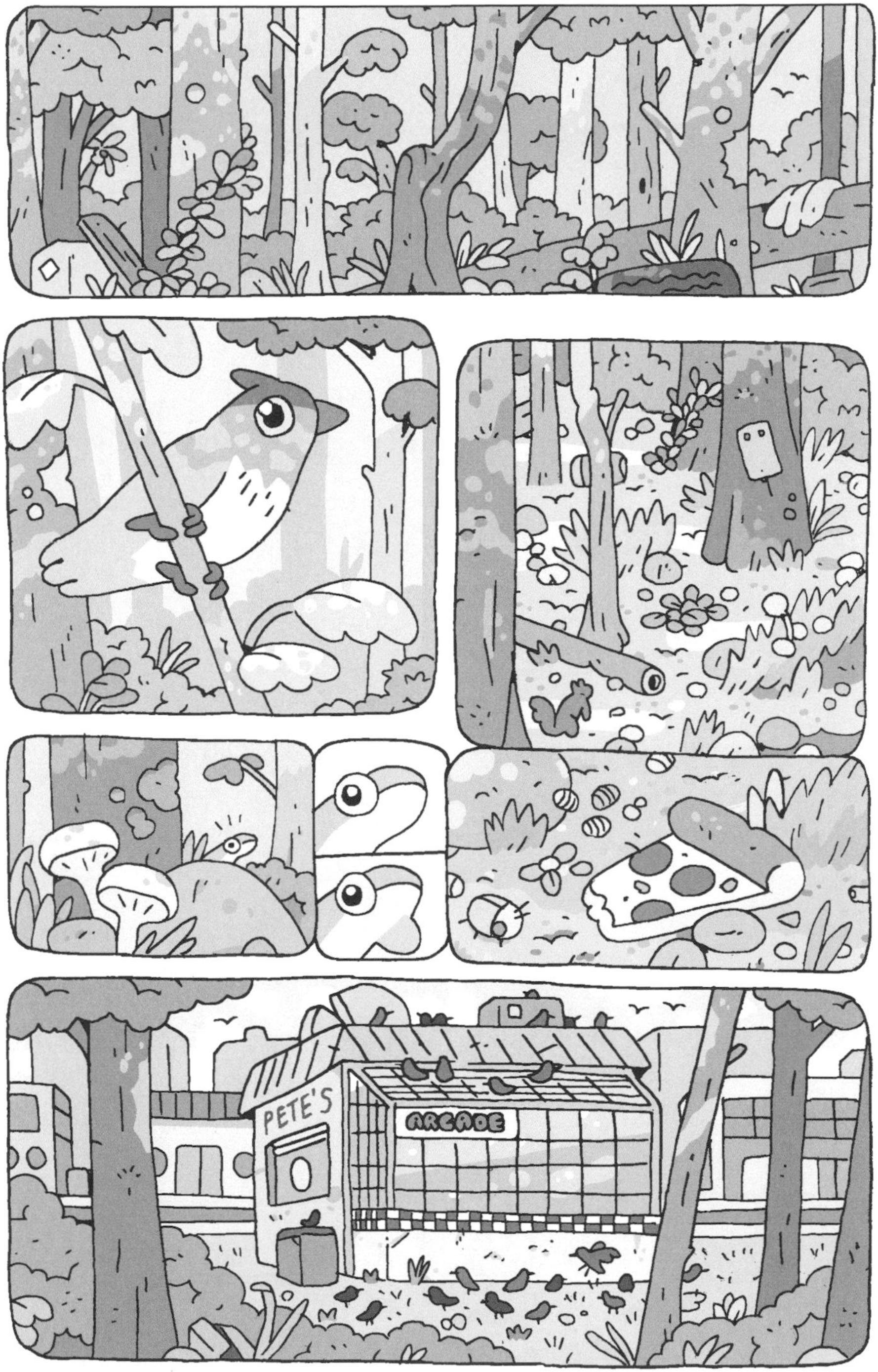
PETE'S
ARCADE

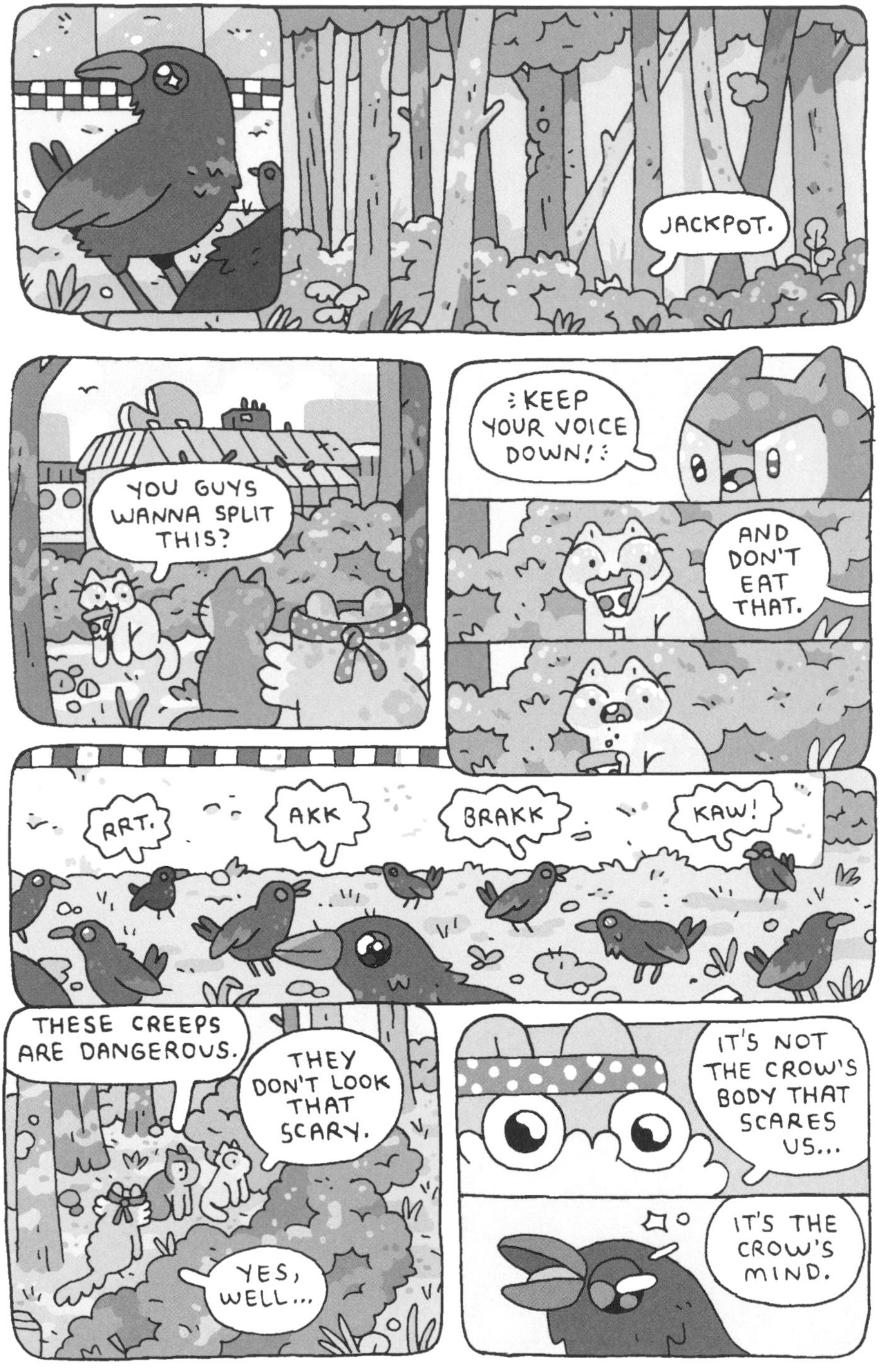
JACKPOT.
YOU GUYS WANNA SPLIT THIS?
KEEP YOUR VOICE DOWN!
AND DON'T EAT THAT.
ART.
AKK
BRAKK
KAW!
THESE CREEPS ARE DANGEROUS.
THEY DON'T LOOK THAT SCARY.
YES, WELL...
IT'S NOT THE CROW'S BODY THAT SCARES US...
IT'S THE CROW'S MIND.

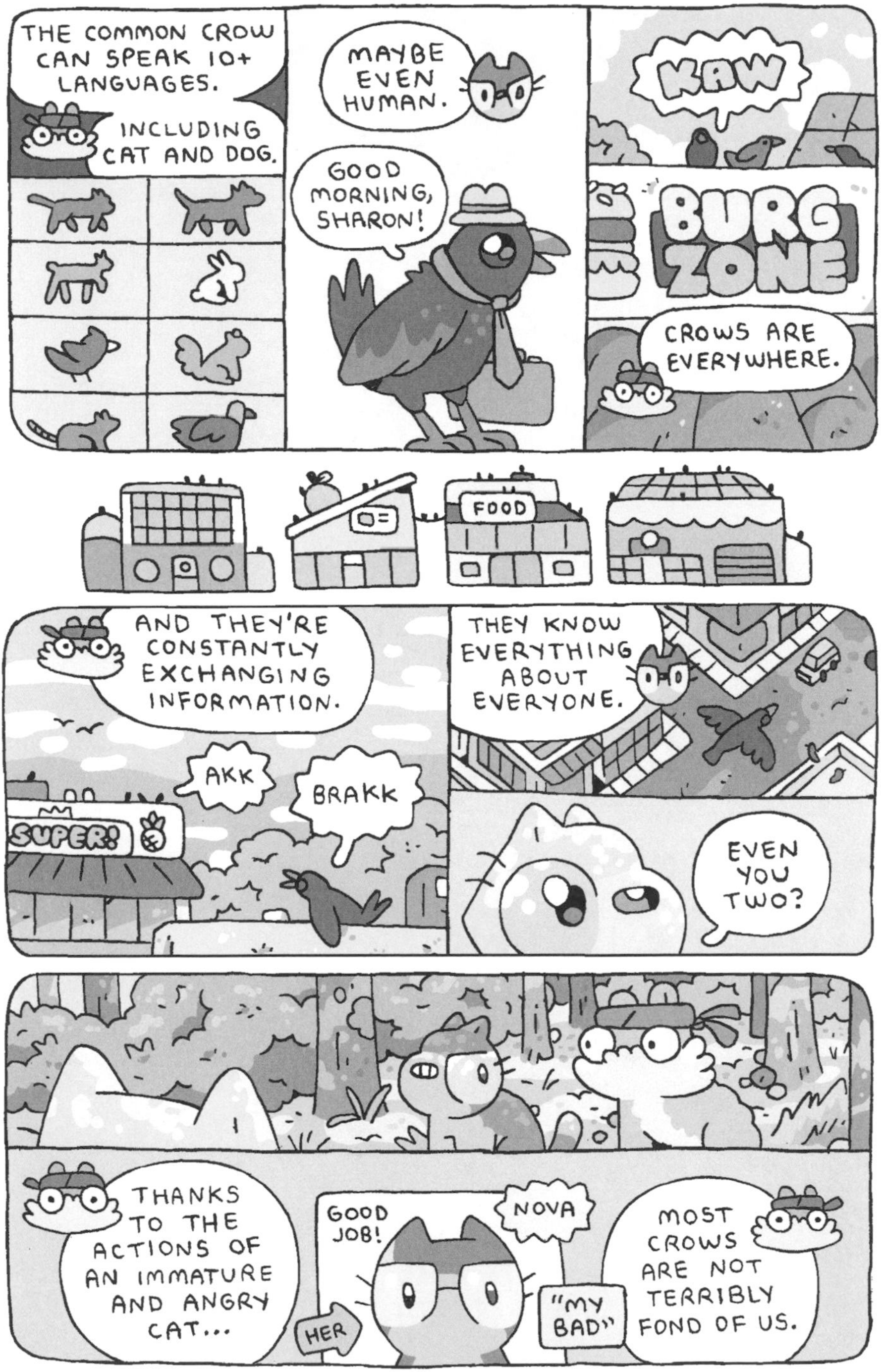
THE COMMON CROW CAN SPEAK 10+ LANGUAGES.
INCLUDING CAT AND DOG.
MAYBE EVEN HUMAN.
GOOD MORNING, SHARON!
KAW
BURG ZONE
CROWS ARE EVERYWHERE.
FOOD
AND THEY'RE CONSTANTLY EXCHANGING INFORMATION.
AKK
BRAKK
SUPER!
THEY KNOW EVERYTHING ABOUT EVERYONE.
EVEN YOU TWO?
THANKS TO THE ACTIONS OF AN IMMATURE AND ANGRY CAT...
GOOD JOB!
NOVA
HER
"MY BAD"
MOST CROWS ARE NOT TERRIBLY FOND OF US.

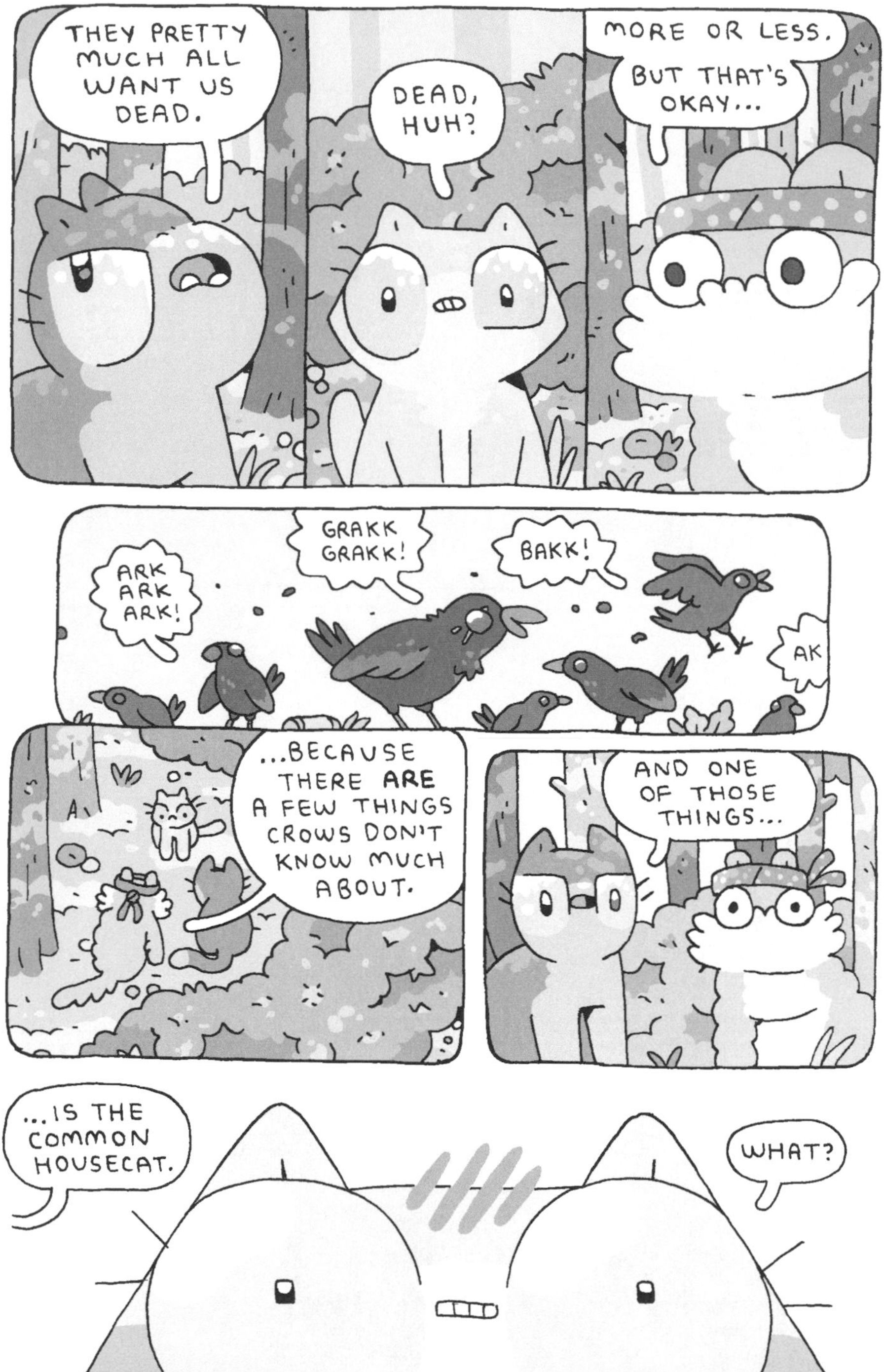
THEY PRETTY MUCH ALL WANT US DEAD.
DEAD, HUH?
MORE OR LESS.
BUT THAT'S OKAY...
ARK ARK ARK!
GRAKK GRAKK!
BAKK!
AK
...BECAUSE THERE **ARE** A FEW THINGS CROWS DON'T KNOW MUCH ABOUT.
AND ONE OF THOSE THINGS...
...IS THE COMMON HOUSECAT.
WHAT?

CHAPTER 3

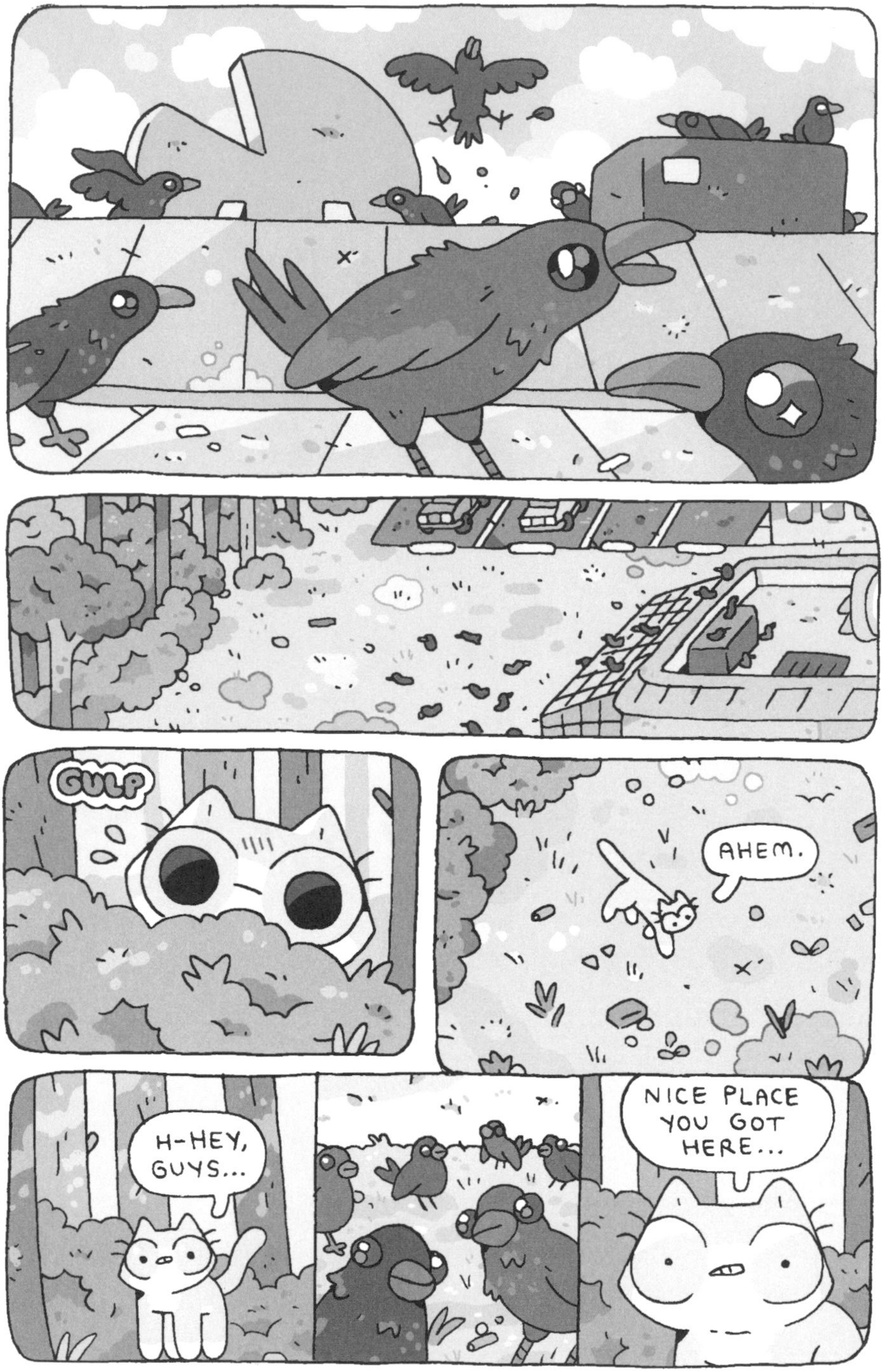
GULP
AHEM.
H-HEY, GUYS...
NICE PLACE YOU GOT HERE...

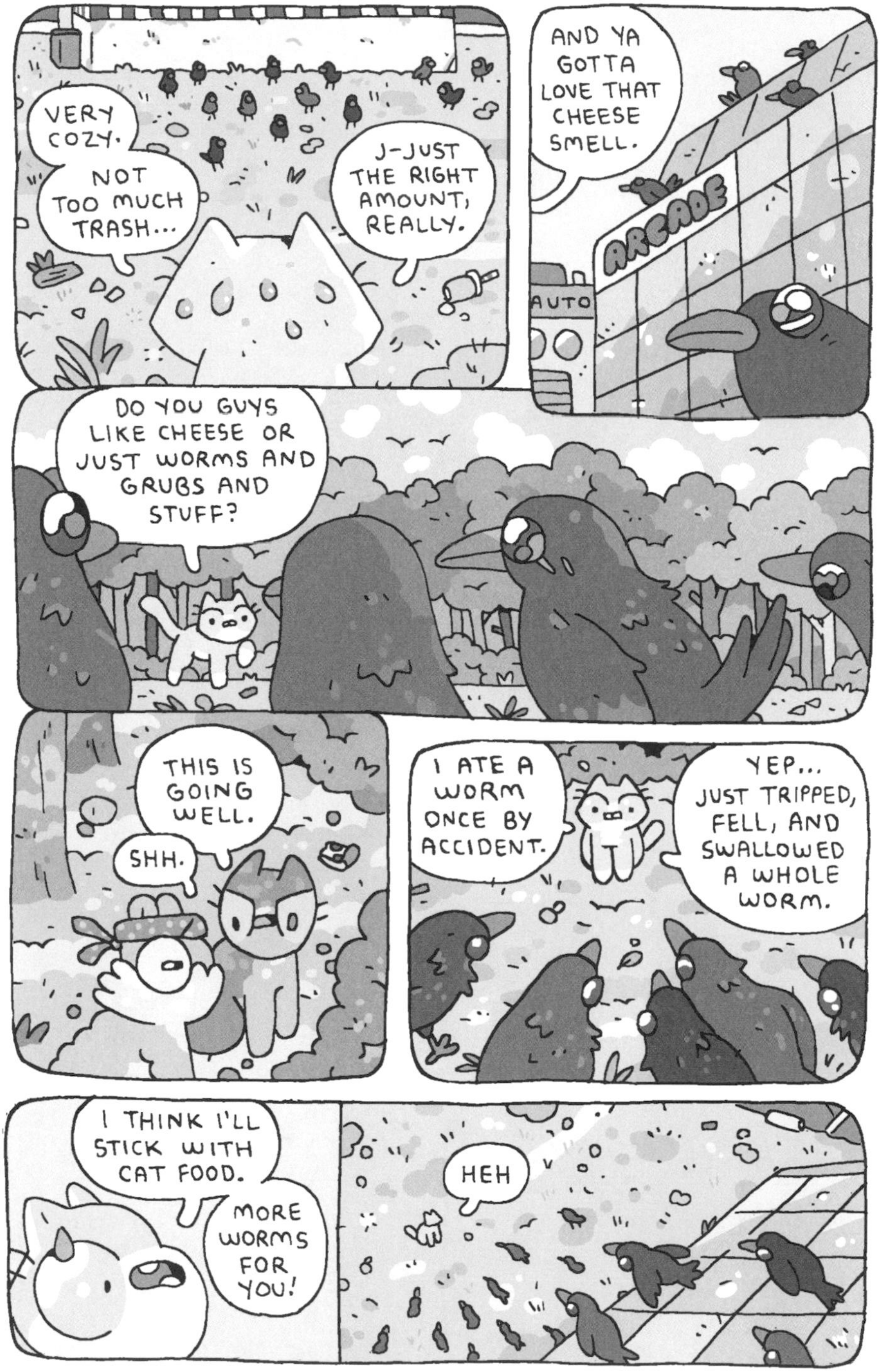
VERY COZY.
NOT TOO MUCH TRASH...
J-JUST THE RIGHT AMOUNT, REALLY.
AND YA GOTTA LOVE THAT CHEESE SMELL.
ARCADE
AUTO
DO YOU GUYS LIKE CHEESE OR JUST WORMS AND GRUBS AND STUFF?
THIS IS GOING WELL.
SHH.
I ATE A WORM ONCE BY ACCIDENT.
YEP... JUST TRIPPED, FELL, AND SWALLOWED A WHOLE WORM.
I THINK I'LL STICK WITH CAT FOOD.
MORE WORMS FOR YOU!
HEH

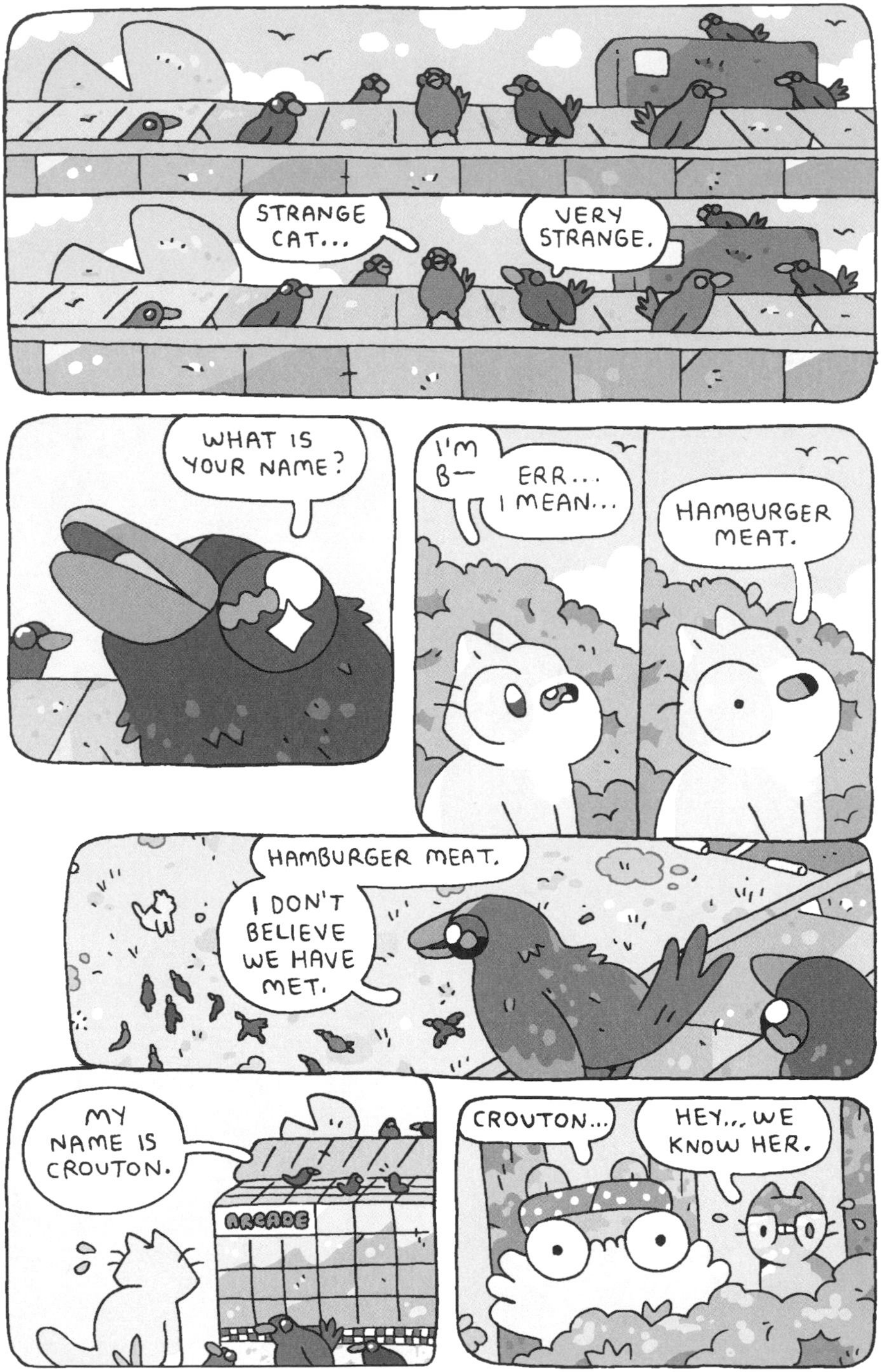
STRANGE CAT...
VERY STRANGE.
WHAT IS YOUR NAME?
I'M B—
ERR... I MEAN...
HAMBURGER MEAT.
HAMBURGER MEAT.
I DON'T BELIEVE WE HAVE MET.
MY NAME IS CROUTON.
ARCADE
CROUTON...
HEY... WE KNOW HER.

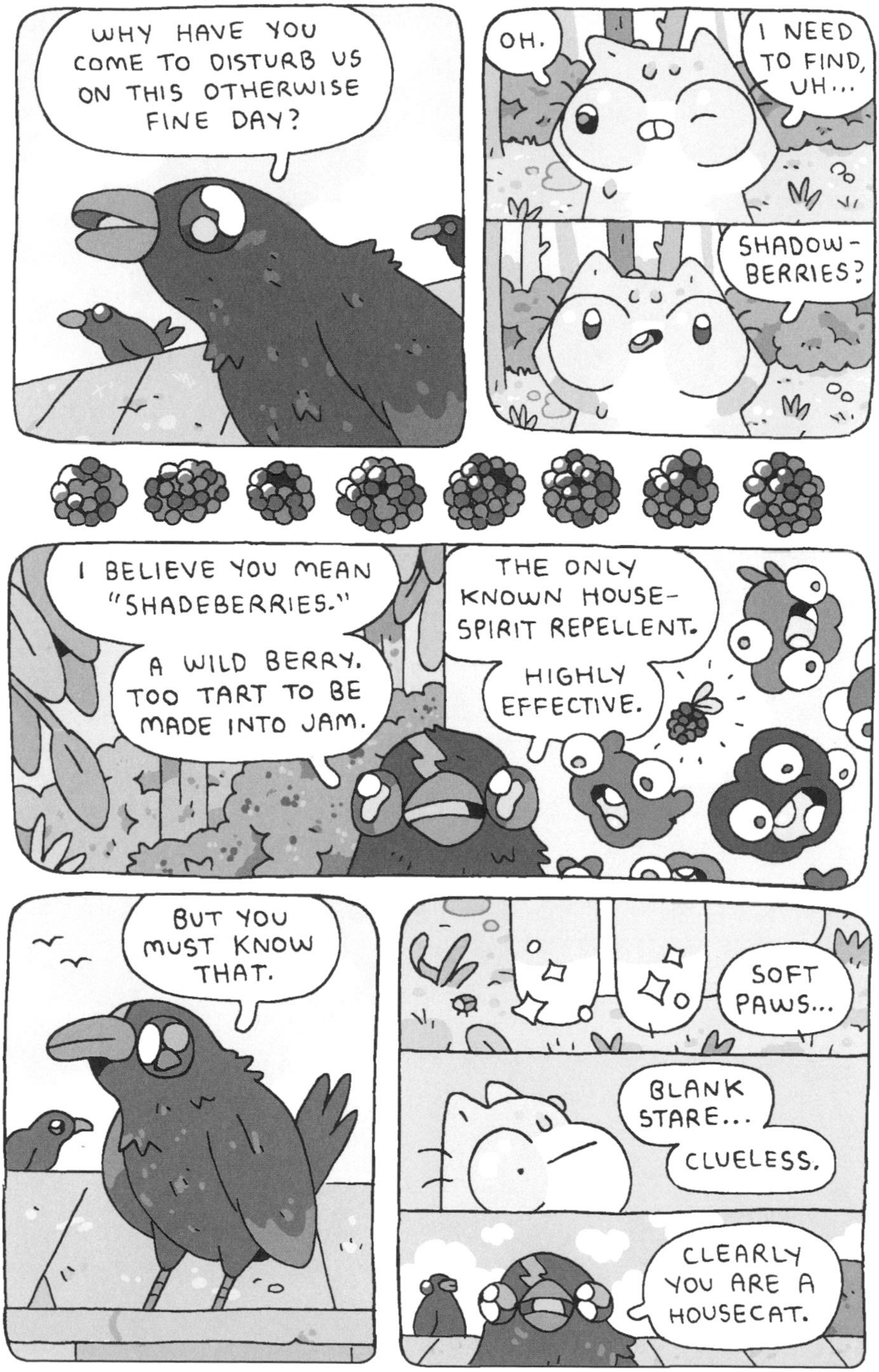
WHY HAVE YOU COME TO DISTURB US ON THIS OTHERWISE FINE DAY?
OH.
I NEED TO FIND, UH...
SHADOW-BERRIES?
I BELIEVE YOU MEAN "SHADEBERRIES."
A WILD BERRY. TOO TART TO BE MADE INTO JAM.
THE ONLY KNOWN HOUSE-SPIRIT REPELLENT.
HIGHLY EFFECTIVE.
BUT YOU MUST KNOW THAT.
SOFT PAWS...
BLANK STARE...
CLUELESS.
CLEARLY YOU ARE A HOUSECAT.

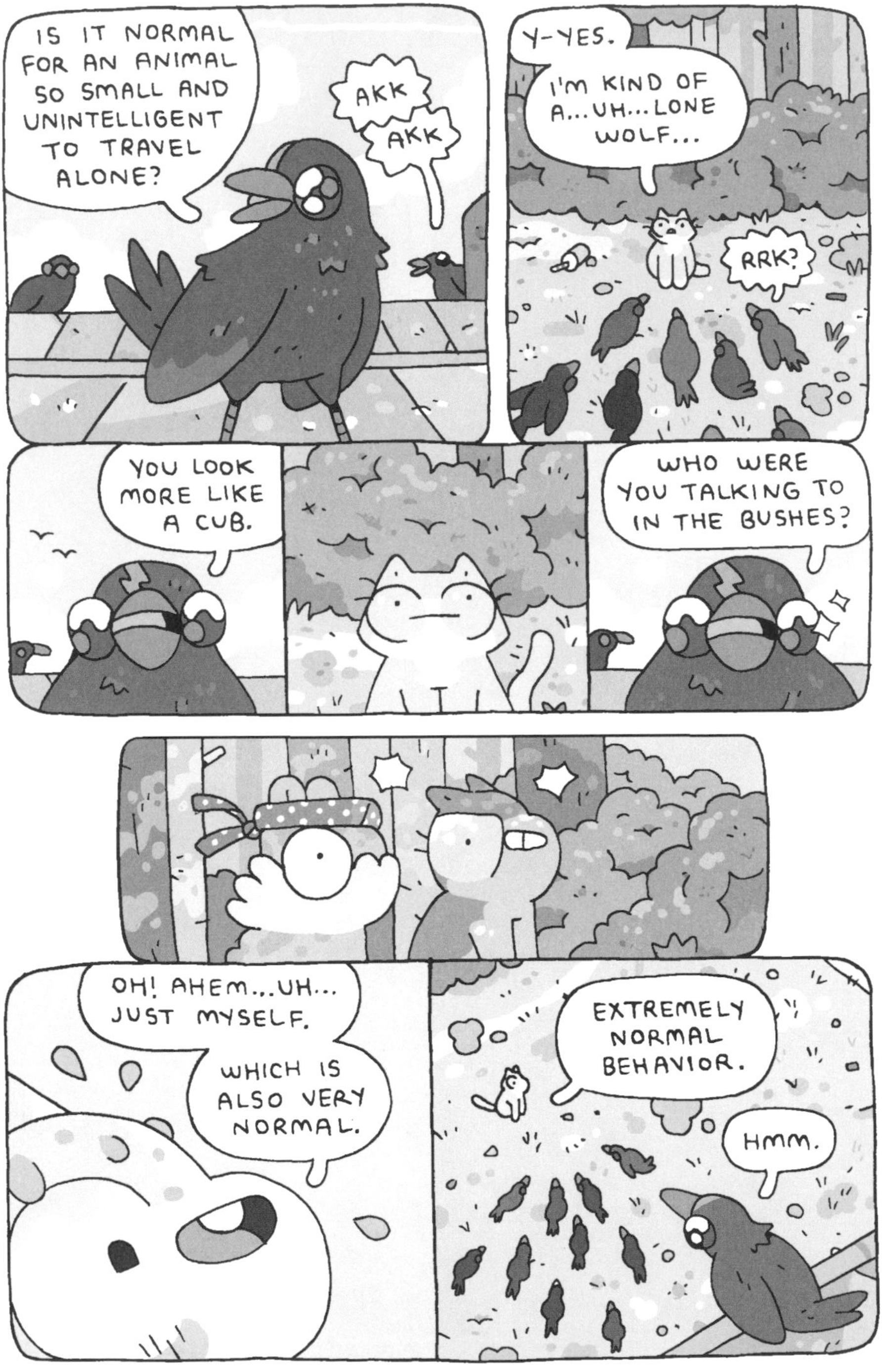
IS IT NORMAL FOR AN ANIMAL SO SMALL AND UNINTELLIGENT TO TRAVEL ALONE?
AKK
AKK
Y-YES.
I'M KIND OF A...UH...LONE WOLF...
RRK?
YOU LOOK MORE LIKE A CUB.
WHO WERE YOU TALKING TO IN THE BUSHES?
OH! AHEM...UH... JUST MYSELF.
WHICH IS ALSO VERY NORMAL.
EXTREMELY NORMAL BEHAVIOR.
HMM.

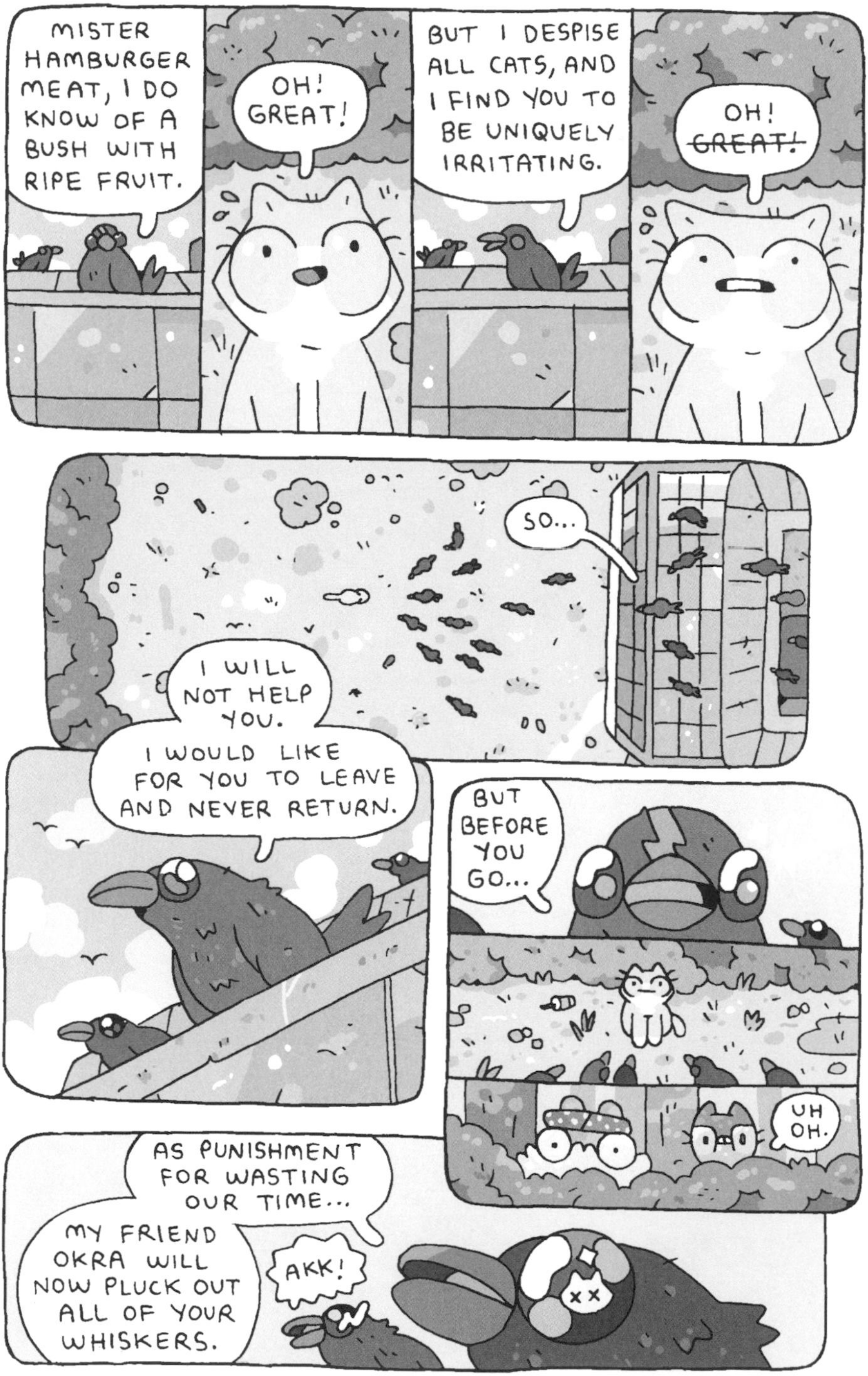
MISTER HAMBURGER MEAT, I DO KNOW OF A BUSH WITH RIPE FRUIT.
OH! GREAT!
BUT I DESPISE ALL CATS, AND I FIND YOU TO BE UNIQUELY IRRITATING.
OH! ~~GREAT!~~
SO...
I WILL NOT HELP YOU.
I WOULD LIKE FOR YOU TO LEAVE AND NEVER RETURN.
BUT BEFORE YOU GO...
UH OH.
AS PUNISHMENT FOR WASTING OUR TIME...
MY FRIEND OKRA WILL NOW PLUCK OUT ALL OF YOUR WHISKERS.
AKK!

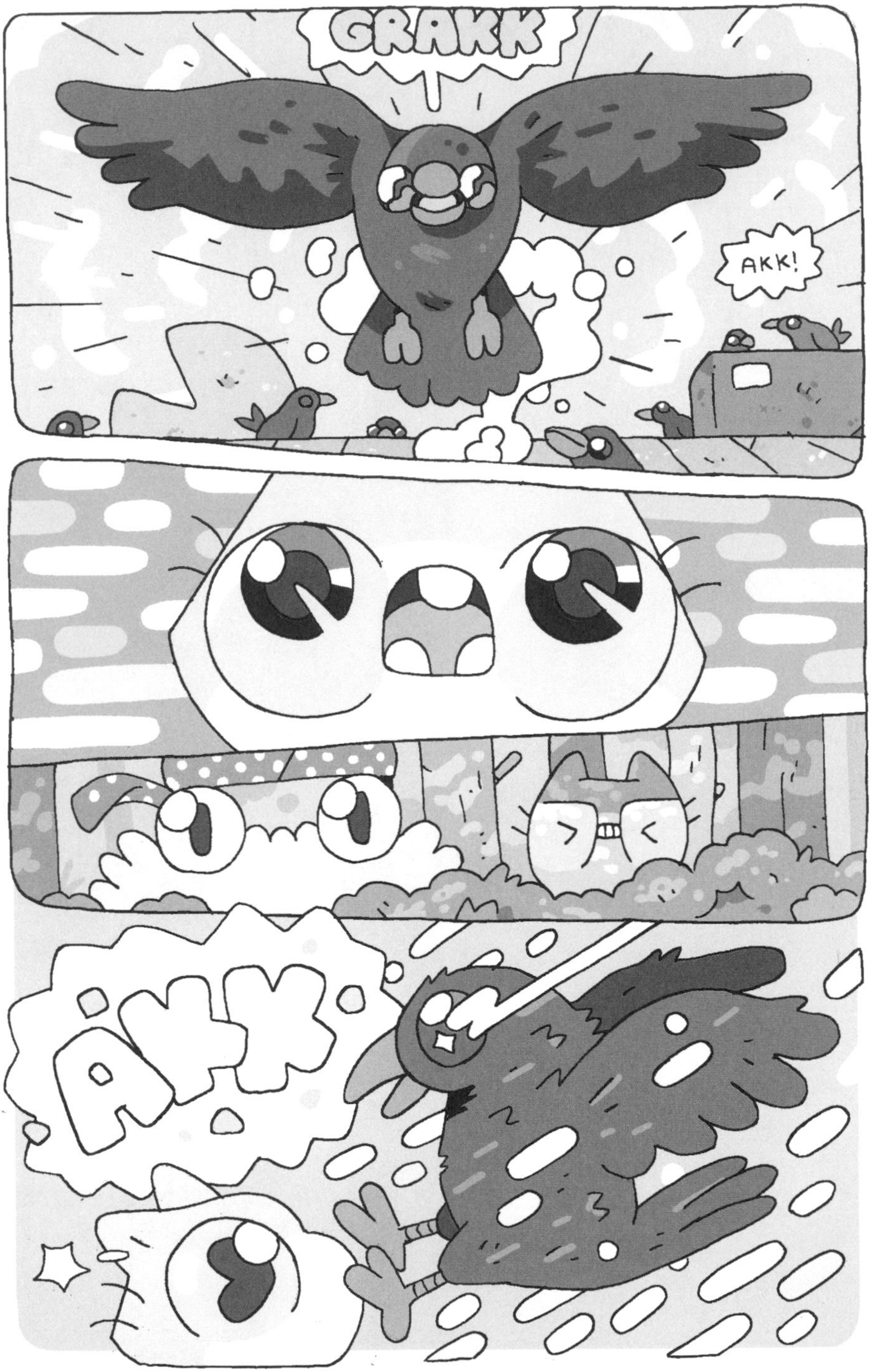
GRAKK
AKK!
AKK

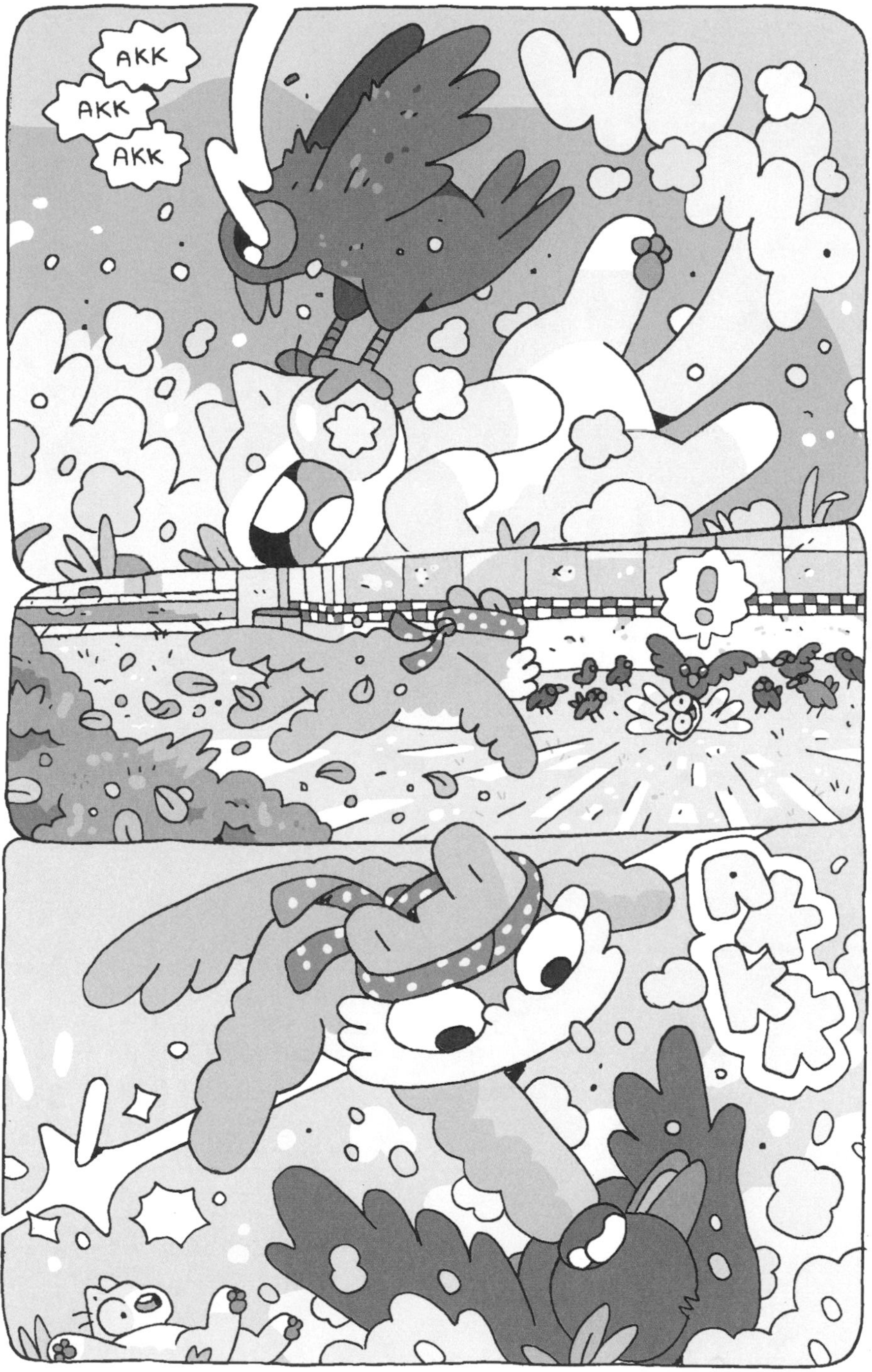

AKK
AKK
AKK
WUMP
!
AKKK

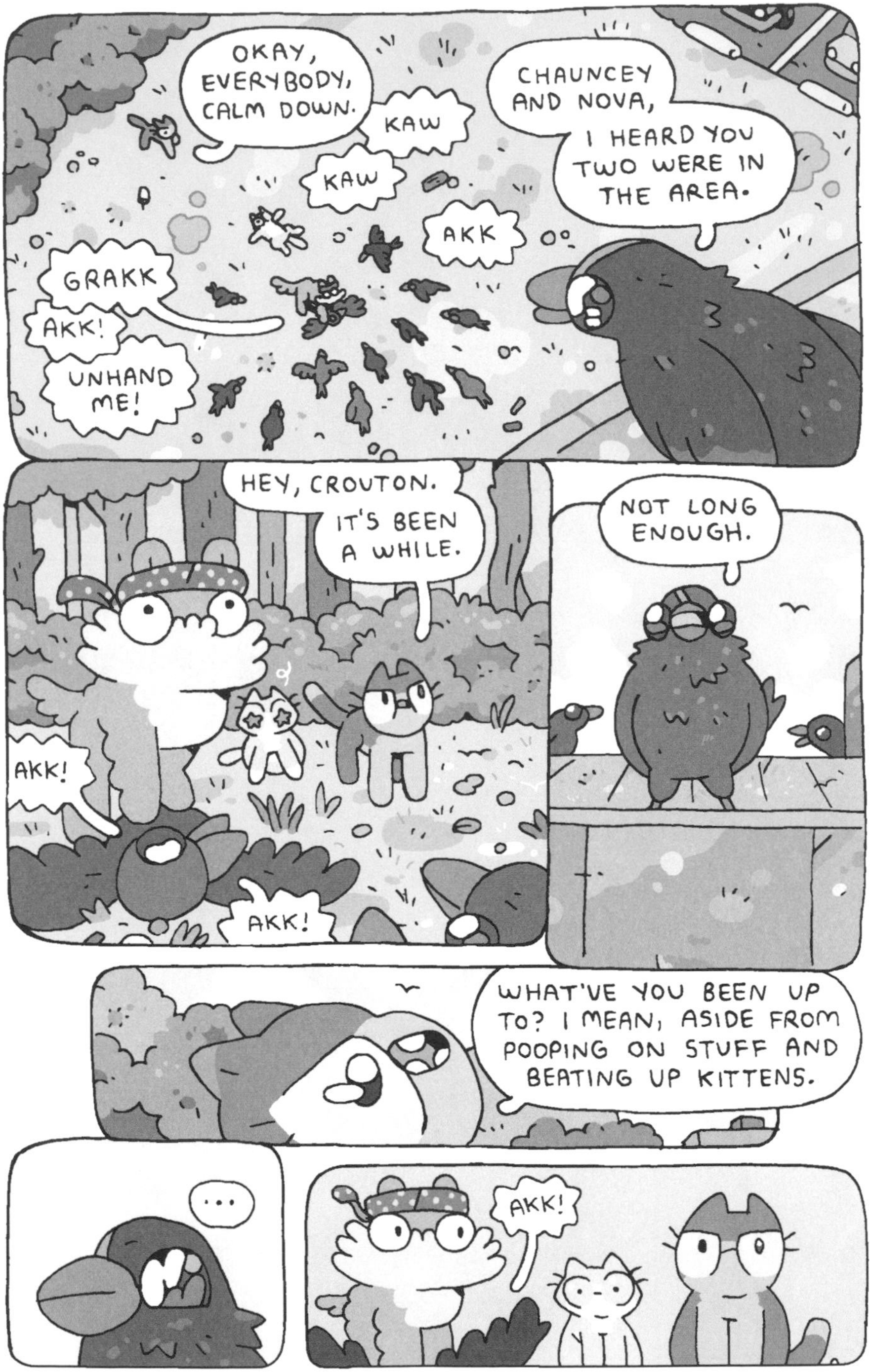
OKAY, EVERYBODY, CALM DOWN.
KAW
KAW
AKK
CHAUNCEY AND NOVA,
I HEARD YOU TWO WERE IN THE AREA.
GRAKK
AKK!
UNHAND ME!
HEY, CROUTON.
IT'S BEEN A WHILE.
AKK!
AKK!
NOT LONG ENOUGH.
WHAT'VE YOU BEEN UP TO? I MEAN, ASIDE FROM POOPING ON STUFF AND BEATING UP KITTENS.
...
AKK!

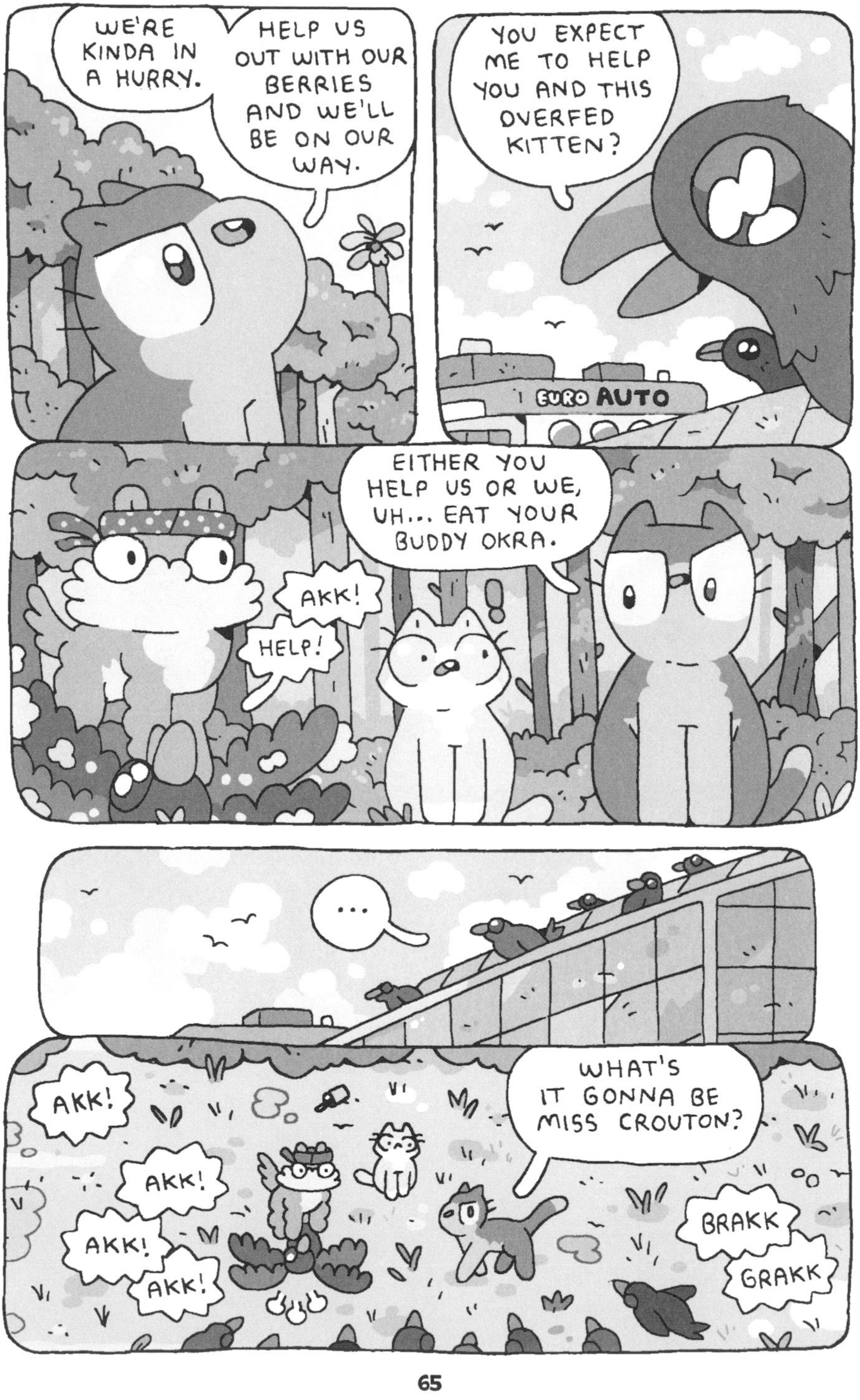
WE'RE KINDA IN A HURRY.
HELP US OUT WITH OUR BERRIES AND WE'LL BE ON OUR WAY.
YOU EXPECT ME TO HELP YOU AND THIS OVERFED KITTEN?
EURO AUTO
EITHER YOU HELP US OR WE, UH... EAT YOUR BUDDY OKRA.
AKK!
HELP!
...
AKK!
WHAT'S IT GONNA BE MISS CROUTON?
AKK!
AKK!
AKK!
BRAKK
GRAKK

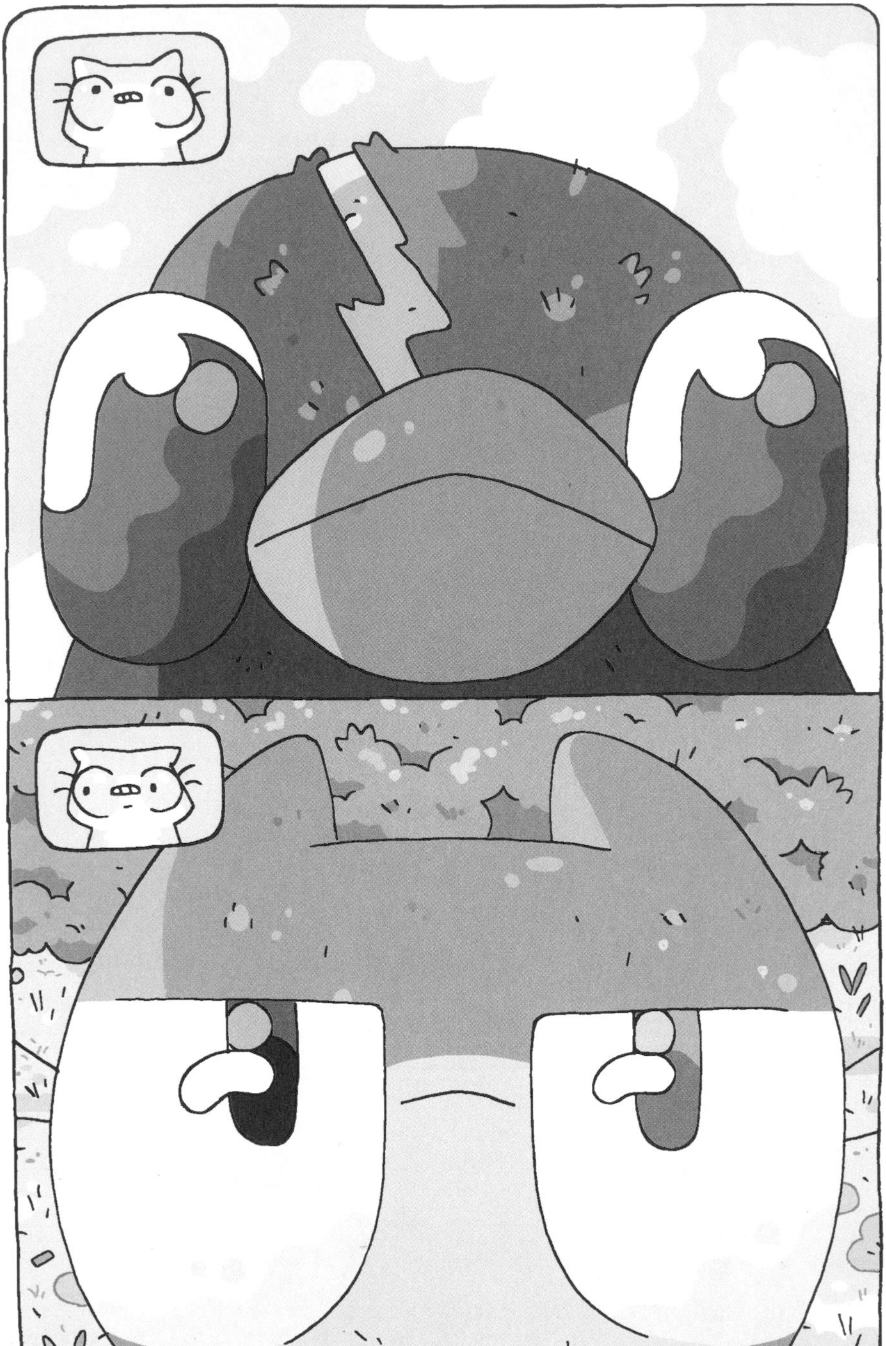

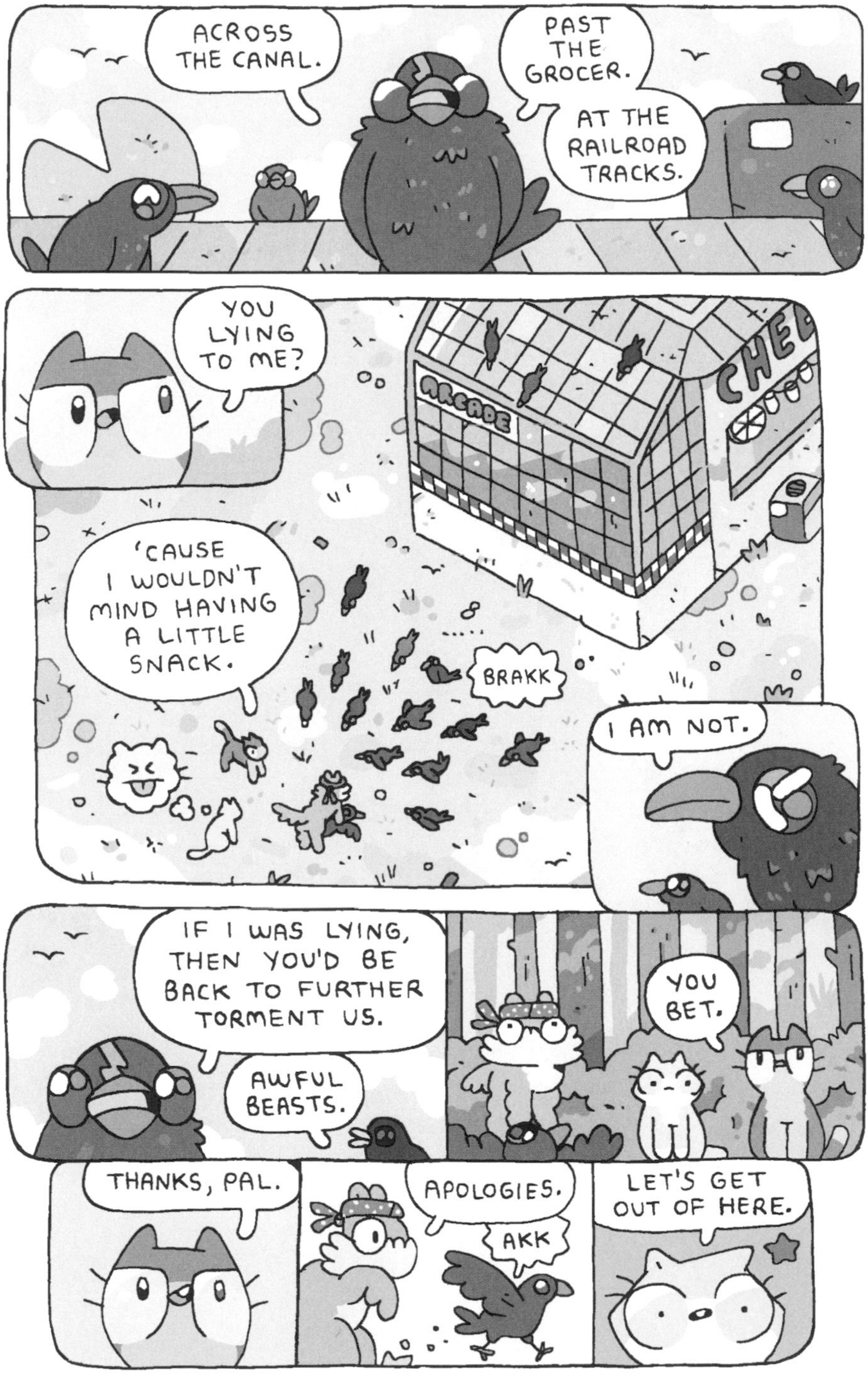
ACROSS THE CANAL.
PAST THE GROCER.
AT THE RAILROAD TRACKS.
YOU LYING TO ME?
ARCADE
CHE
'CAUSE I WOULDN'T MIND HAVING A LITTLE SNACK.
BRAKK
I AM NOT.
IF I WAS LYING, THEN YOU'D BE BACK TO FURTHER TORMENT US.
AWFUL BEASTS.
YOU BET.
THANKS, PAL.
APOLOGIES.
AKK
LET'S GET OUT OF HERE.

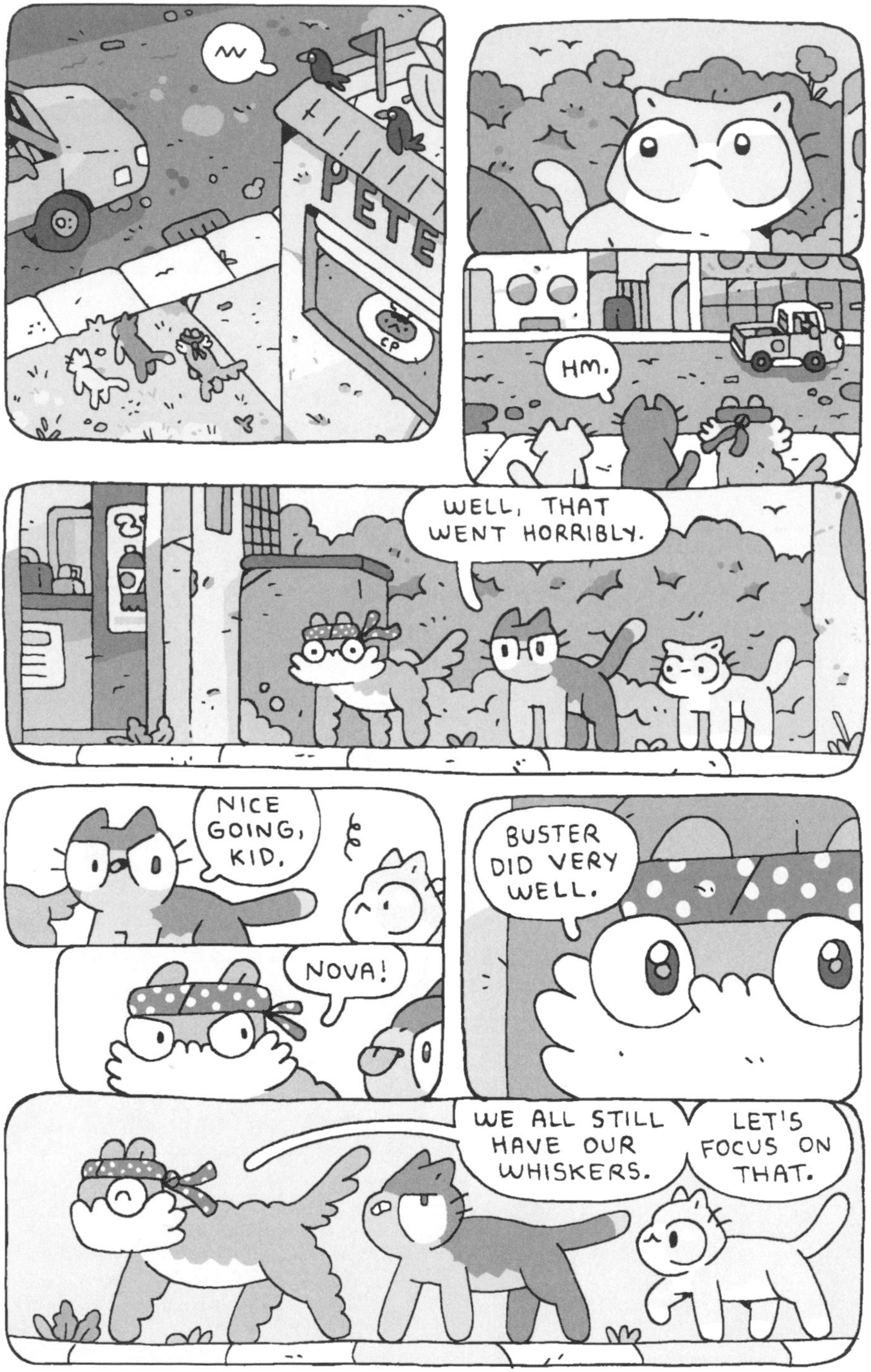

PETE
HM.
WELL, THAT WENT HORRIBLY.
NICE GOING, KID.
NOVA!
BUSTER DID VERY WELL.
WE ALL STILL HAVE OUR WHISKERS.
LET'S FOCUS ON THAT.

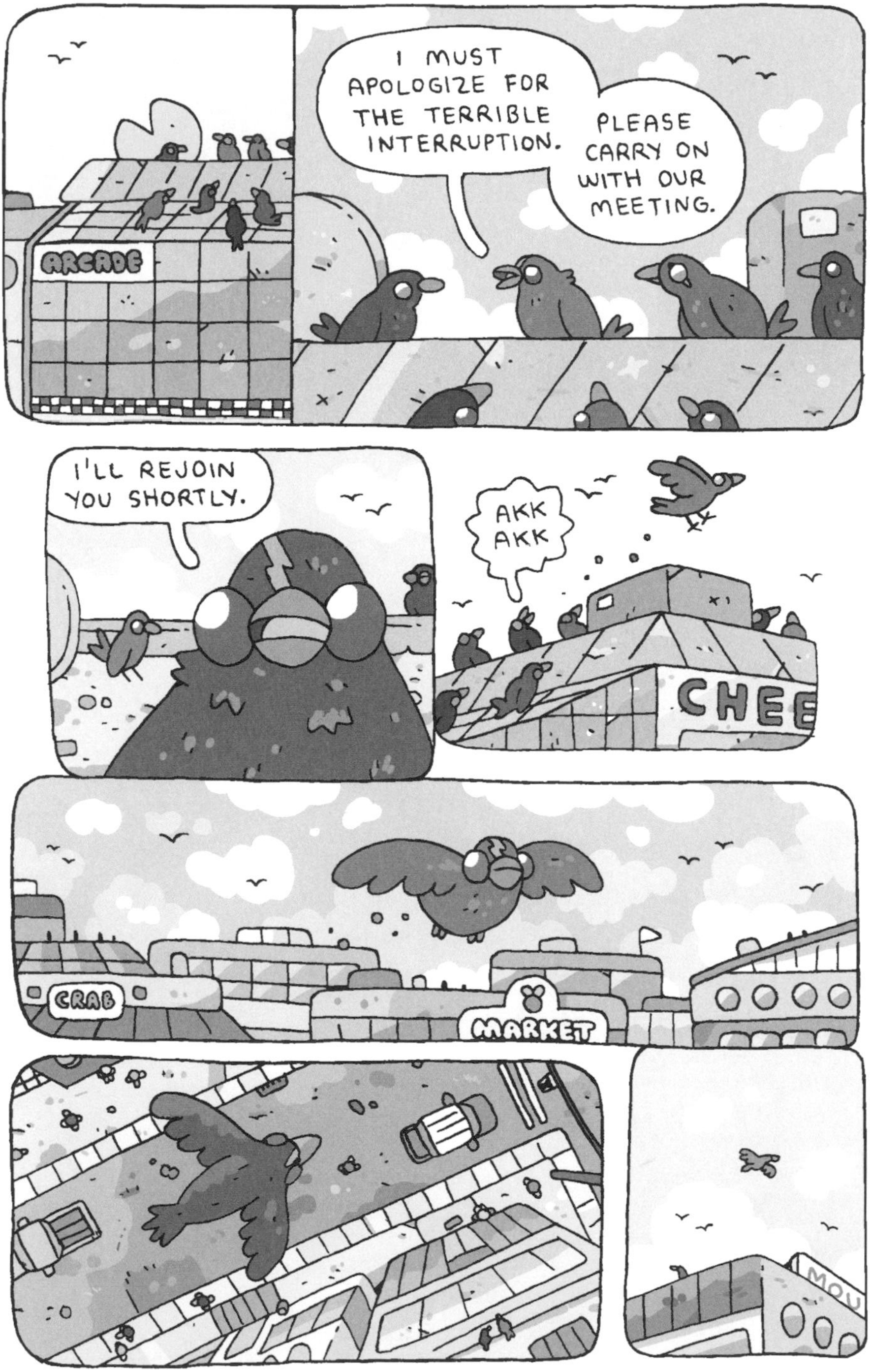
ARCADE
I MUST APOLOGIZE FOR THE TERRIBLE INTERRUPTION.
PLEASE CARRY ON WITH OUR MEETING.
I'LL REJOIN YOU SHORTLY.
AKK AKK
CHEE
CRAB
MARKET
MOU

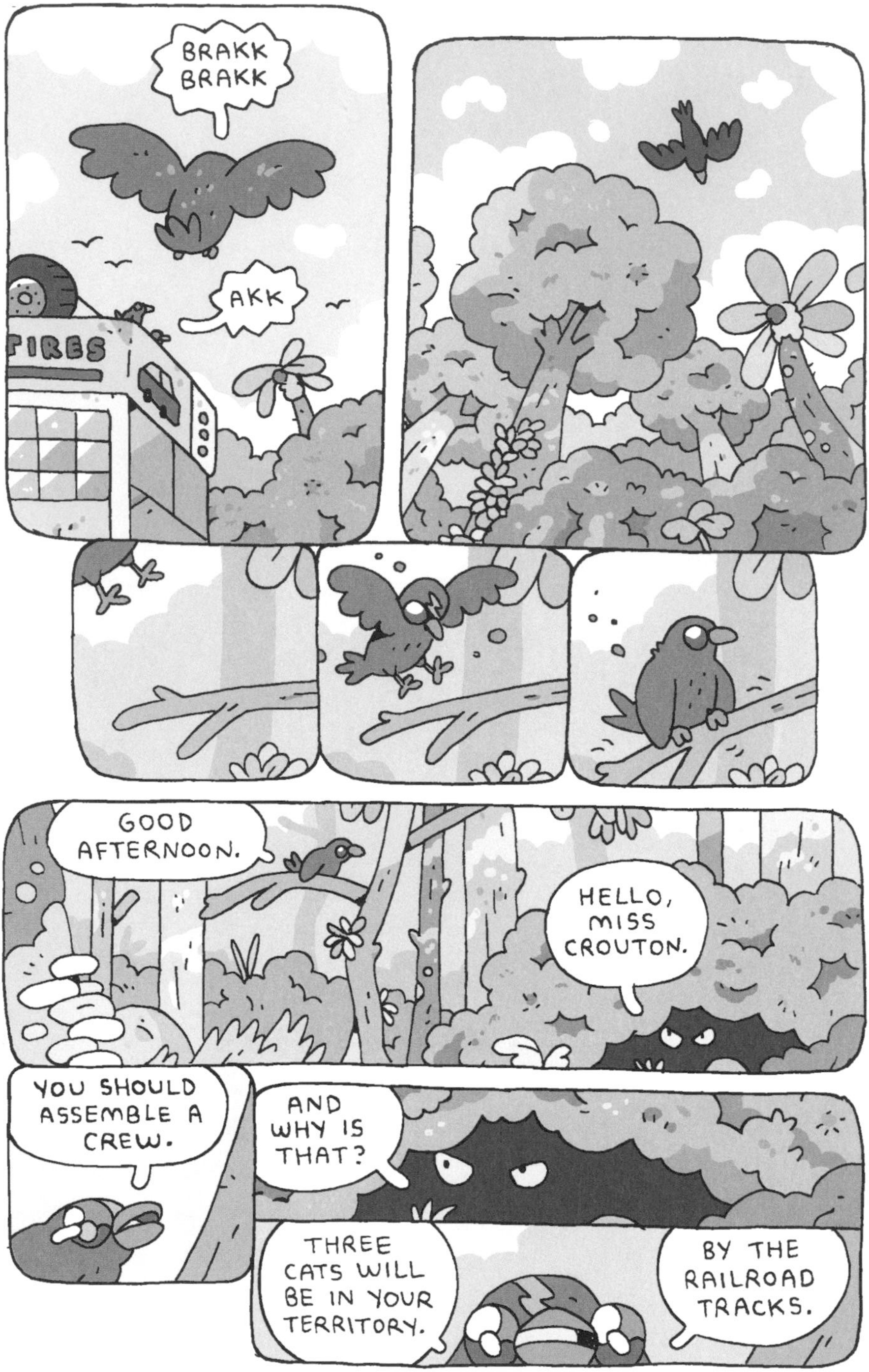
BRAKK BRAKK
AKK
TIRES
GOOD AFTERNOON.
HELLO, MISS CROUTON.
YOU SHOULD ASSEMBLE A CREW.
AND WHY IS THAT?
THREE CATS WILL BE IN YOUR TERRITORY.
BY THE RAILROAD TRACKS.

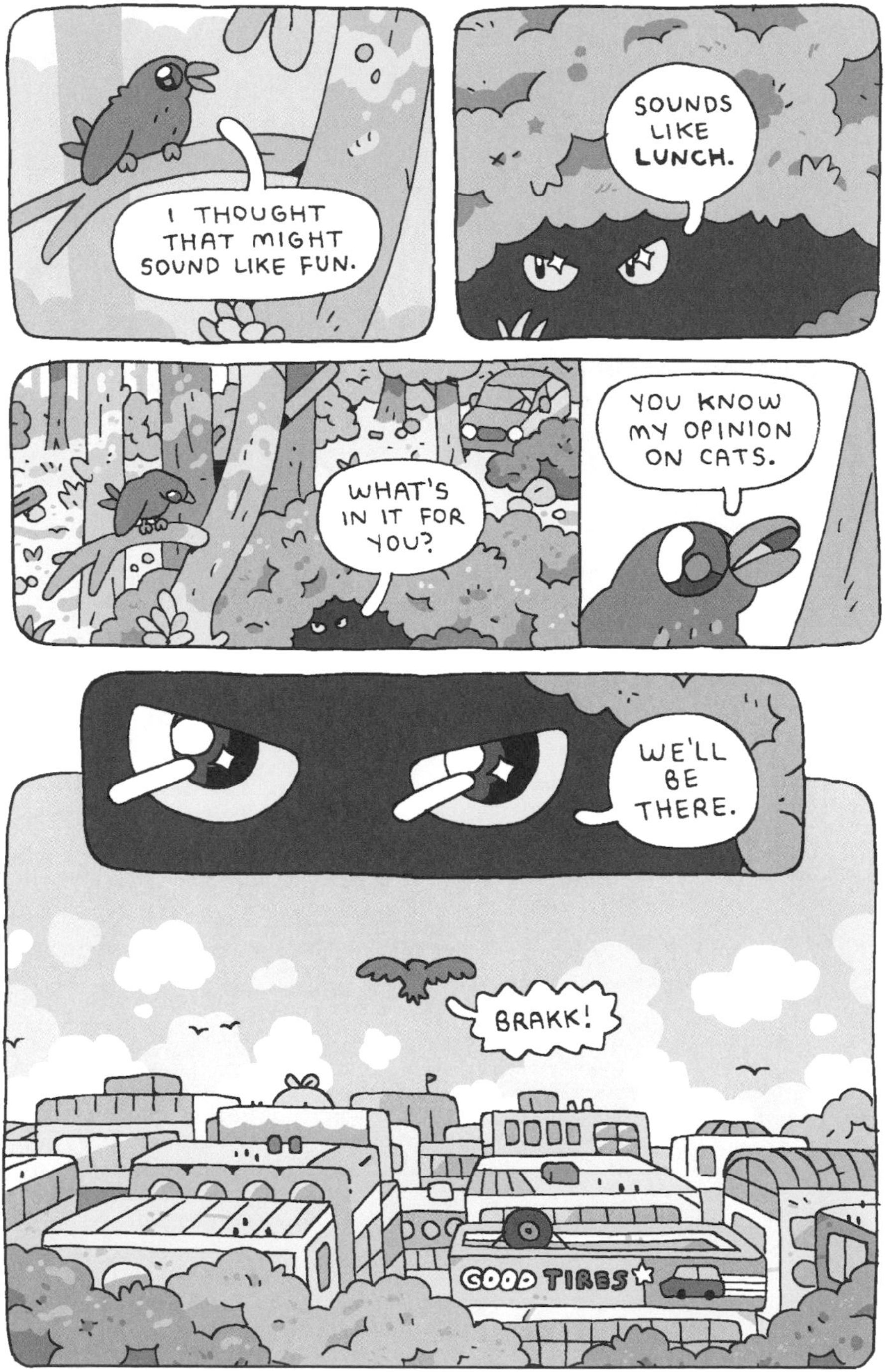
I THOUGHT THAT MIGHT SOUND LIKE FUN.
SOUNDS LIKE **LUNCH.**
WHAT'S IN IT FOR YOU?
YOU KNOW MY OPINION ON CATS.
WE'LL BE THERE.
BRAKK!
GOOD TIRES

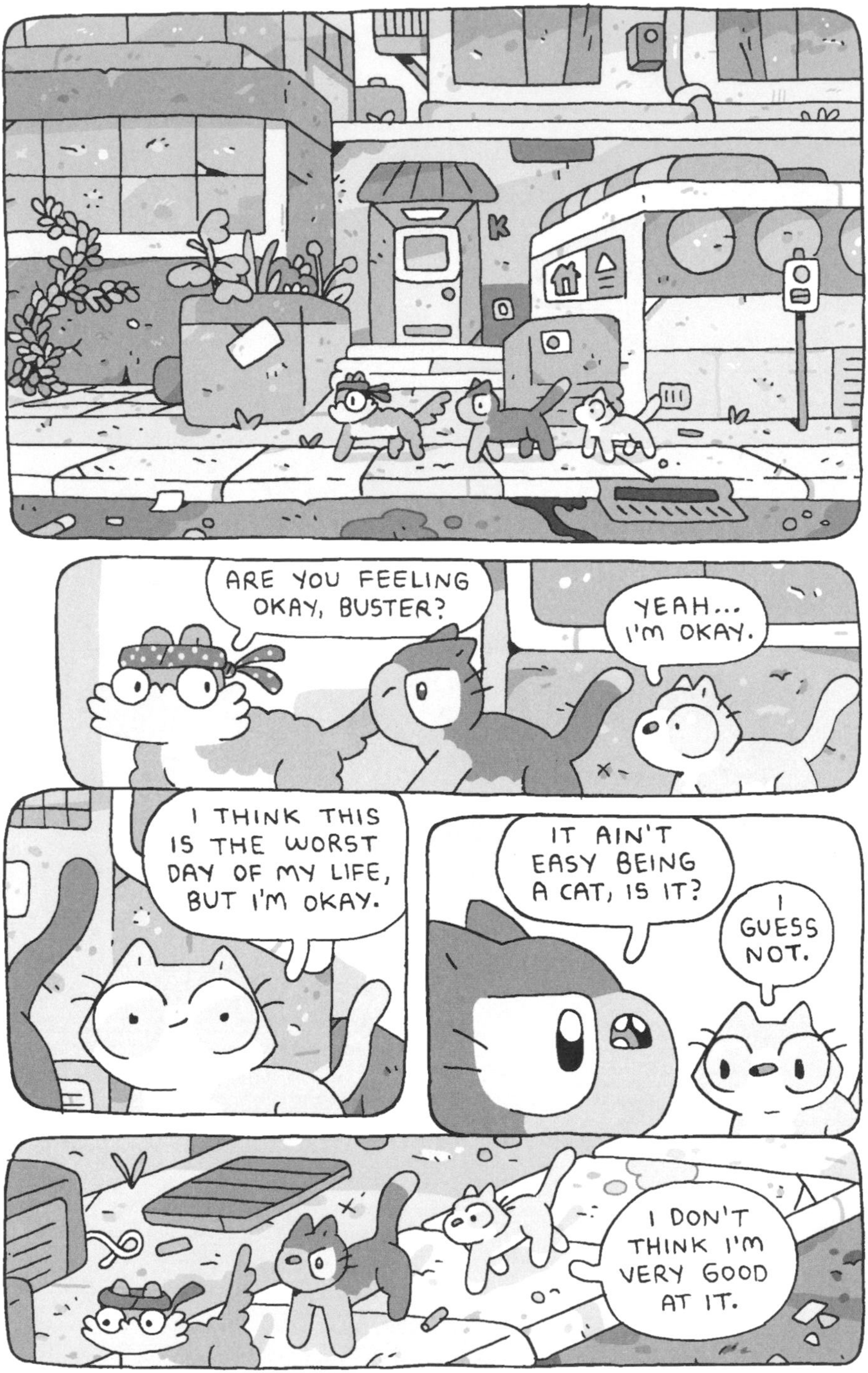
ARE YOU FEELING OKAY, BUSTER?
YEAH... I'M OKAY.
I THINK THIS IS THE WORST DAY OF MY LIFE, BUT I'M OKAY.
IT AIN'T EASY BEING A CAT, IS IT?
I GUESS NOT.
I DON'T THINK I'M VERY GOOD AT IT.

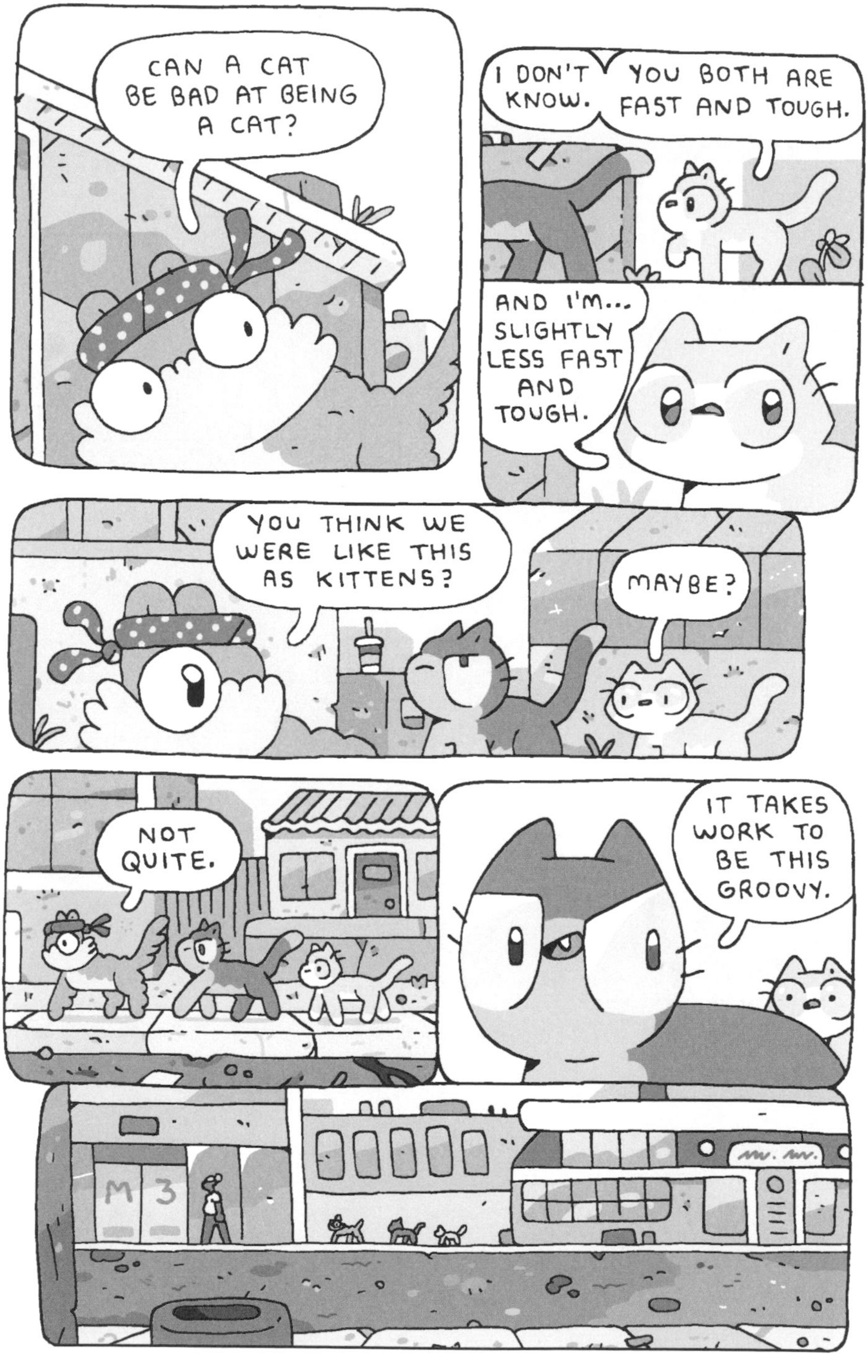
CAN A CAT BE BAD AT BEING A CAT?
I DON'T KNOW.
YOU BOTH ARE FAST AND TOUGH.
AND I'M... SLIGHTLY LESS FAST AND TOUGH.
YOU THINK WE WERE LIKE THIS AS KITTENS?
MAYBE?
NOT QUITE.
IT TAKES WORK TO BE THIS GROOVY.
M 3

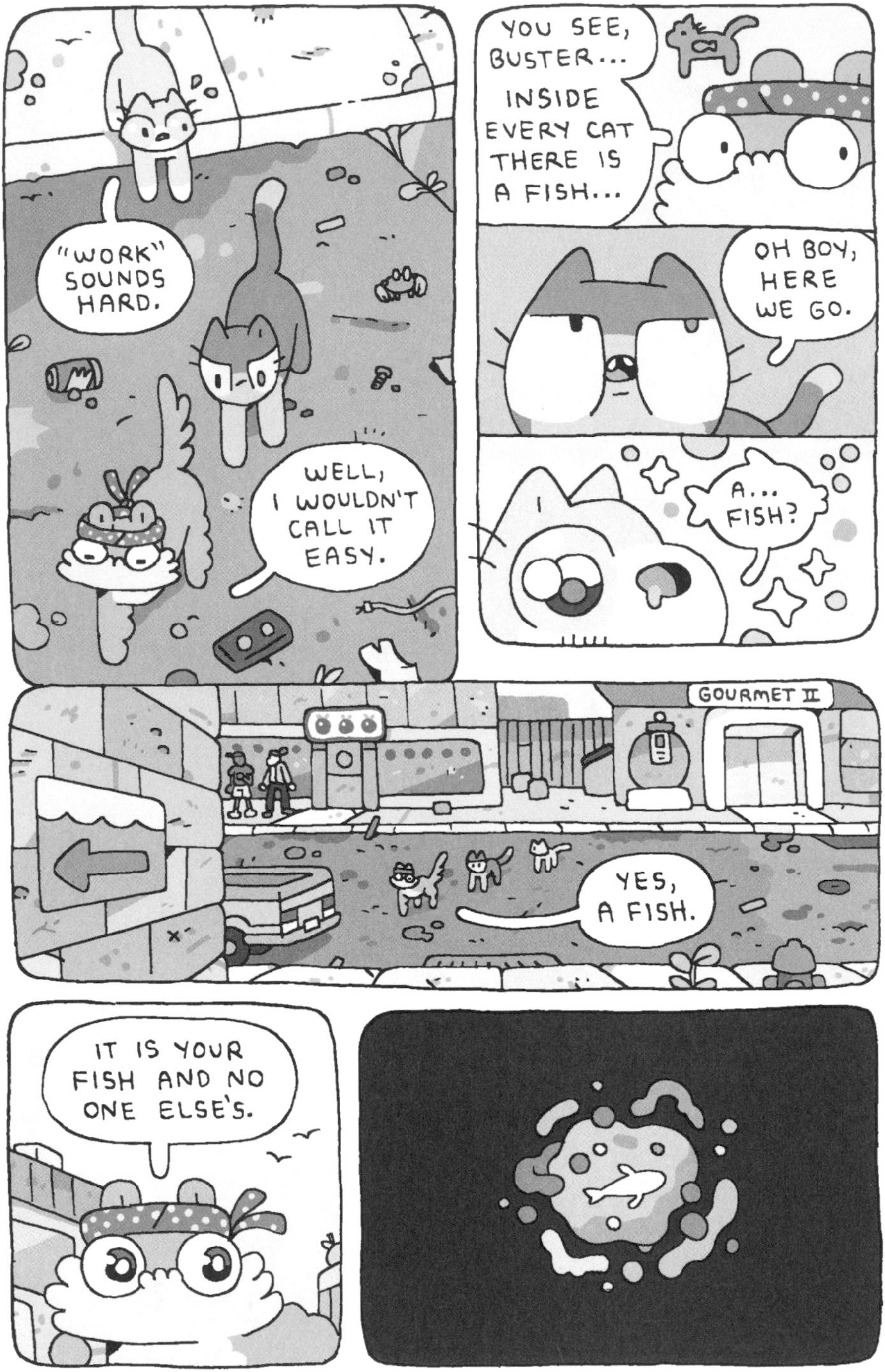
"WORK" SOUNDS HARD.
WELL, I WOULDN'T CALL IT EASY.
YOU SEE, BUSTER...
INSIDE EVERY CAT THERE IS A FISH...
OH BOY, HERE WE GO.
A... FISH?
GOURMET II
YES, A FISH.
IT IS YOUR FISH AND NO ONE ELSE'S.

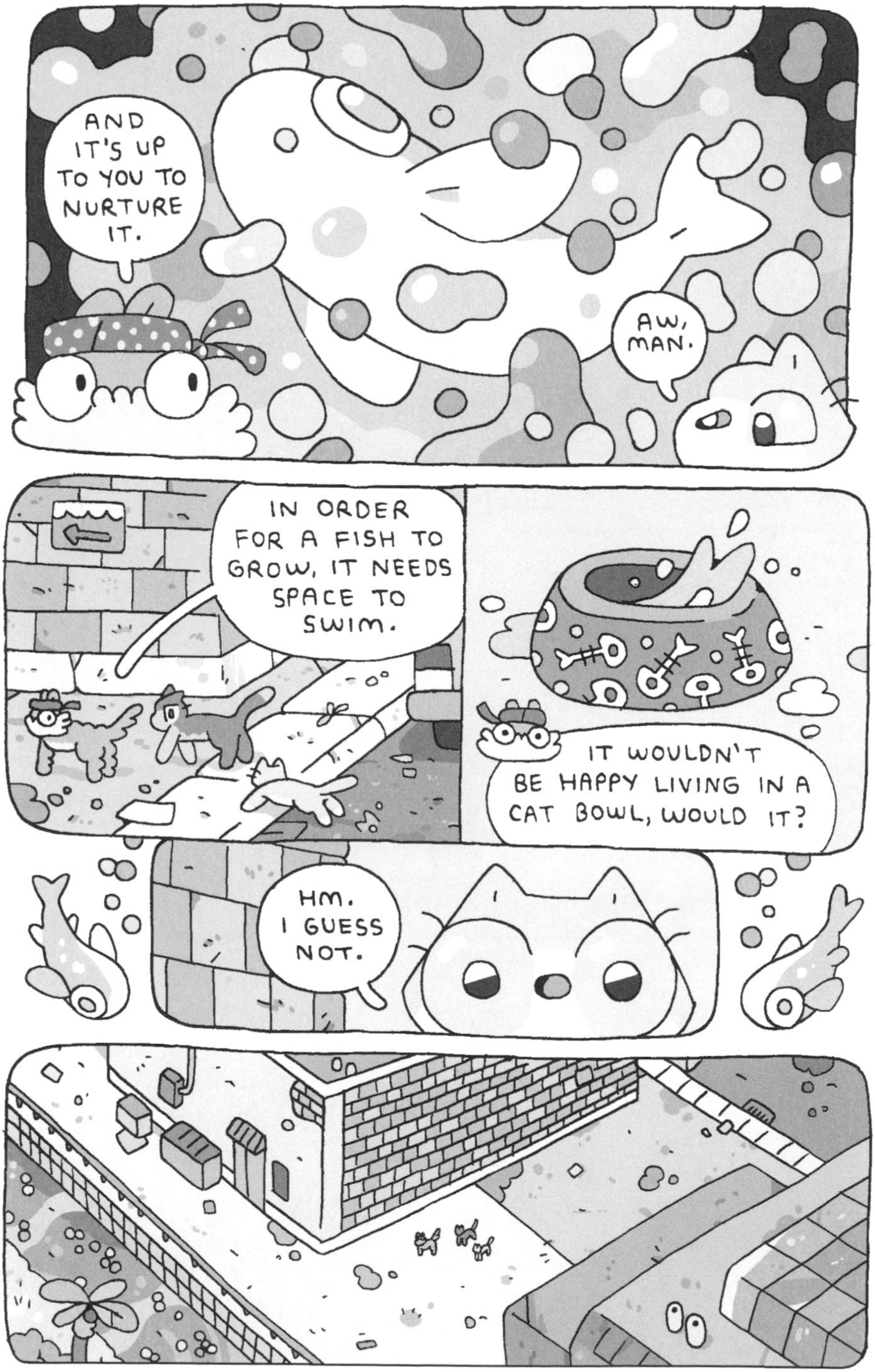
AND IT'S UP TO YOU TO NURTURE IT.
AW, MAN.
IN ORDER FOR A FISH TO GROW, IT NEEDS SPACE TO SWIM.
IT WOULDN'T BE HAPPY LIVING IN A CAT BOWL, WOULD IT?
HM. I GUESS NOT.

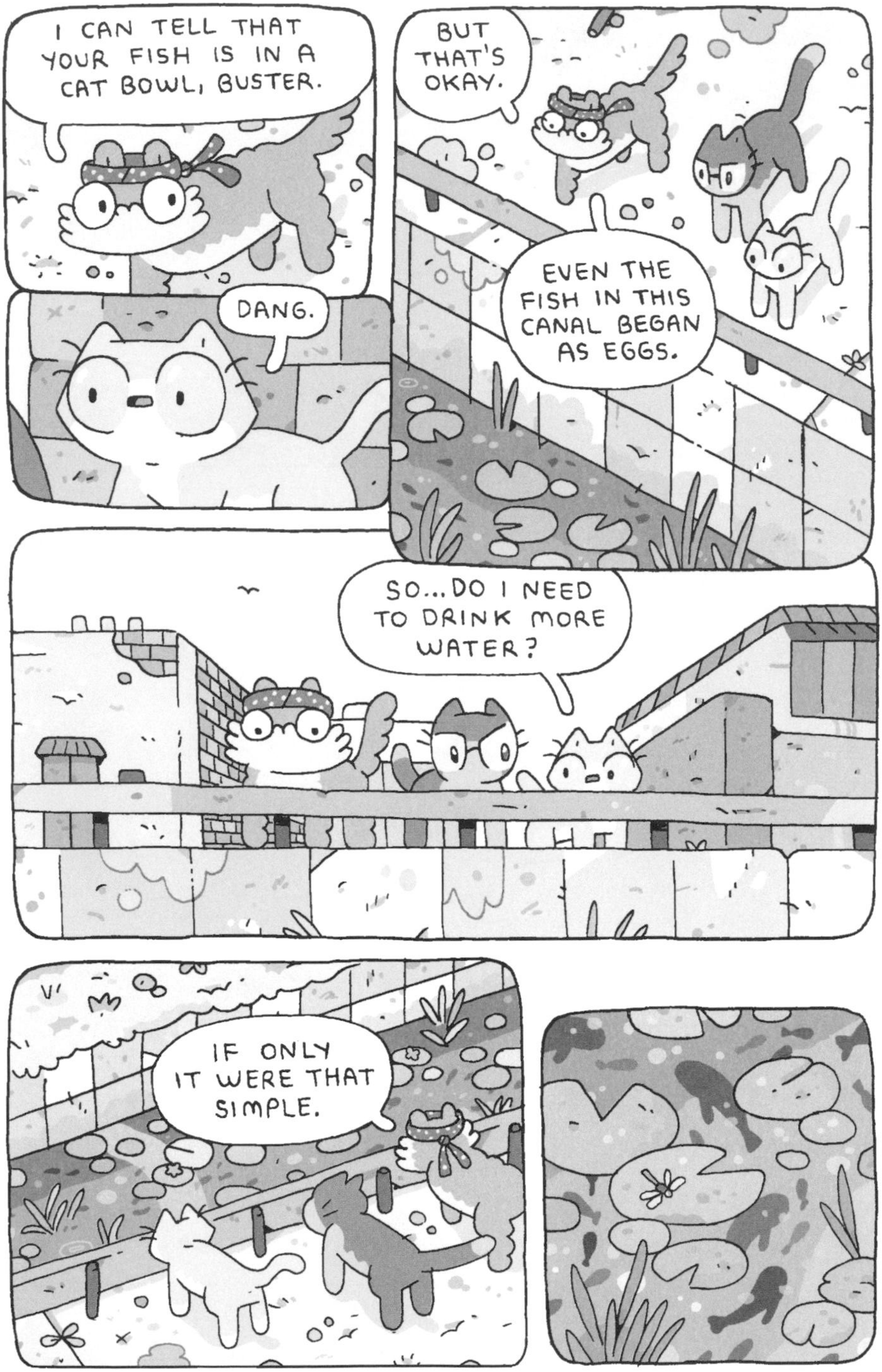
I CAN TELL THAT YOUR FISH IS IN A CAT BOWL, BUSTER.
DANG.
BUT THAT'S OKAY.
EVEN THE FISH IN THIS CANAL BEGAN AS EGGS.
SO...DO I NEED TO DRINK MORE WATER?
IF ONLY IT WERE THAT SIMPLE.

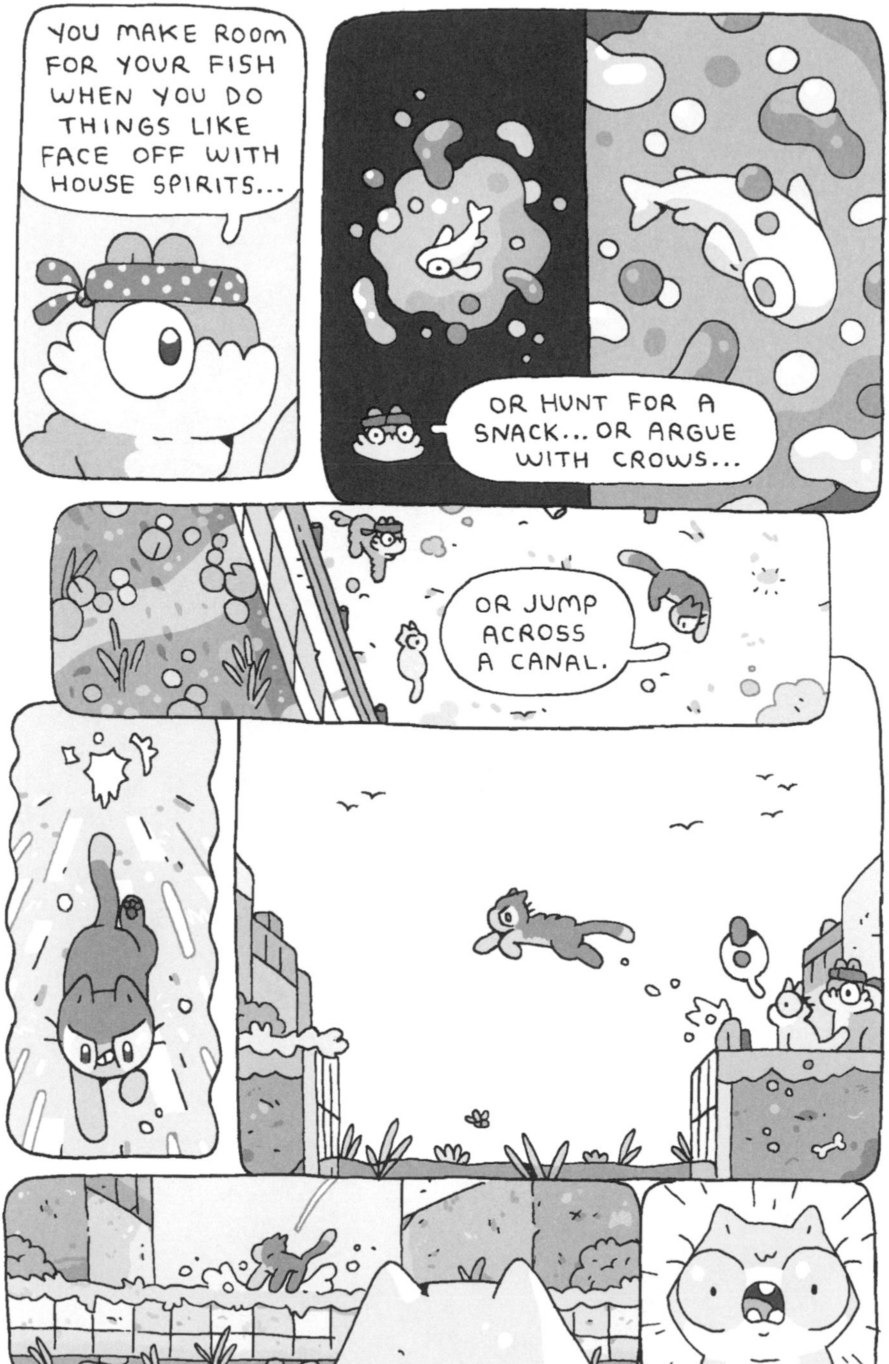
YOU MAKE ROOM FOR YOUR FISH WHEN YOU DO THINGS LIKE FACE OFF WITH HOUSE SPIRITS...
OR HUNT FOR A SNACK... OR ARGUE WITH CROWS...
OR JUMP ACROSS A CANAL.

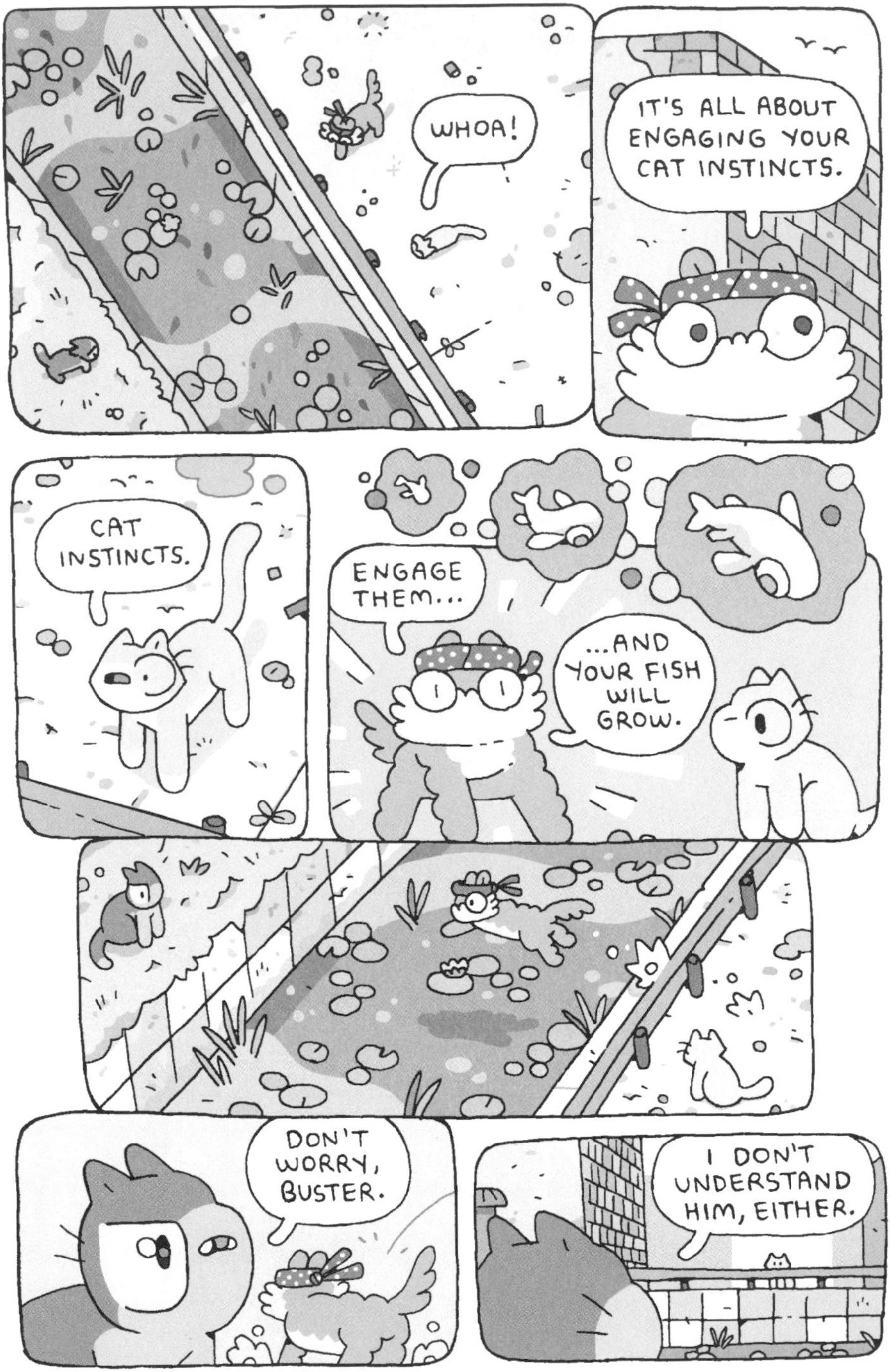
WHOA!
IT'S ALL ABOUT ENGAGING YOUR CAT INSTINCTS.
CAT INSTINCTS.
ENGAGE THEM...
...AND YOUR FISH WILL GROW.
DON'T WORRY, BUSTER.
I DON'T UNDERSTAND HIM, EITHER.

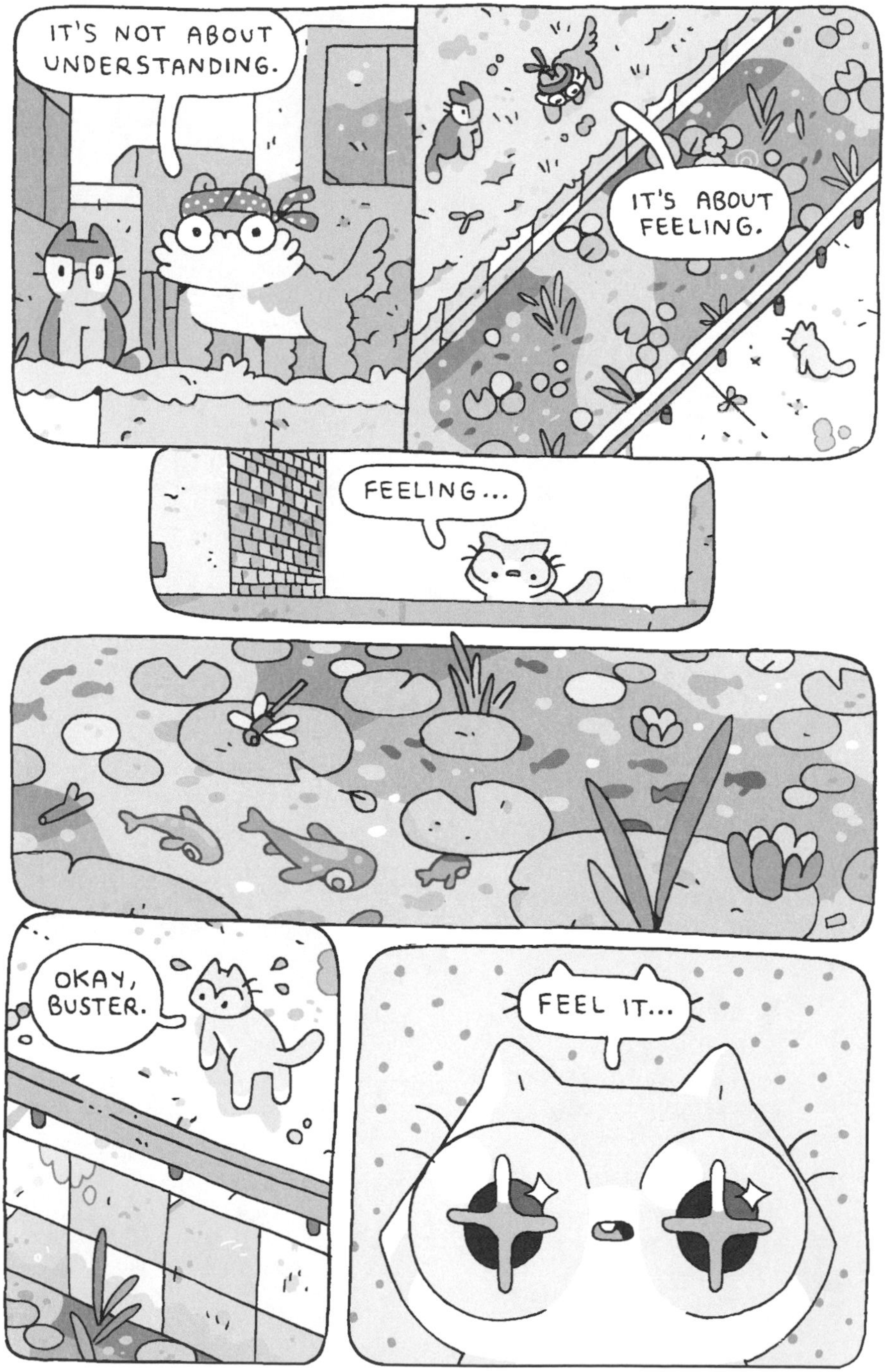
IT'S NOT ABOUT UNDERSTANDING.
IT'S ABOUT FEELING.
FEELING...
OKAY, BUSTER.
FEEL IT...

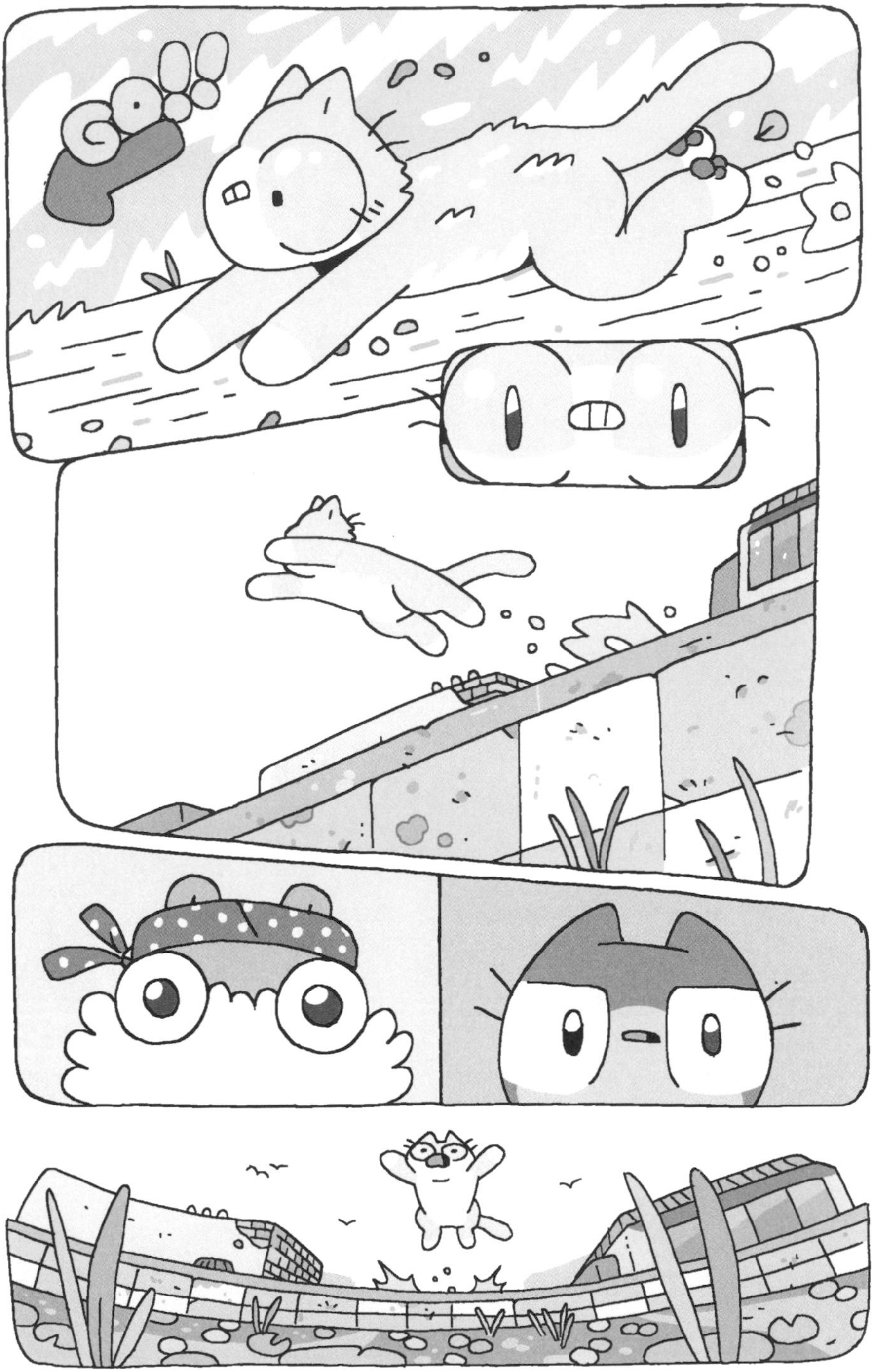
GO!!

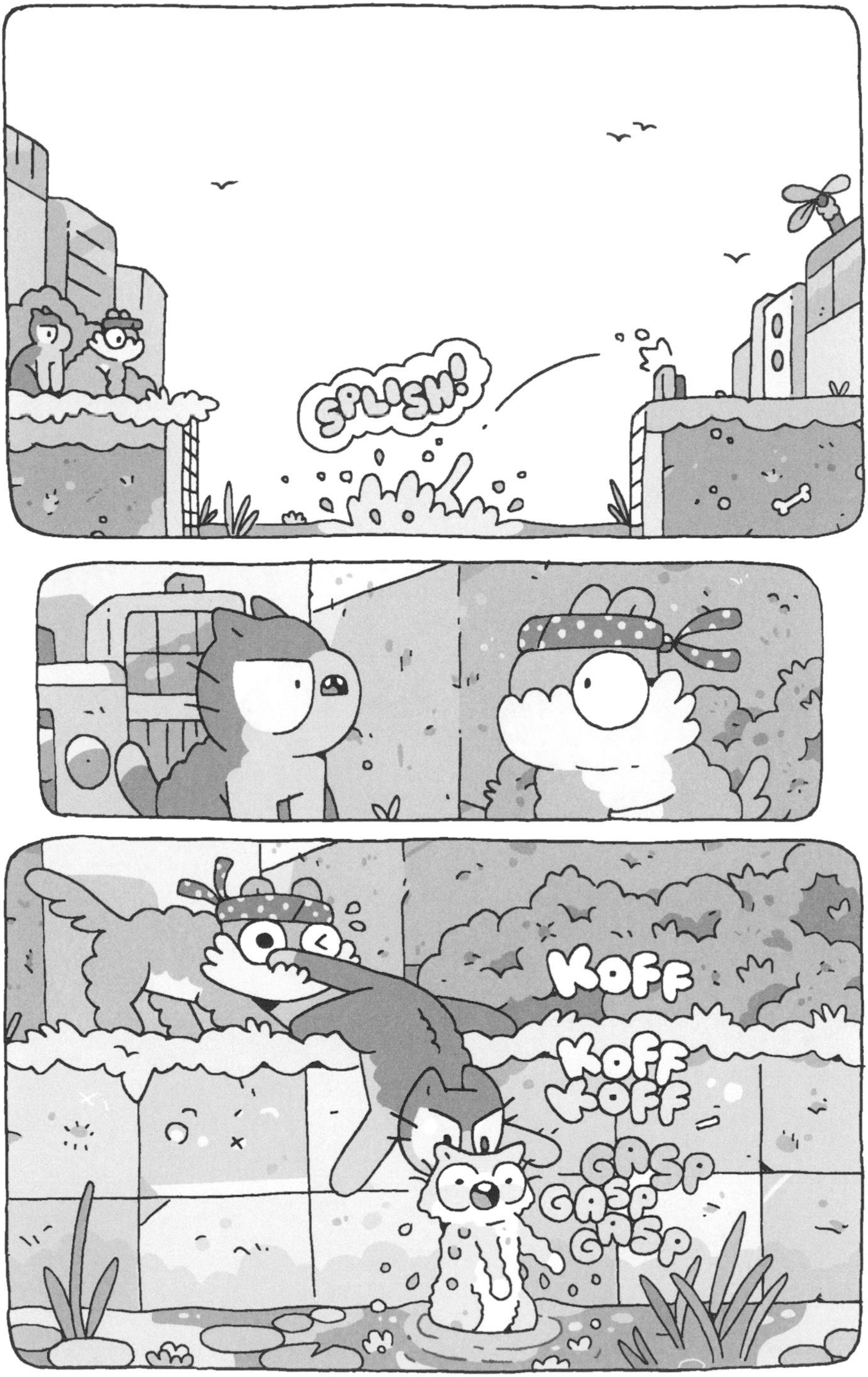
SPLISH!
KOFF
KOFF
KOFF
GASP
GASP
GASP

CHAPTER 4

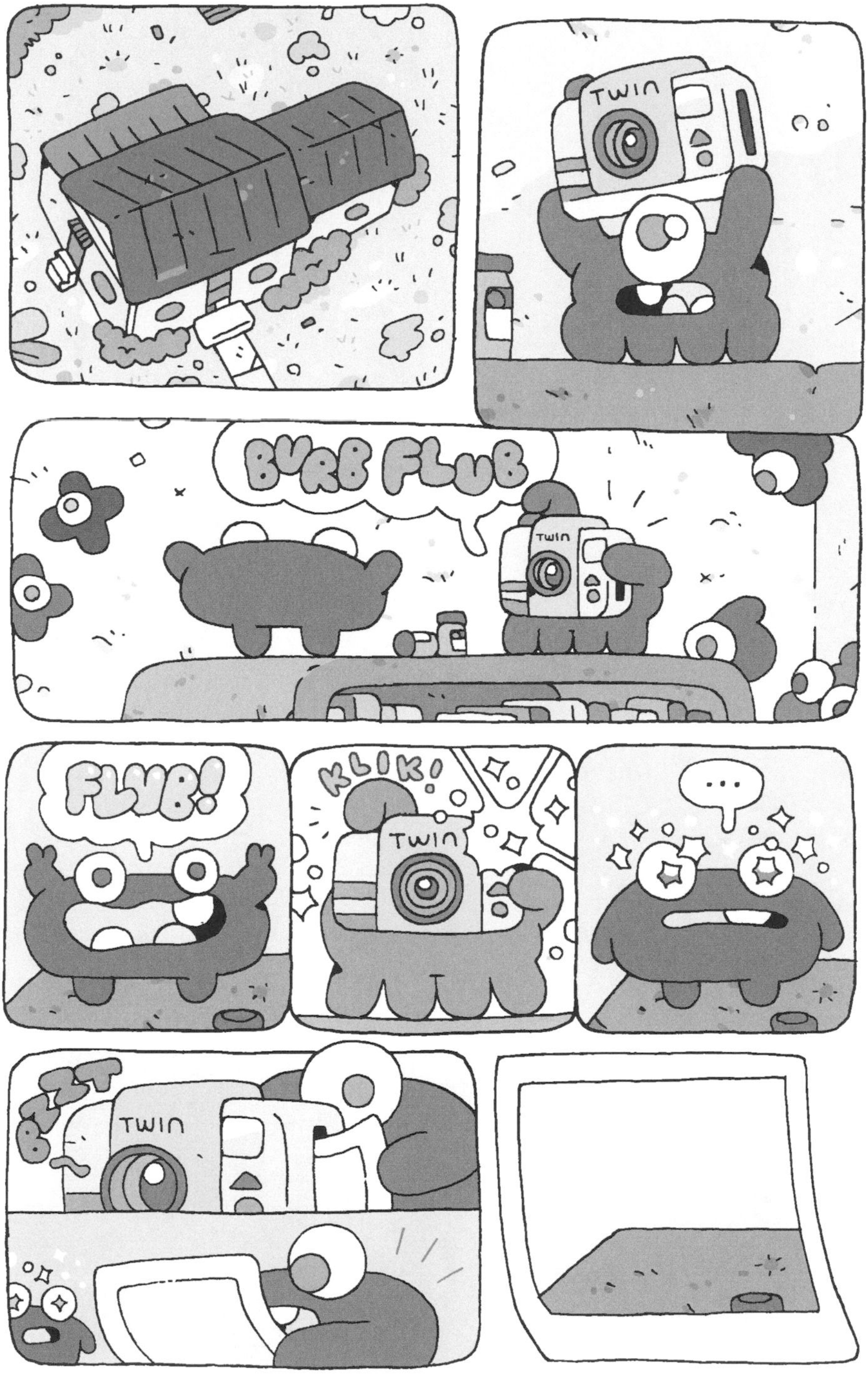
TWIN
BURB FLUB
TWIN
FLUB!
KLIK!
TWIN
...
BZZT
TWIN

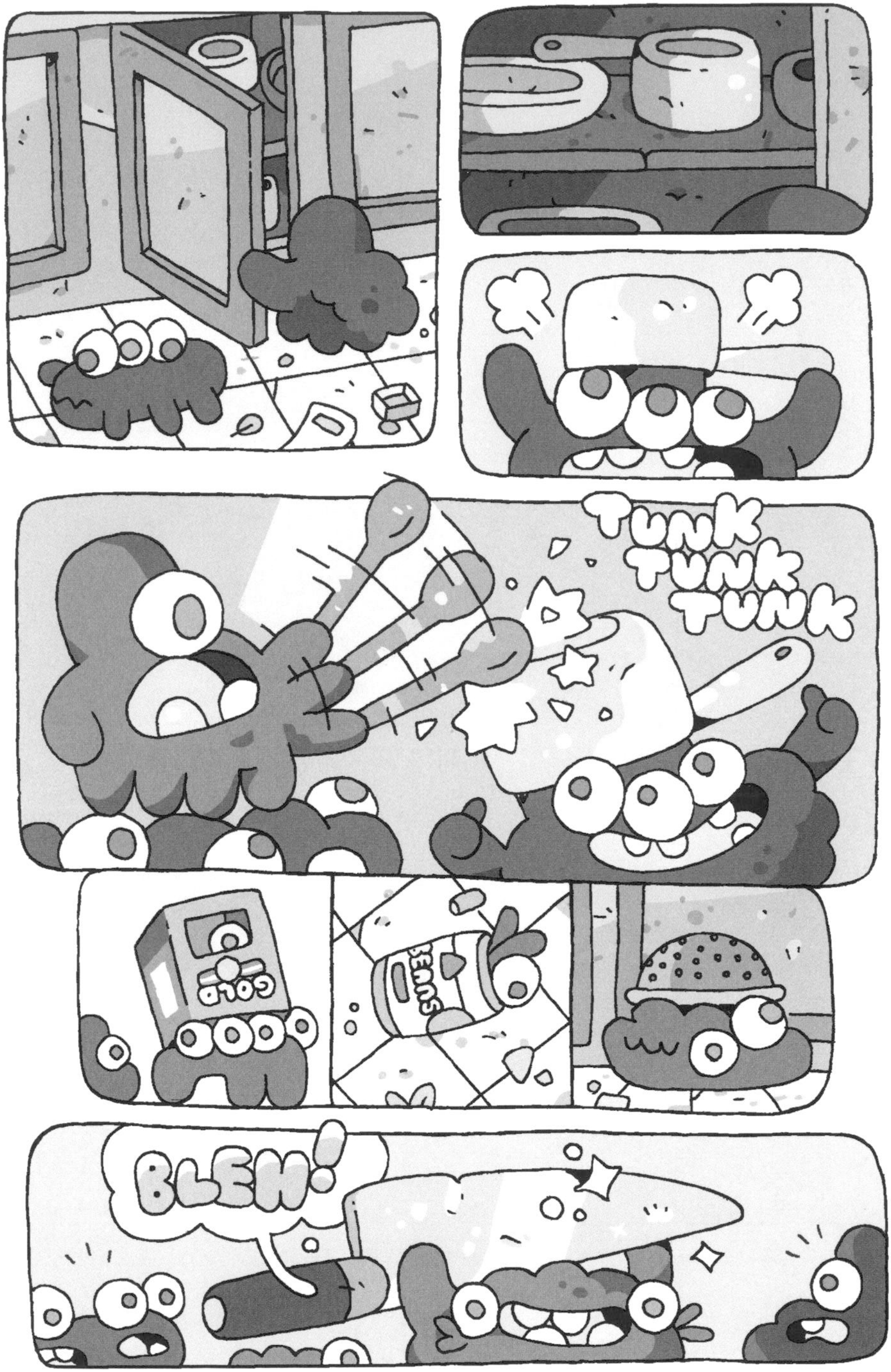
TUNK
TUNK
TUNK
GOLD
BEANS
BLEH!

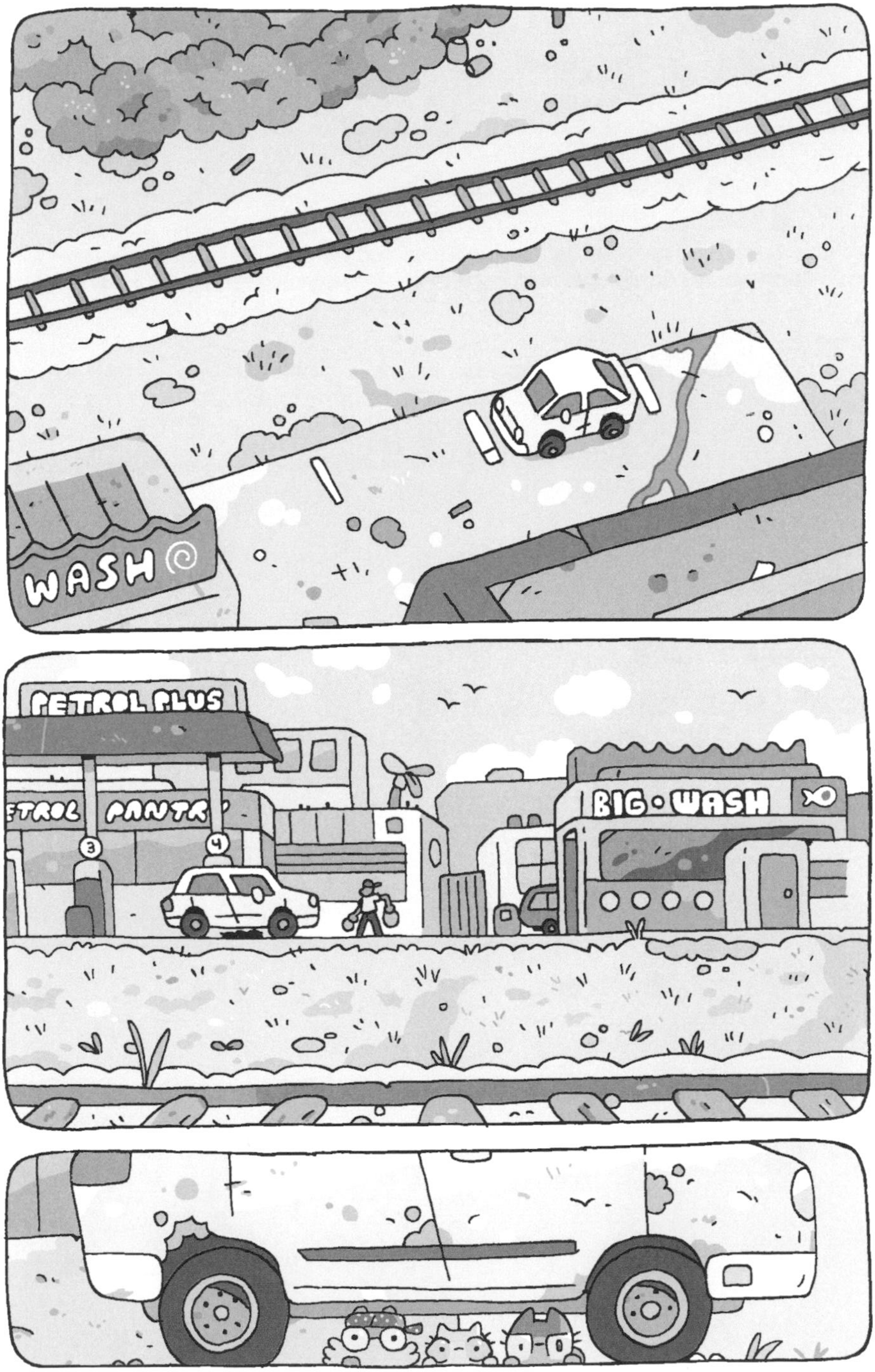
WASH
PETROL PLUS
ETROL PANTR
3
4
BIG • WASH

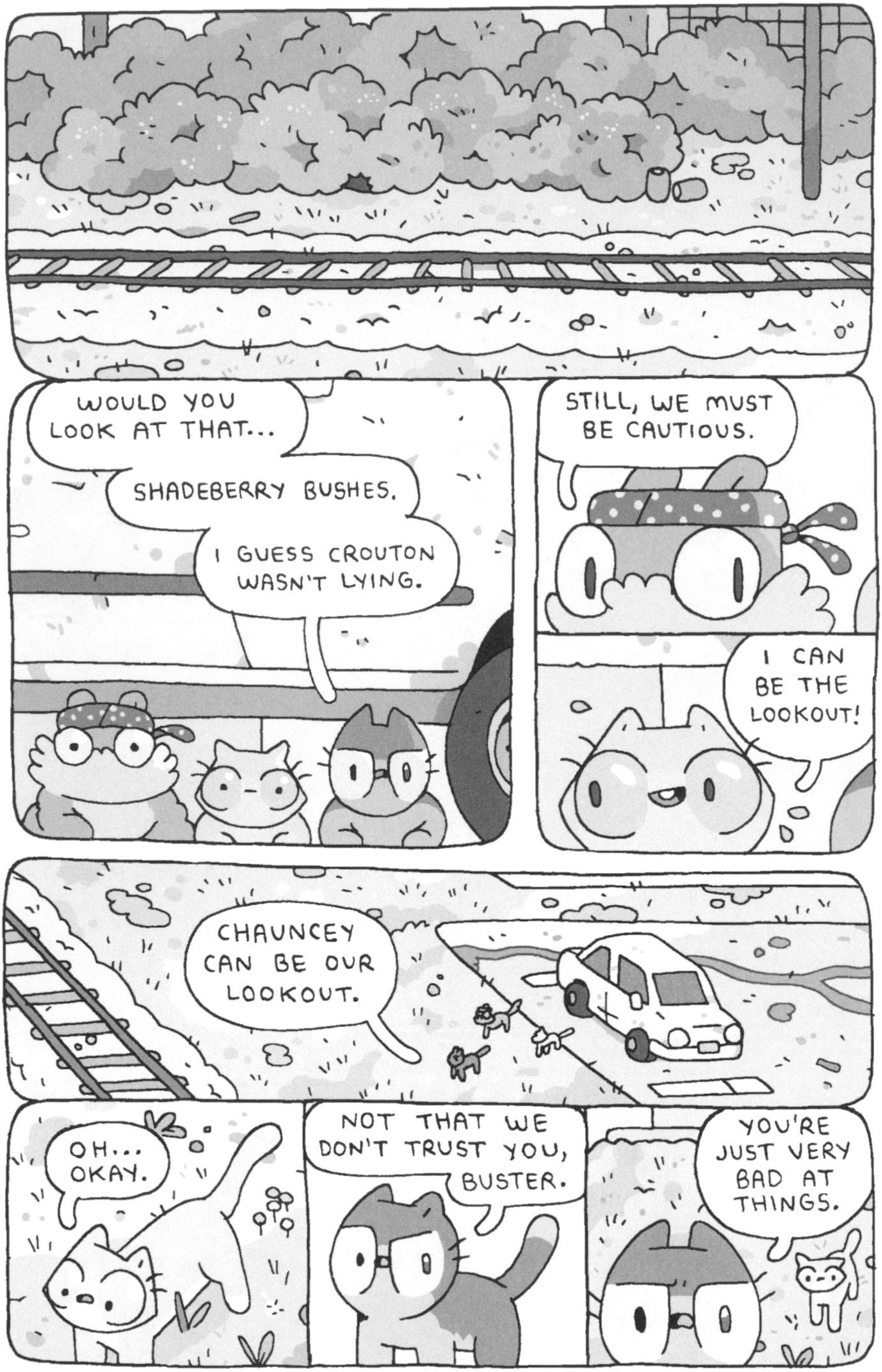

WOULD YOU LOOK AT THAT...
SHADEBERRY BUSHES.
I GUESS CROUTON WASN'T LYING.
STILL, WE MUST BE CAUTIOUS.
I CAN BE THE LOOKOUT!
CHAUNCEY CAN BE OUR LOOKOUT.
OH... OKAY.
NOT THAT WE DON'T TRUST YOU, BUSTER.
YOU'RE JUST VERY BAD AT THINGS.

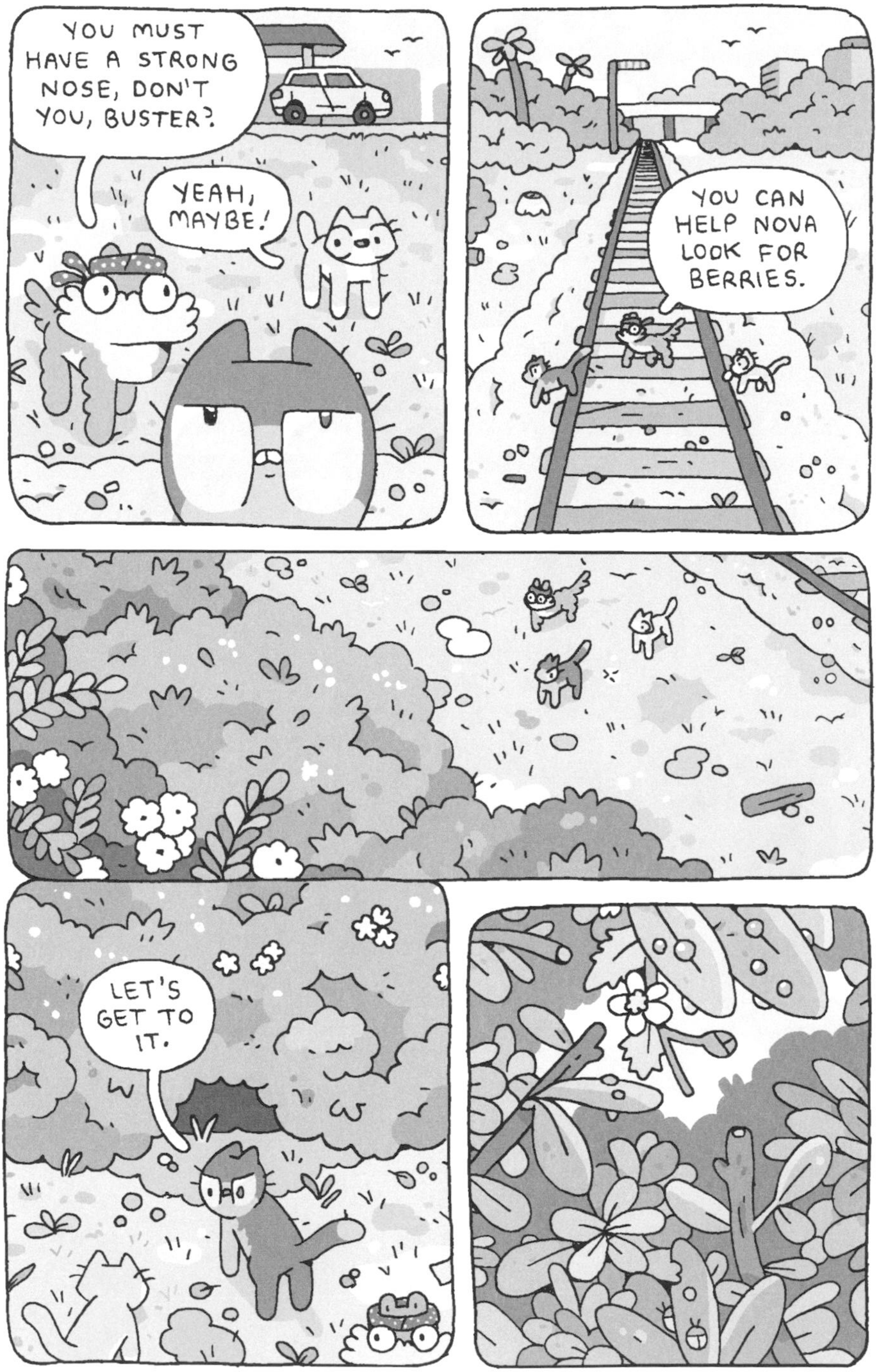
YOU MUST HAVE A STRONG NOSE, DON'T YOU, BUSTER?
YEAH, MAYBE!
YOU CAN HELP NOVA LOOK FOR BERRIES.
LET'S GET TO IT.

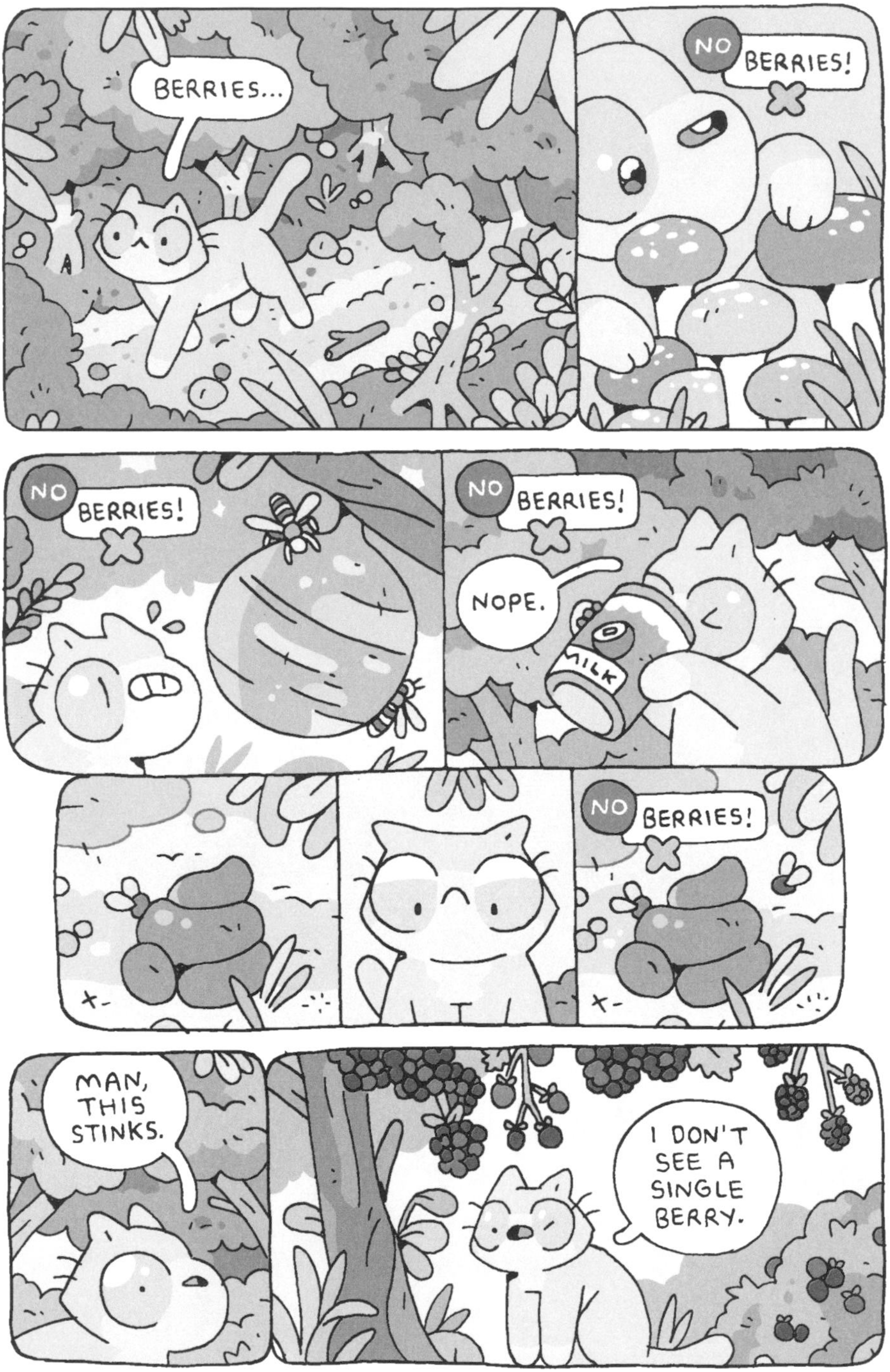
BERRIES...
NO BERRIES!
NO BERRIES!
NO BERRIES!
NOPE.
MILK
NO BERRIES!
MAN, THIS STINKS.
I DON'T SEE A SINGLE BERRY.

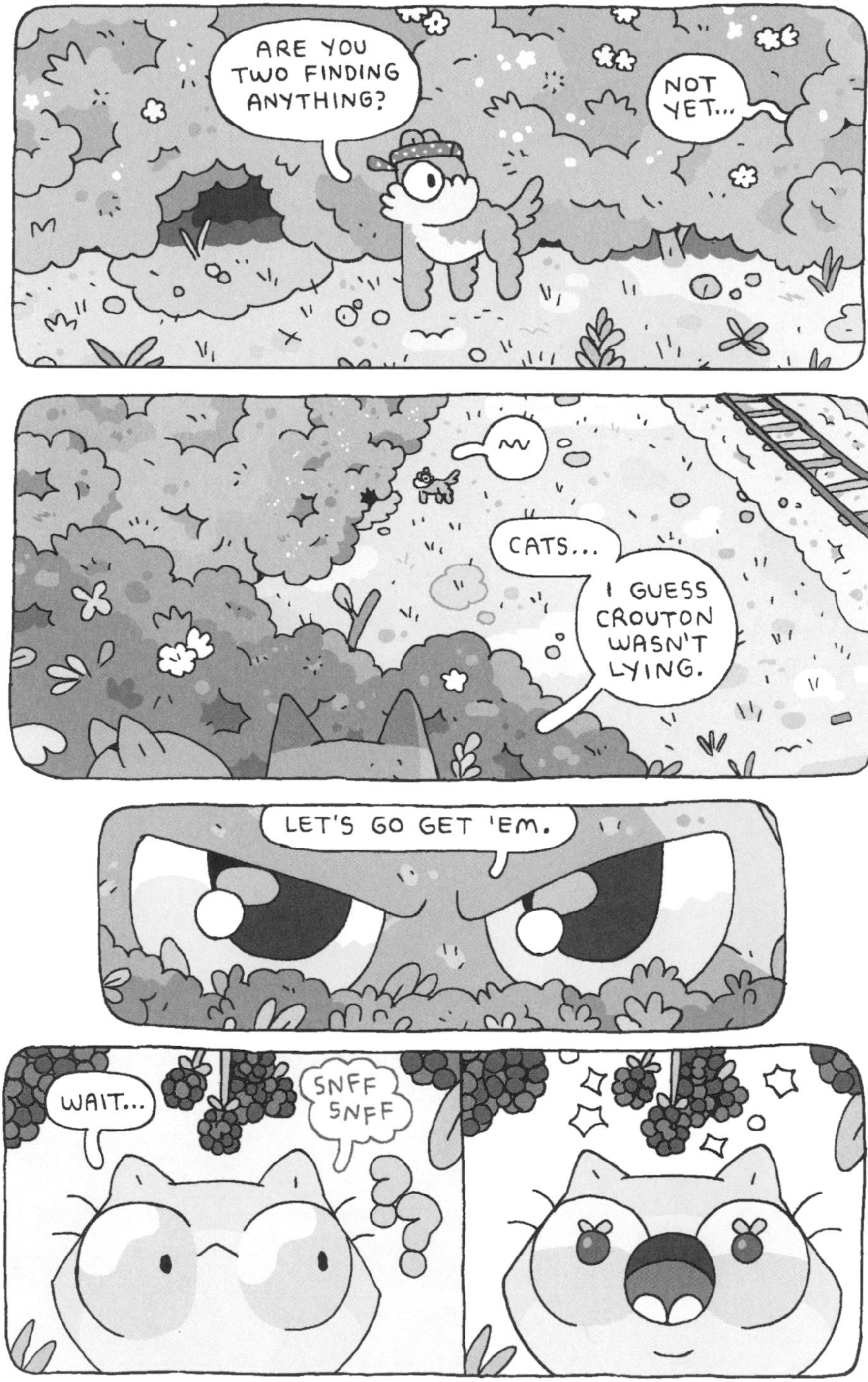
ARE YOU TWO FINDING ANYTHING?
NOT YET...
~
CATS...
I GUESS CROUTON WASN'T LYING.
LET'S GO GET 'EM.
WAIT...
SNFF SNFF

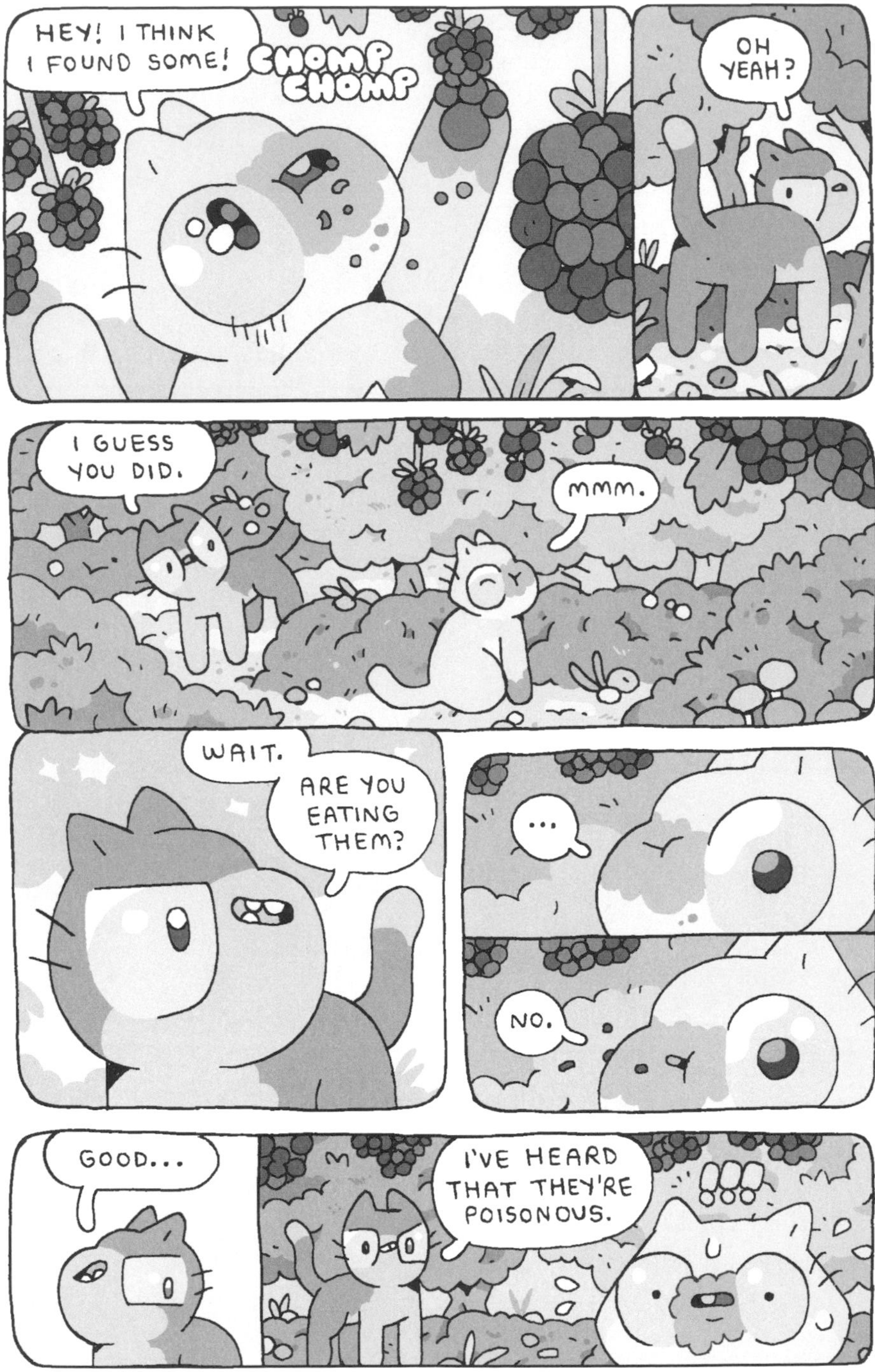
HEY! I THINK I FOUND SOME!
CHOMP CHOMP
OH YEAH?
I GUESS YOU DID.
MMM.
WAIT.
ARE YOU EATING THEM?
...
NO.
GOOD...
I'VE HEARD THAT THEY'RE POISONOUS.

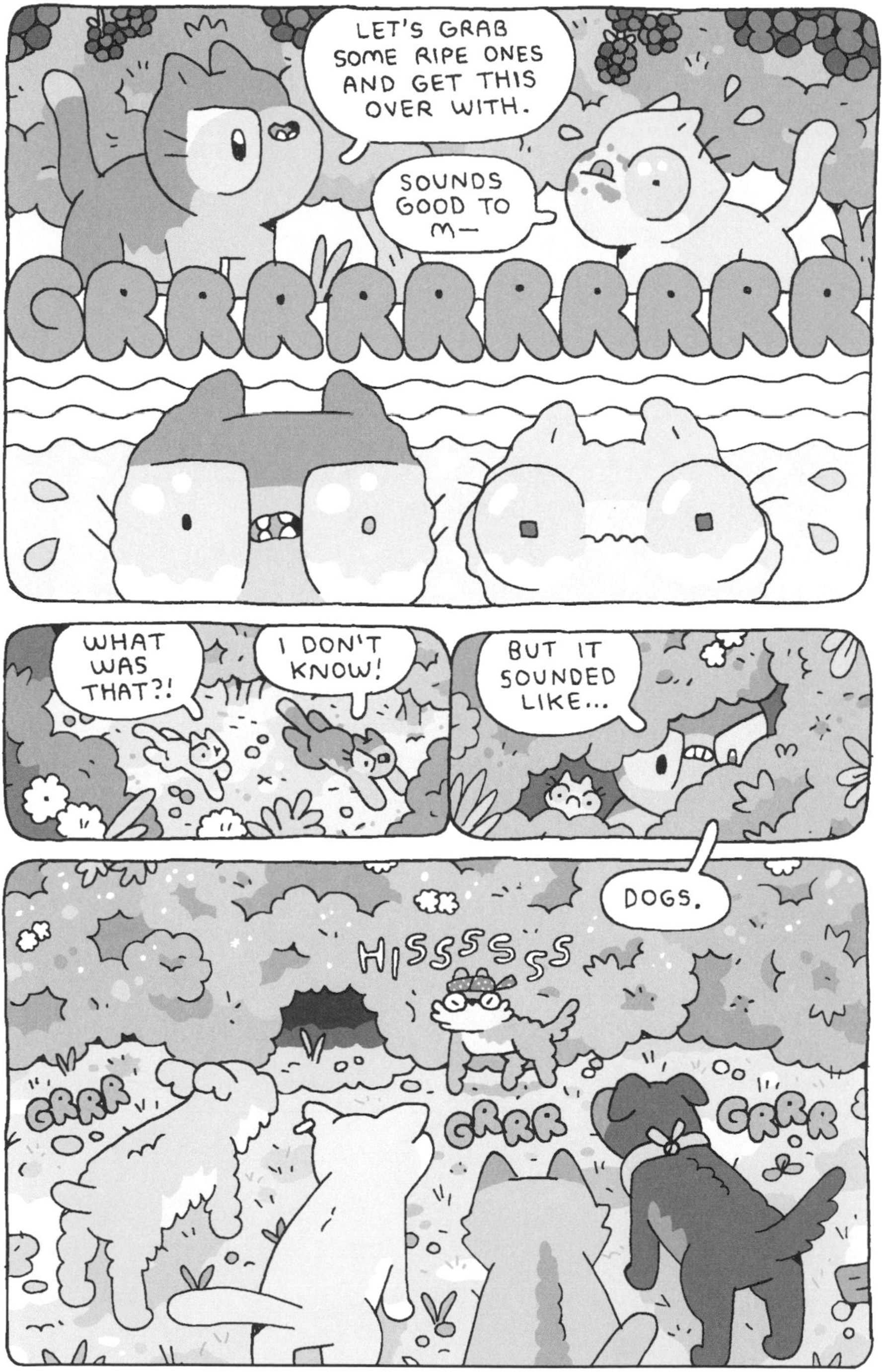
LET'S GRAB SOME RIPE ONES AND GET THIS OVER WITH.
SOUNDS GOOD TO M—
GRRRRRRRRRR
WHAT WAS THAT?!
I DON'T KNOW!
BUT IT SOUNDED LIKE...
DOGS.
HISSSSSSS
GRRR
GRRR
GRRR

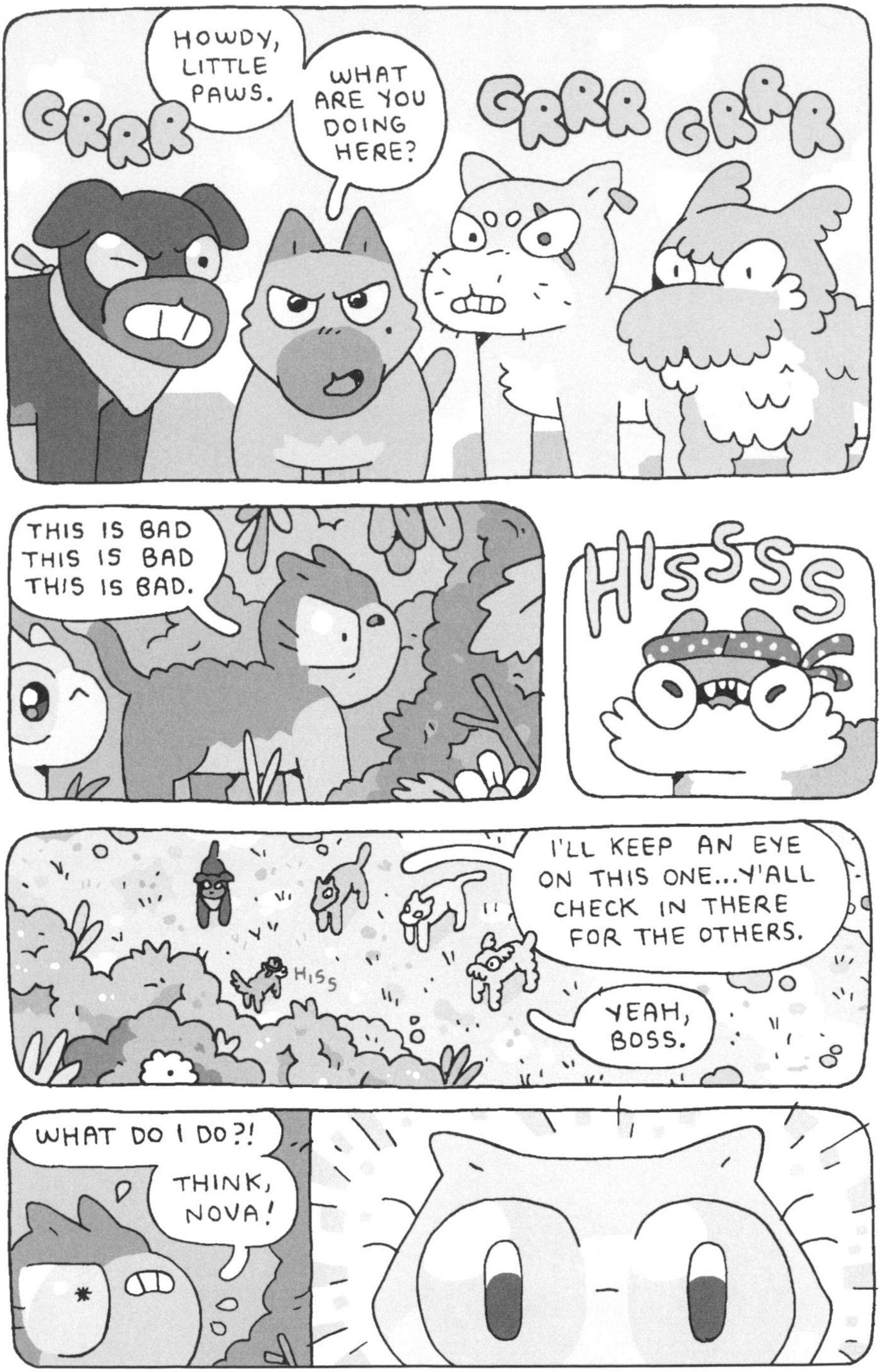
GRRR
HOWDY, LITTLE PAWS.
WHAT ARE YOU DOING HERE?
GRRR GRRR
THIS IS BAD THIS IS BAD THIS IS BAD.
HISSSS
HISS
I'LL KEEP AN EYE ON THIS ONE...Y'ALL CHECK IN THERE FOR THE OTHERS.
YEAH, BOSS.
WHAT DO I DO?!
THINK, NOVA!

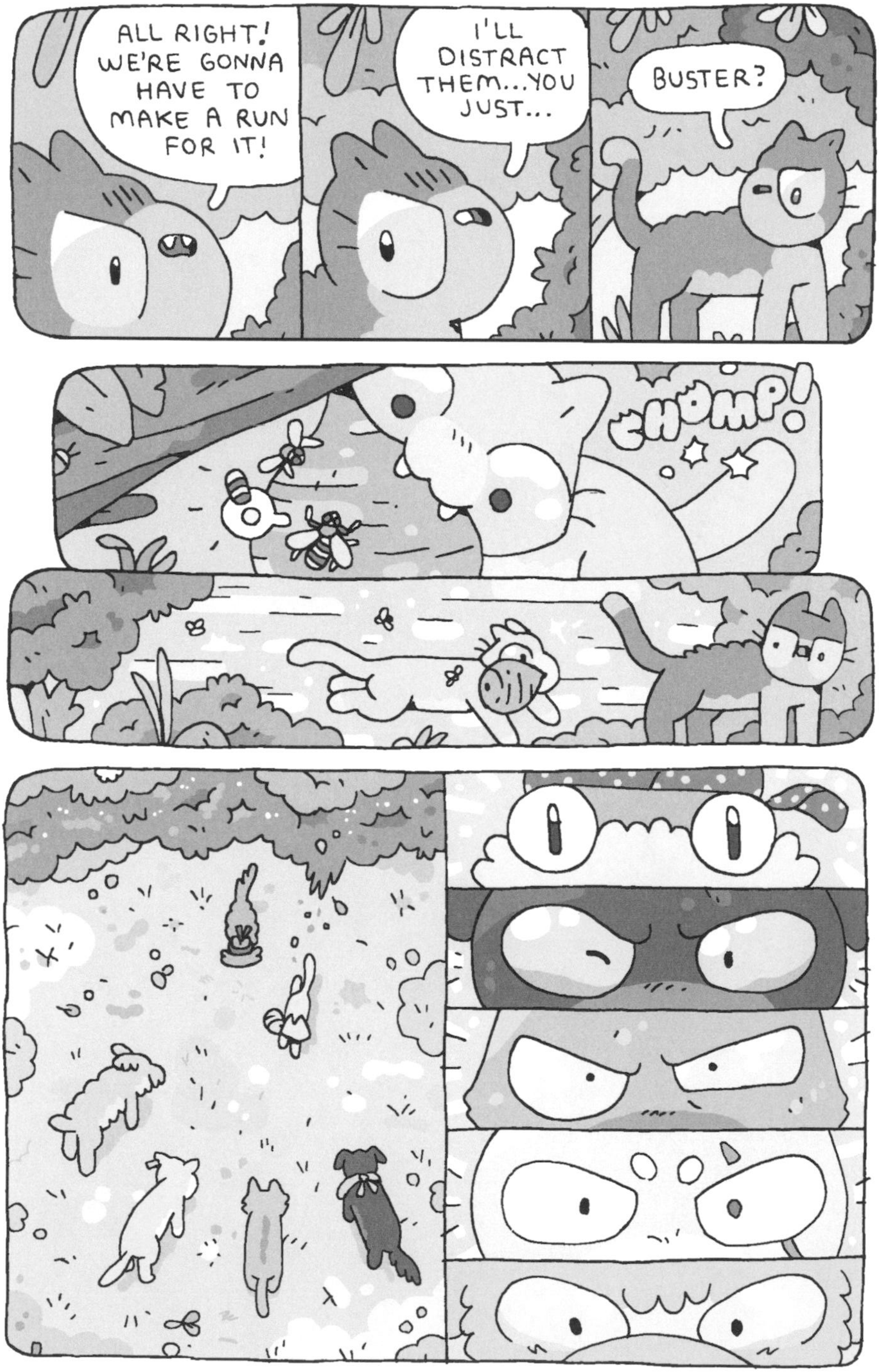

ALL RIGHT! WE'RE GONNA HAVE TO MAKE A RUN FOR IT!
I'LL DISTRACT THEM...YOU JUST...
BUSTER?
CHOMP!

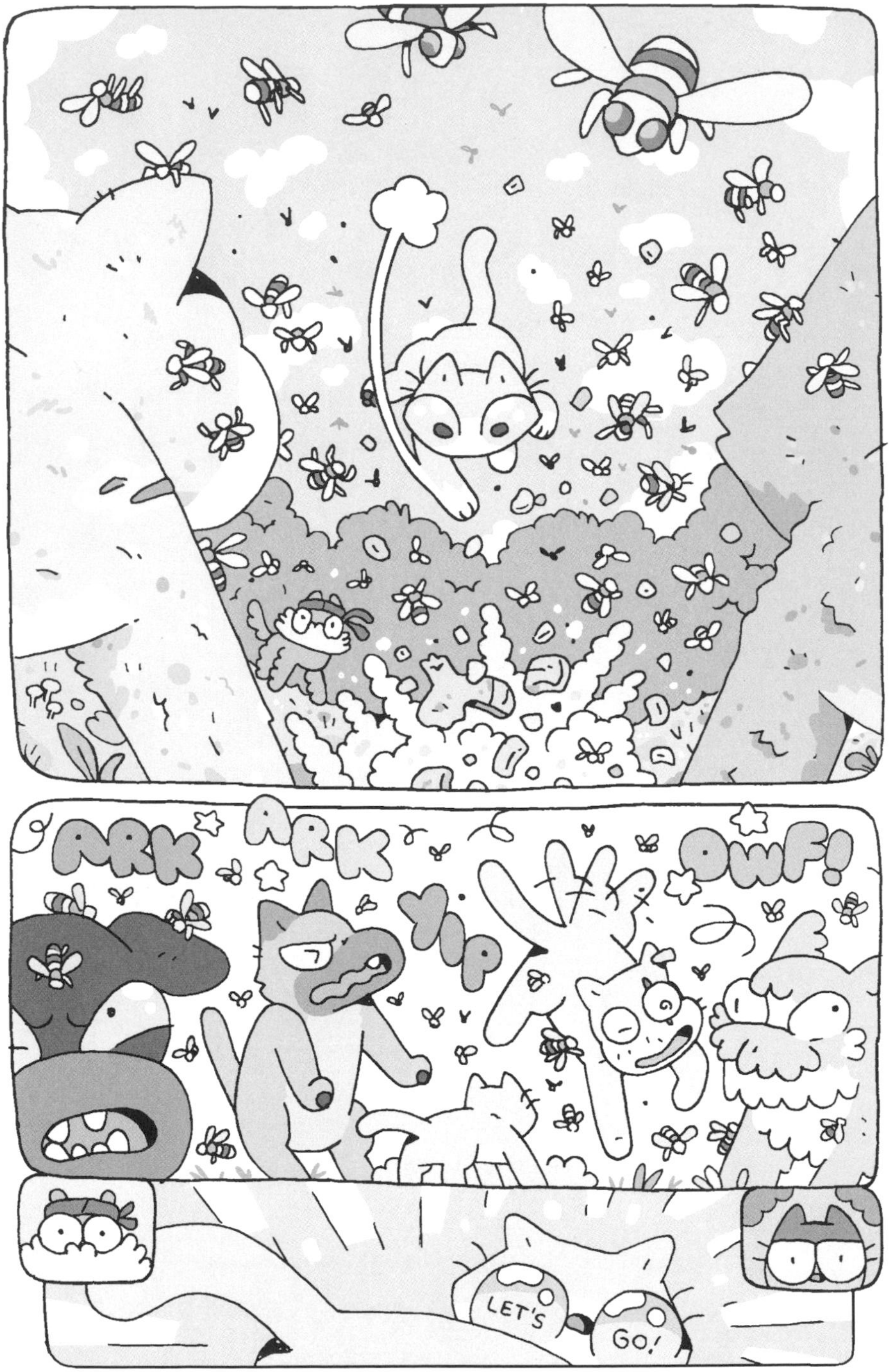
ARK ARK
YIP
OWF!
LET'S
GO!

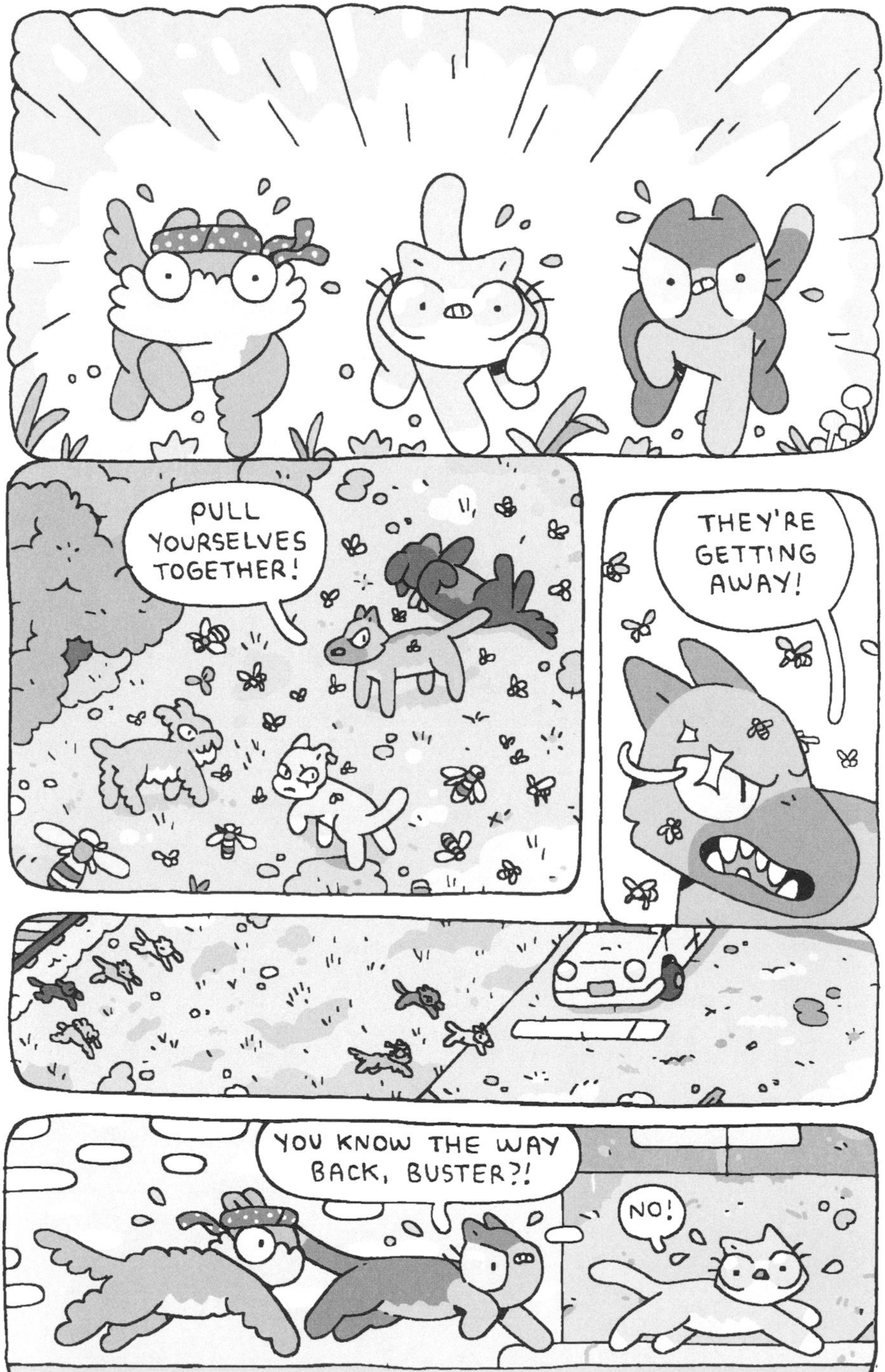
PULL YOURSELVES TOGETHER!
THEY'RE GETTING AWAY!
YOU KNOW THE WAY BACK, BUSTER?!
NO!

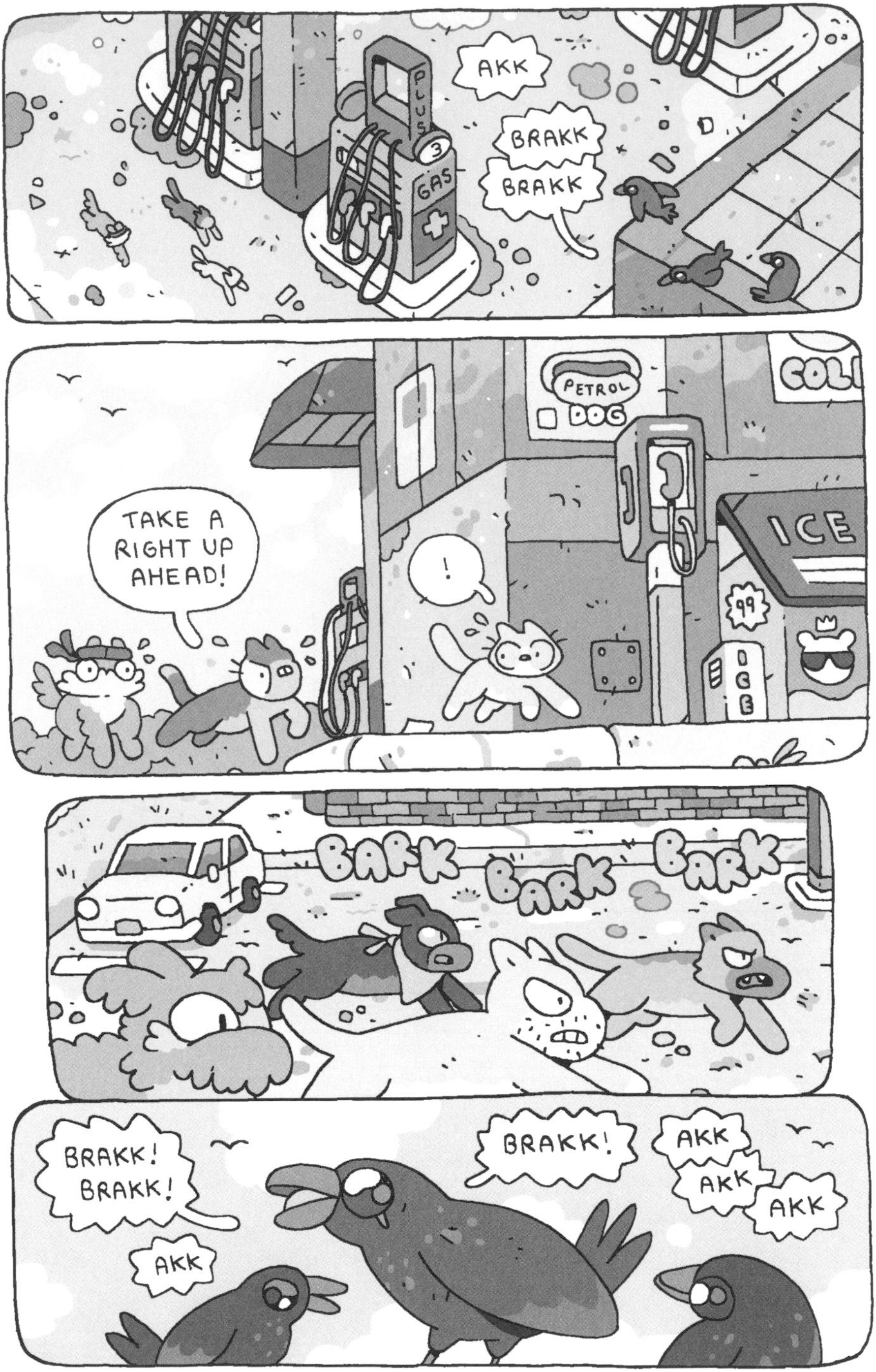
AKK
BRAKK
BRAKK
PLUS
3
GAS
PETROL
DOG
COL
TAKE A RIGHT UP AHEAD!
!
ICE
99
BARK
BARK
BARK
BRAKK! BRAKK!
BRAKK!
AKK
AKK
AKK
AKK

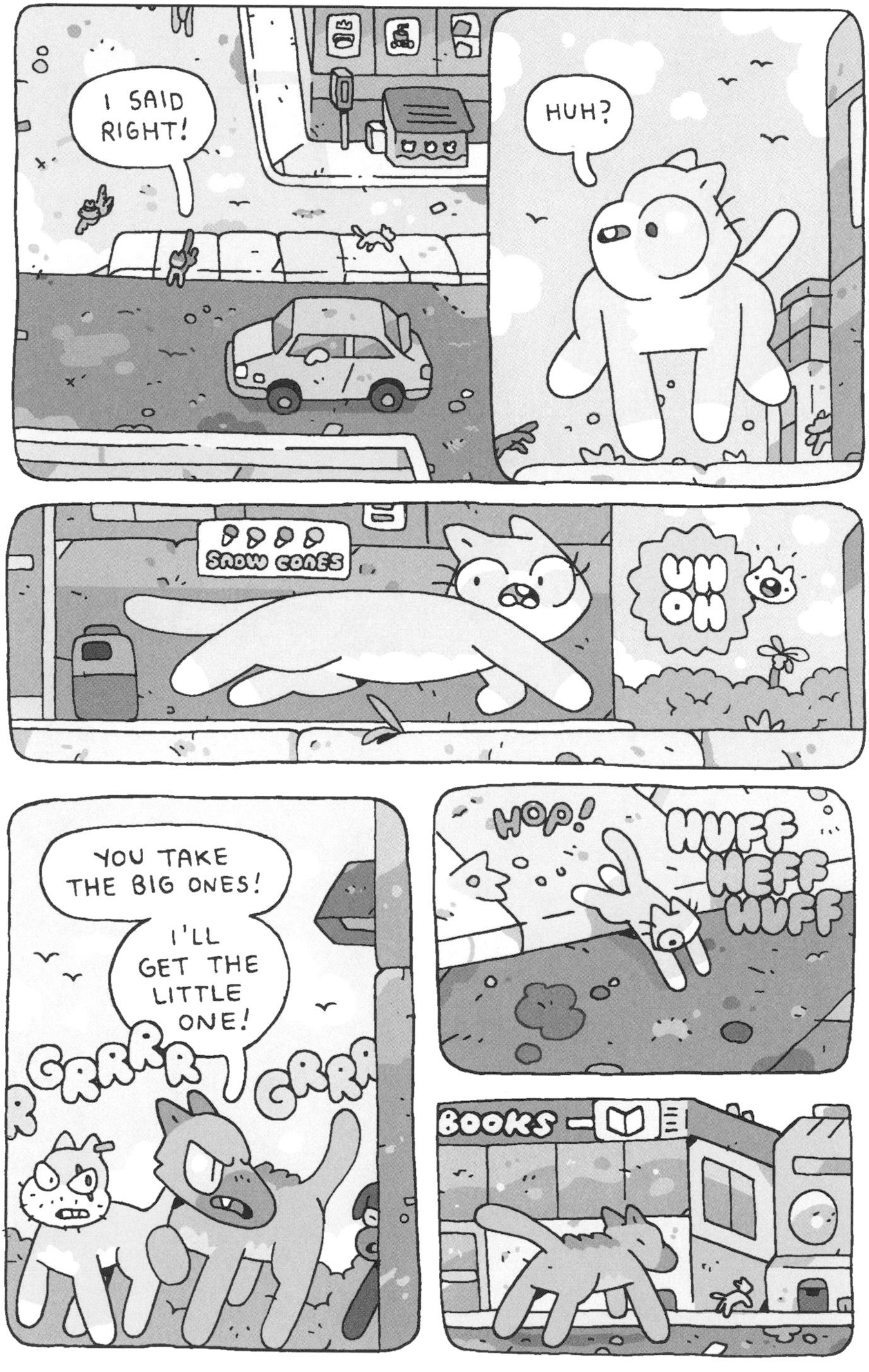
I SAID RIGHT!
HUH?
SNOW CONES
UH OH
YOU TAKE THE BIG ONES!
I'LL GET THE LITTLE ONE!
GRRRR
GRRR
HOP!
HUFF HEFF HUFF
BOOKS

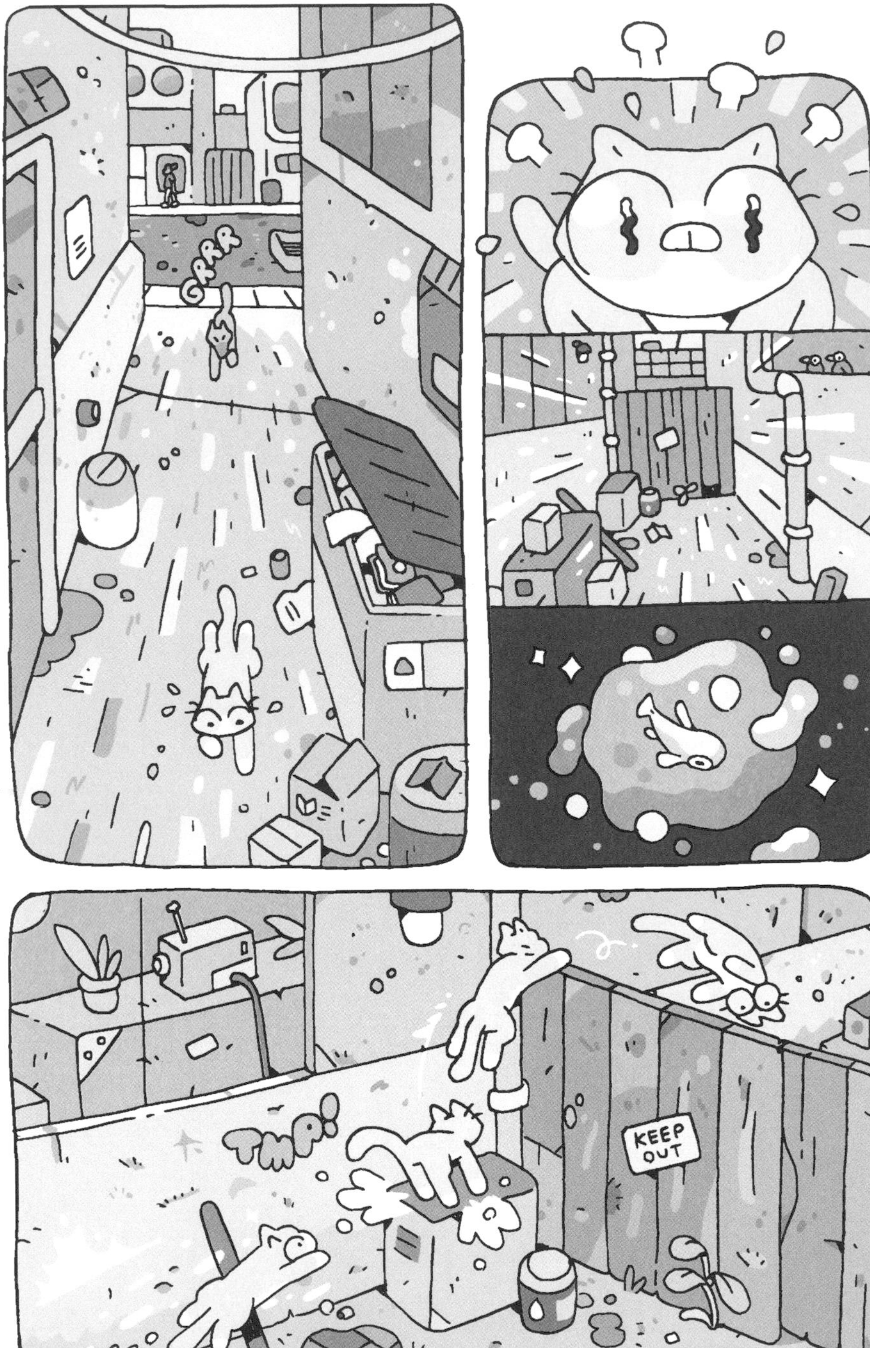
GRRR
TMP!
KEEP OUT

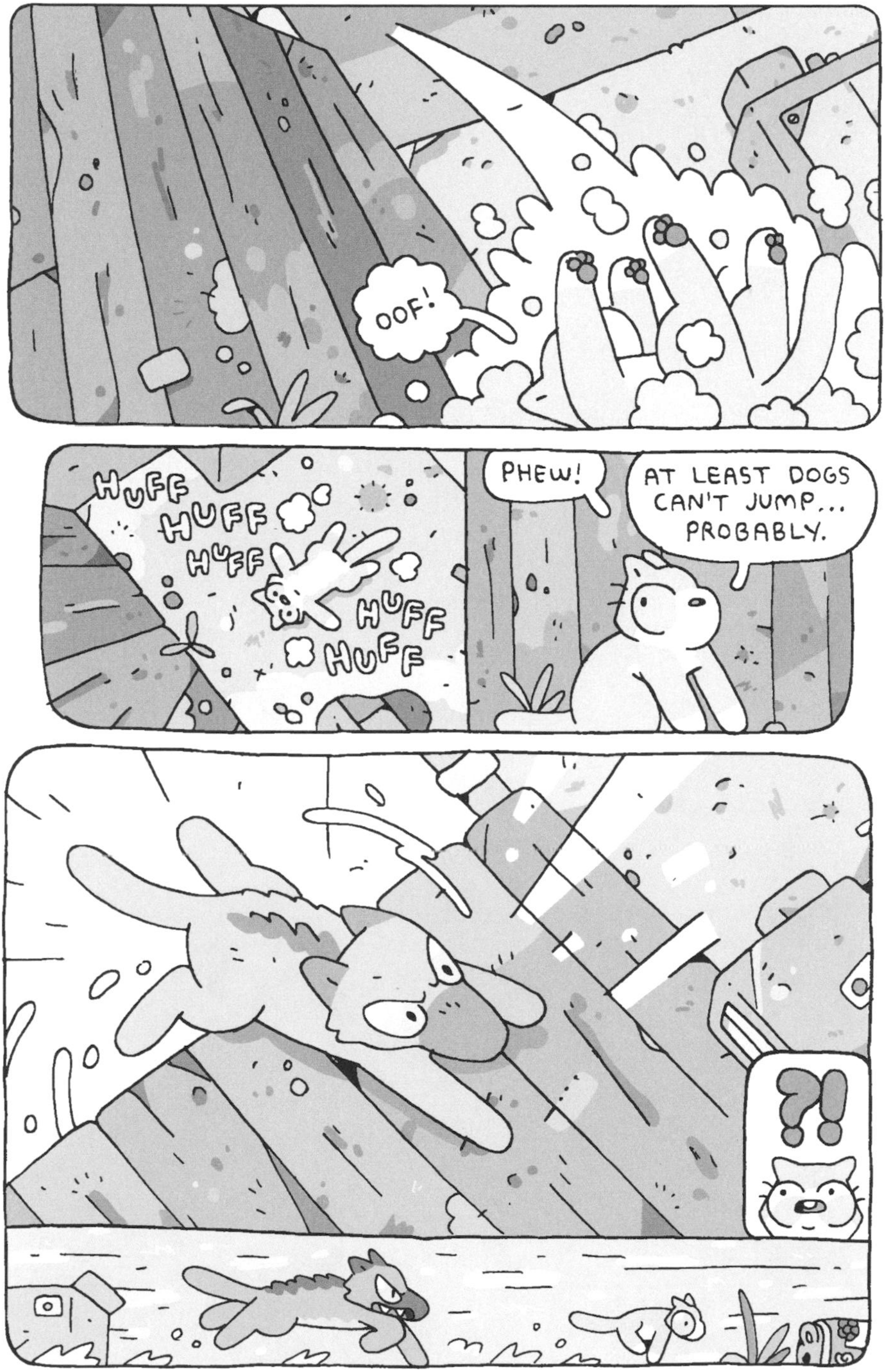

OOF!
HUFF
HUFF
HUFF
HUFF
HUFF
PHEW!
AT LEAST DOGS CAN'T JUMP... PROBABLY.
?!

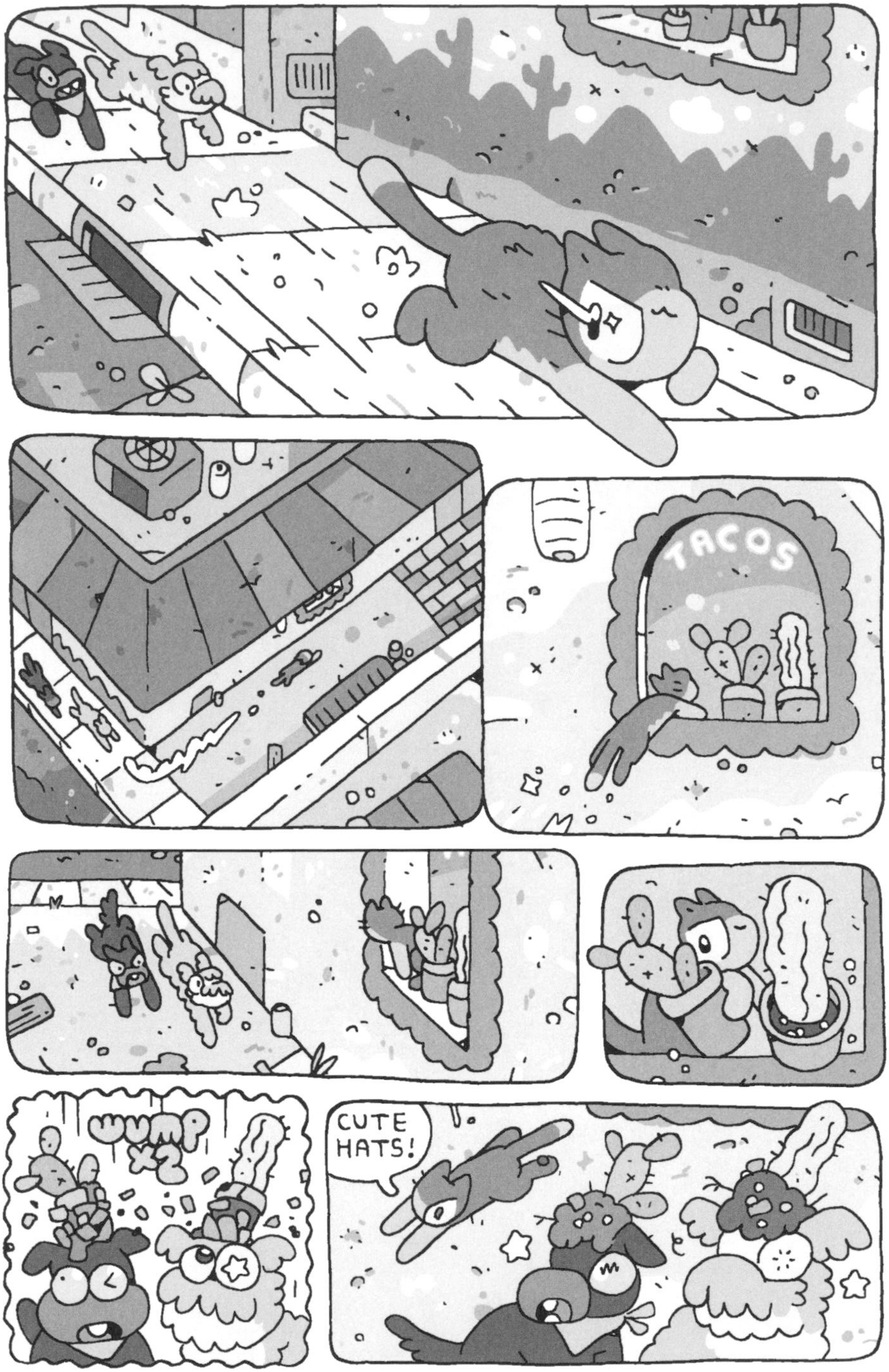
TACOS
WUMP x2
CUTE HATS!

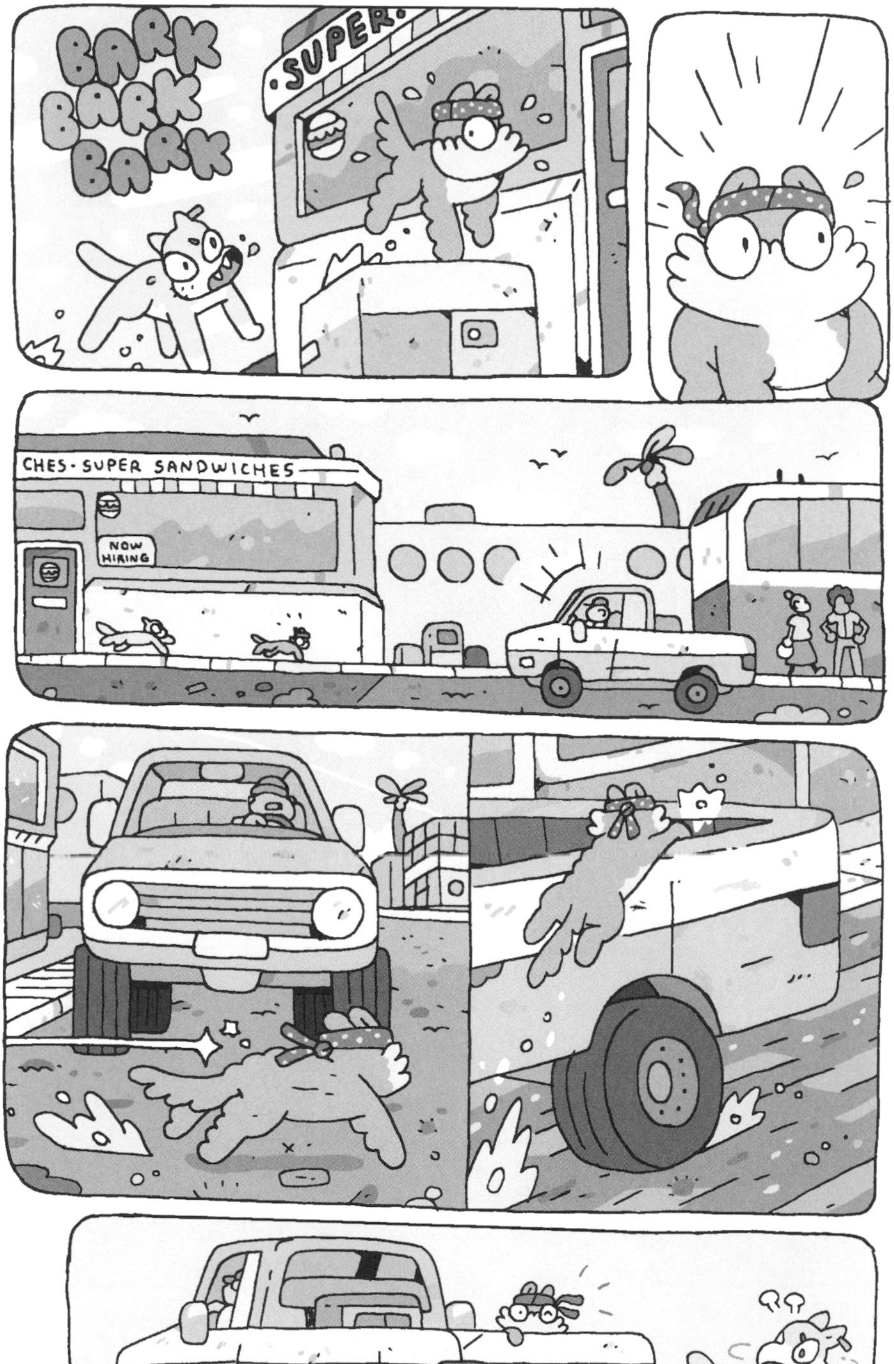
BARK
BARK
BARK
SUPER
CHES-SUPER SANDWICHES
NOW HIRING
BFF

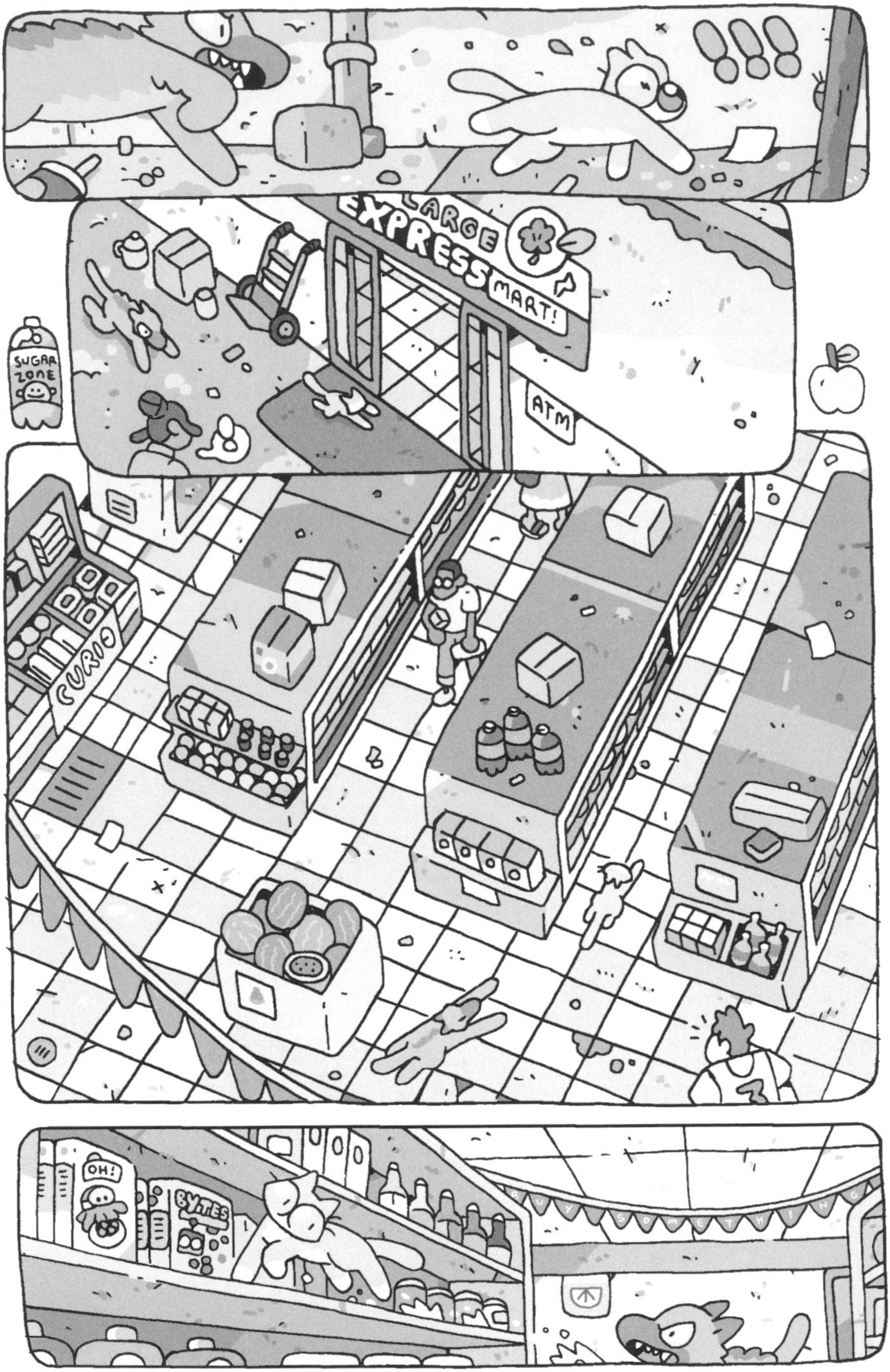
LARGE
EXPRESS
MART!
ATM
SUGAR ZONE
CURIO
OH!
BYTES
BUY SOMETHING

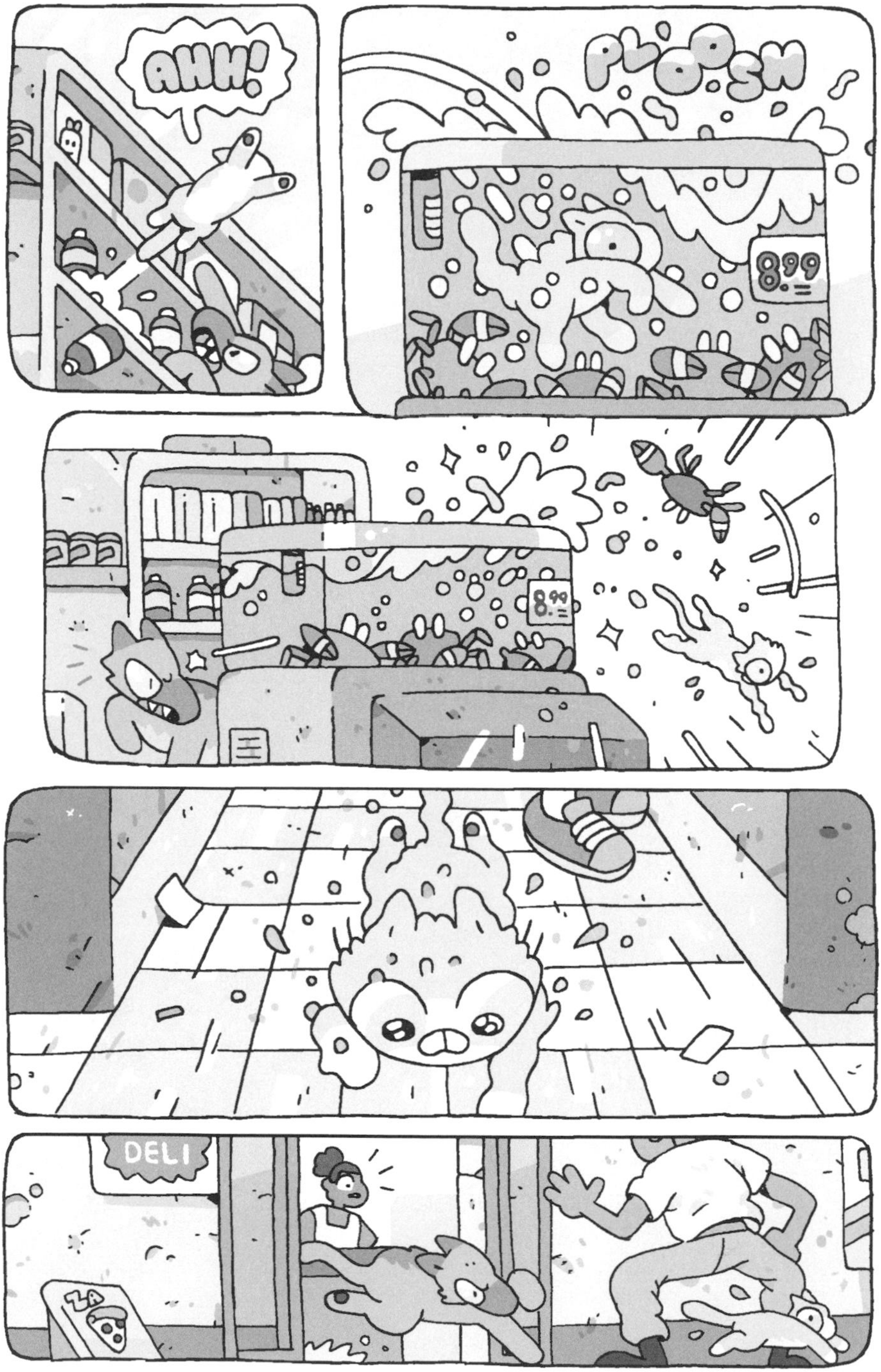
AHH!
PLOOSH
8.99
8.99
DELI
ZA

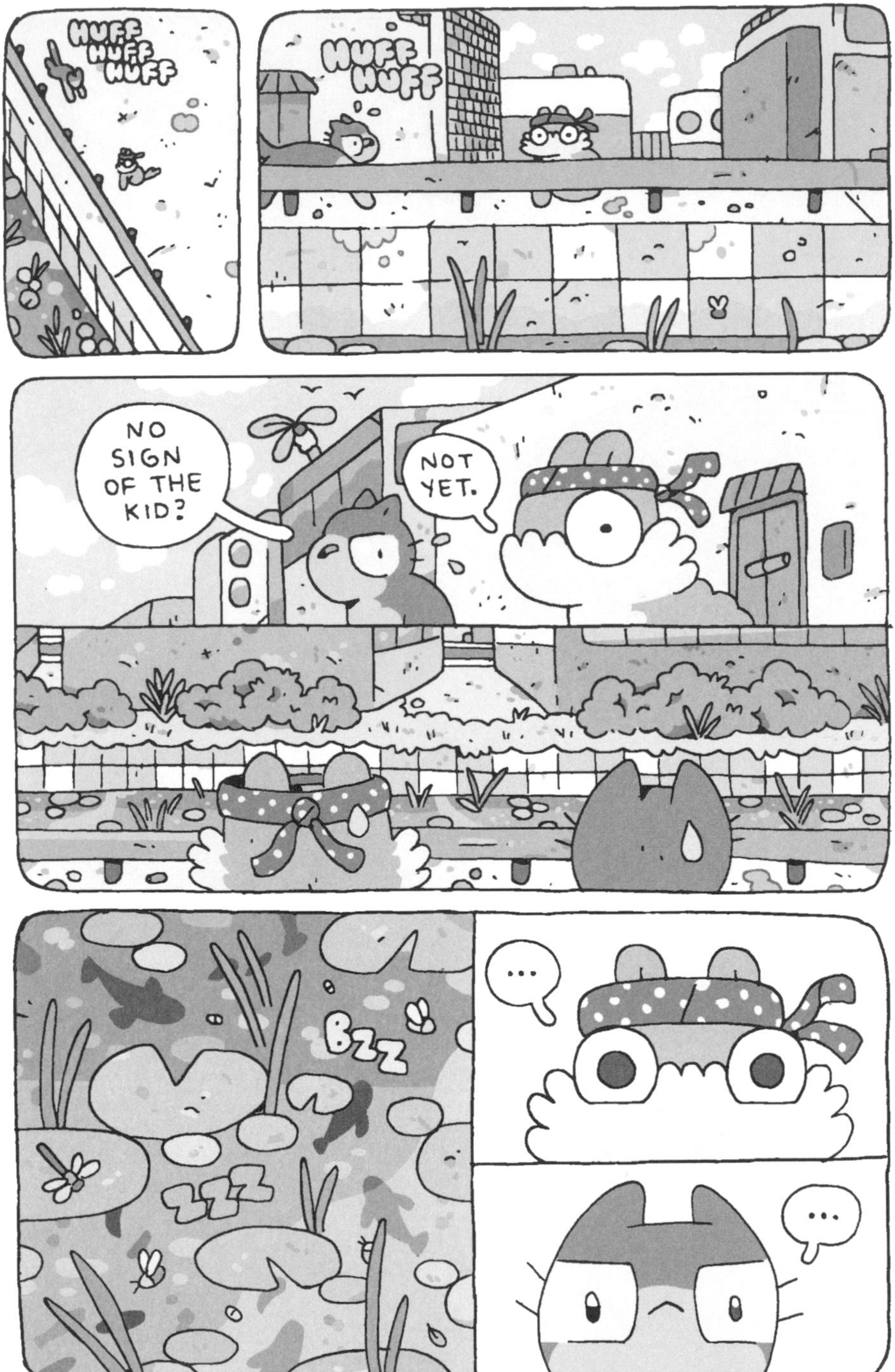
HUFF HUFF HUFF
HUFF HUFF
NO SIGN OF THE KID?
NOT YET.
BZZ
ZZZ
...
...

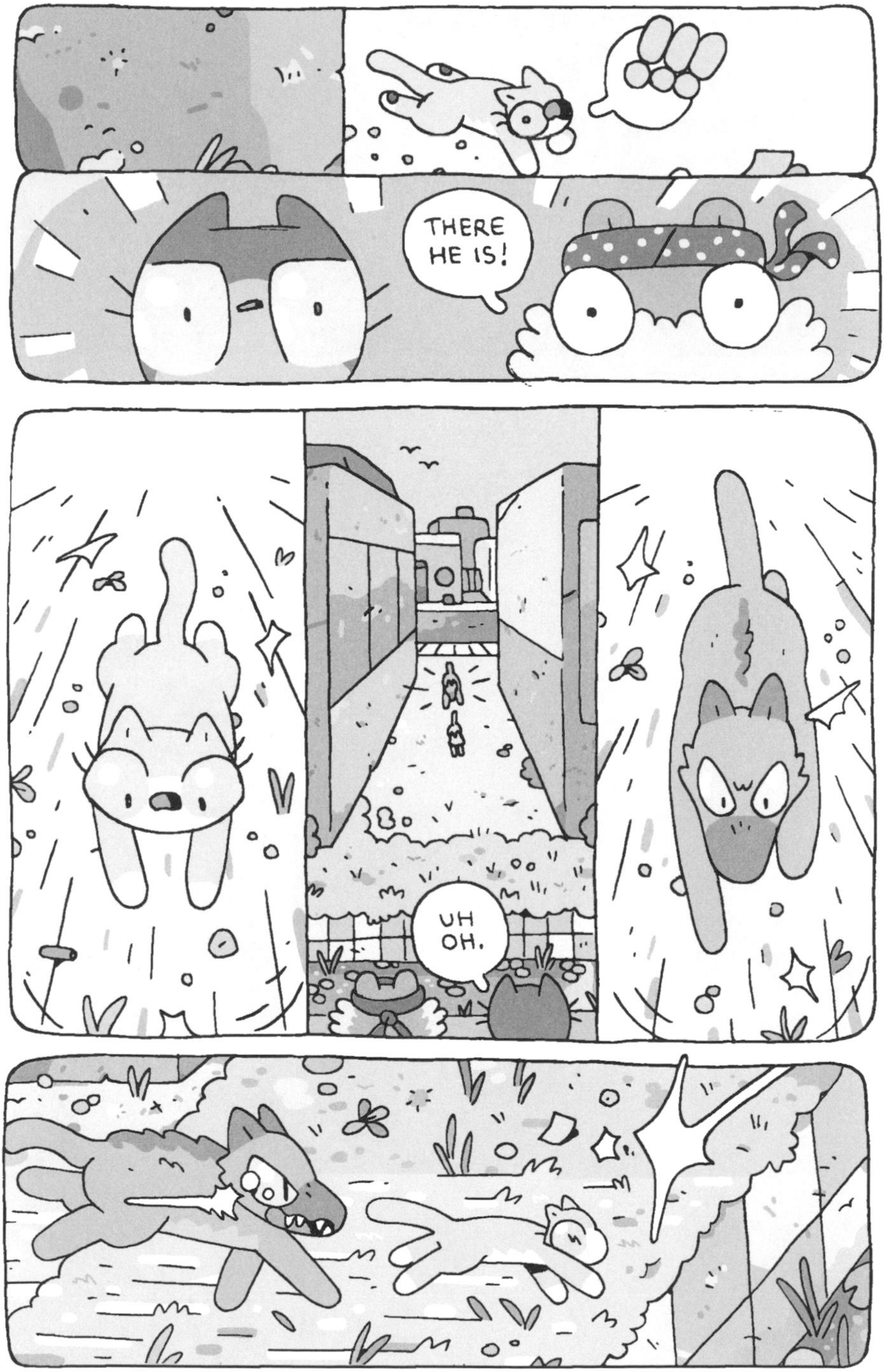
THERE HE IS!
UH OH.

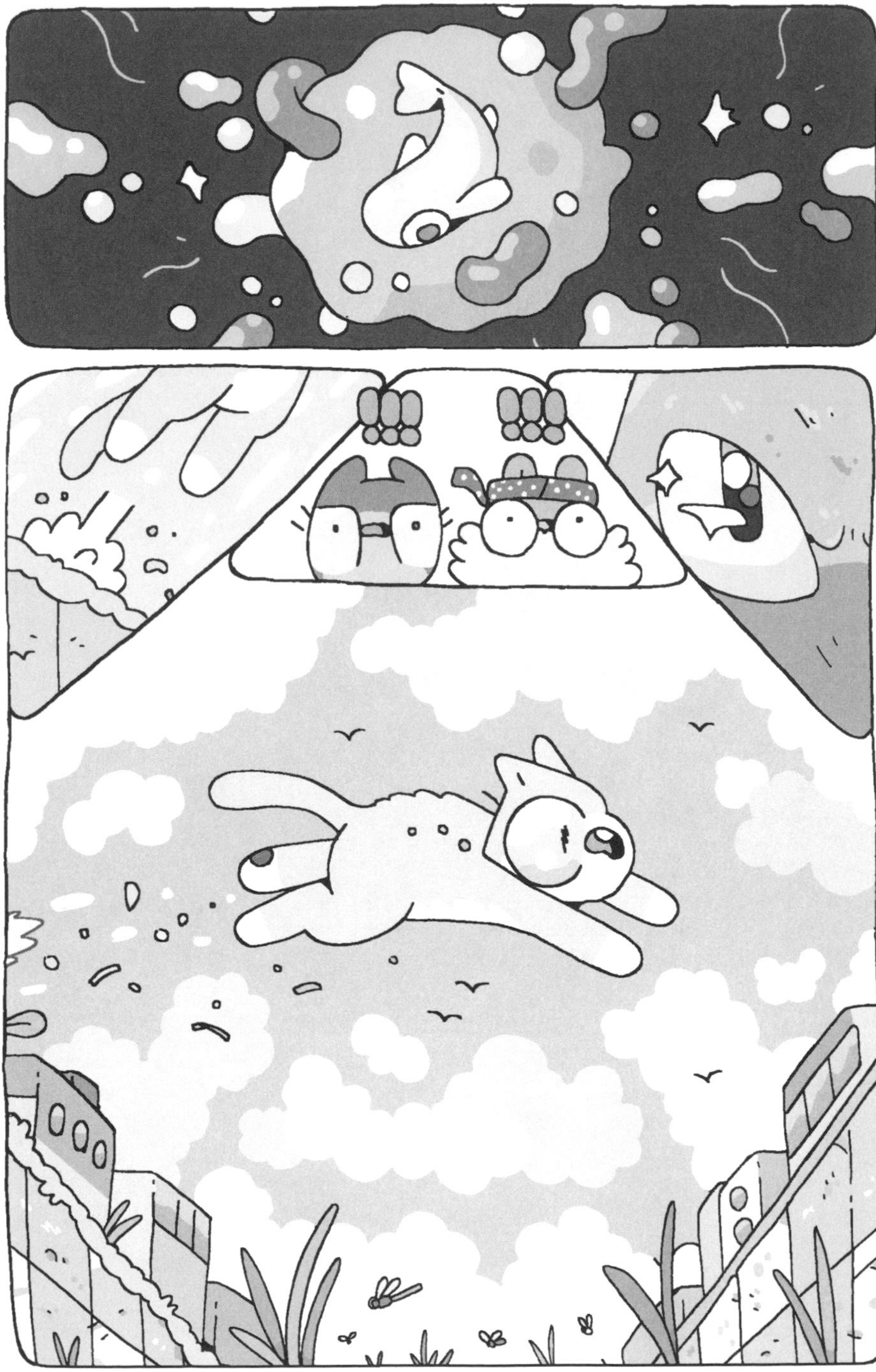

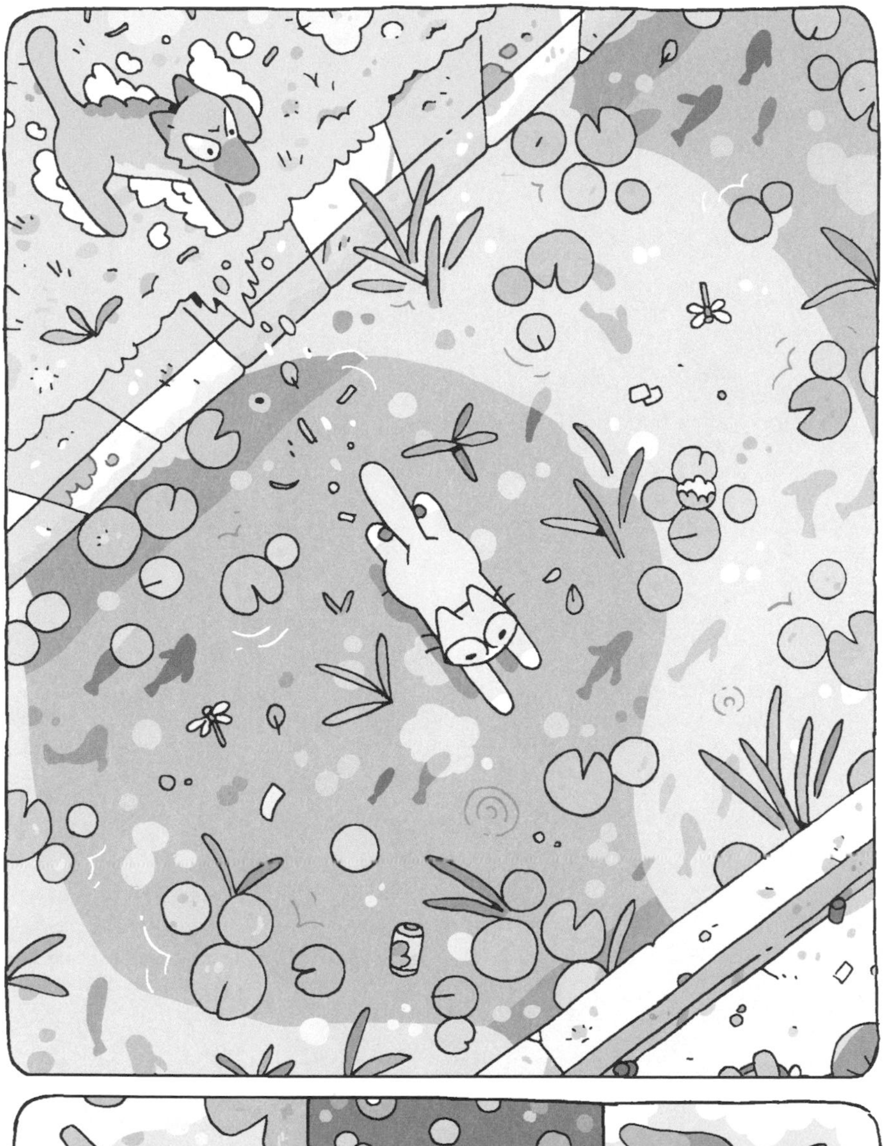

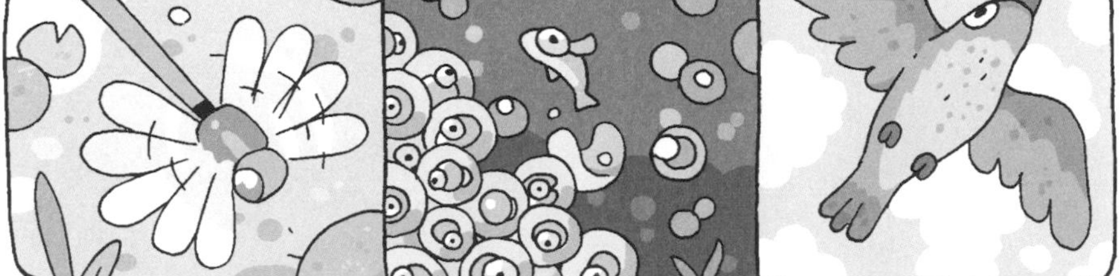

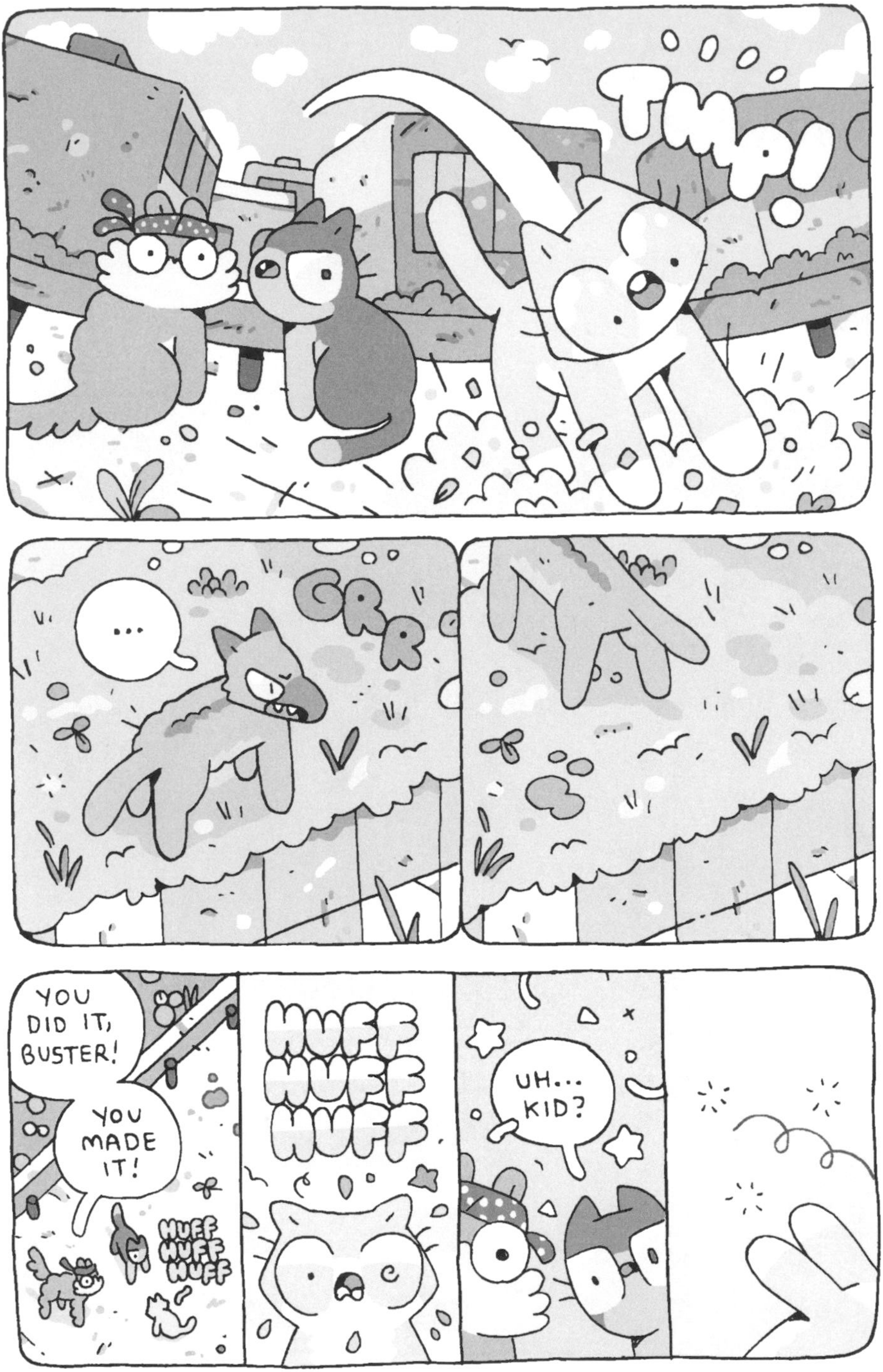
THMP!
...
GRR
YOU DID IT, BUSTER!
YOU MADE IT!
HUFF HUFF HUFF
HUFF HUFF HUFF
UH... KID?

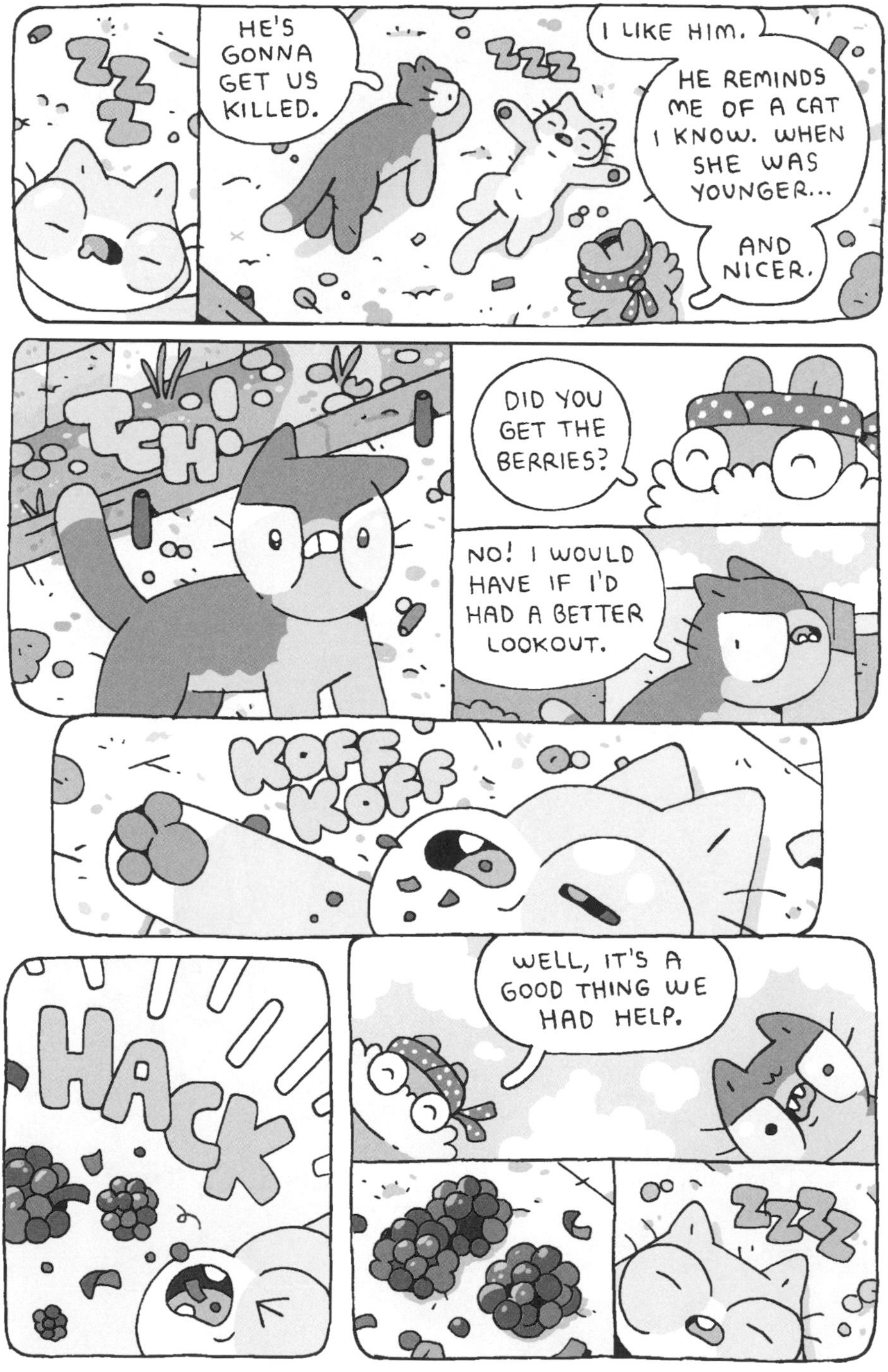
ZZZ
HE'S GONNA GET US KILLED.
ZZZ
I LIKE HIM.
HE REMINDS ME OF A CAT I KNOW. WHEN SHE WAS YOUNGER...
AND NICER.
TCH!
DID YOU GET THE BERRIES?
NO! I WOULD HAVE IF I'D HAD A BETTER LOOKOUT.
KOFF KOFF
HACK
WELL, IT'S A GOOD THING WE HAD HELP.
ZZZZ

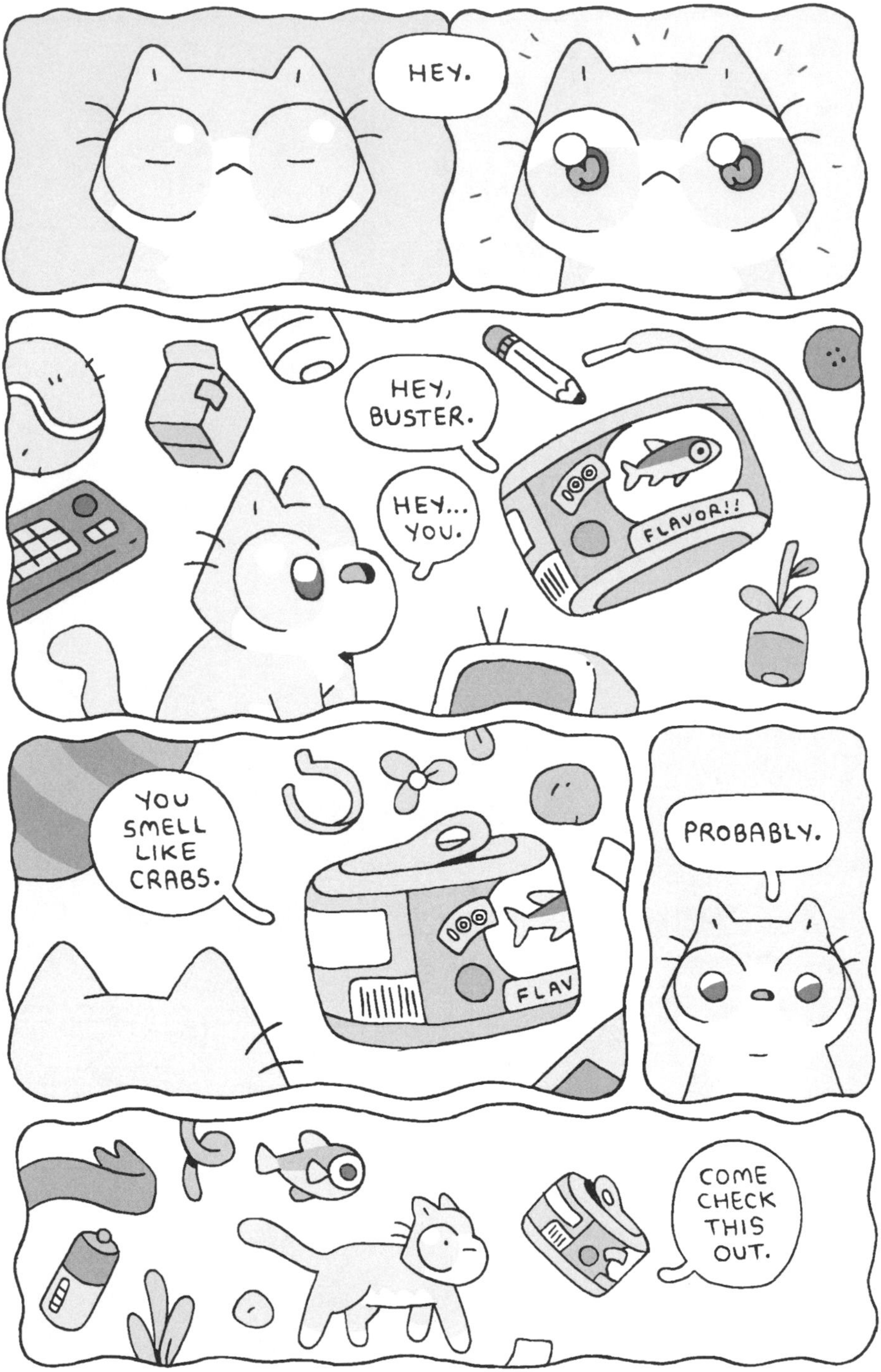
HEY.
HEY, BUSTER.
HEY... YOU.
FLAVOR!!
YOU SMELL LIKE CRABS.
FLAV
PROBABLY.
COME CHECK THIS OUT.

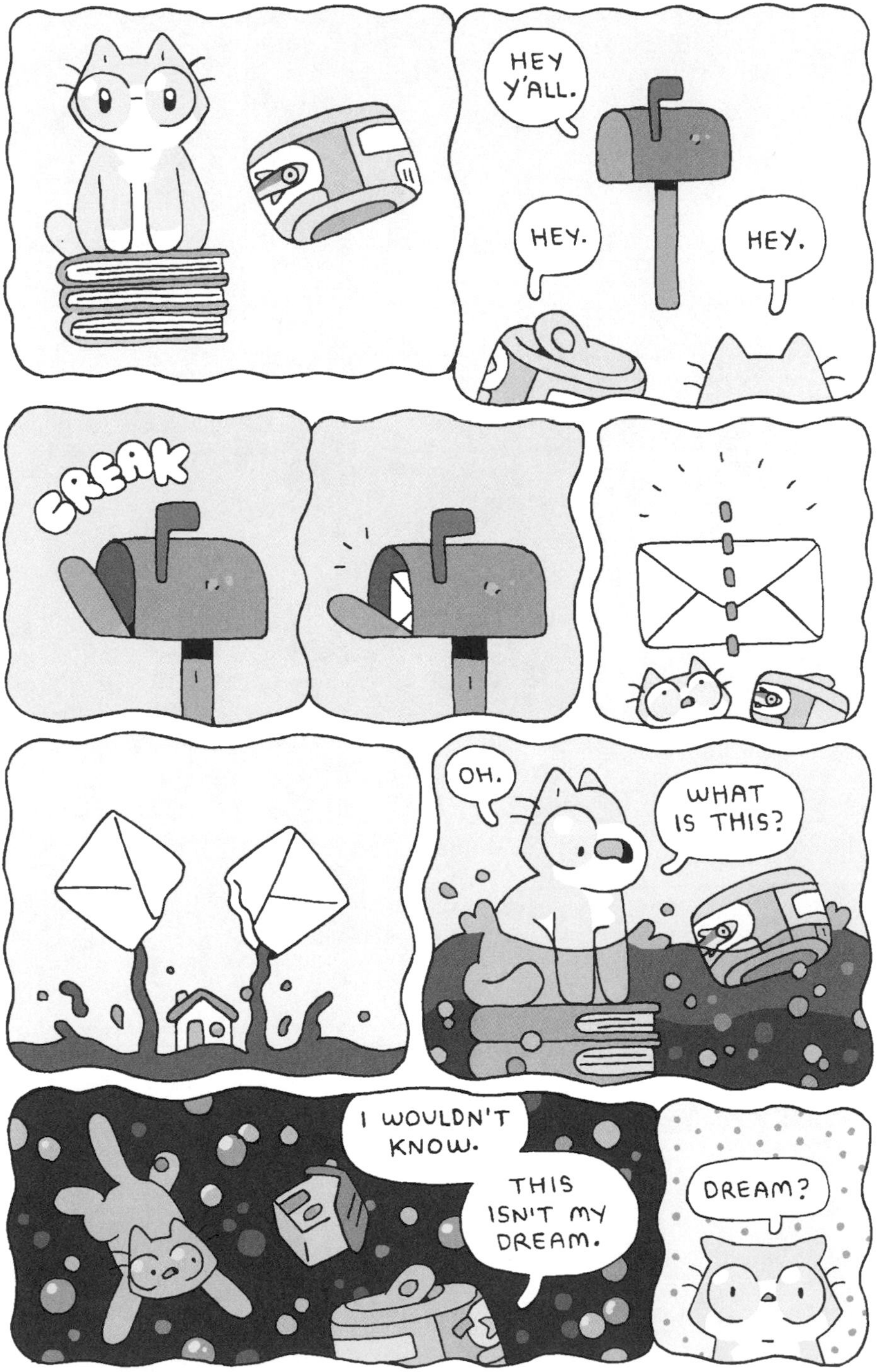
HEY Y'ALL.
HEY.
HEY.
CREAK
OH.
WHAT IS THIS?
I WOULDN'T KNOW.
THIS ISN'T MY DREAM.
DREAM?

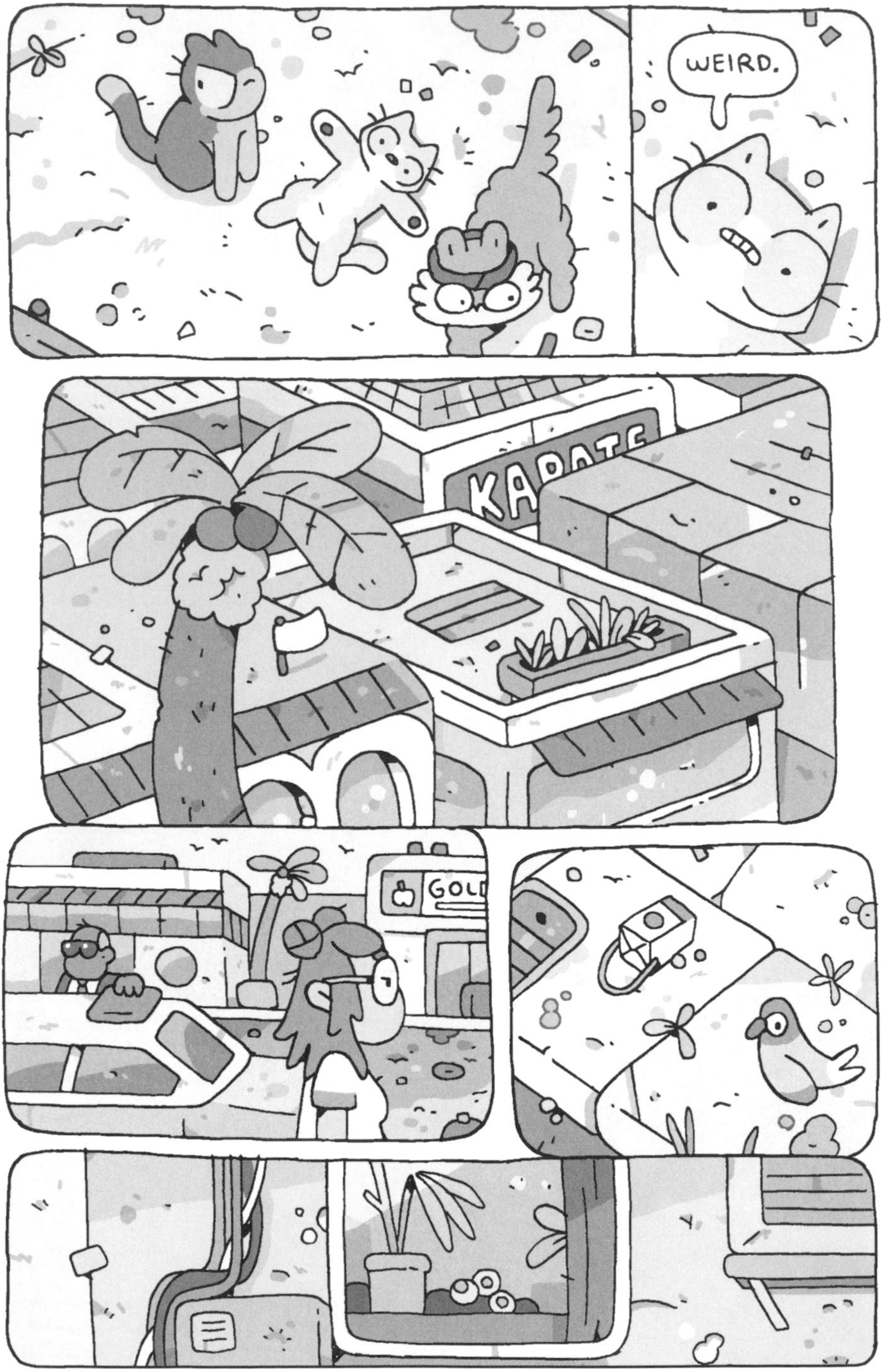
WEIRD.
KARATE
GOLD

CHAPTER 5

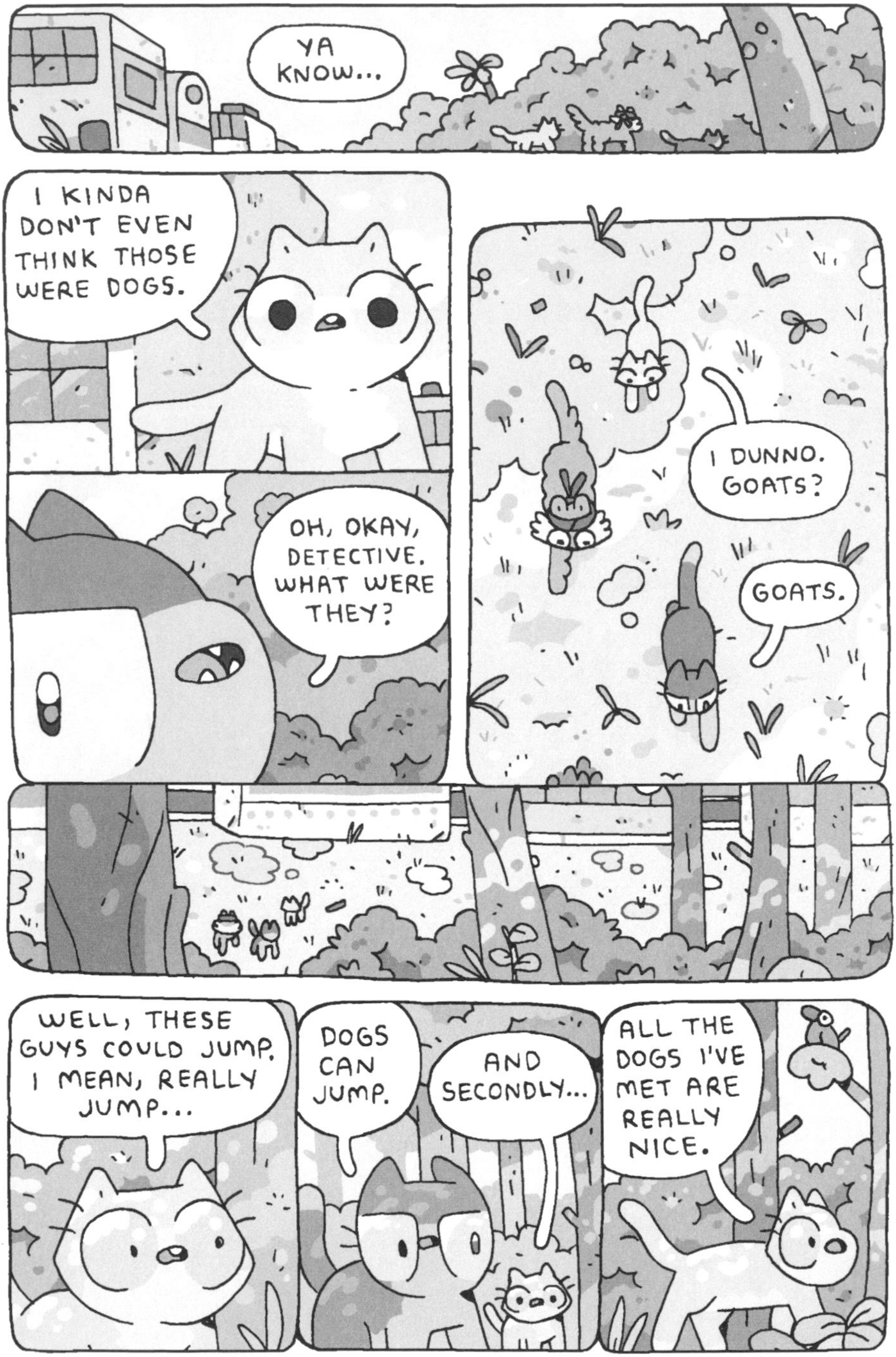
YA KNOW...
I KINDA DON'T EVEN THINK THOSE WERE DOGS.
OH, OKAY, DETECTIVE. WHAT WERE THEY?
I DUNNO. GOATS?
GOATS.
WELL, THESE GUYS COULD JUMP. I MEAN, REALLY JUMP...
DOGS CAN JUMP.
AND SECONDLY...
ALL THE DOGS I'VE MET ARE REALLY NICE.

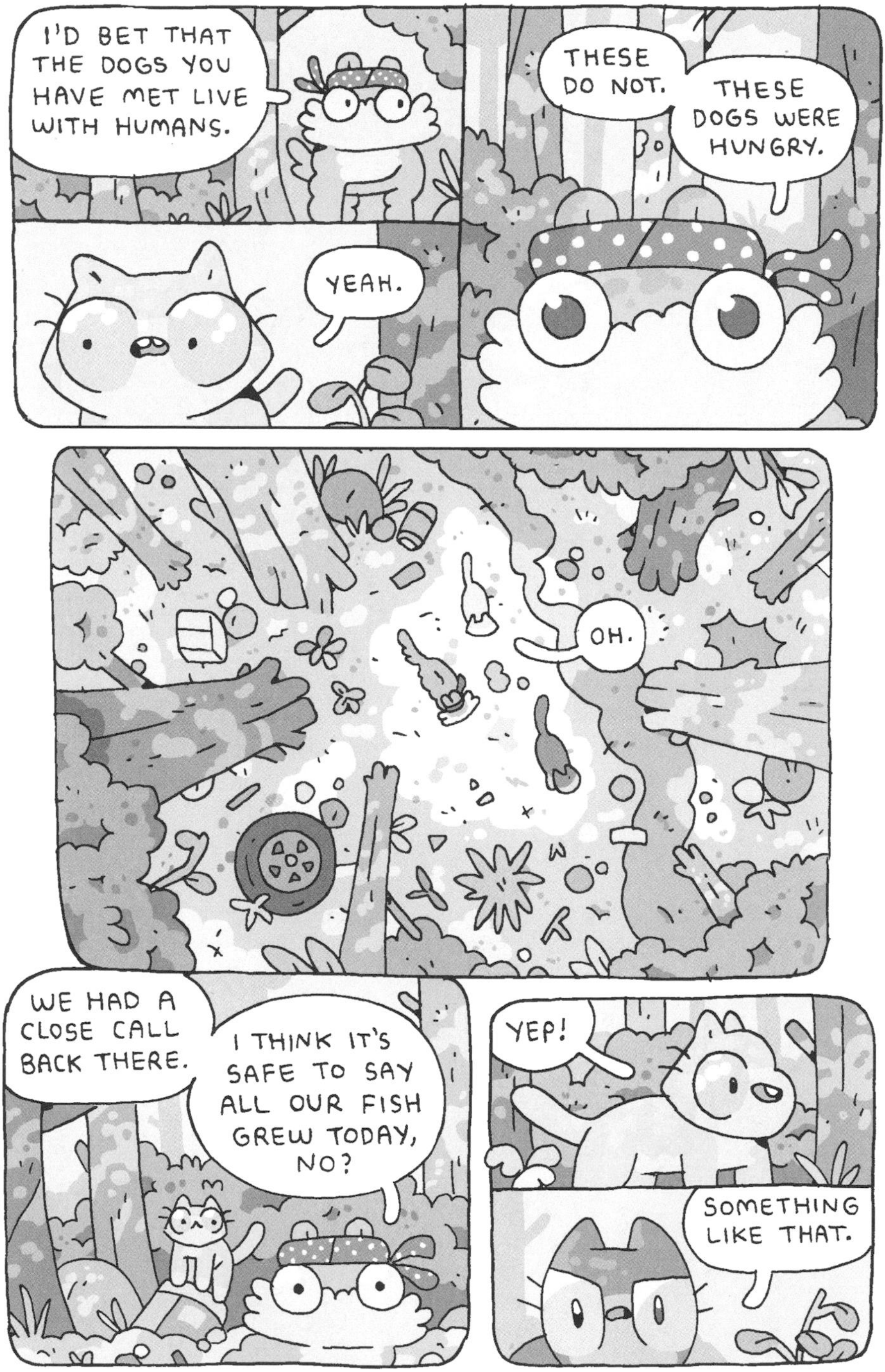
I'D BET THAT THE DOGS YOU HAVE MET LIVE WITH HUMANS.
THESE DO NOT.
THESE DOGS WERE HUNGRY.
YEAH.
OH.
WE HAD A CLOSE CALL BACK THERE.
I THINK IT'S SAFE TO SAY ALL OUR FISH GREW TODAY, NO?
YEP!
SOMETHING LIKE THAT.

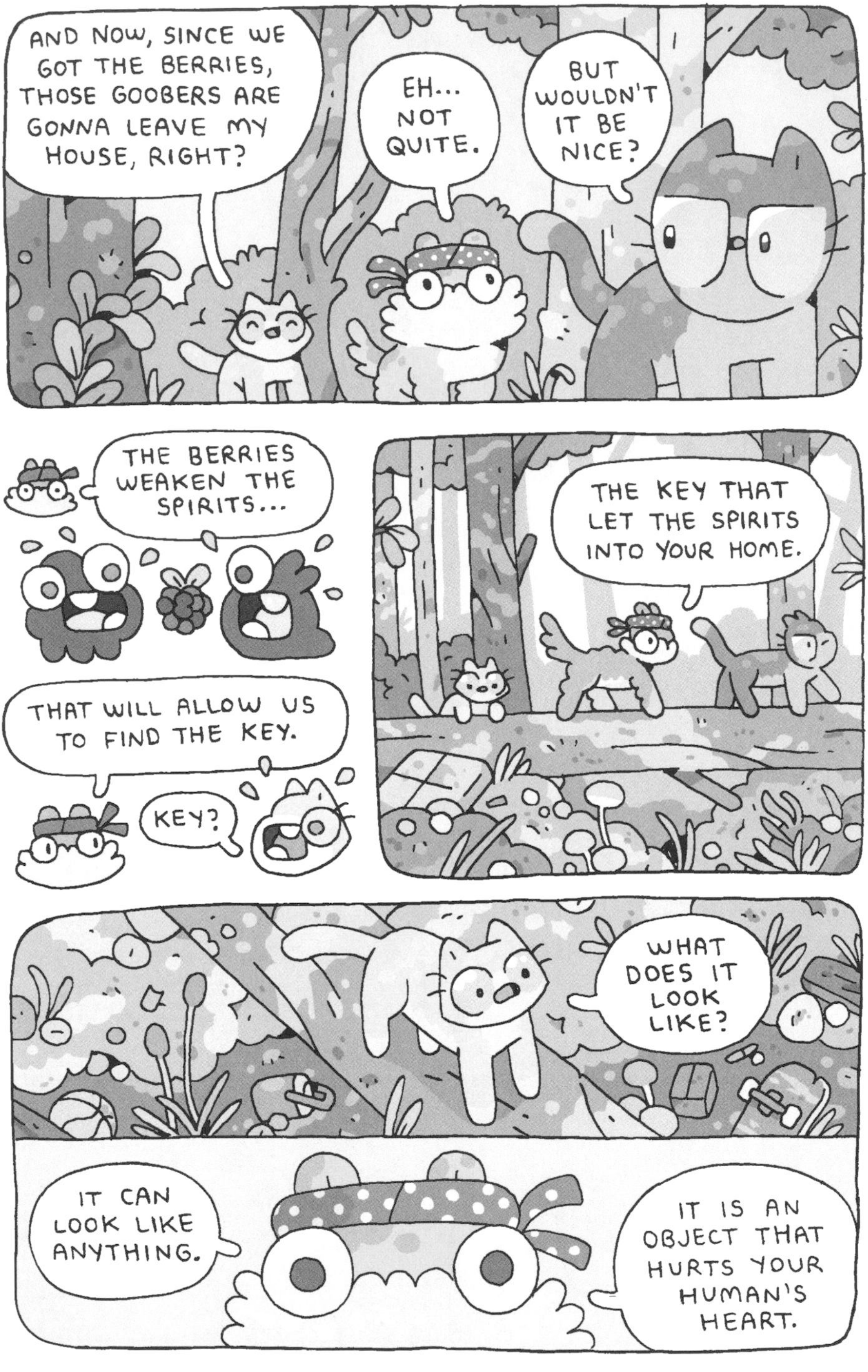
AND NOW, SINCE WE GOT THE BERRIES, THOSE GOOBERS ARE GONNA LEAVE MY HOUSE, RIGHT?
EH... NOT QUITE.
BUT WOULDN'T IT BE NICE?
THE BERRIES WEAKEN THE SPIRITS...
THAT WILL ALLOW US TO FIND THE KEY.
KEY?
THE KEY THAT LET THE SPIRITS INTO YOUR HOME.
WHAT DOES IT LOOK LIKE?
IT CAN LOOK LIKE ANYTHING.
IT IS AN OBJECT THAT HURTS YOUR HUMAN'S HEART.

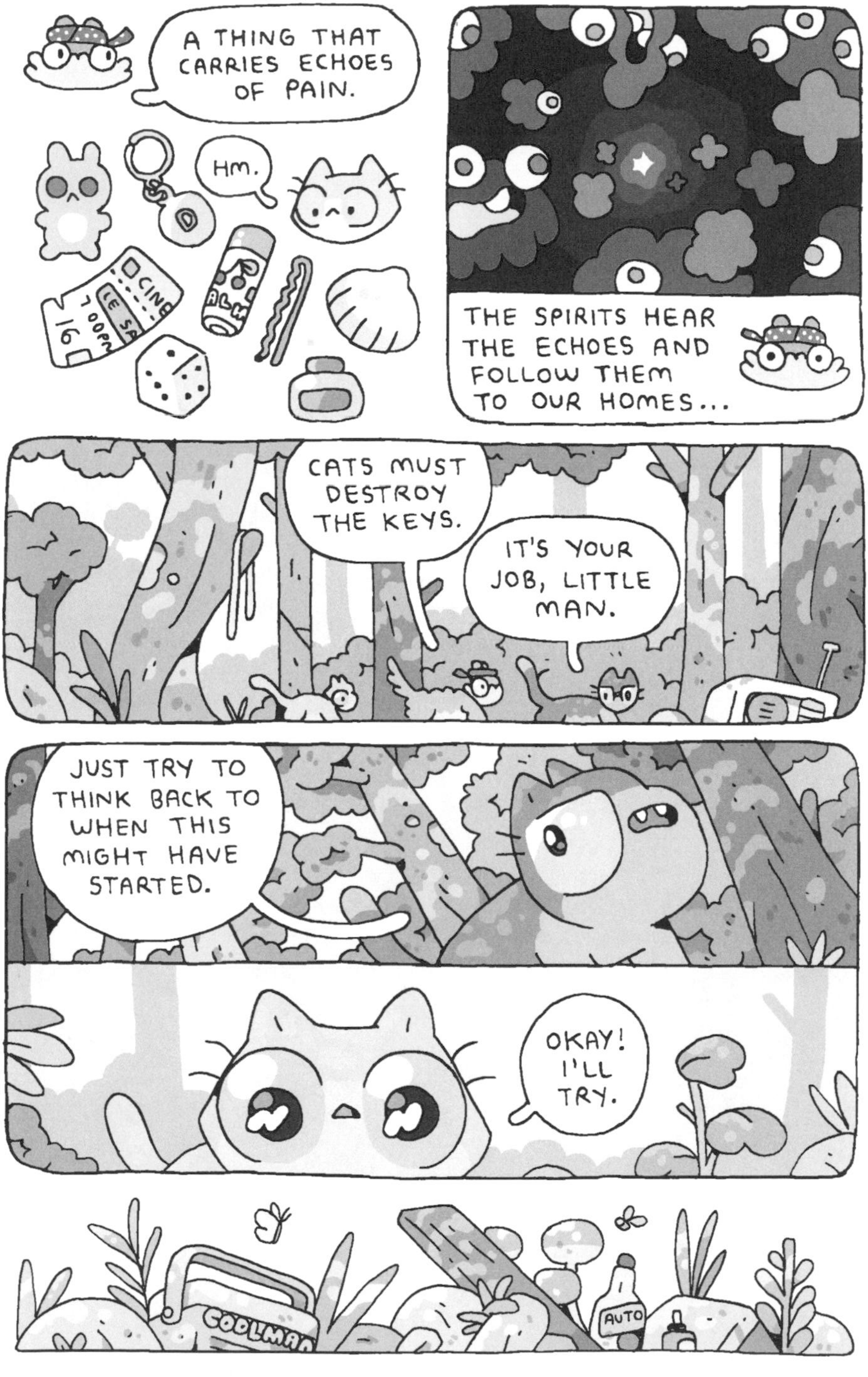
A THING THAT CARRIES ECHOES OF PAIN.
Hm.
THE SPIRITS HEAR THE ECHOES AND FOLLOW THEM TO OUR HOMES...
CATS MUST DESTROY THE KEYS.
IT'S YOUR JOB, LITTLE MAN.
JUST TRY TO THINK BACK TO WHEN THIS MIGHT HAVE STARTED.
OKAY! I'LL TRY.
AUTO

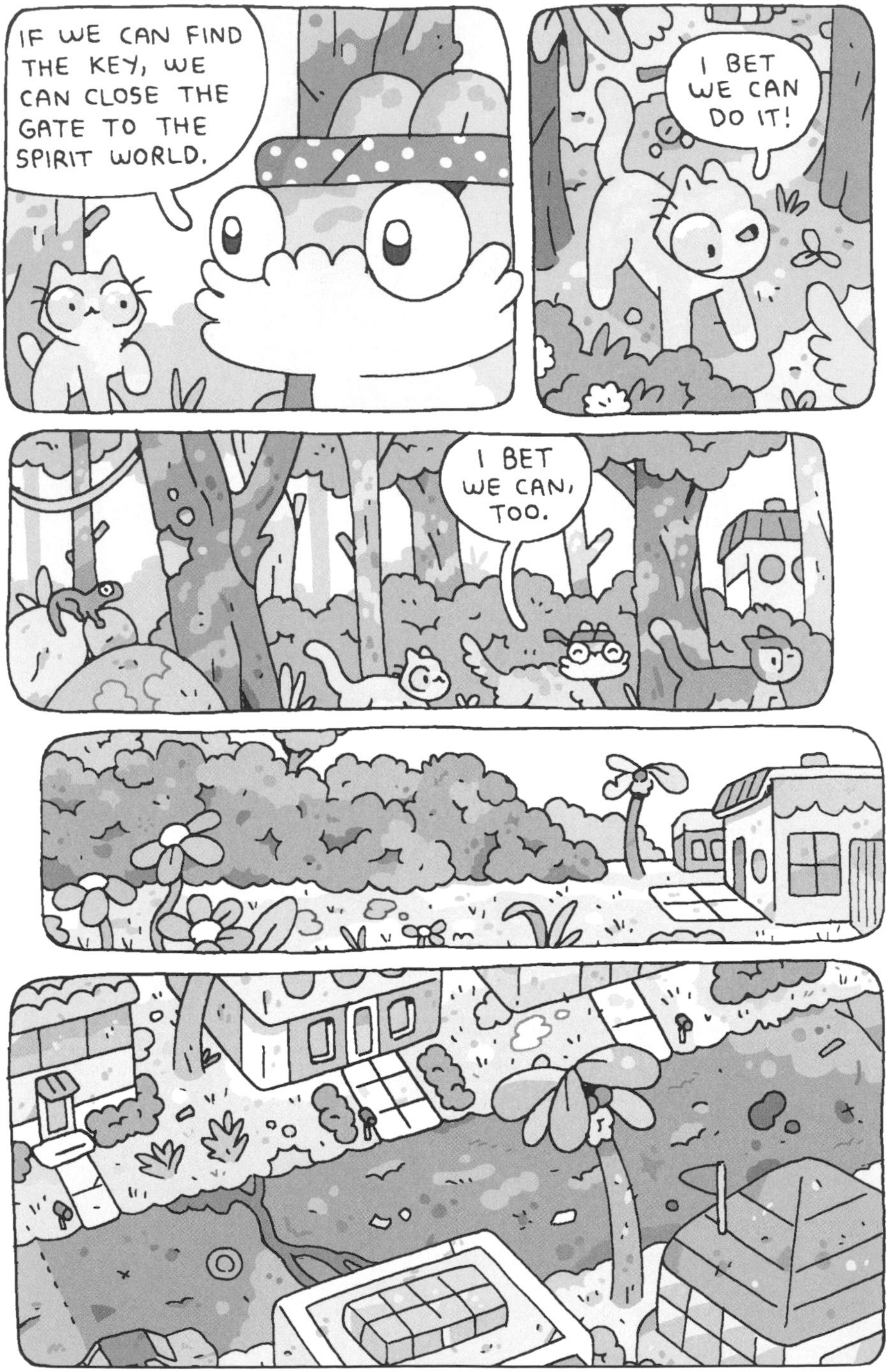
IF WE CAN FIND THE KEY, WE CAN CLOSE THE GATE TO THE SPIRIT WORLD.
I BET WE CAN DO IT!
I BET WE CAN, TOO.

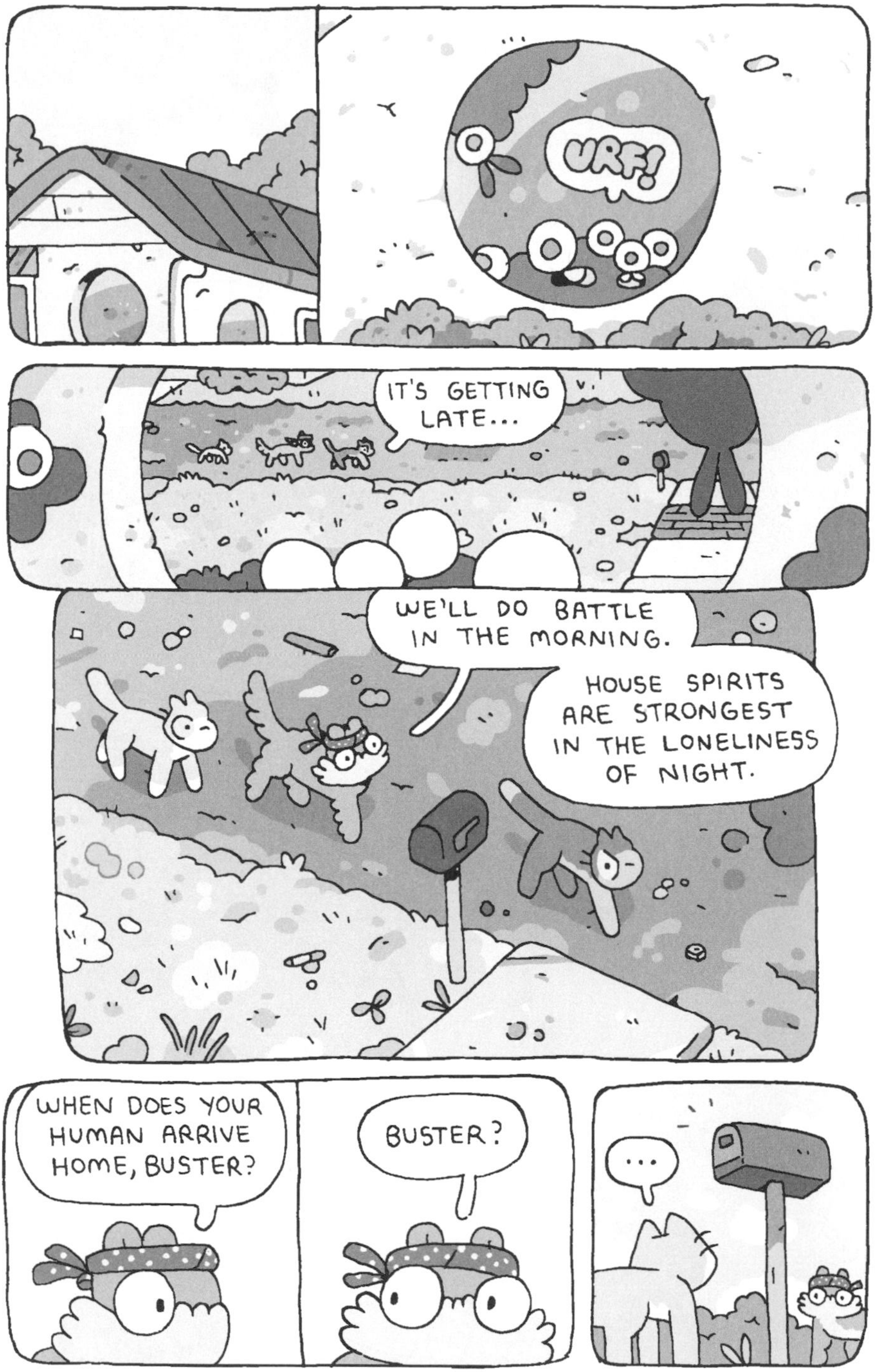
URF!
IT'S GETTING LATE...
WE'LL DO BATTLE IN THE MORNING.
HOUSE SPIRITS ARE STRONGEST IN THE LONELINESS OF NIGHT.
WHEN DOES YOUR HUMAN ARRIVE HOME, BUSTER?
BUSTER?
...

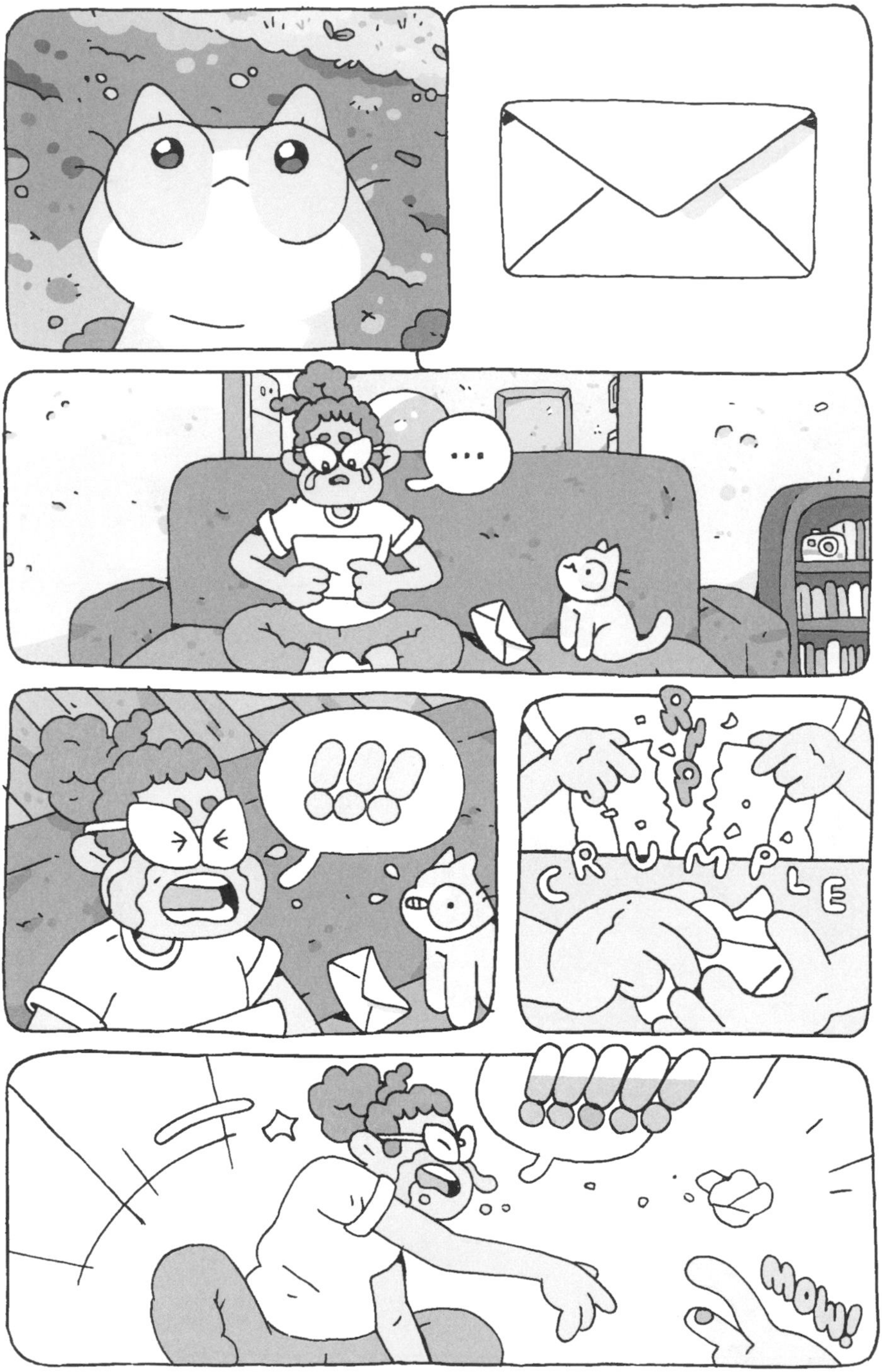
...
!!!
RIP
CRUMPLE
!!!!!
MOW!

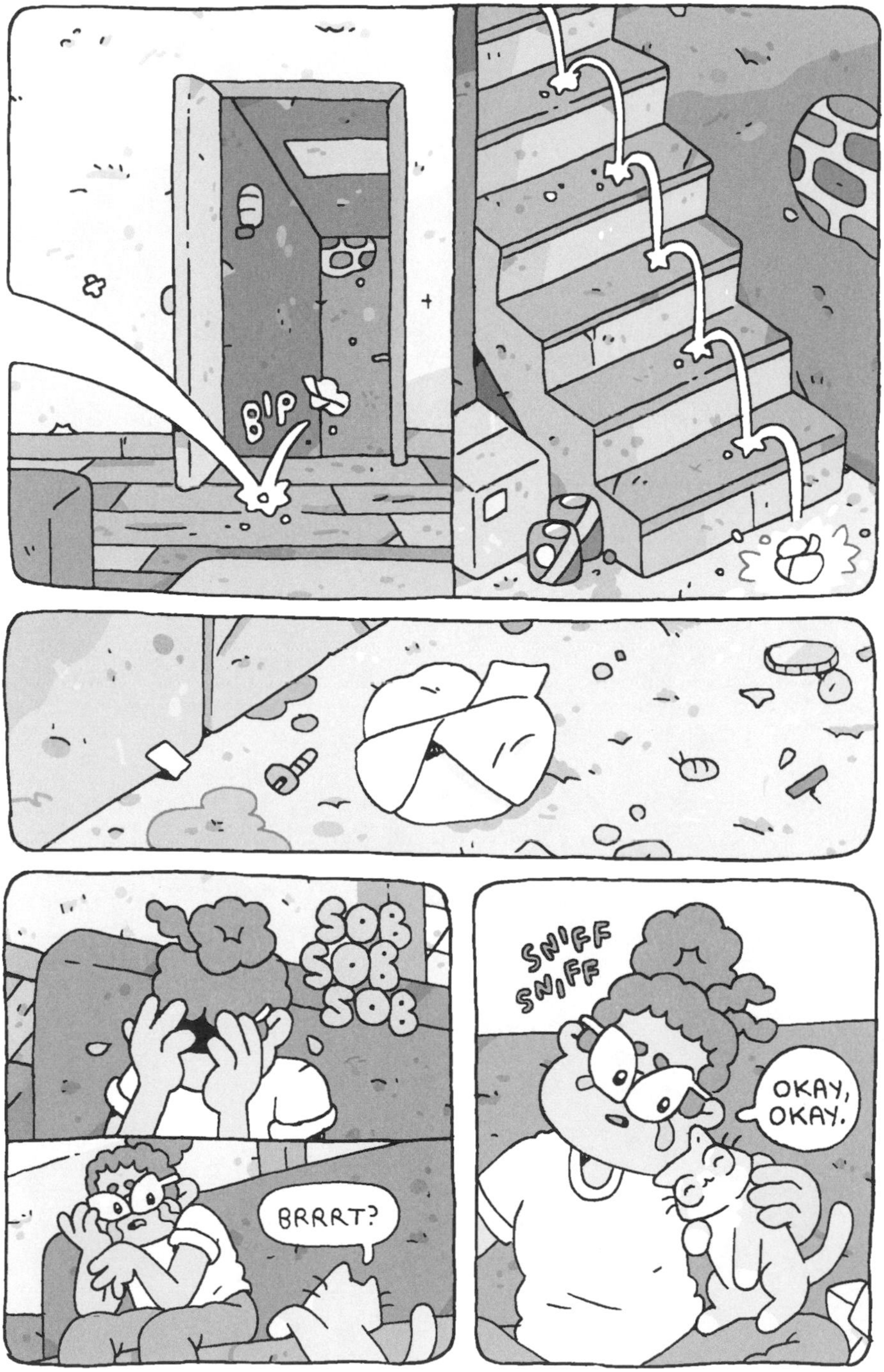
BIP
SOB SOB SOB
BRRRT?
SNIFF SNIFF
OKAY, OKAY.

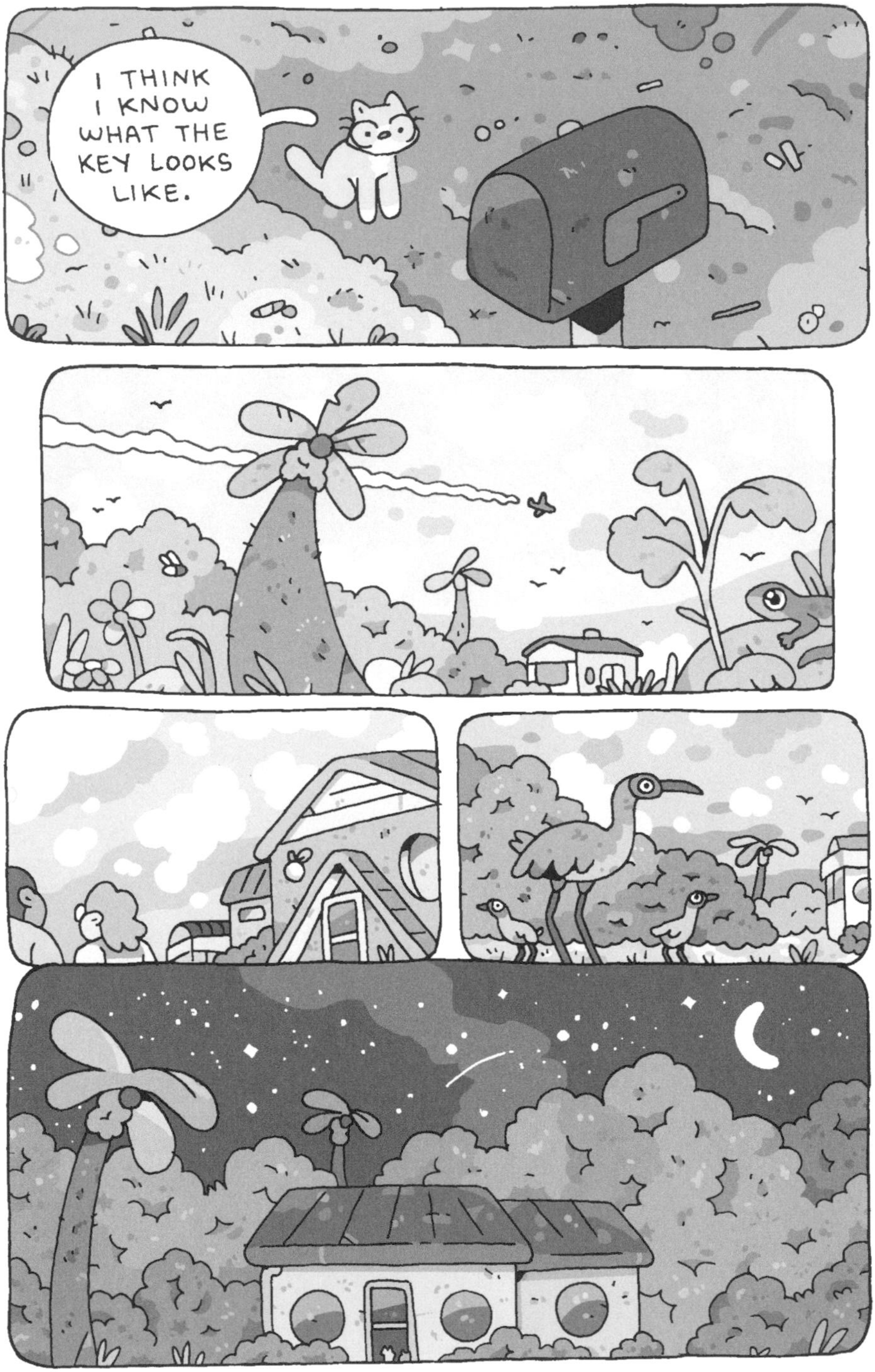
I THINK I KNOW WHAT THE KEY LOOKS LIKE.

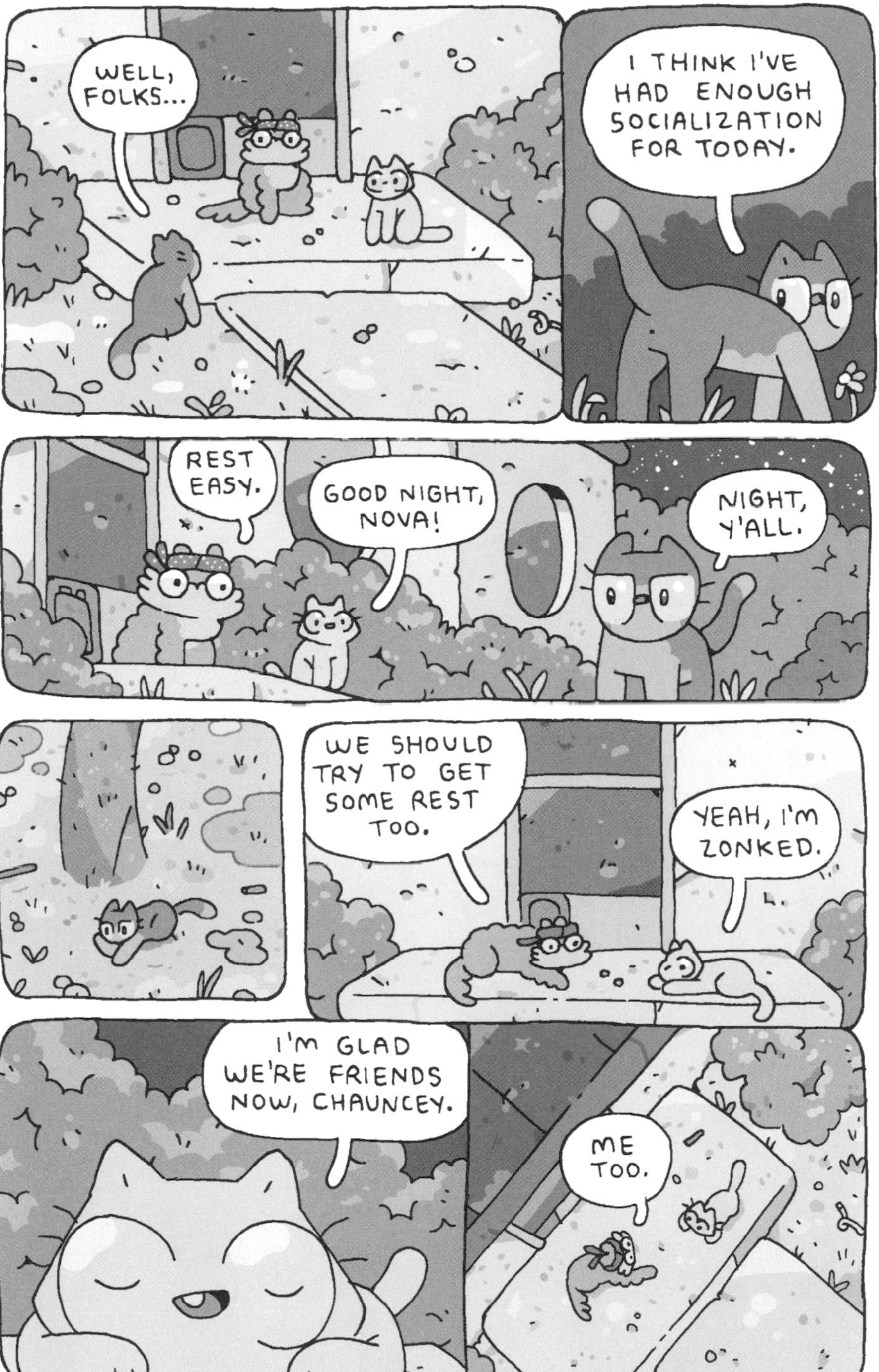
WELL, FOLKS...
I THINK I'VE HAD ENOUGH SOCIALIZATION FOR TODAY.
REST EASY.
GOOD NIGHT, NOVA!
NIGHT, Y'ALL.
WE SHOULD TRY TO GET SOME REST TOO.
YEAH, I'M ZONKED.
I'M GLAD WE'RE FRIENDS NOW, CHAUNCEY.
ME TOO.

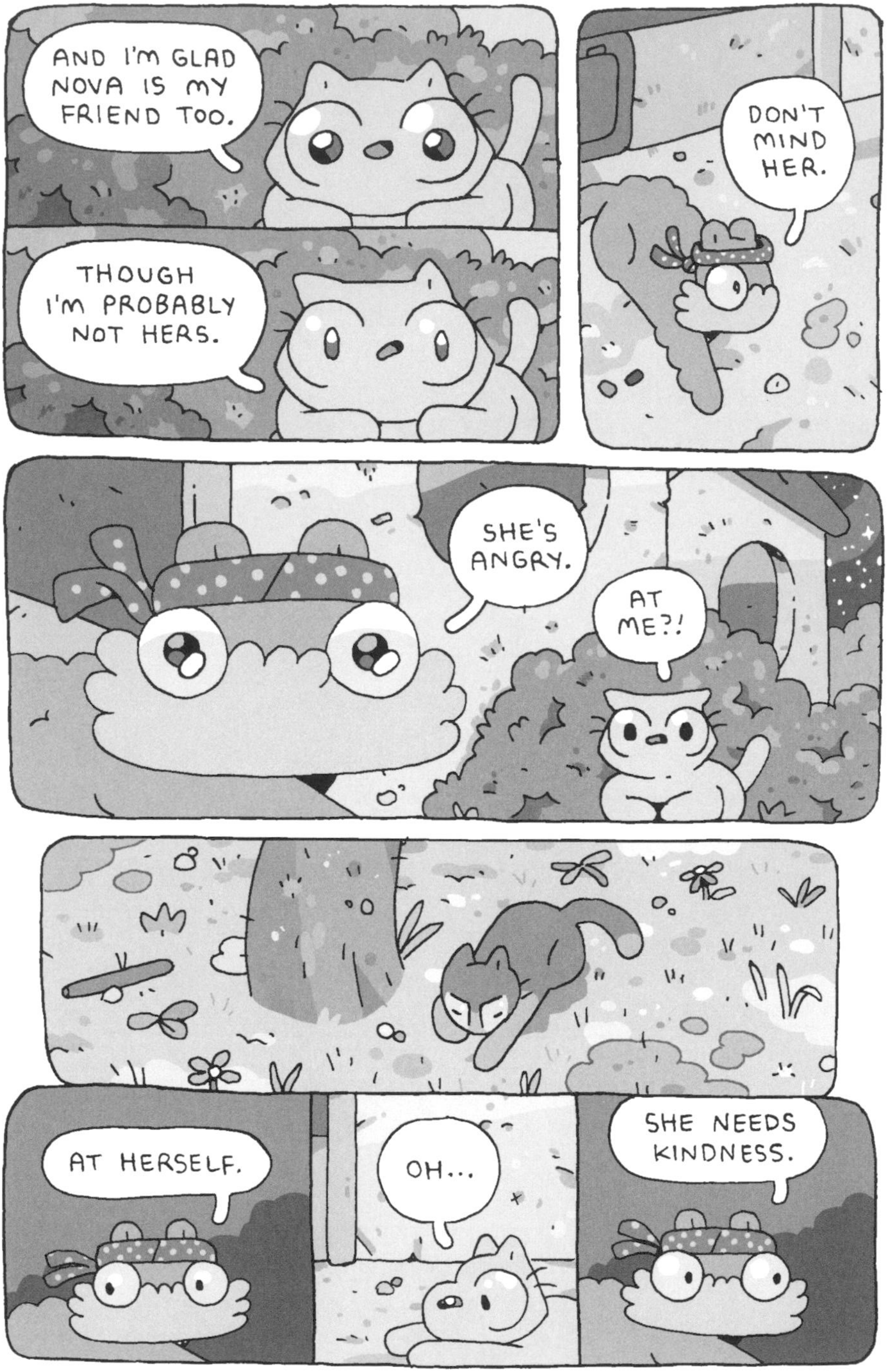
AND I'M GLAD NOVA IS MY FRIEND TOO.
THOUGH I'M PROBABLY NOT HERS.
DON'T MIND HER.
SHE'S ANGRY.
AT ME?!
AT HERSELF.
OH...
SHE NEEDS KINDNESS.

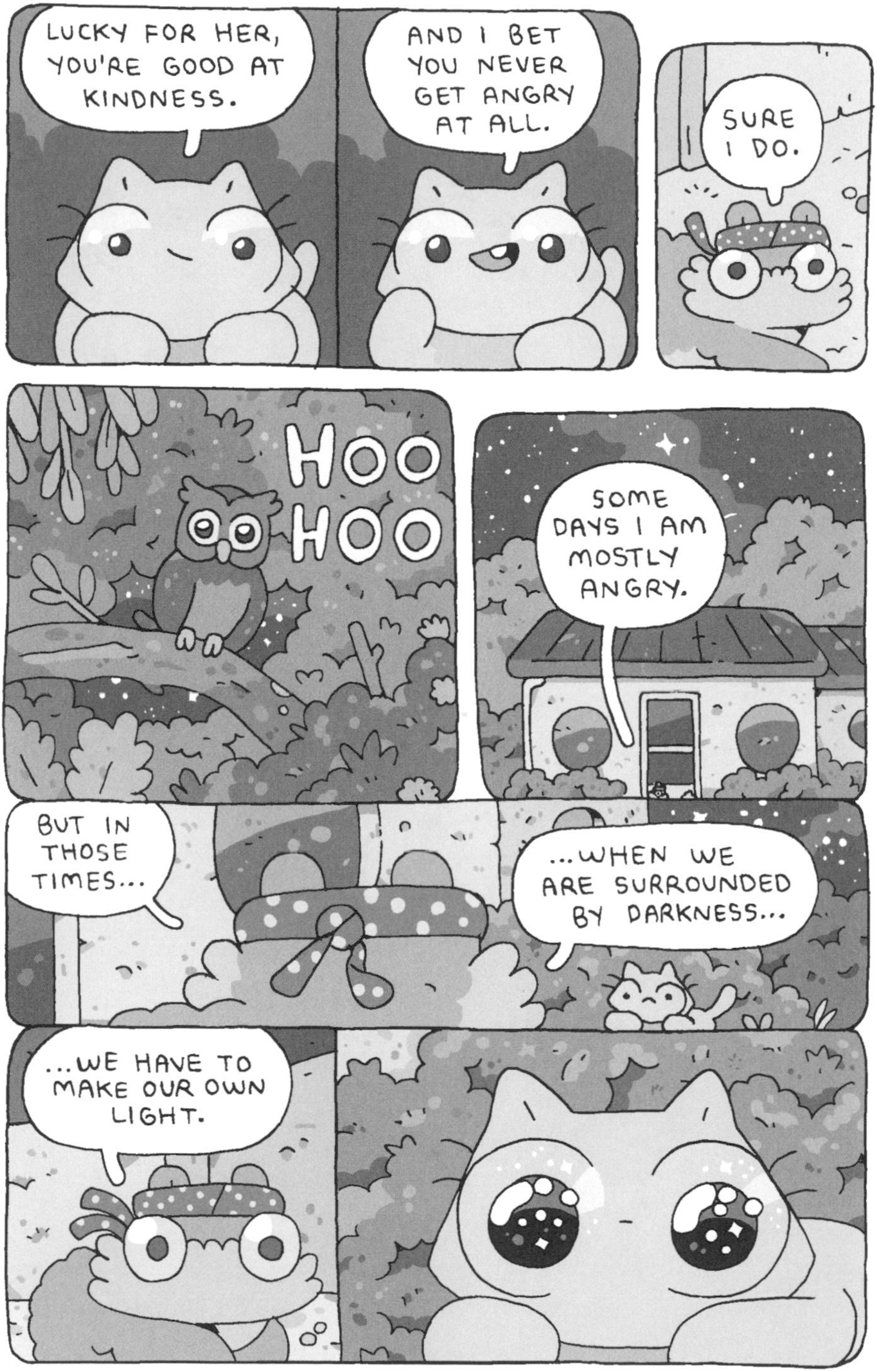
LUCKY FOR HER, YOU'RE GOOD AT KINDNESS.
AND I BET YOU NEVER GET ANGRY AT ALL.
SURE I DO.
HOO HOO
SOME DAYS I AM MOSTLY ANGRY.
BUT IN THOSE TIMES...
...WHEN WE ARE SURROUNDED BY DARKNESS...
...WE HAVE TO MAKE OUR OWN LIGHT.

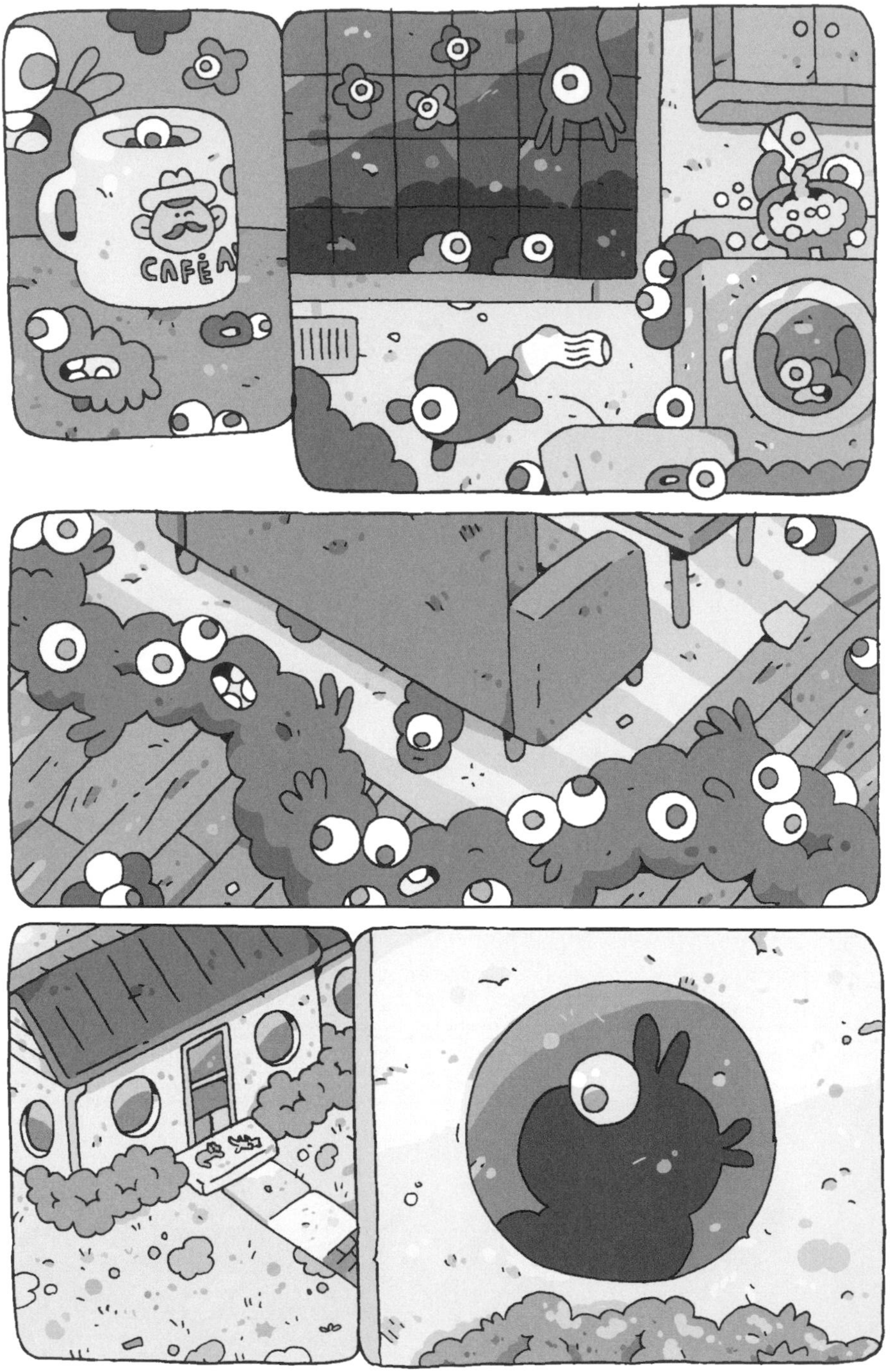
CAFÉ

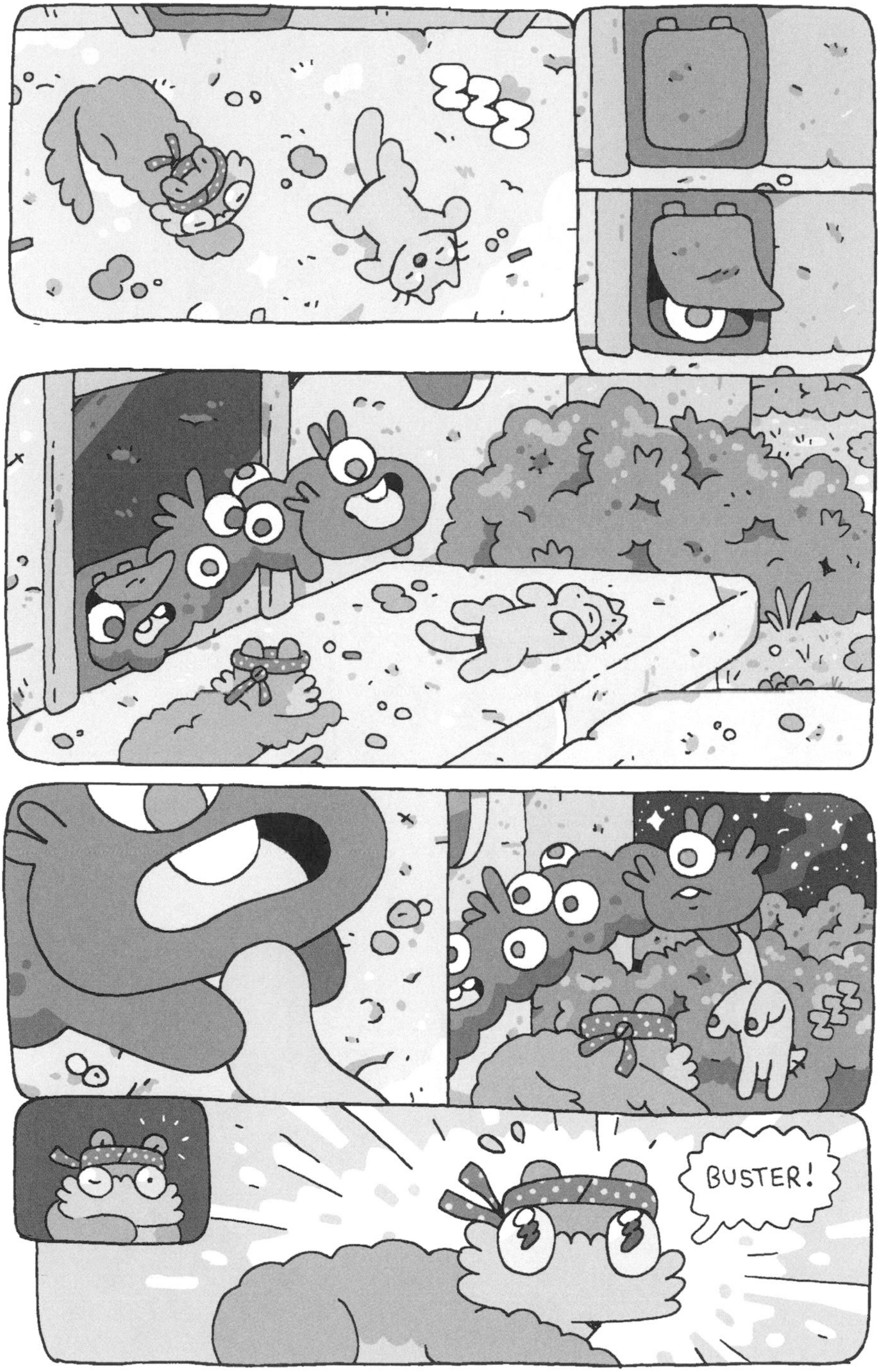
ZZZ
ZZZ
BUSTER!

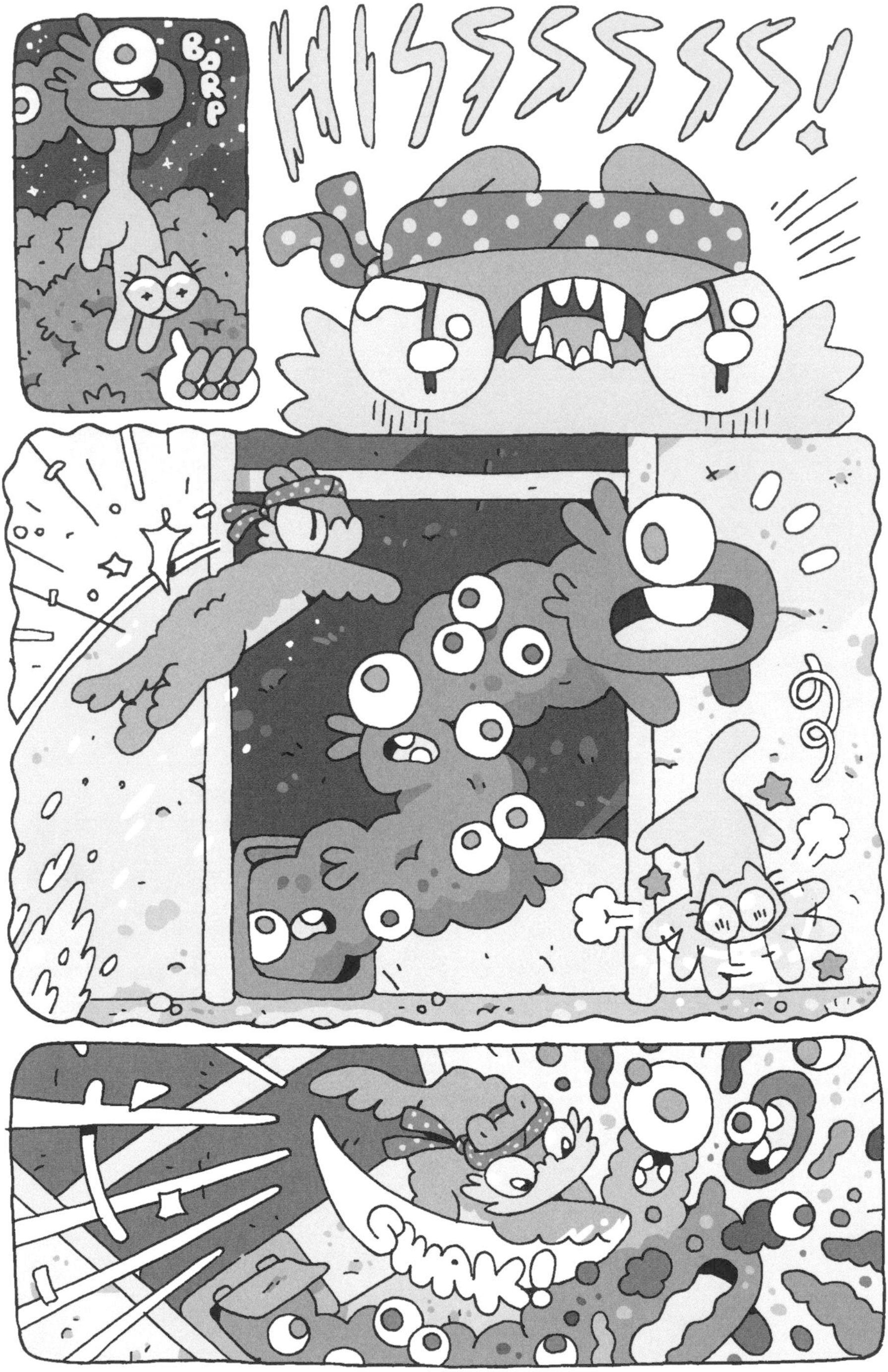
BORP
HISSSSSSS!
SHWAK!

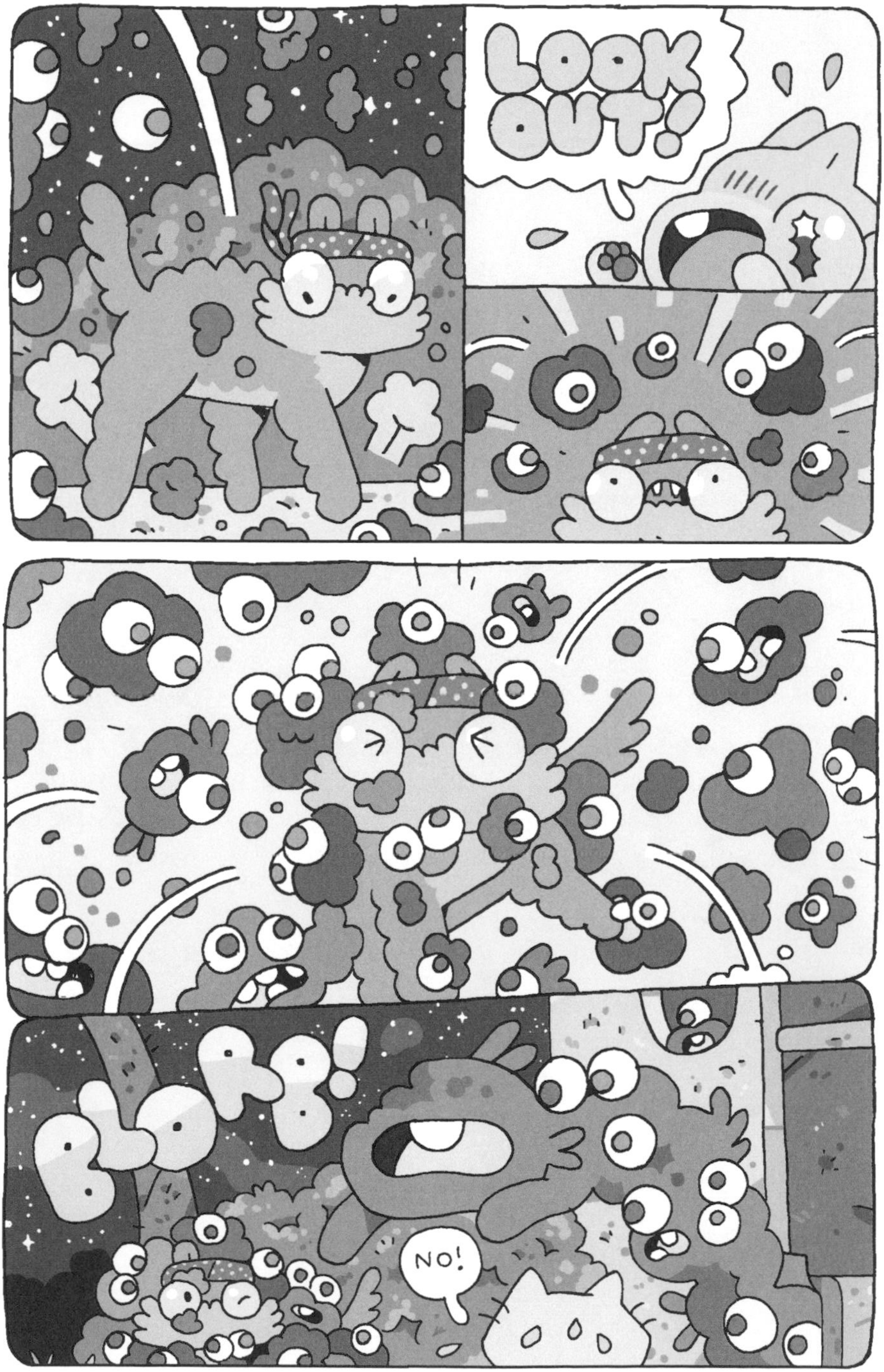
LOOK OUT!
BLORP!
NO!

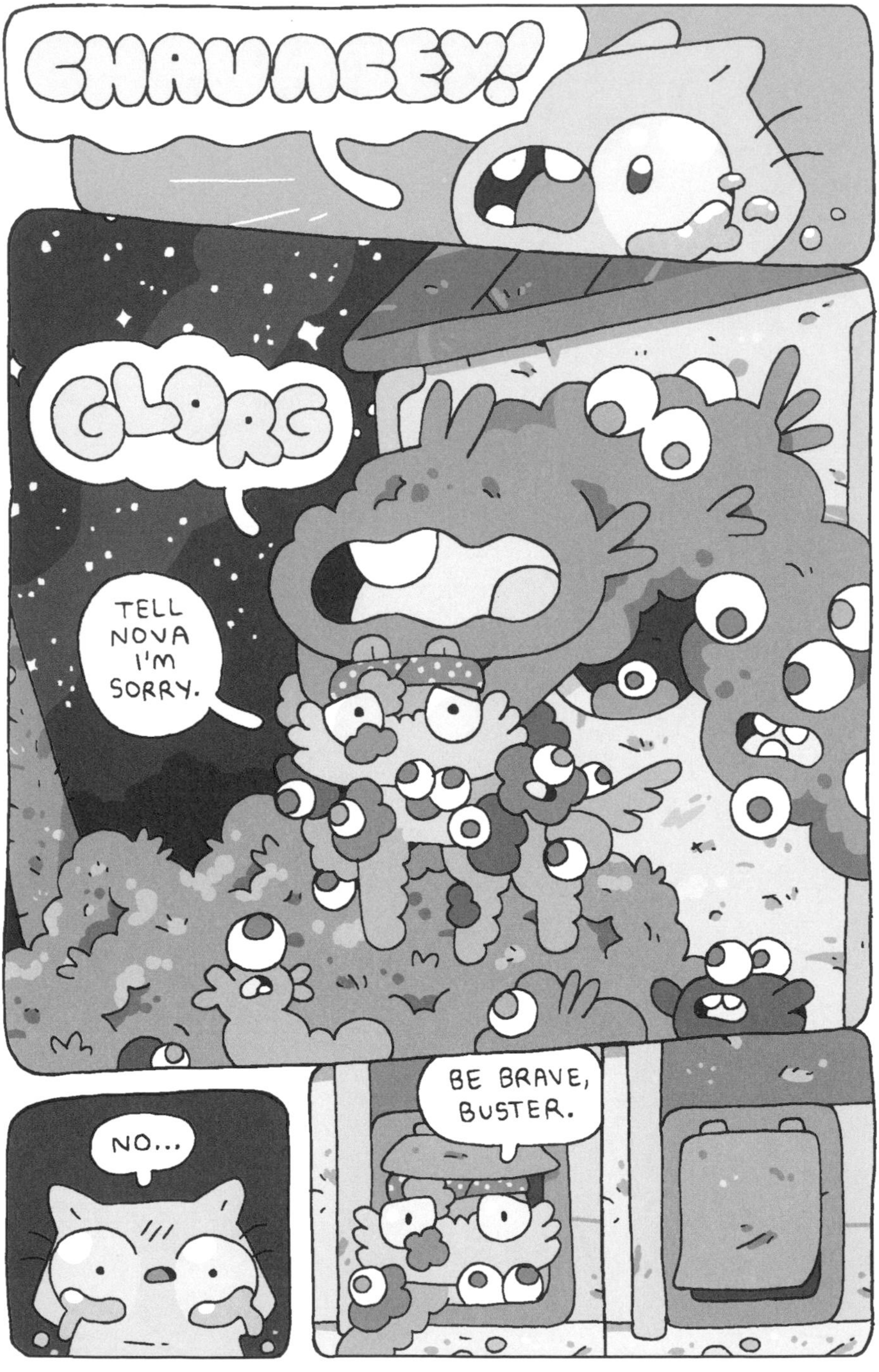
CHAUNCEY!
GLORG
TELL NOVA I'M SORRY.
NO...
BE BRAVE, BUSTER.

CHAPTER 6

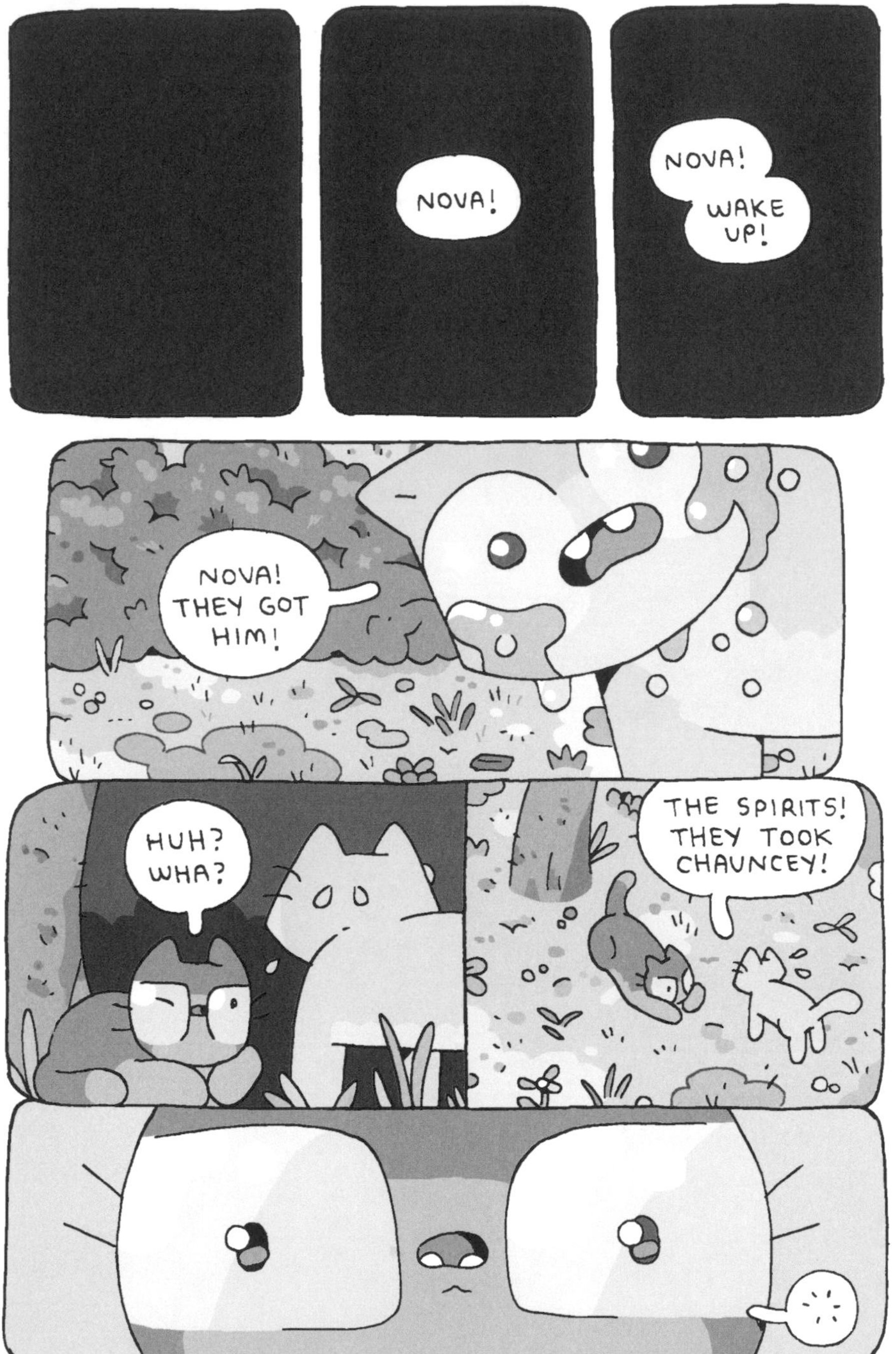
NOVA!
NOVA!
WAKE UP!
NOVA! THEY GOT HIM!
HUH? WHA?
THE SPIRITS! THEY TOOK CHAUNCEY!

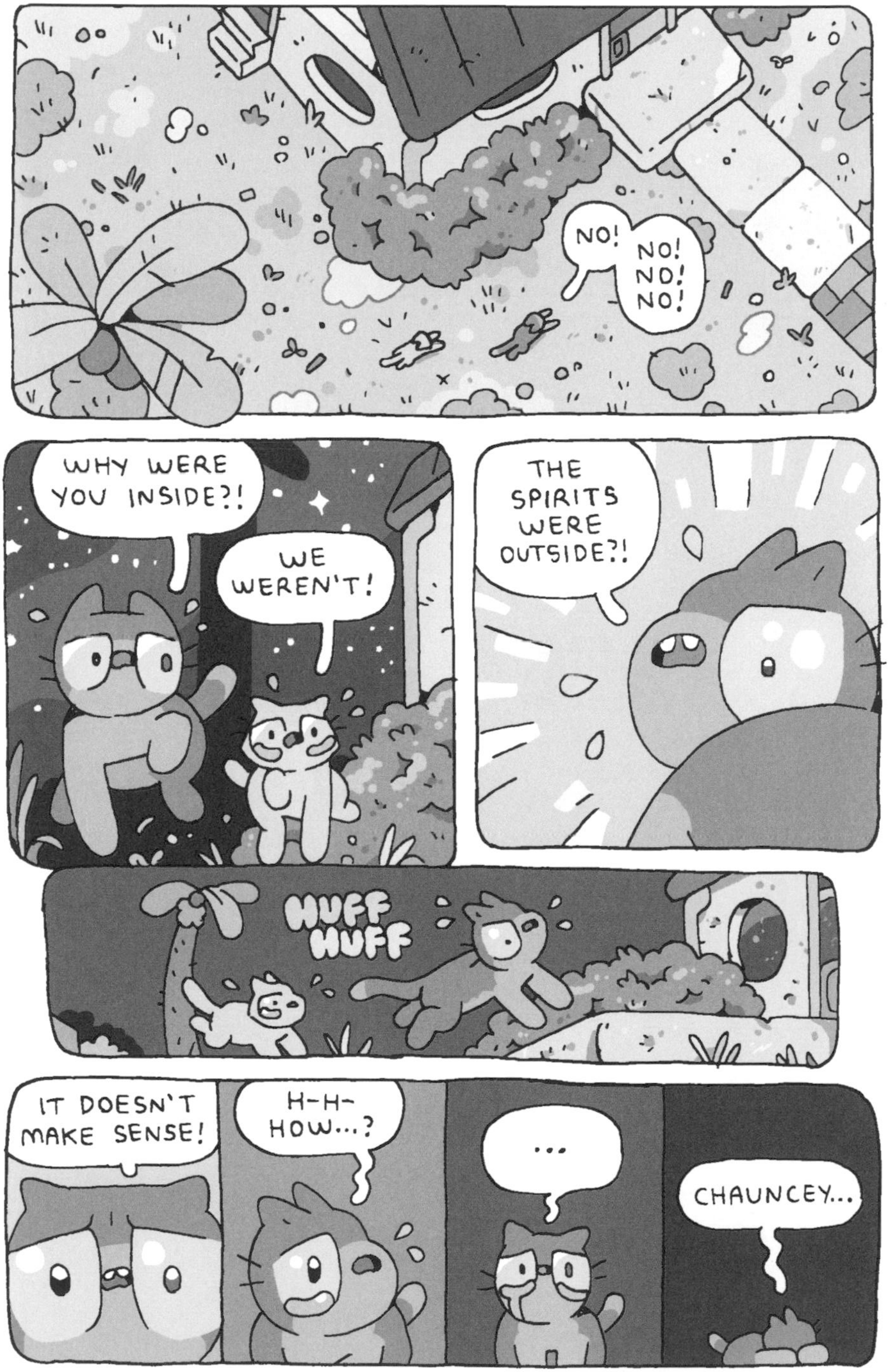
NO!
NO!
NO!
NO!
WHY WERE YOU INSIDE?!
WE WEREN'T!
THE SPIRITS WERE OUTSIDE?!
HUFF HUFF
IT DOESN'T MAKE SENSE!
H-H-HOW...?
...
CHAUNCEY...

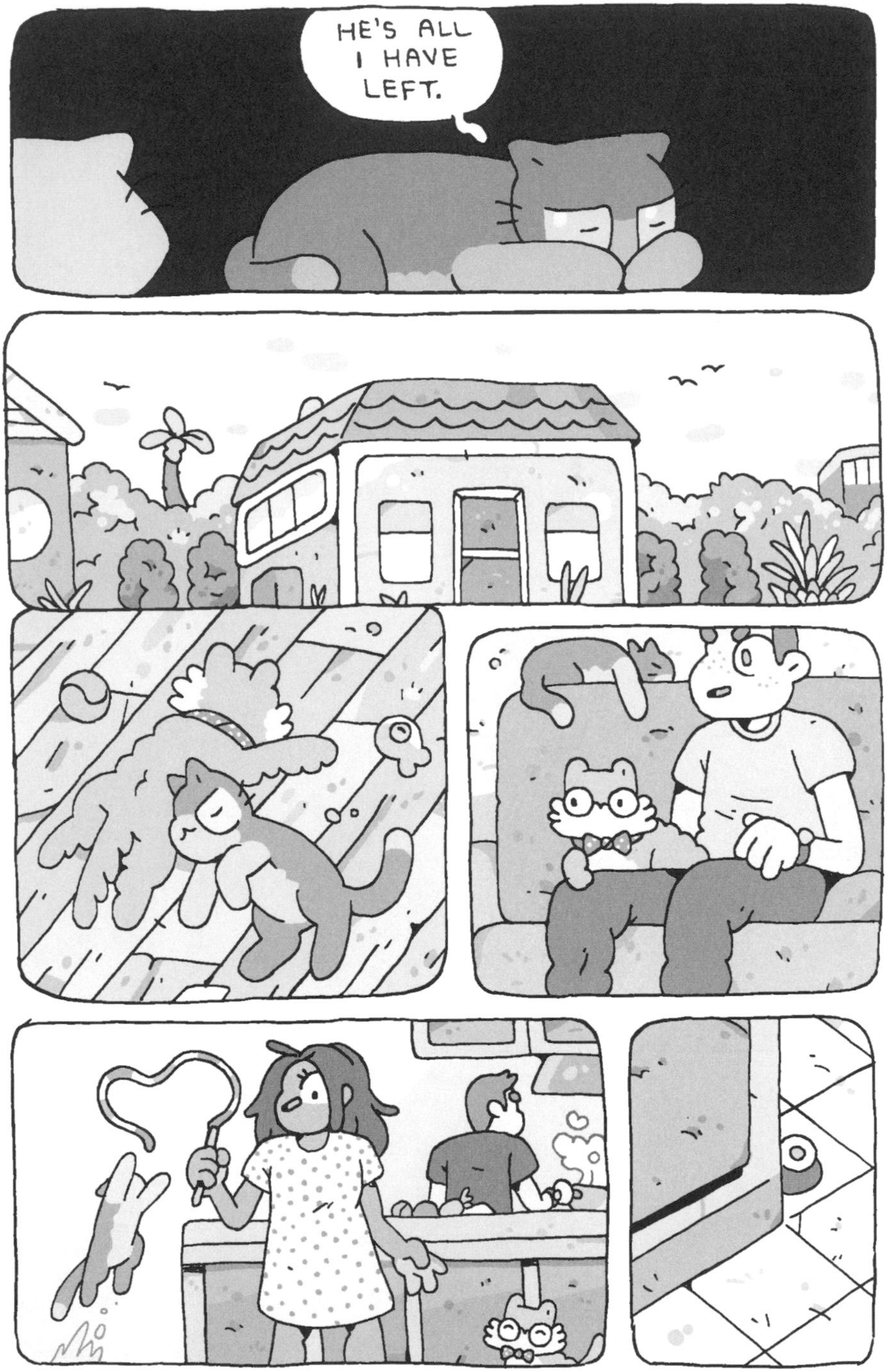
HE'S ALL
I HAVE
LEFT.

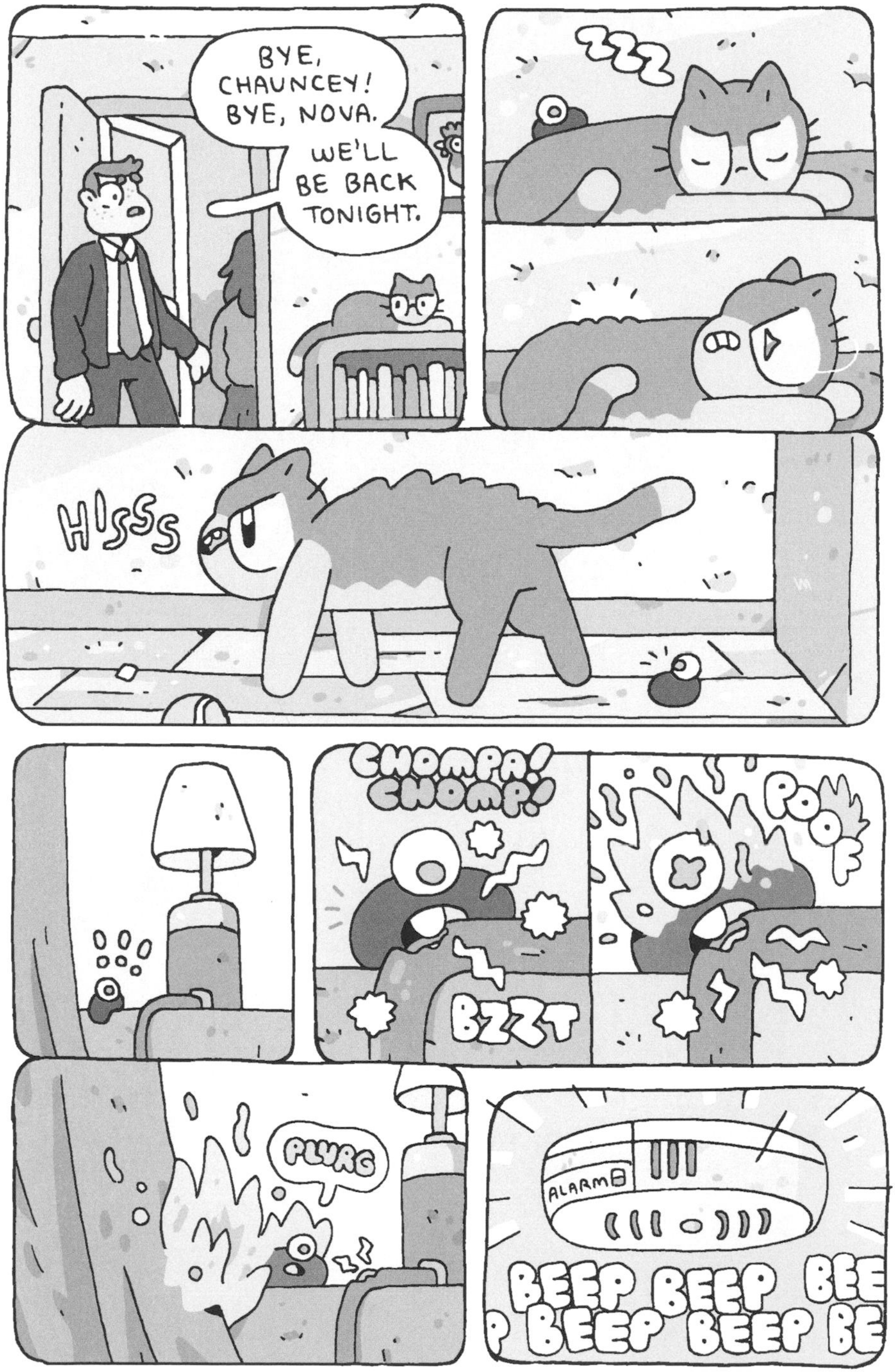
BYE, CHAUNCEY! BYE, NOVA.
WE'LL BE BACK TONIGHT.
ZZZ
HISSS
CHOMPA! CHOMP!
BZZT
POOF
PLURG
ALARM
BEEP BEEP BEE
P BEEP BEEP BE

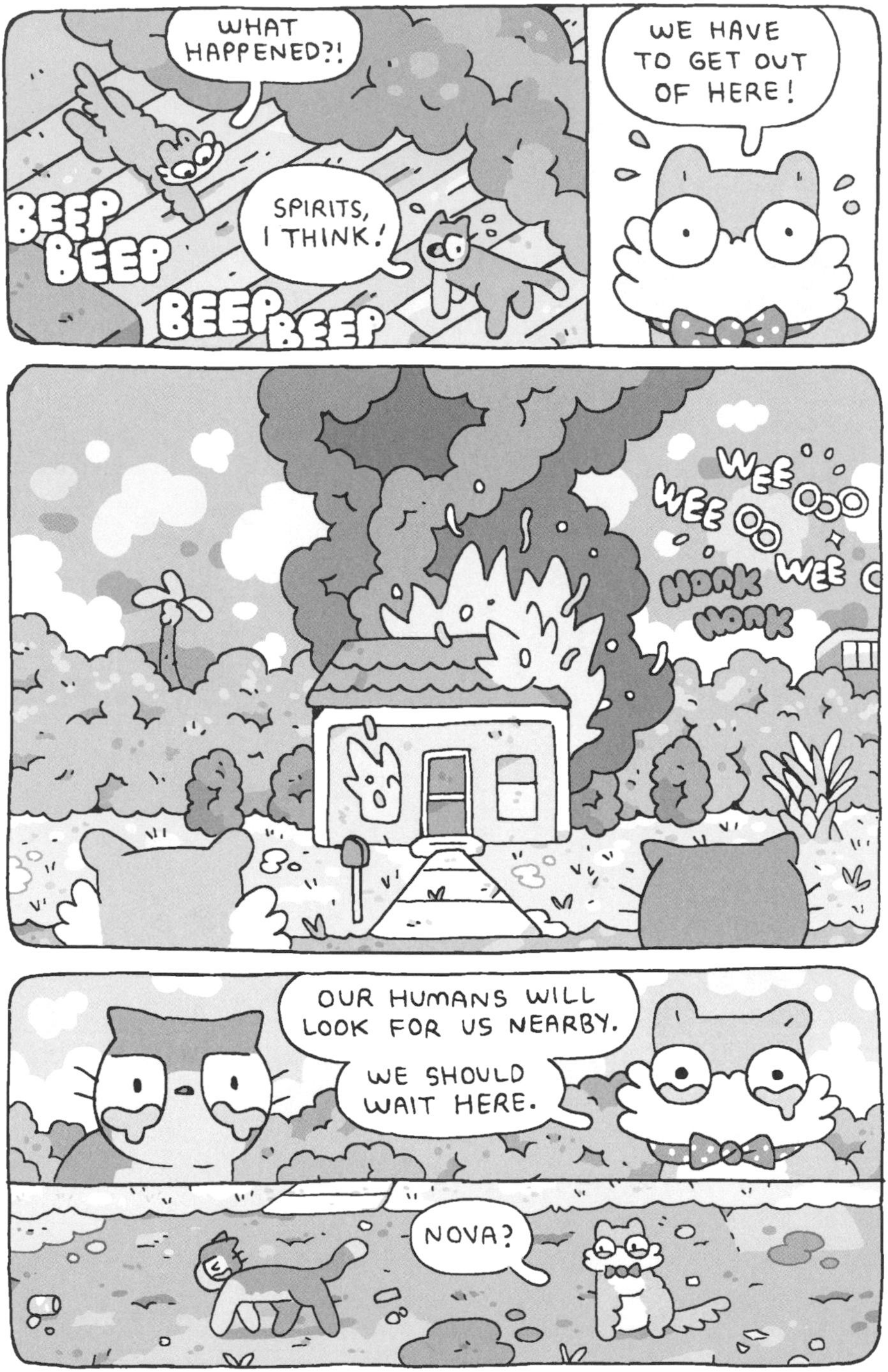
WHAT HAPPENED?!
SPIRITS, I THINK!
BEEP BEEP BEEP BEEP
WE HAVE TO GET OUT OF HERE!
WEE OOO WEE OO WEE
HONK HONK
OUR HUMANS WILL LOOK FOR US NEARBY.
WE SHOULD WAIT HERE.
NOVA?

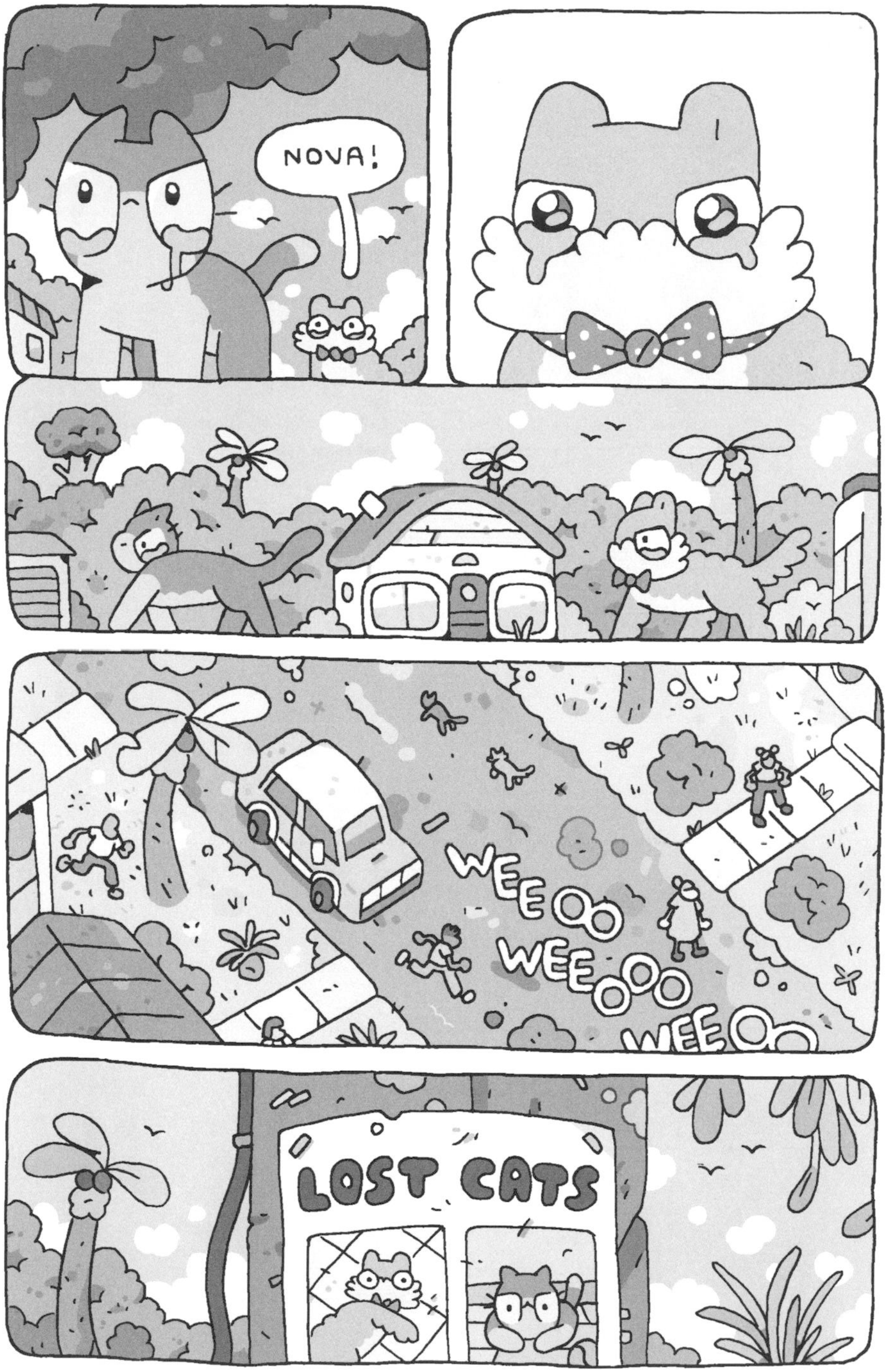
NOVA!
WEEOO
WEEOOO
WEEOO
LOST CATS

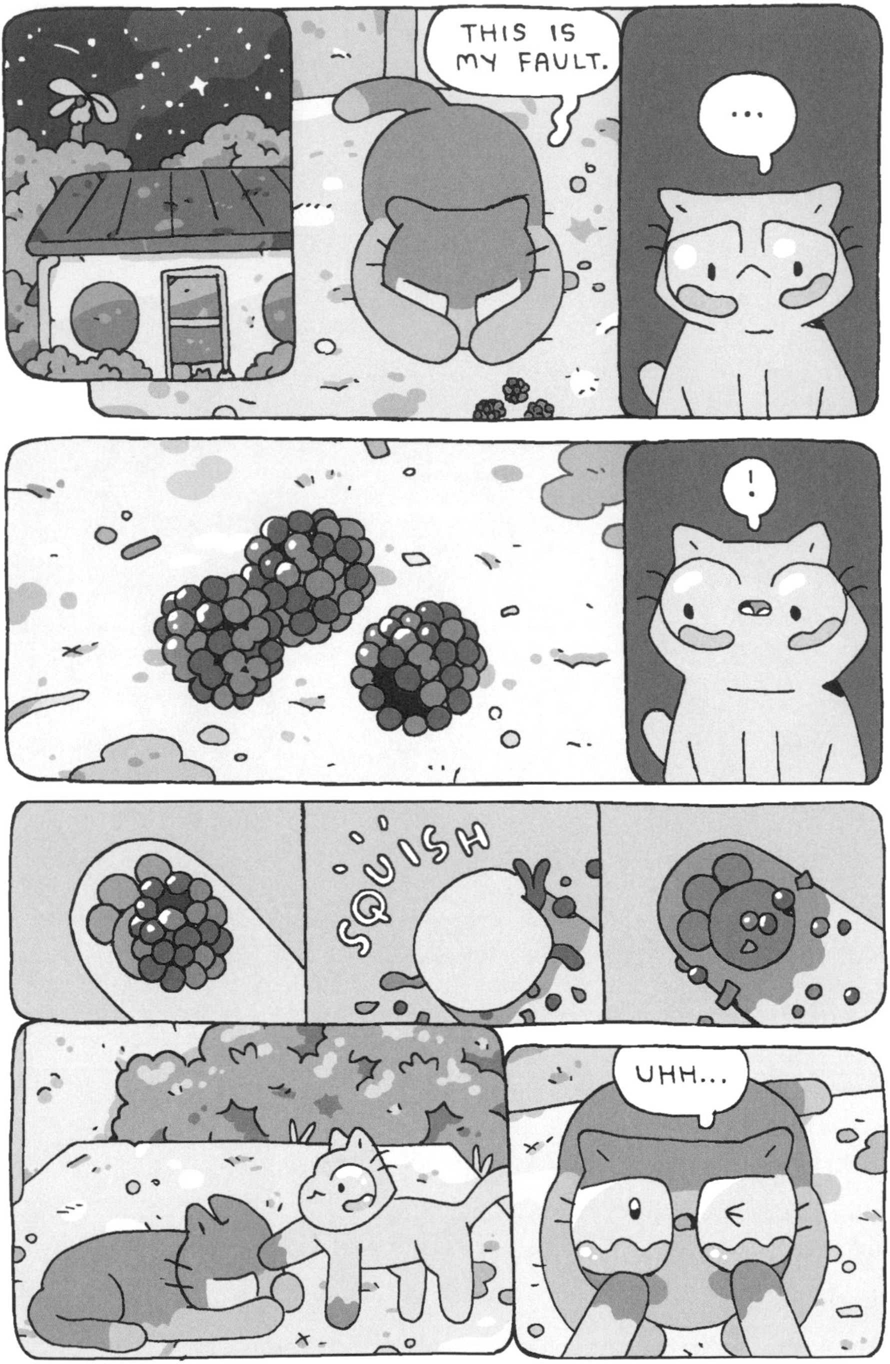
THIS IS MY FAULT.
...
!
SQUISH
UHH...

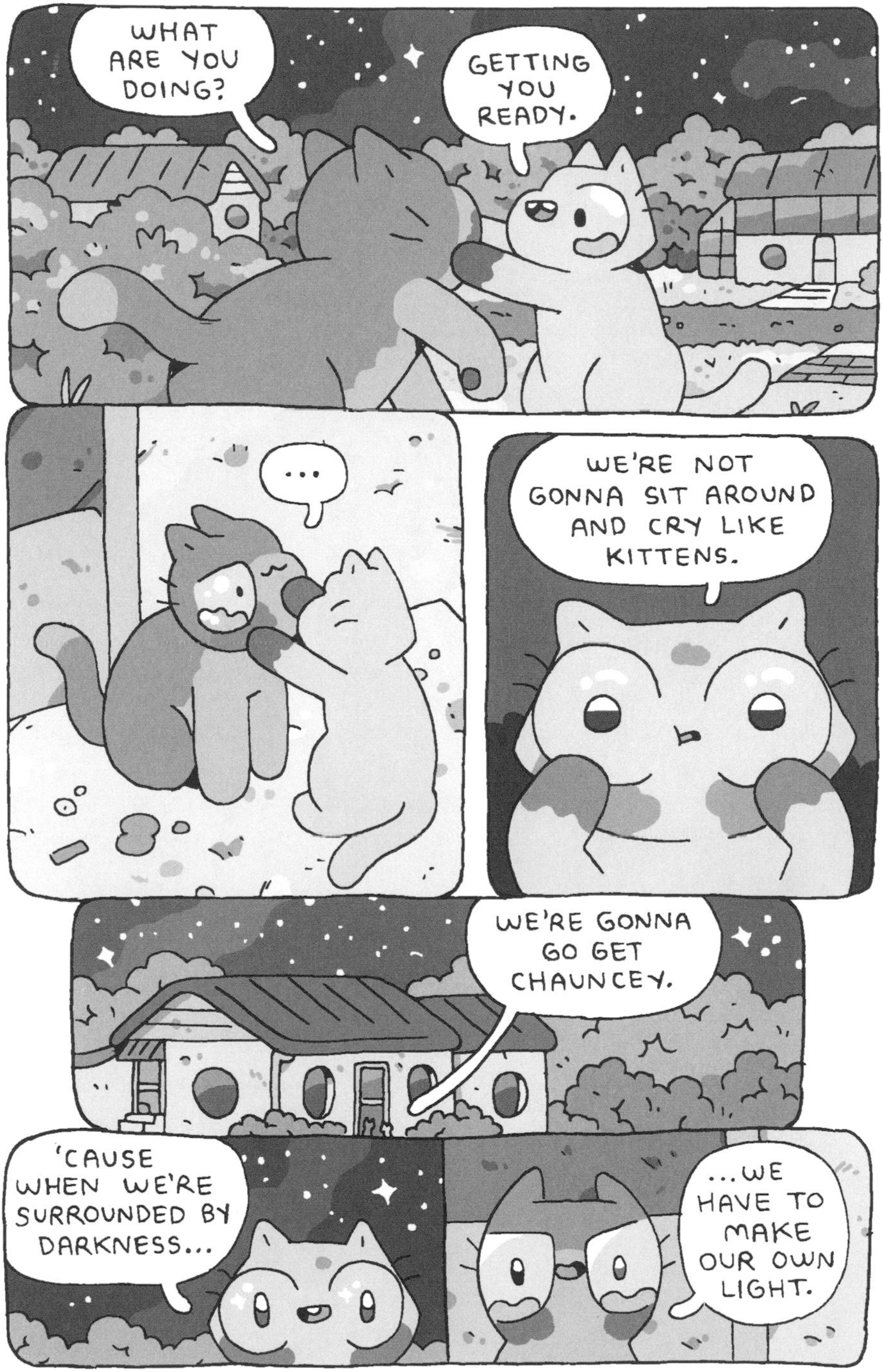
WHAT ARE YOU DOING?
GETTING YOU READY.
...
WE'RE NOT GONNA SIT AROUND AND CRY LIKE KITTENS.
WE'RE GONNA GO GET CHAUNCEY.
'CAUSE WHEN WE'RE SURROUNDED BY DARKNESS...
...WE HAVE TO MAKE OUR OWN LIGHT.

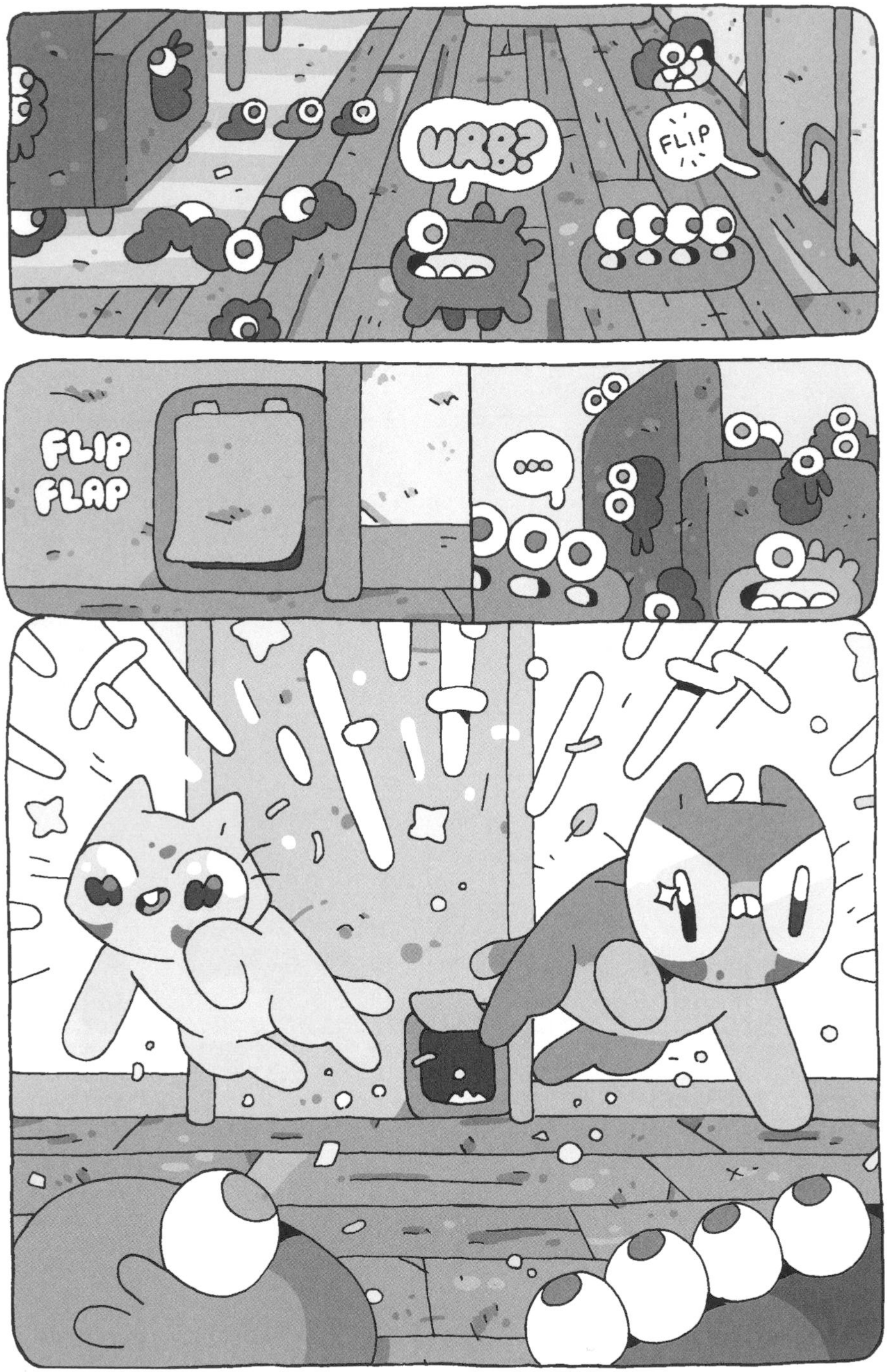
URB?
FLIP
FLIP
FLAP
ooo

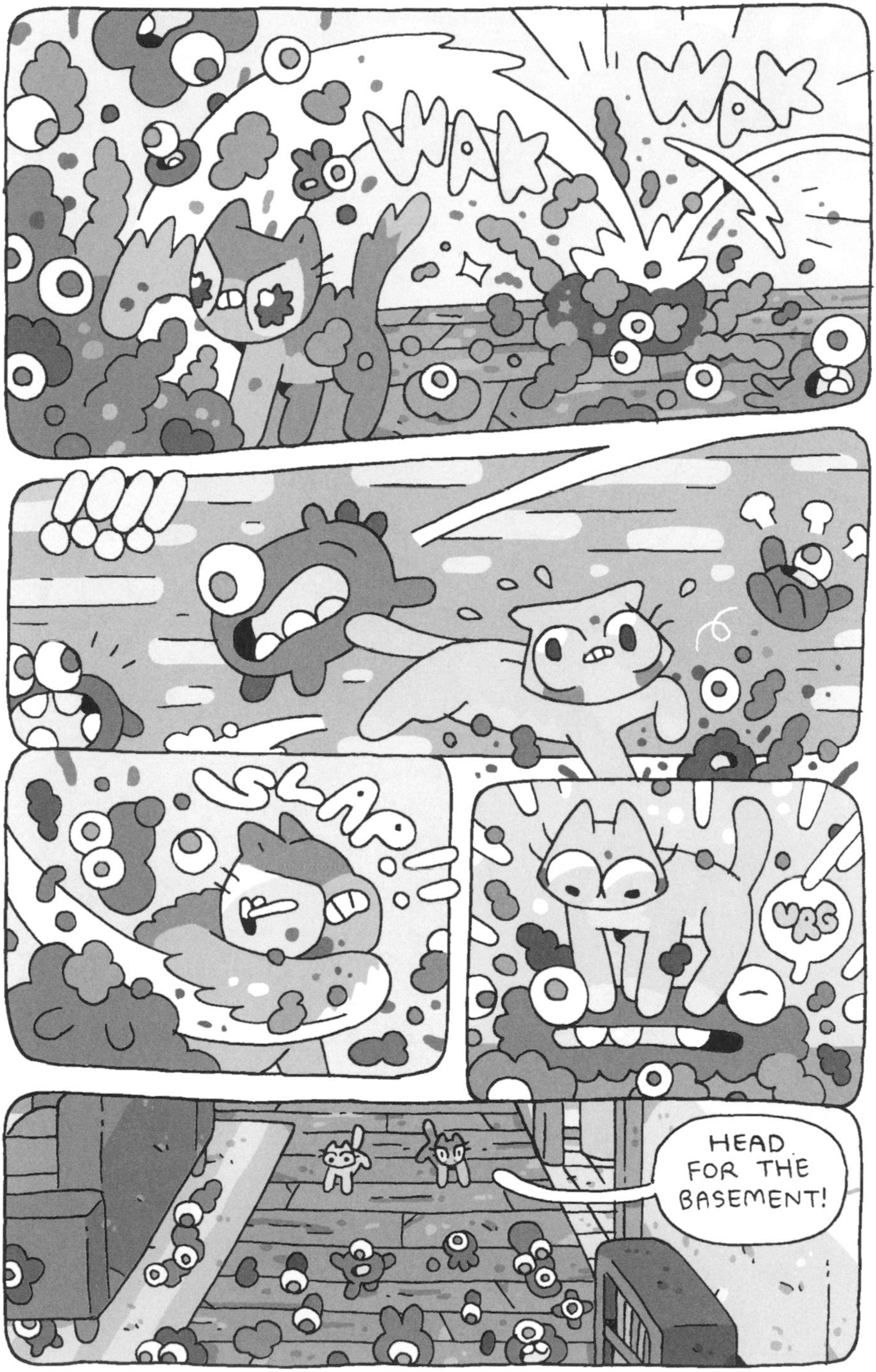
WAK
WAK
SLAP
URG
HEAD FOR THE BASEMENT!

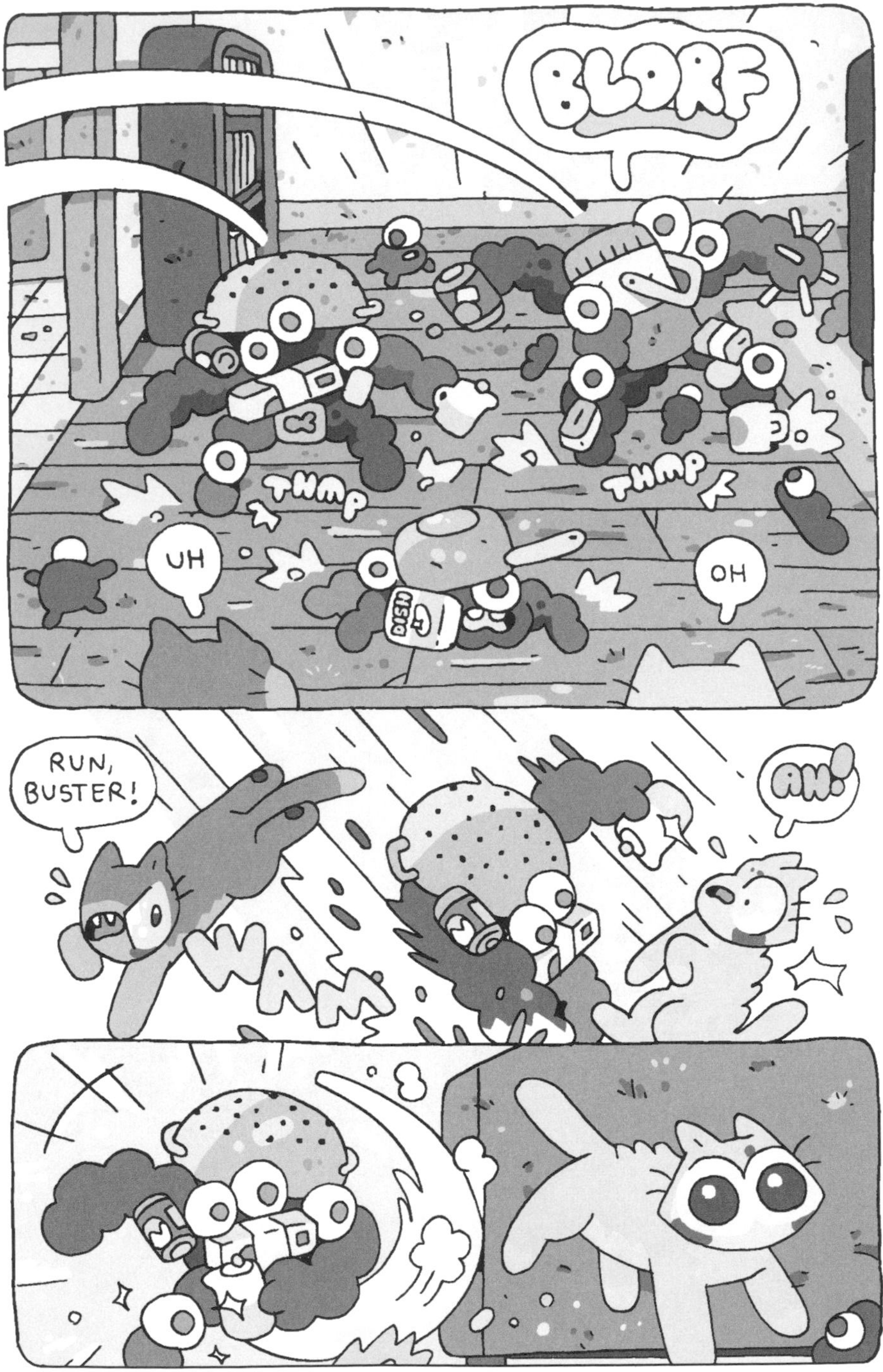
BLORF
THMP
THMP
UH
OH
RUN, BUSTER!
AH!
WAM

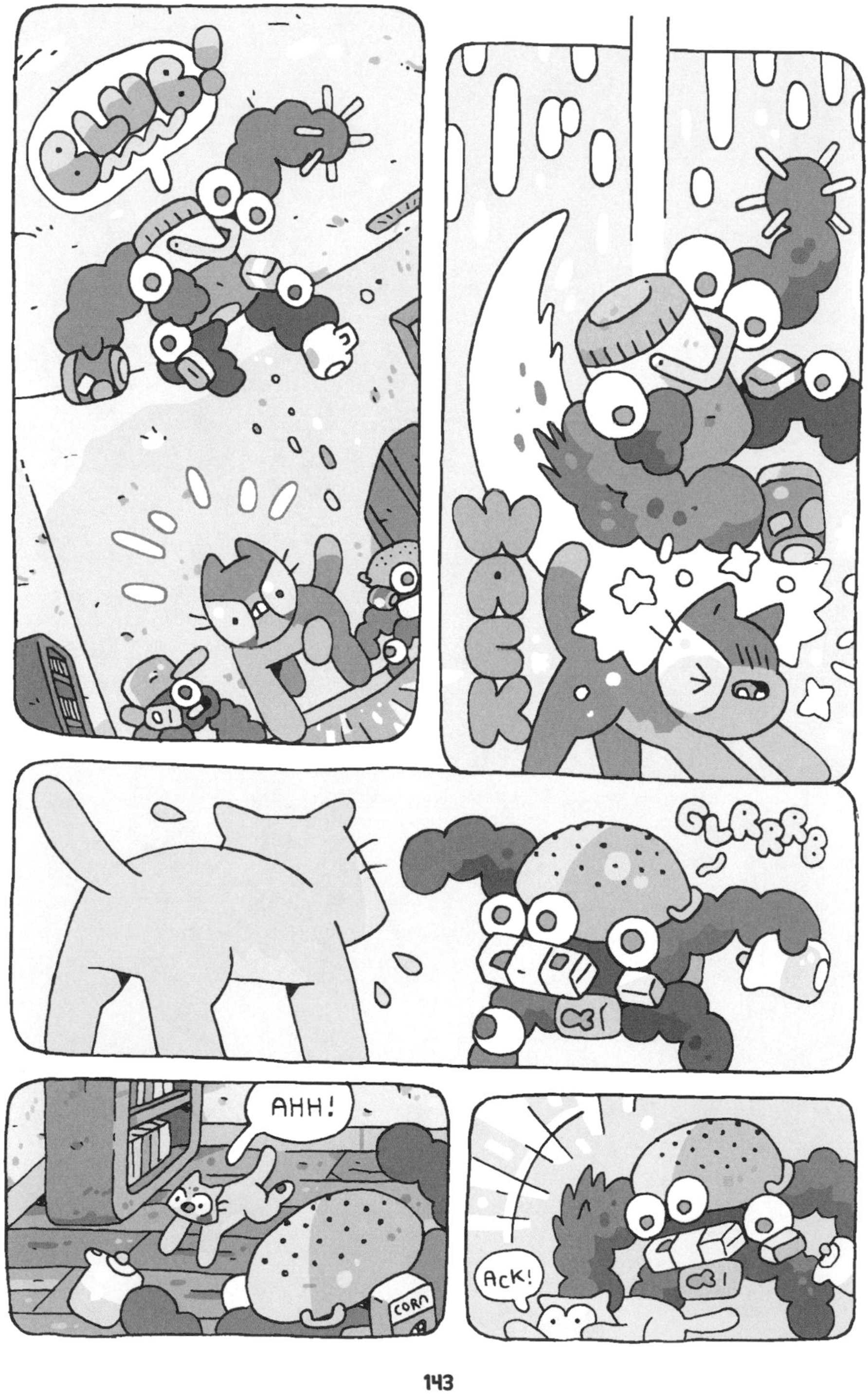
BLUB!
WACK
GLRRRB
AHH!
ACK!
CORN

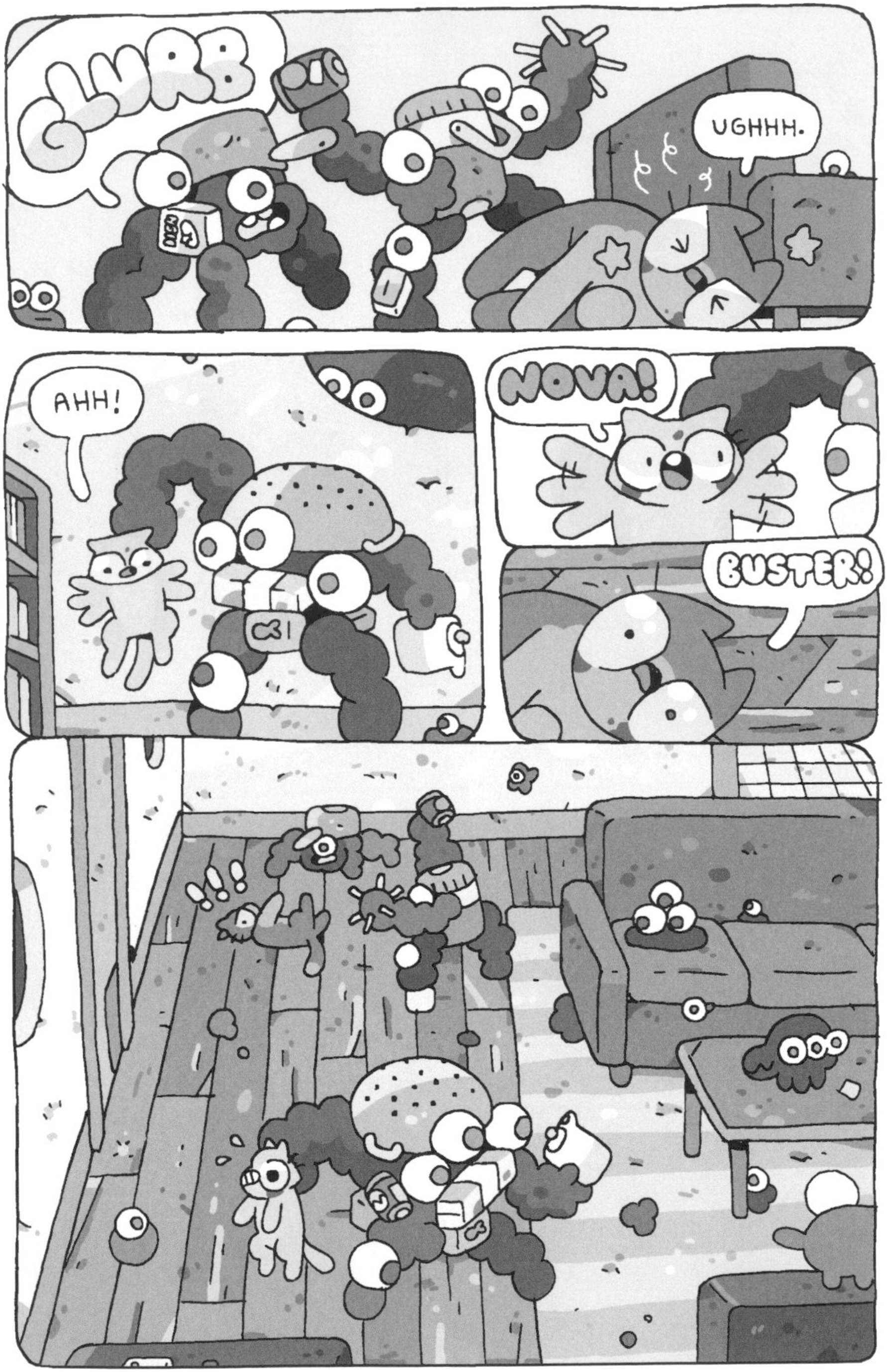
GLURB
UGHHH.
AHH!
NOVA!
BUSTER!

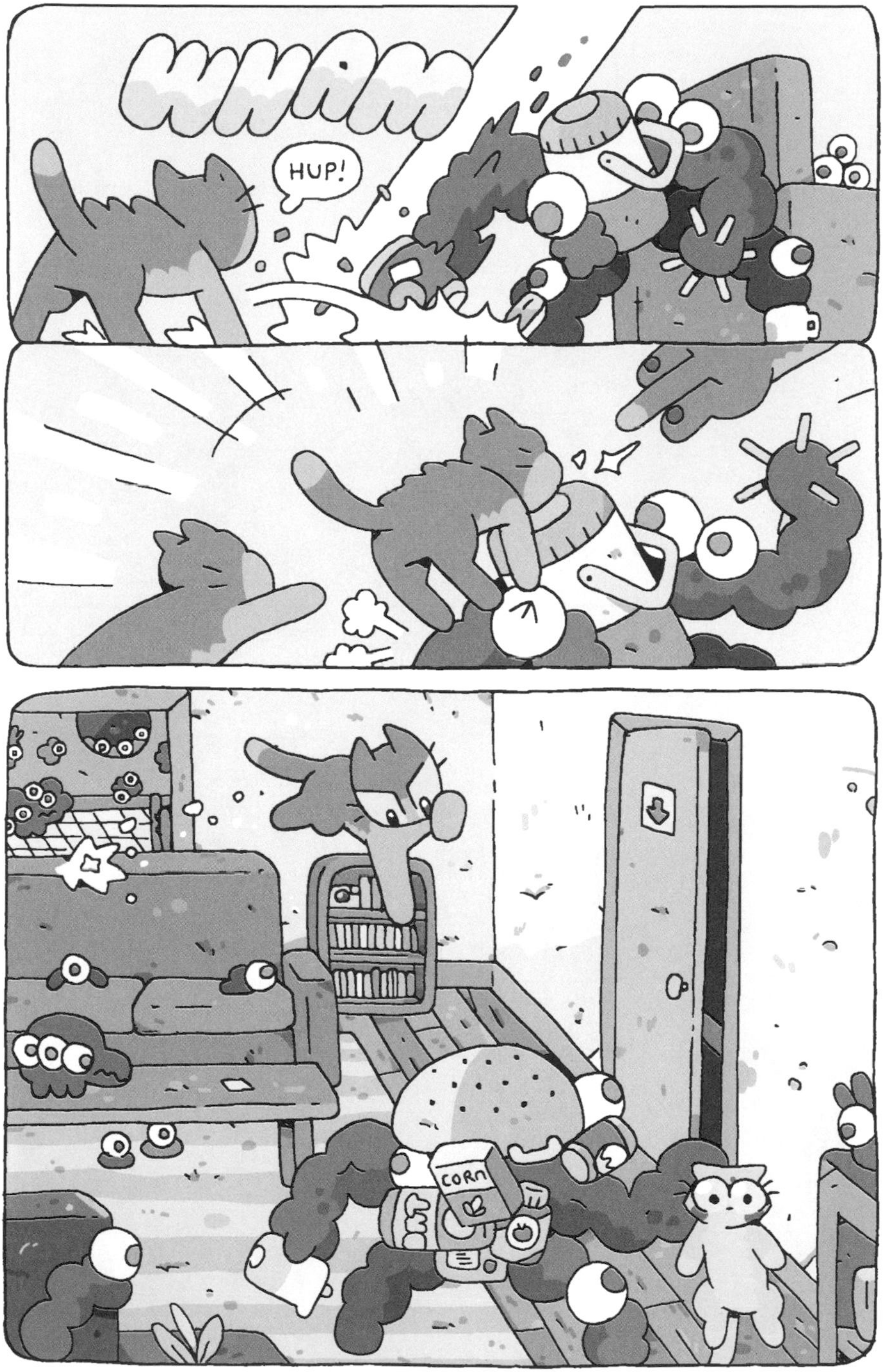
WHAM
HUP!
CORN

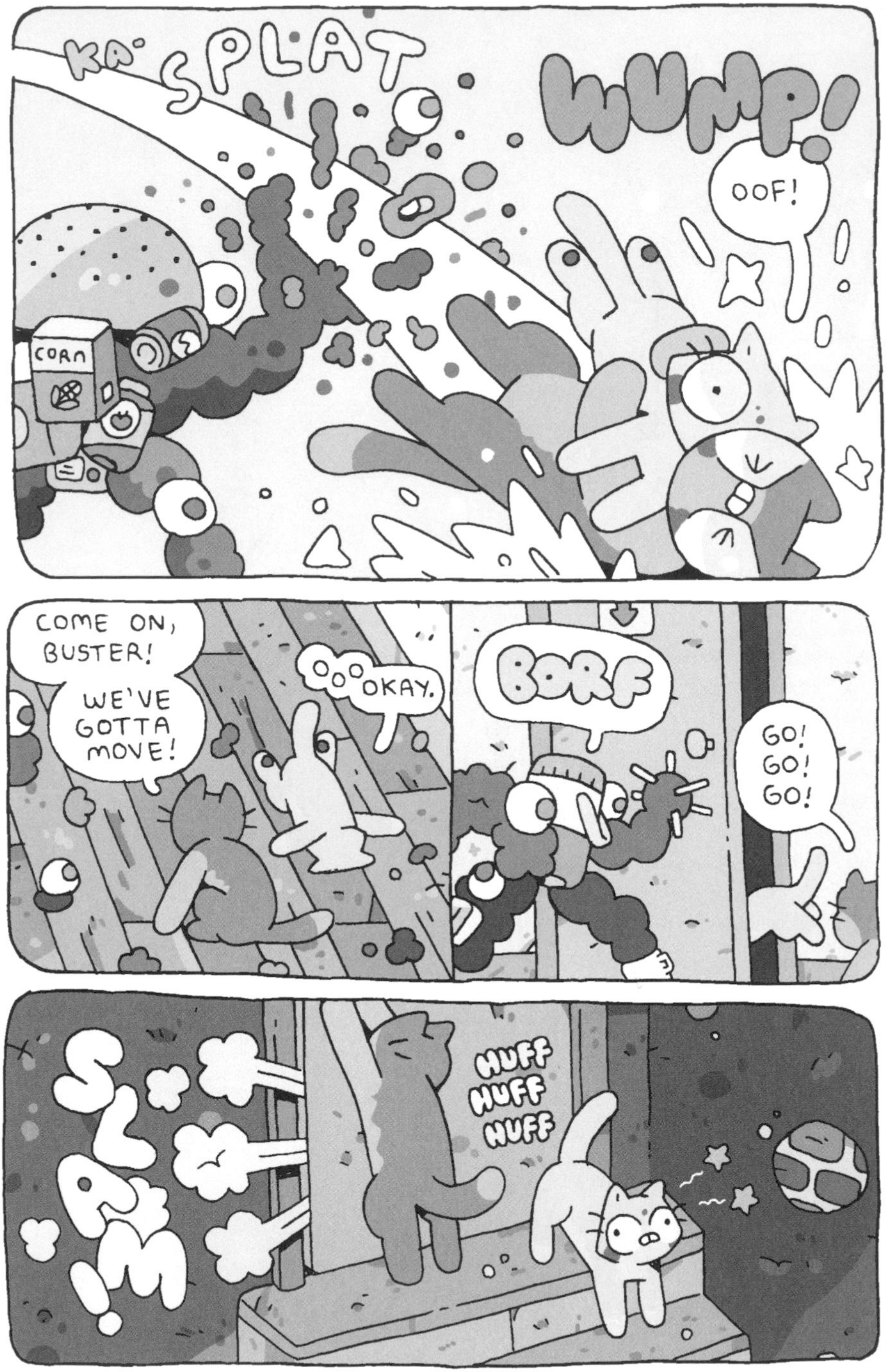
KA-SPLAT
WUMP!
OOF!
COME ON, BUSTER!
WE'VE GOTTA MOVE!
OOOOKAY.
BORF
GO! GO! GO!
SLAM!
HUFF HUFF HUFF

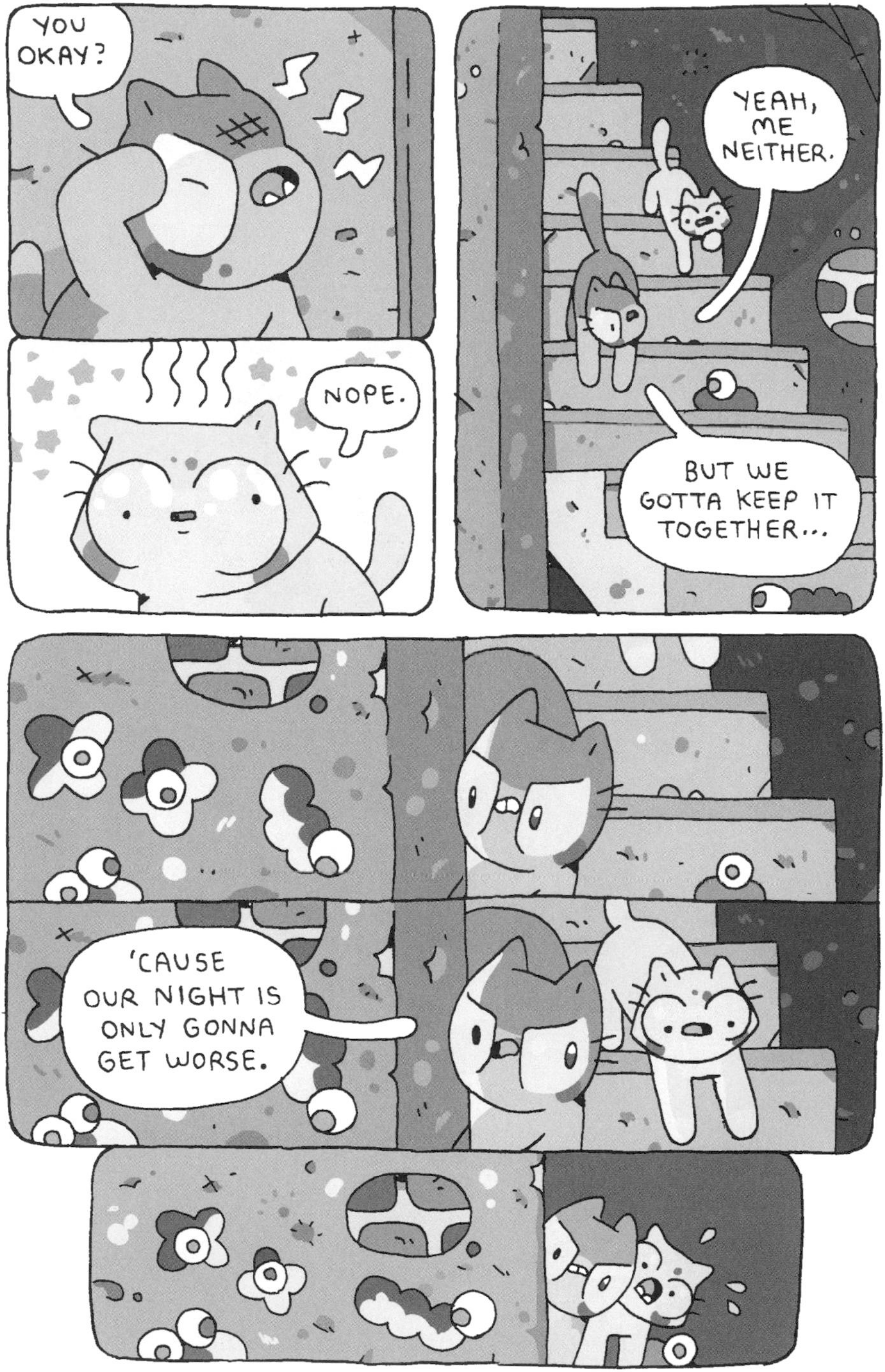
YOU OKAY?
NOPE.
YEAH, ME NEITHER.
BUT WE GOTTA KEEP IT TOGETHER...
'CAUSE OUR NIGHT IS ONLY GONNA GET WORSE.

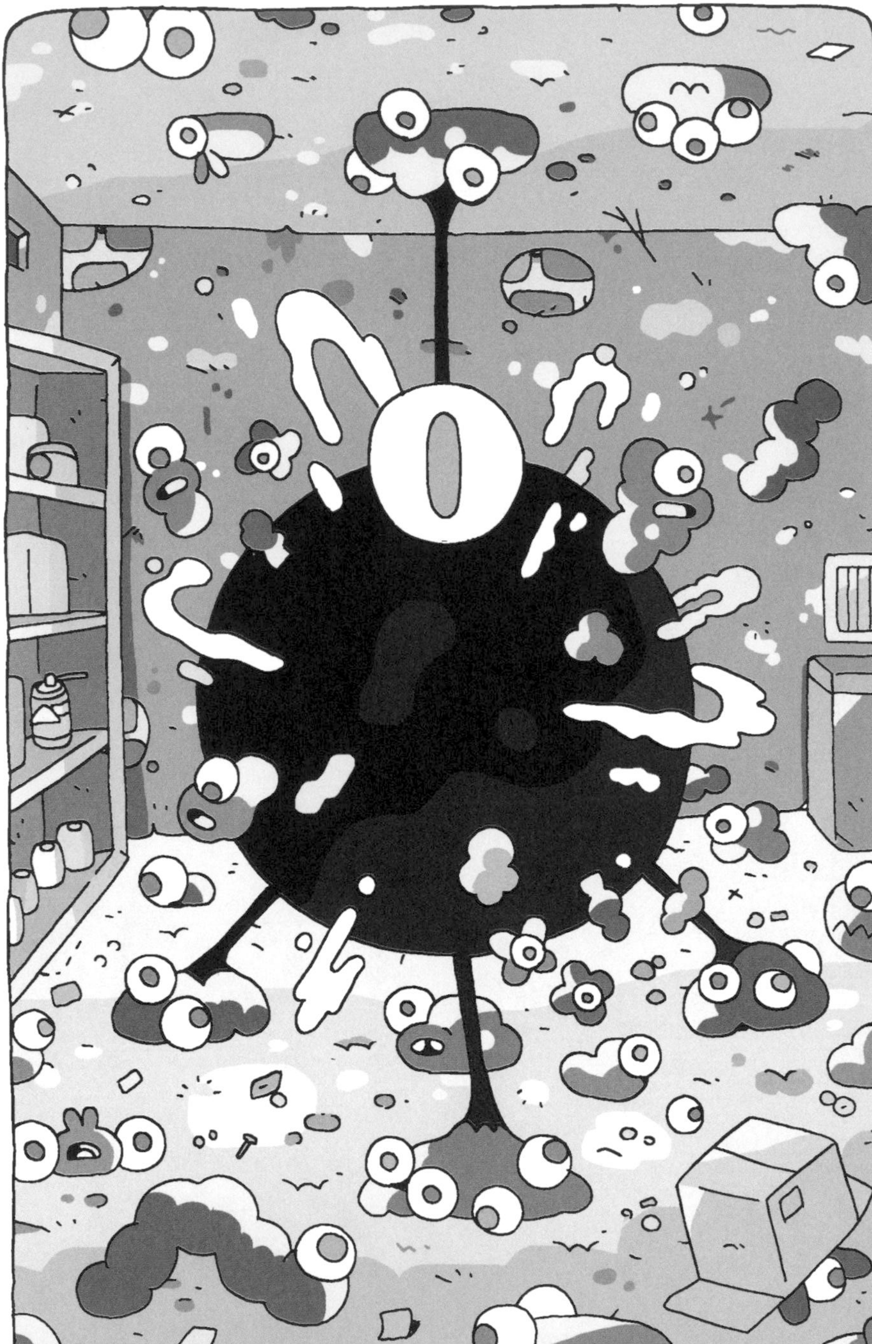

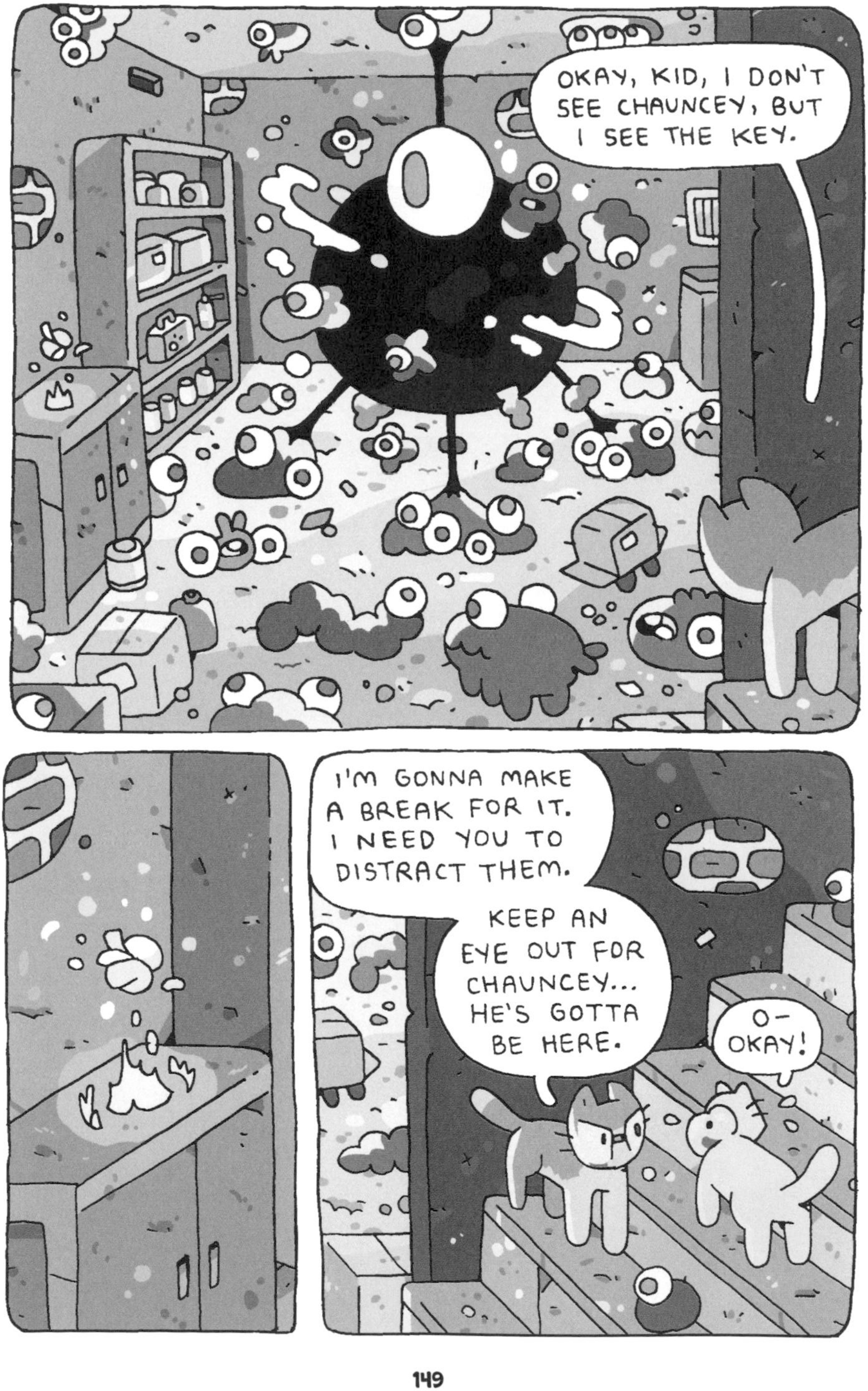

OKAY, KID, I DON'T SEE CHAUNCEY, BUT I SEE THE KEY.
I'M GONNA MAKE A BREAK FOR IT. I NEED YOU TO DISTRACT THEM.
KEEP AN EYE OUT FOR CHAUNCEY... HE'S GOTTA BE HERE.
O-OKAY!

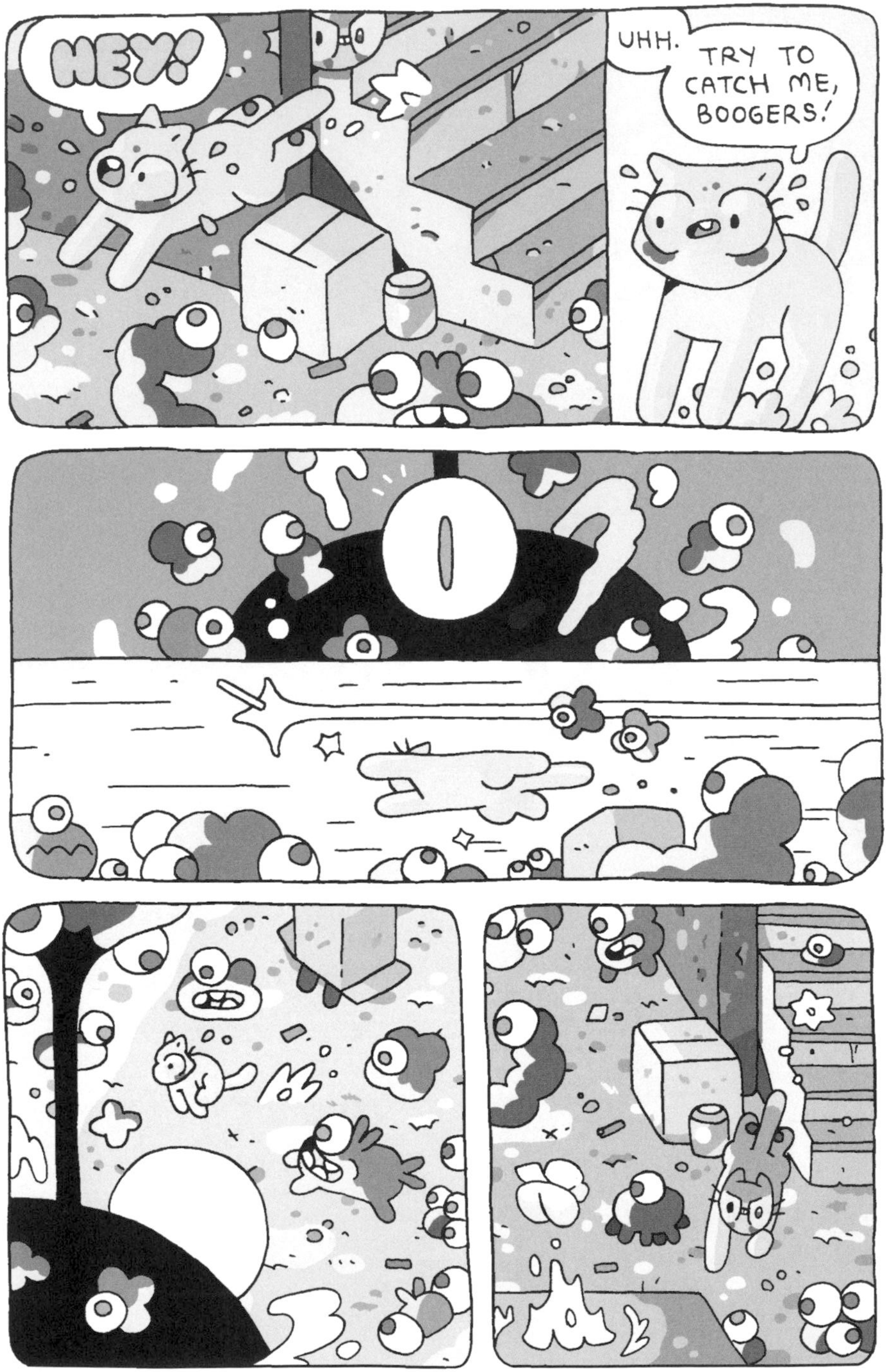
HEY!
UHH.
TRY TO CATCH ME, BOOGERS!

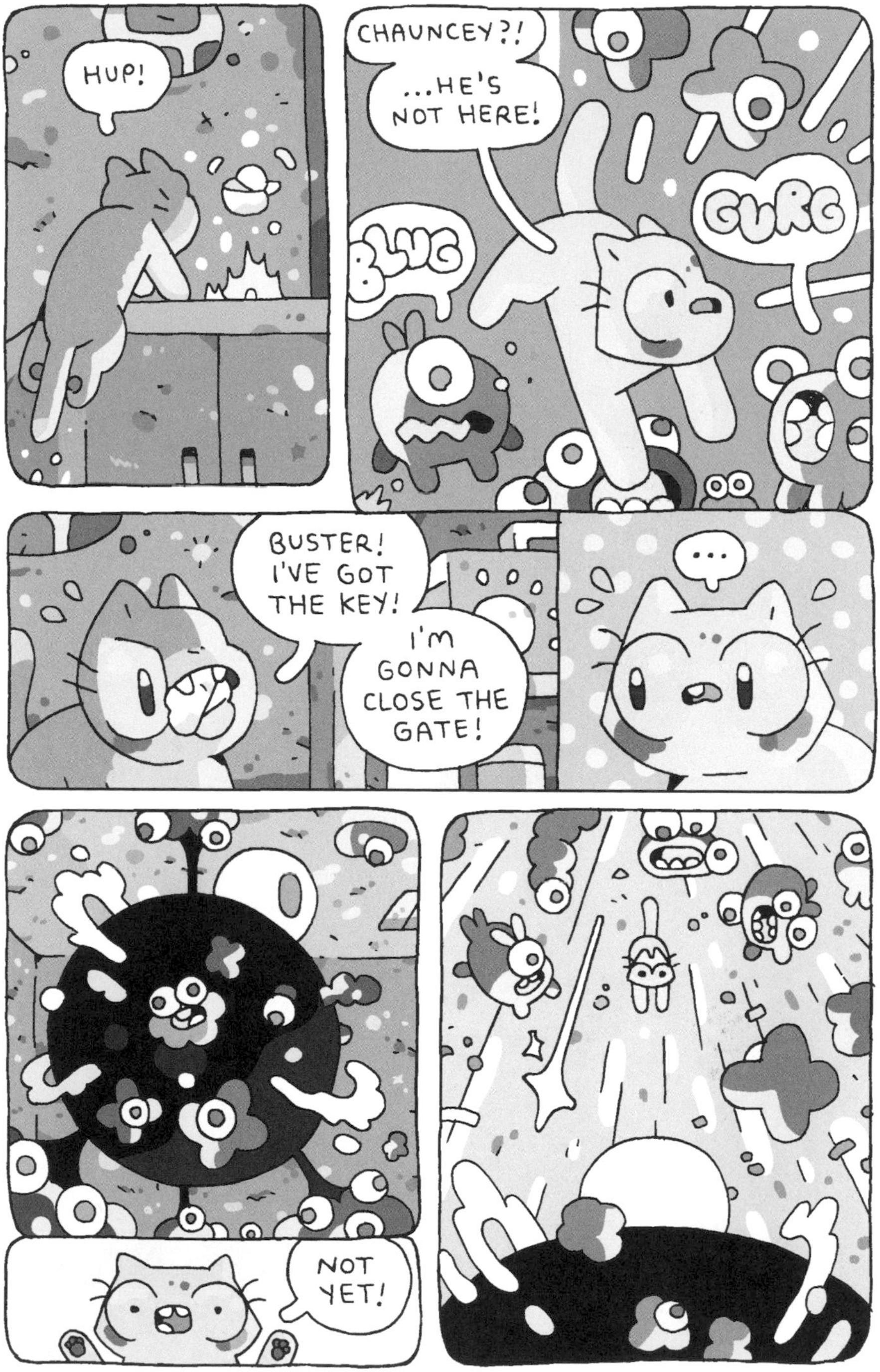
HUP!
CHAUNCEY?!
...HE'S NOT HERE!
BLUG
GURG
BUSTER! I'VE GOT THE KEY!
I'M GONNA CLOSE THE GATE!
...
NOT YET!

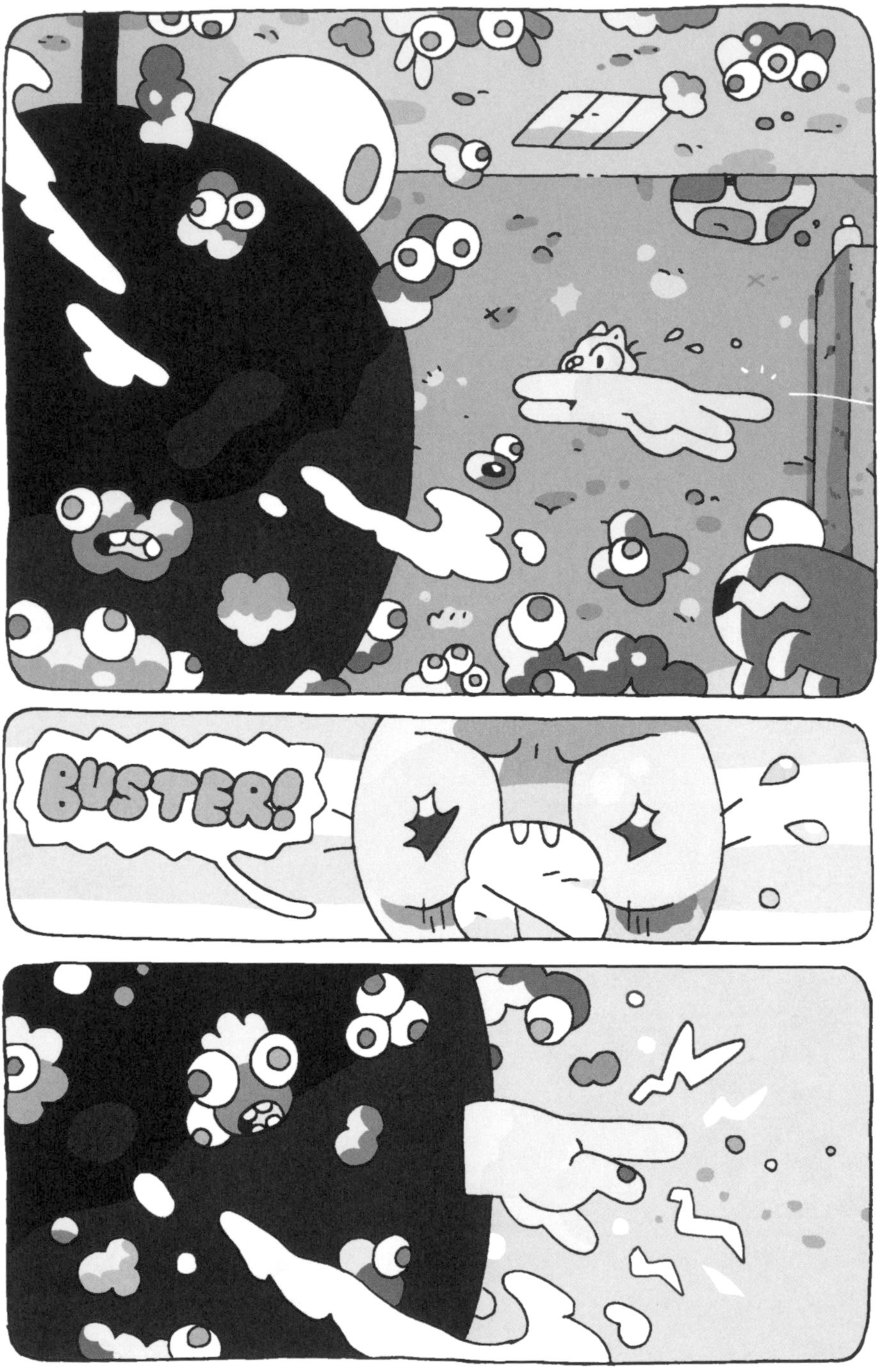
BUSTER!

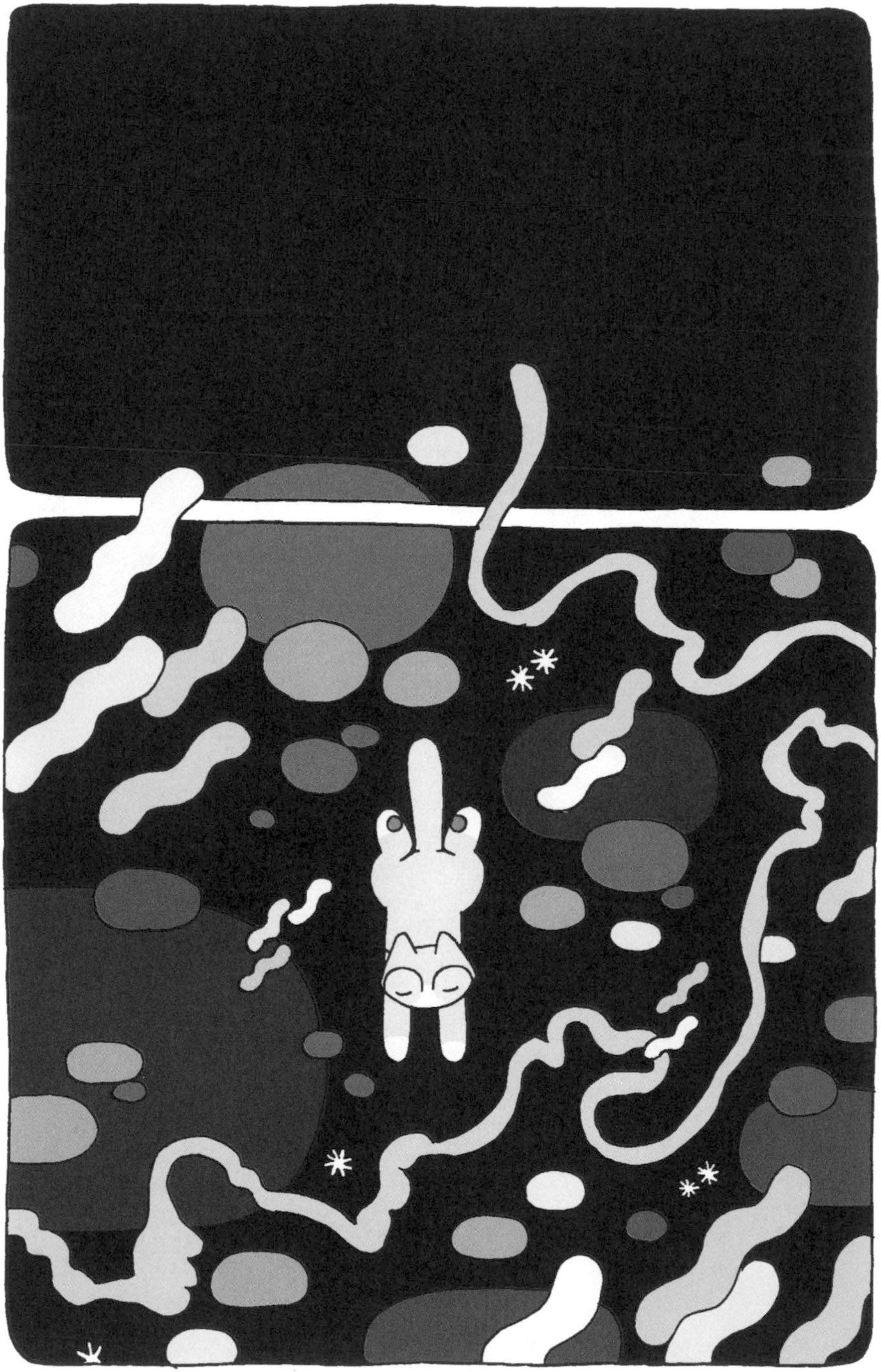

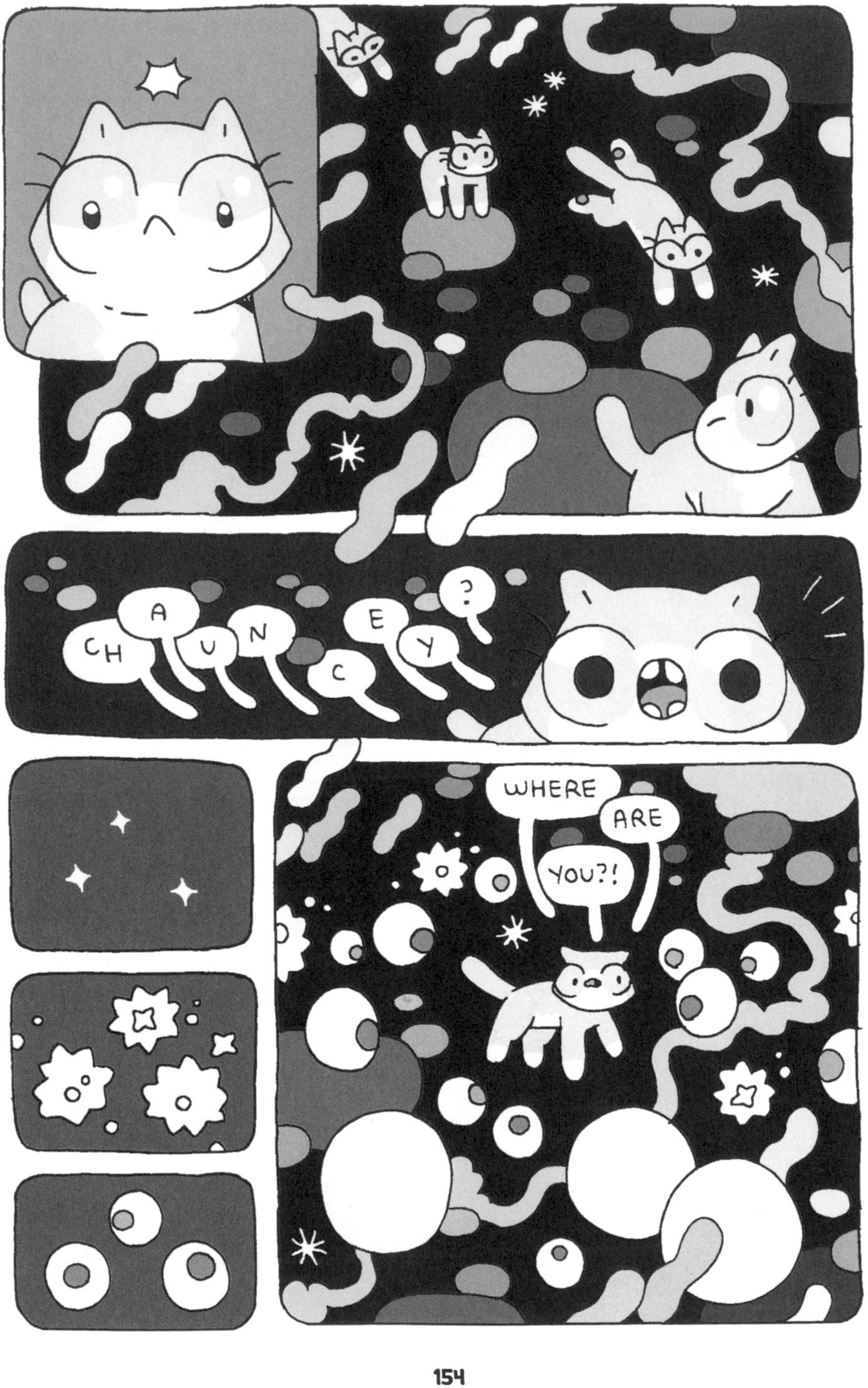
CH A U N C E Y ?
WHERE
ARE
YOU?!

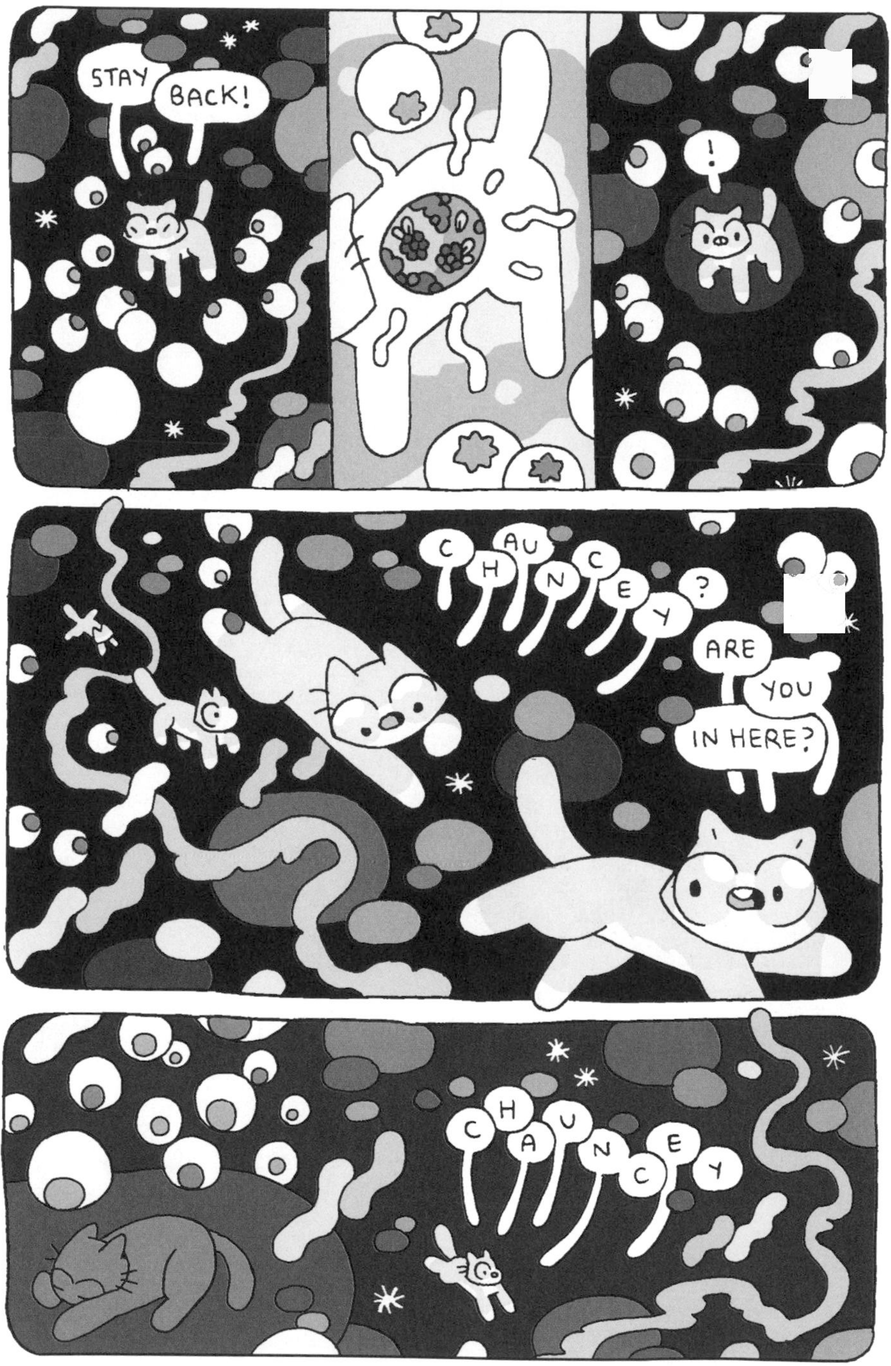
STAY
BACK!
!
CHAUNCEY?
ARE YOU IN HERE?
CHAUNCEY

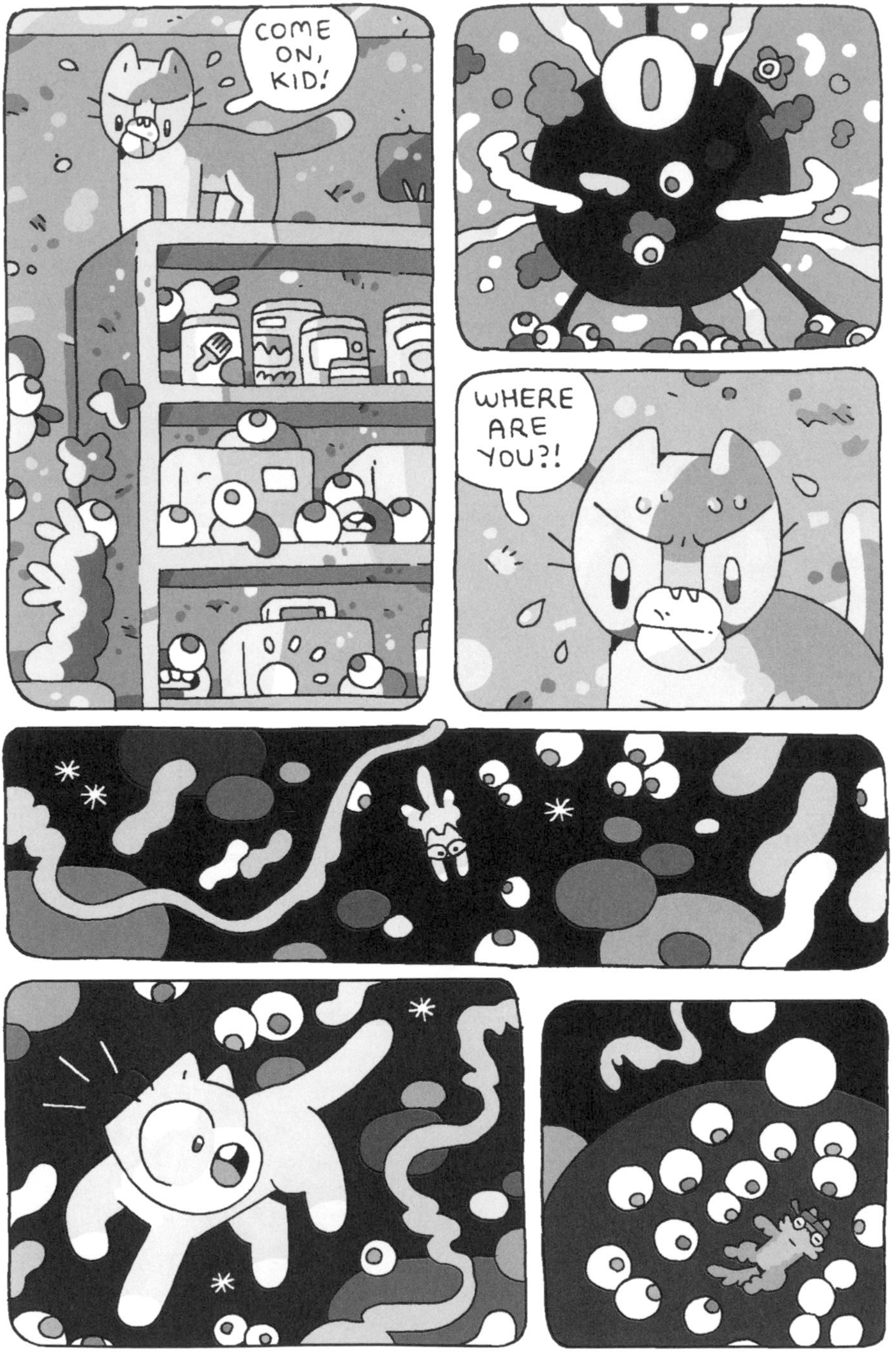
COME ON, KID!
WHERE ARE YOU?!

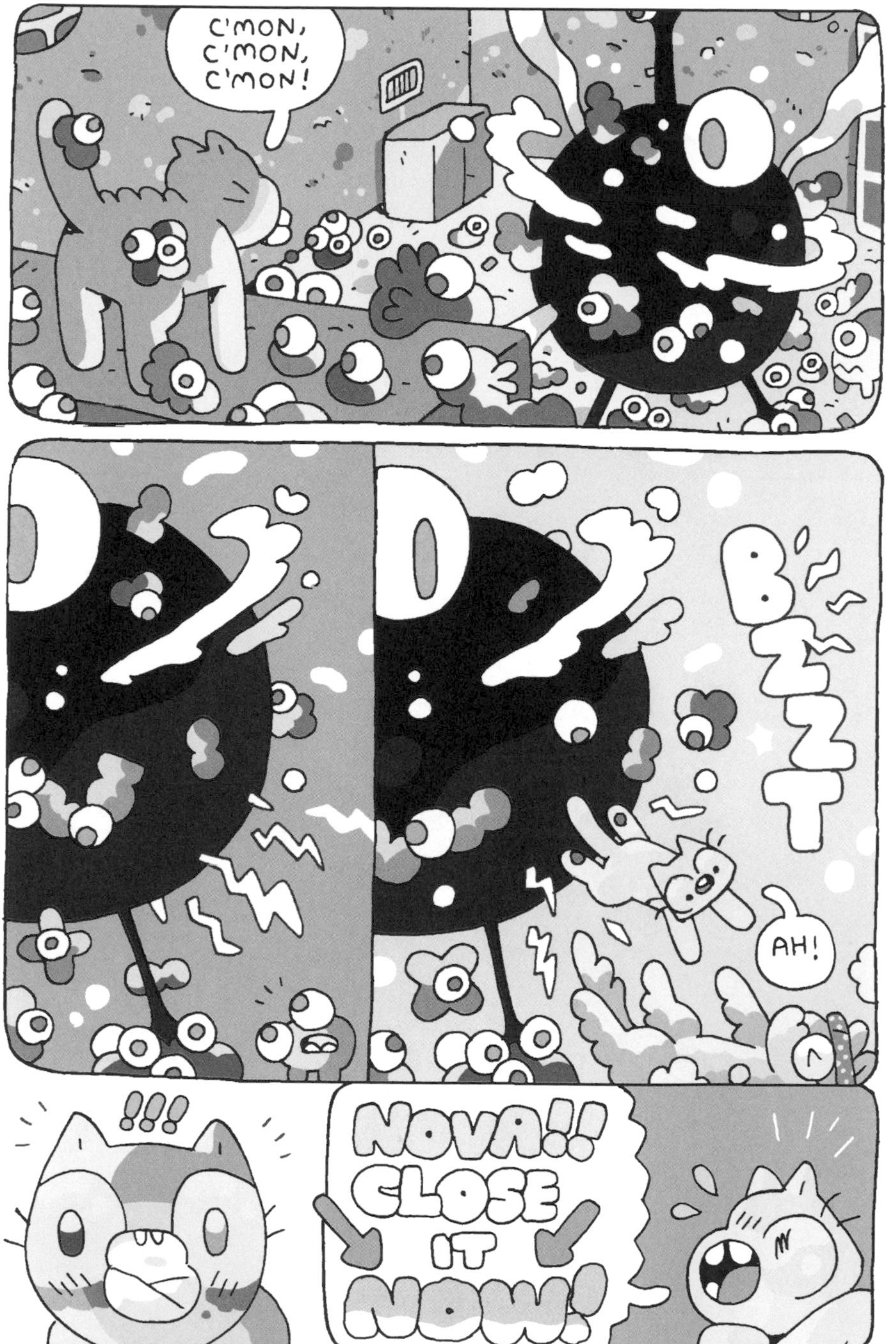

C'MON, C'MON, C'MON!
BZZZT
AH!
!!!
NOVA!! CLOSE IT NOW!

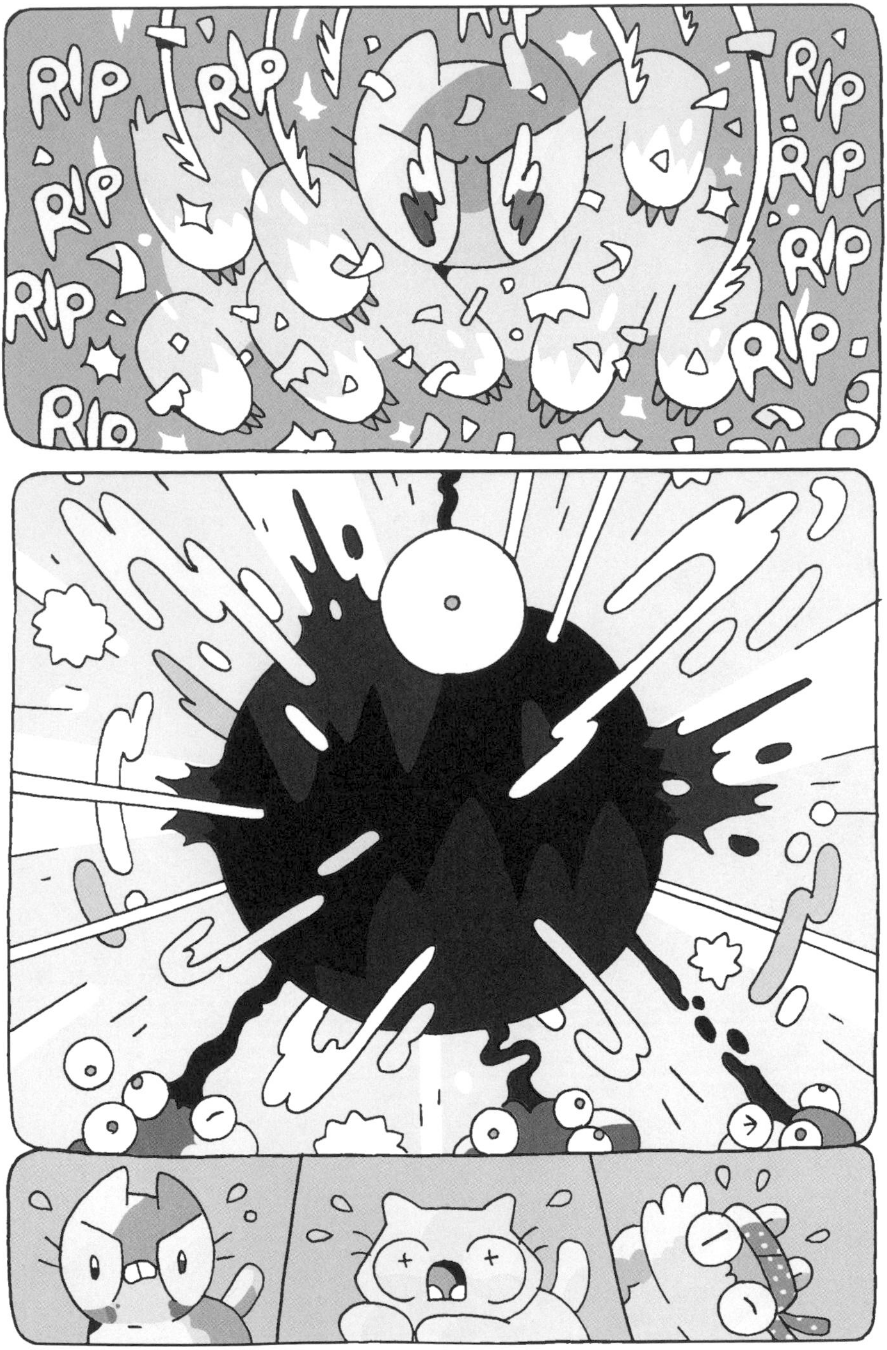
RIP
RIP
RIP
RIP
RIP
RIP
RIP
RIP
RIP

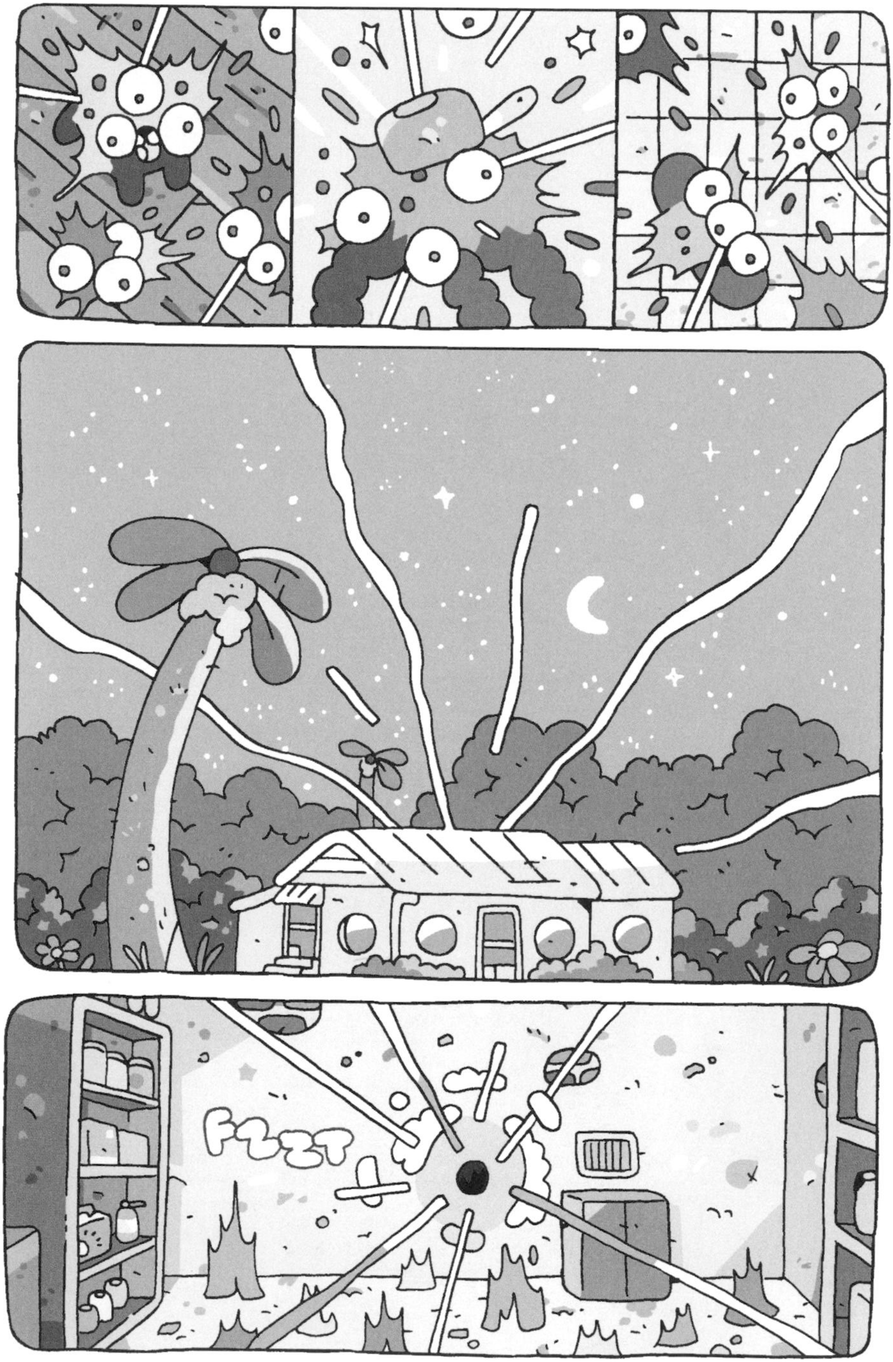
FZZT

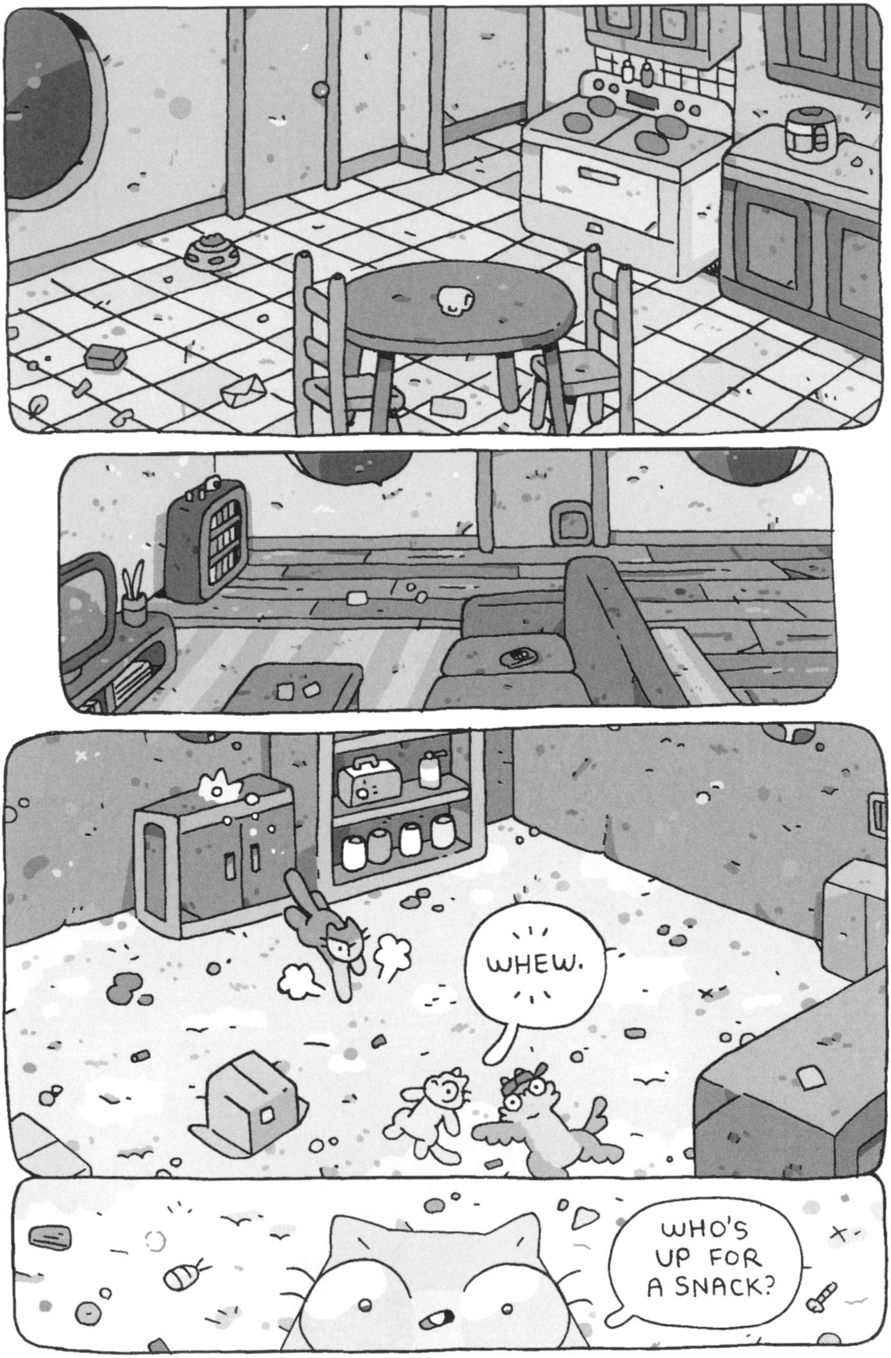
WHEW.
WHO'S UP FOR A SNACK?

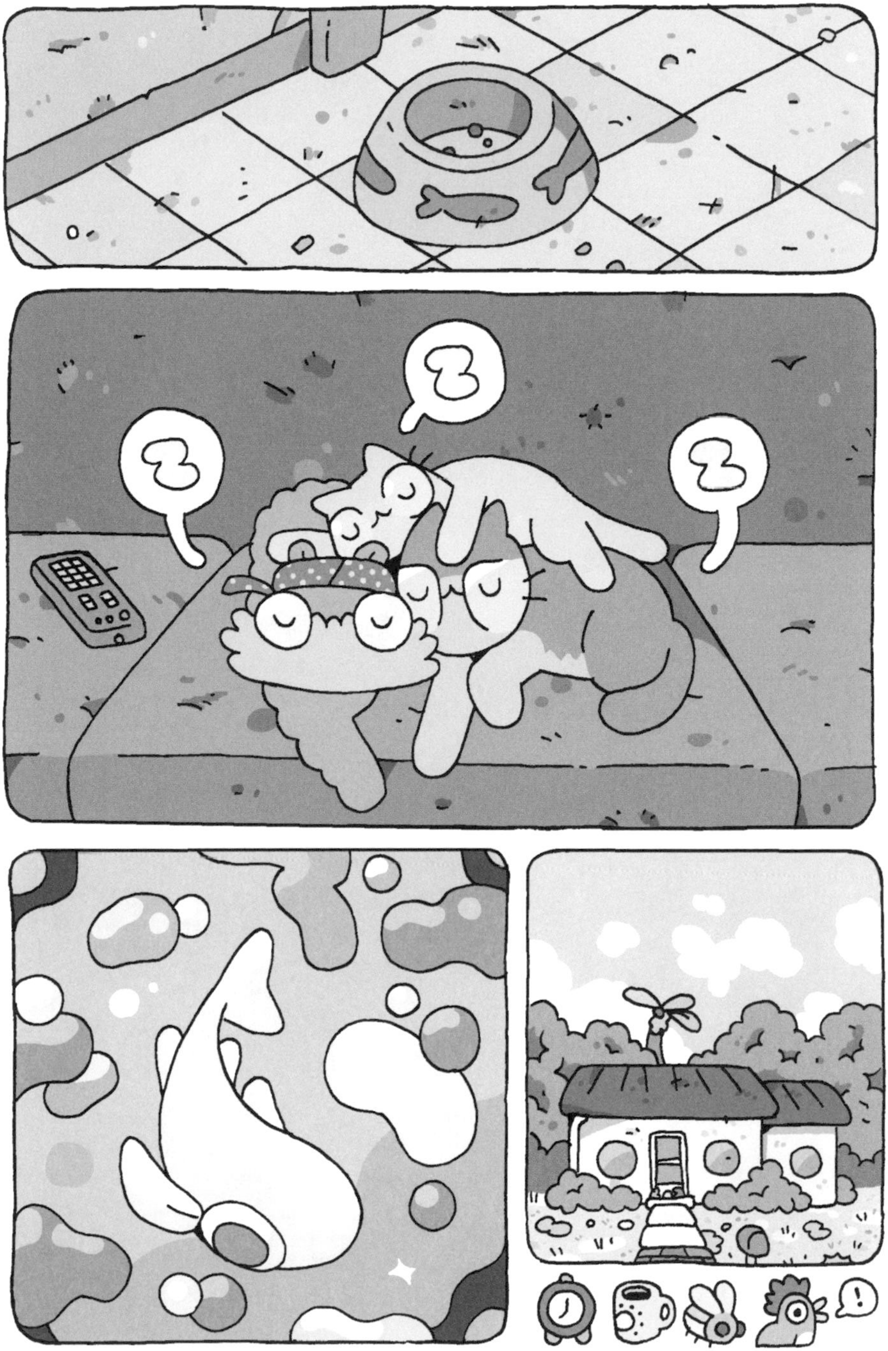
Z
Z
Z
!

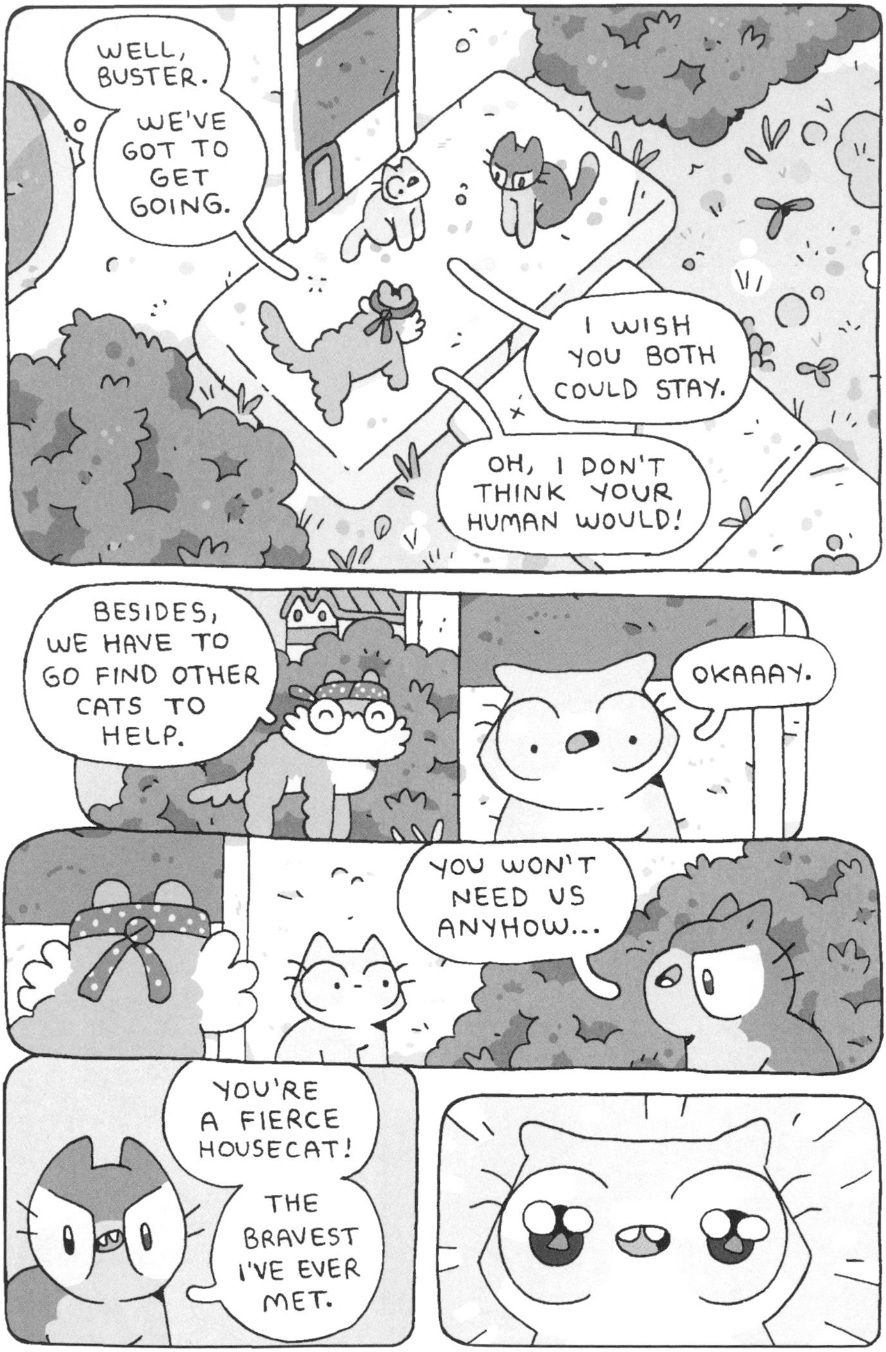
WELL, BUSTER.
WE'VE GOT TO GET GOING.
I WISH YOU BOTH COULD STAY.
OH, I DON'T THINK YOUR HUMAN WOULD!
BESIDES, WE HAVE TO GO FIND OTHER CATS TO HELP.
OKAAAY.
YOU WON'T NEED US ANYHOW...
YOU'RE A FIERCE HOUSECAT!
THE BRAVEST I'VE EVER MET.

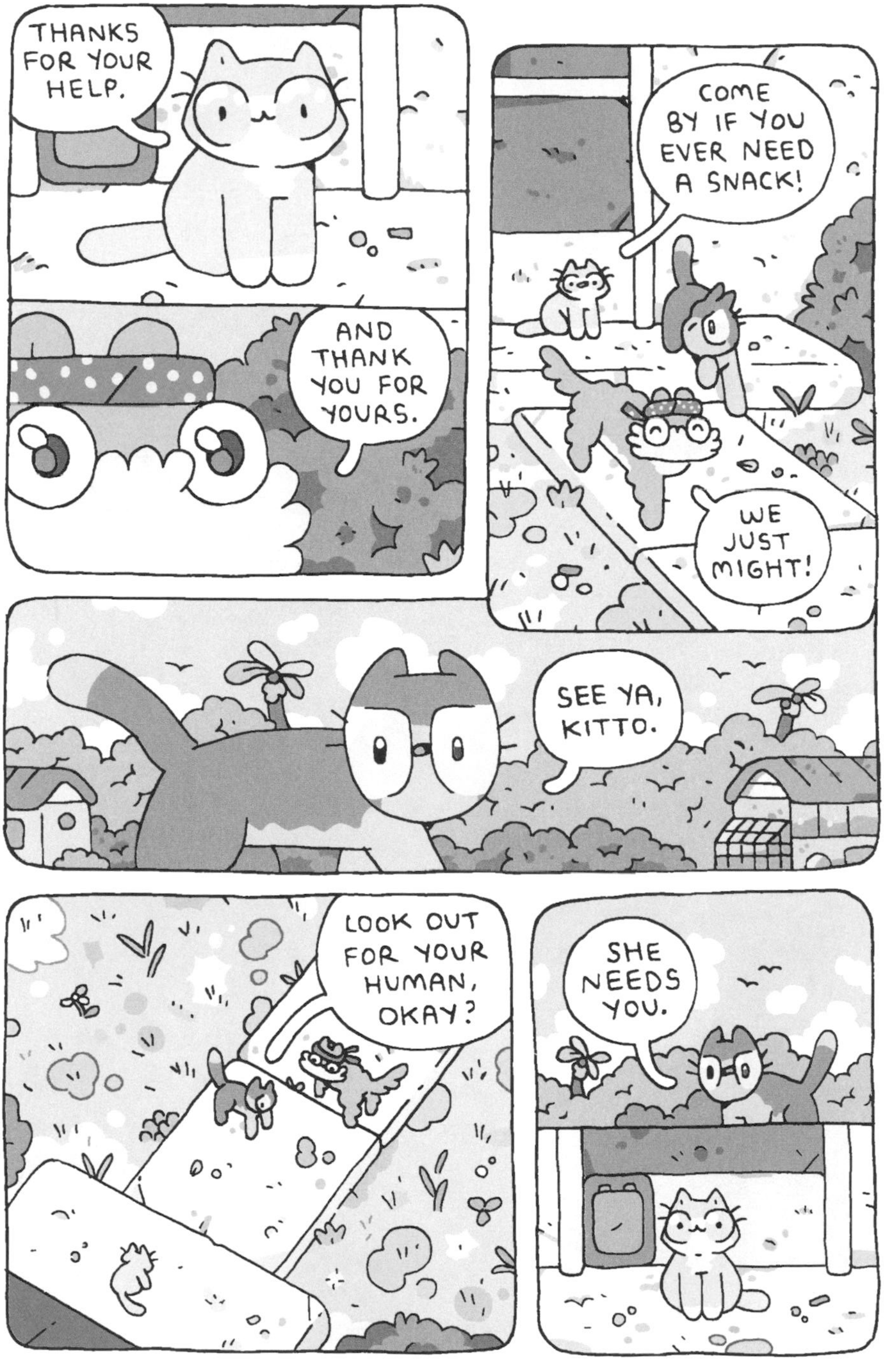
THANKS FOR YOUR HELP.
AND THANK YOU FOR YOURS.
COME BY IF YOU EVER NEED A SNACK!
WE JUST MIGHT!
SEE YA, KITTO.
LOOK OUT FOR YOUR HUMAN, OKAY?
SHE NEEDS YOU.

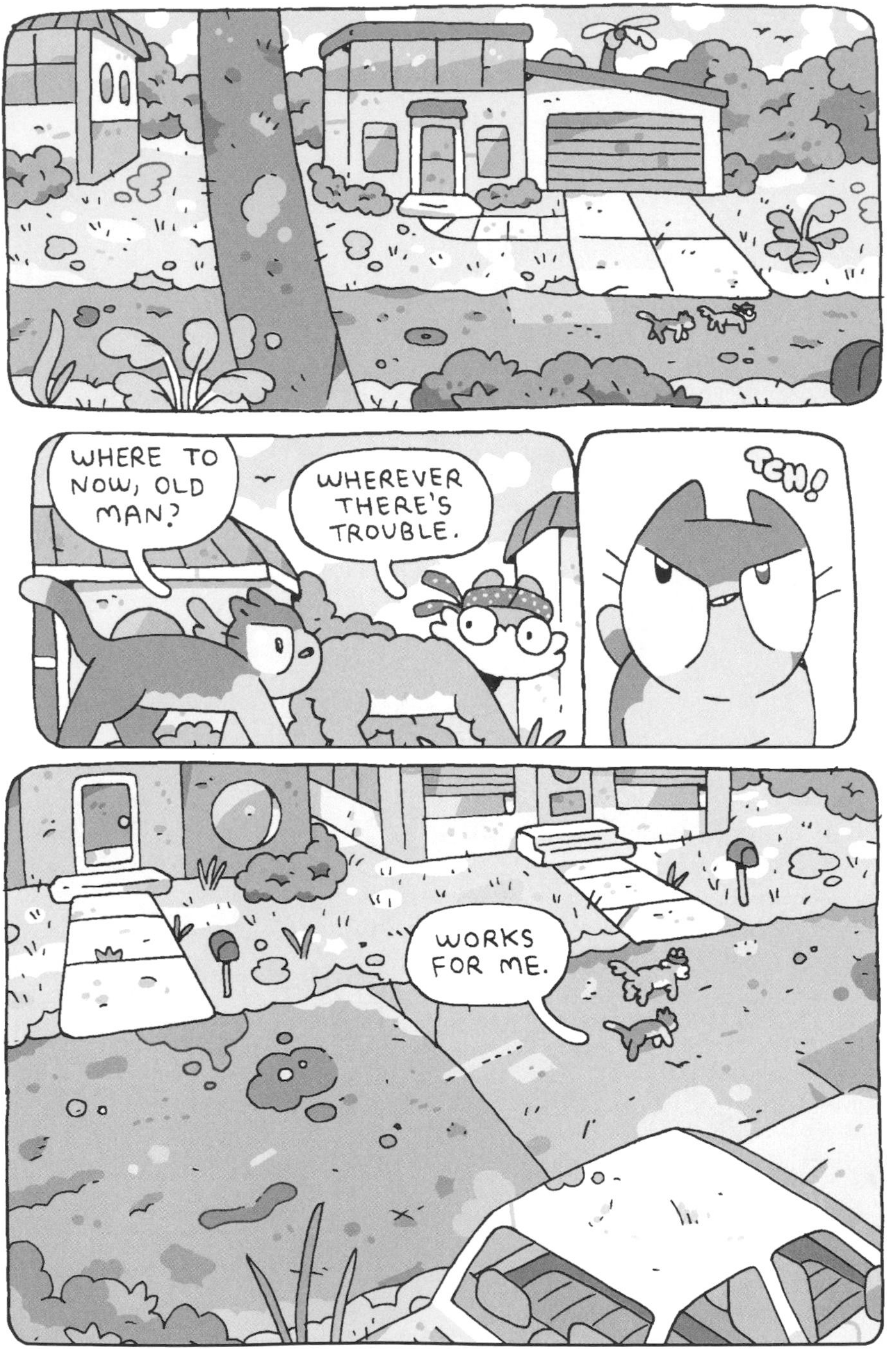
WHERE TO NOW, OLD MAN?
WHEREVER THERE'S TROUBLE.
TCH!
WORKS FOR ME.

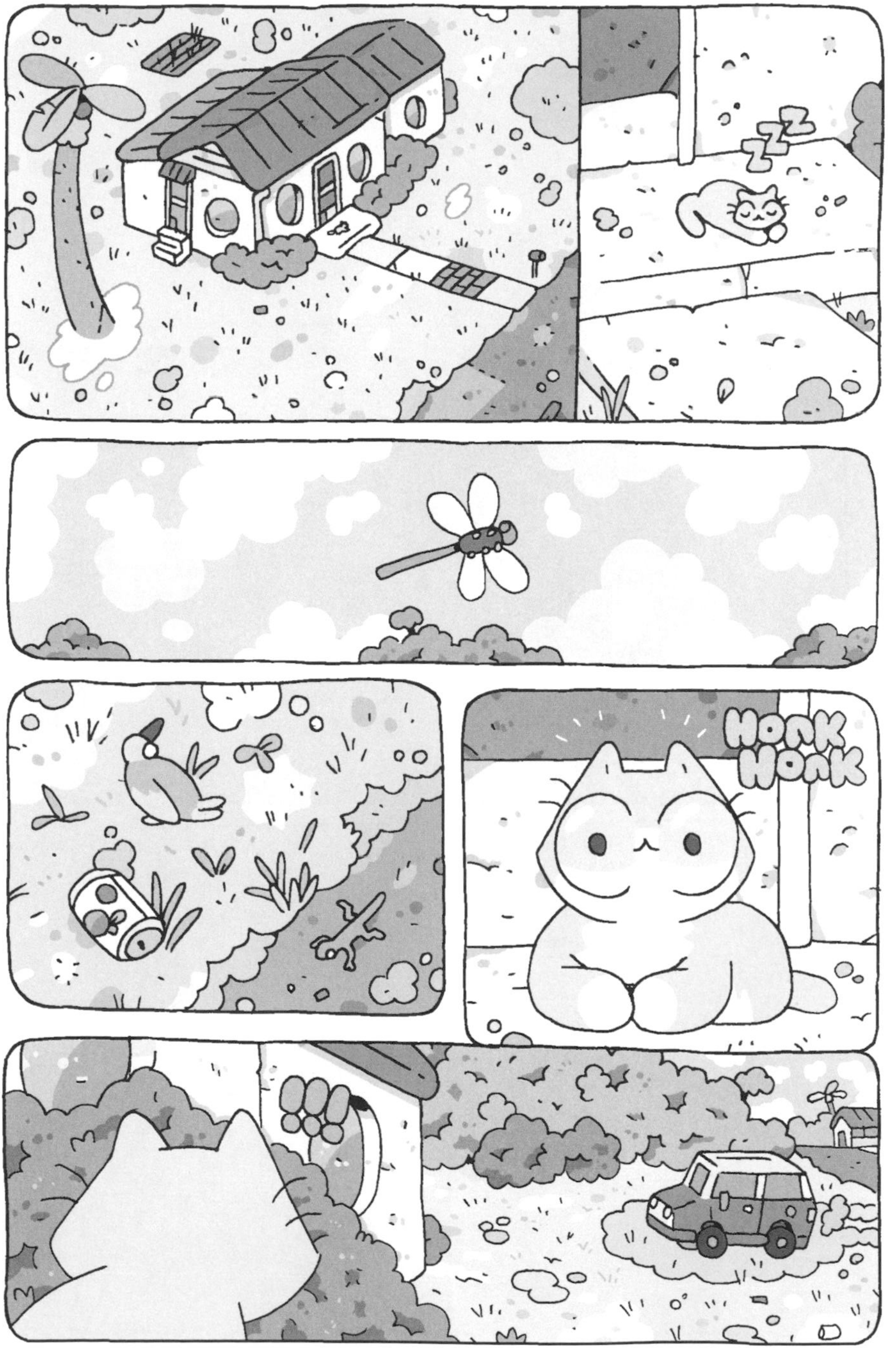
ZZZ
HONK
HONK

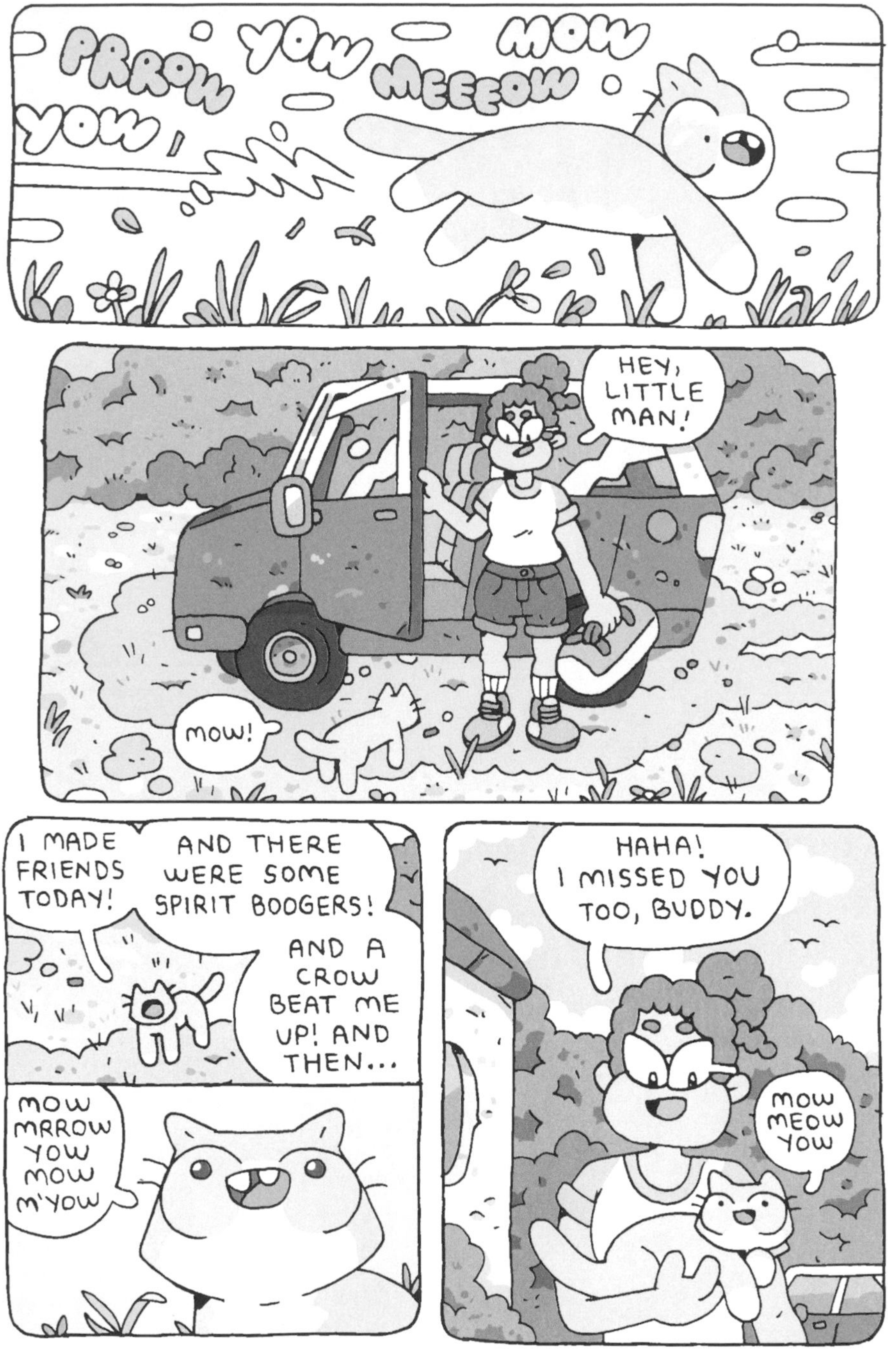
PRROW YOW YOW MEEEOW MOW YOW
HEY, LITTLE MAN!
MOW!
I MADE FRIENDS TODAY!
AND THERE WERE SOME SPIRIT BOOGERS!
AND A CROW BEAT ME UP! AND THEN...
MOW MRROW YOW MOW M'YOW
HAHA! I MISSED YOU TOO, BUDDY.
MOW MEOW YOW

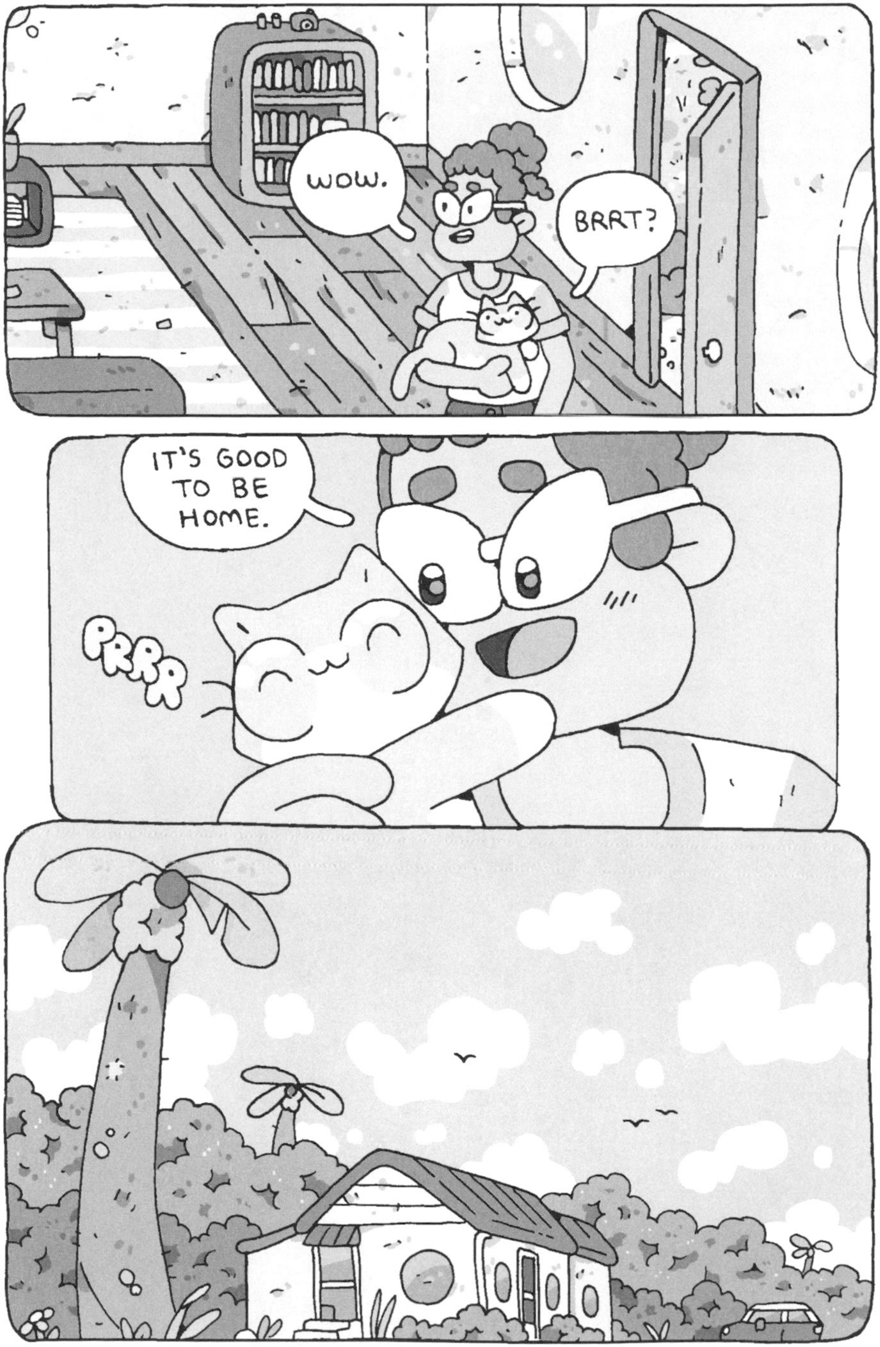
WOW.
BRRT?
IT'S GOOD TO BE HOME.
PRRR

ACKNOWLEDGMENTS

Thank you to my family, for your constant love and support.

Thanks also to Brid, Nathan, Ben, Chris, Mike, Zach, Jordan, Jennie and Ommy, Dustin Harbin, Ben Sears, Woolly Press, Travis at 641RPM, Devon Tuttle, Annie Koyama, Rico Renzi, and anyone who has ever bought one of my comics, prints, or shirts.

Special thanks to my editor, Whitney Leopard, and my designer, Patrick Crotty, as well as Gina Gagliano and the rest of the team at Random House Graphic for helping me make this book.

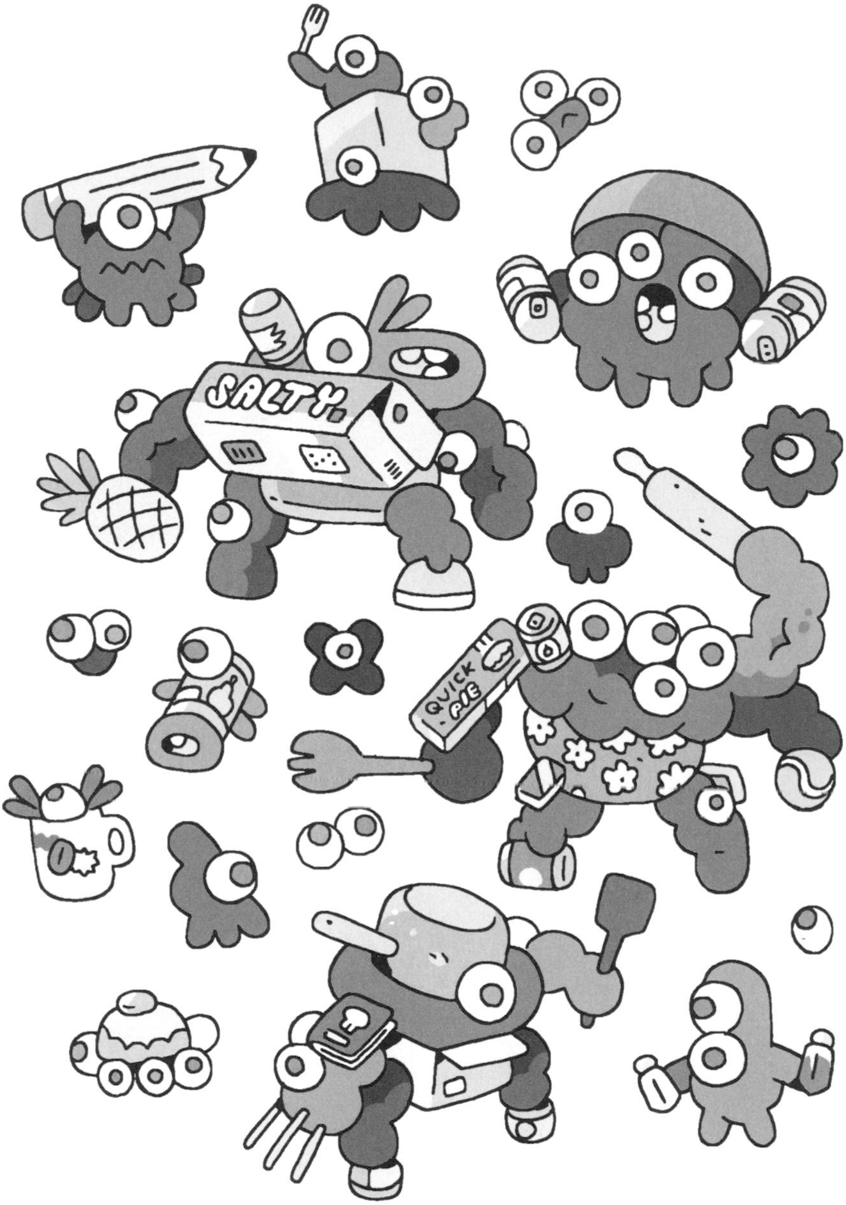
SALTY
QUICK PIE

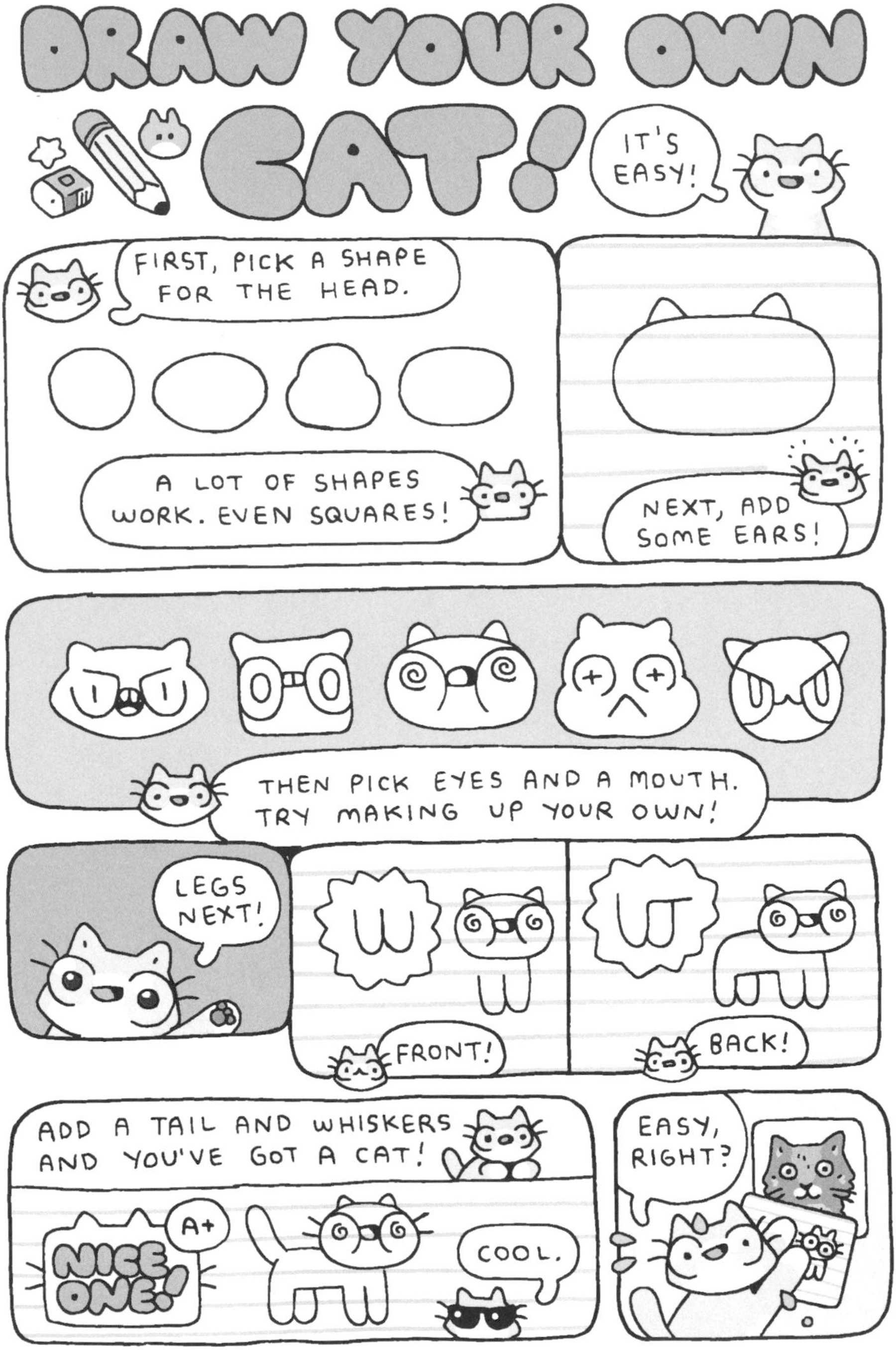
DRAW YOUR OWN CAT!
IT'S EASY!
FIRST, PICK A SHAPE FOR THE HEAD.
A LOT OF SHAPES WORK. EVEN SQUARES!
NEXT, ADD SOME EARS!
THEN PICK EYES AND A MOUTH. TRY MAKING UP YOUR OWN!
LEGS NEXT!
FRONT!
BACK!
ADD A TAIL AND WHISKERS AND YOU'VE GOT A CAT!
A+
NICE ONE!
COOL.
EASY, RIGHT?

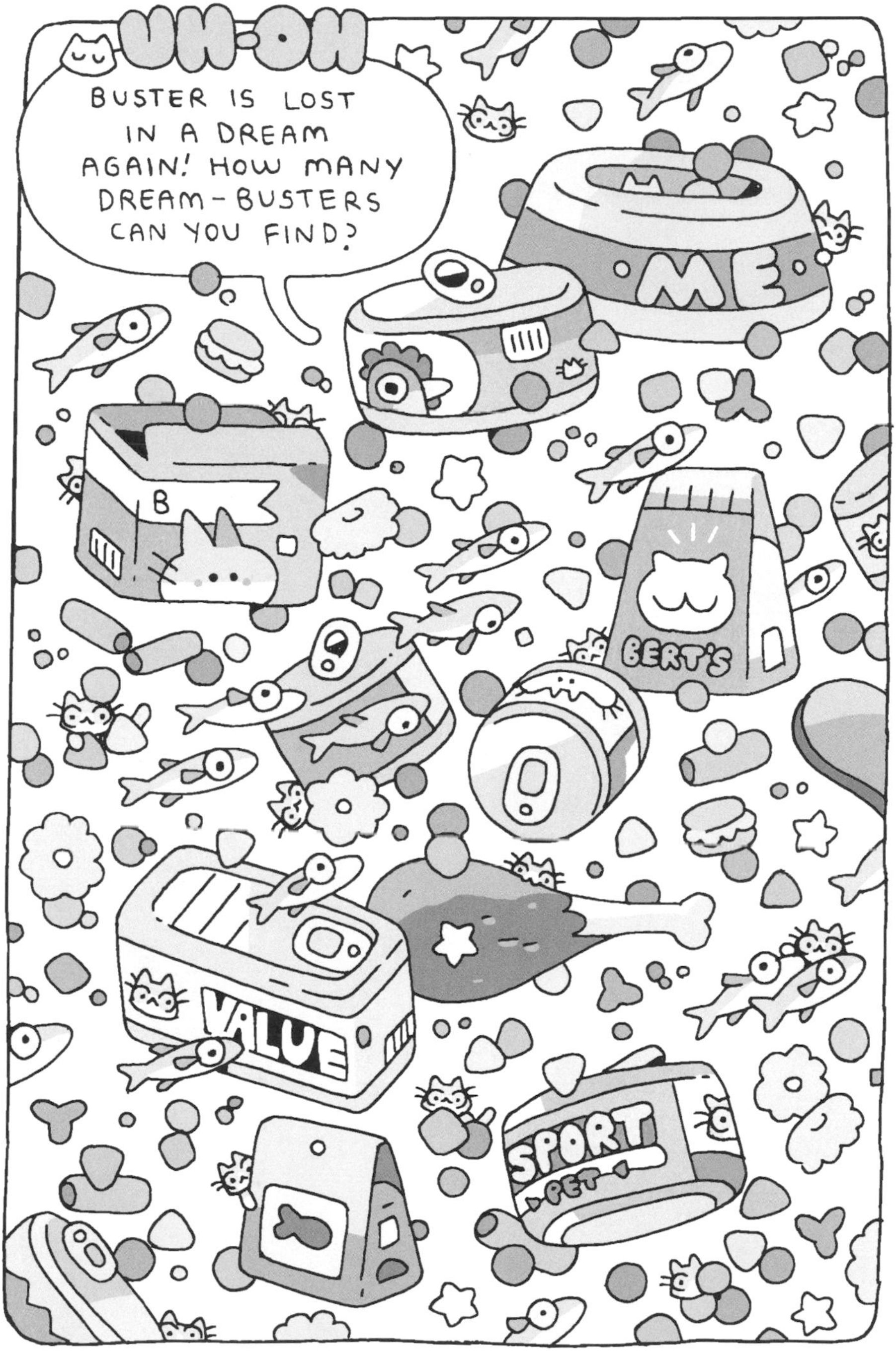
UH-OH
BUSTER IS LOST IN A DREAM AGAIN! HOW MANY DREAM-BUSTERS CAN YOU FIND?
ME
B
BERT'S
VALUE
SPORT
PET

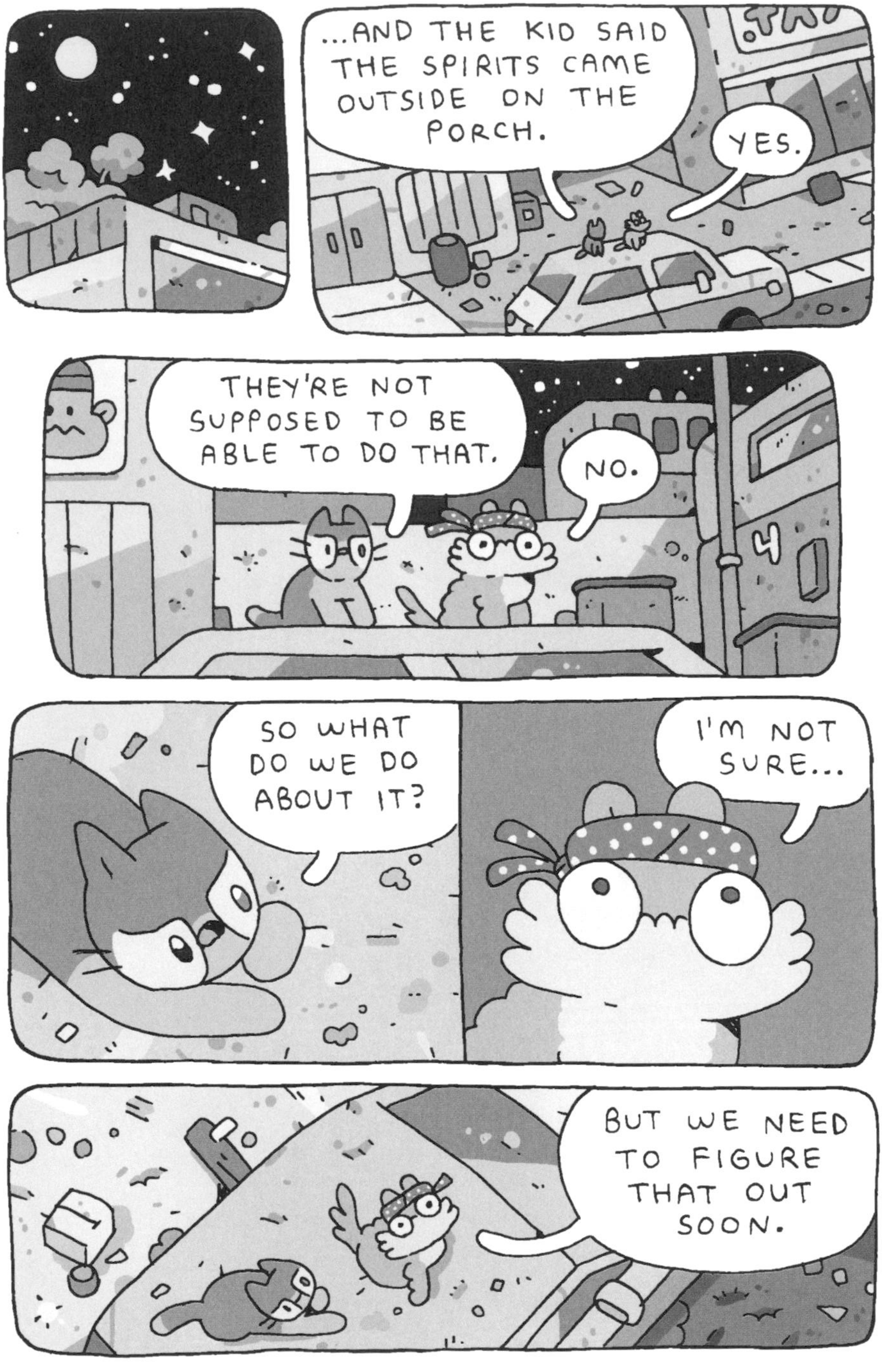
...AND THE KID SAID THE SPIRITS CAME OUTSIDE ON THE PORCH.
YES.
THEY'RE NOT SUPPOSED TO BE ABLE TO DO THAT.
NO.
SO WHAT DO WE DO ABOUT IT?
I'M NOT SURE...
BUT WE NEED TO FIGURE THAT OUT SOON.

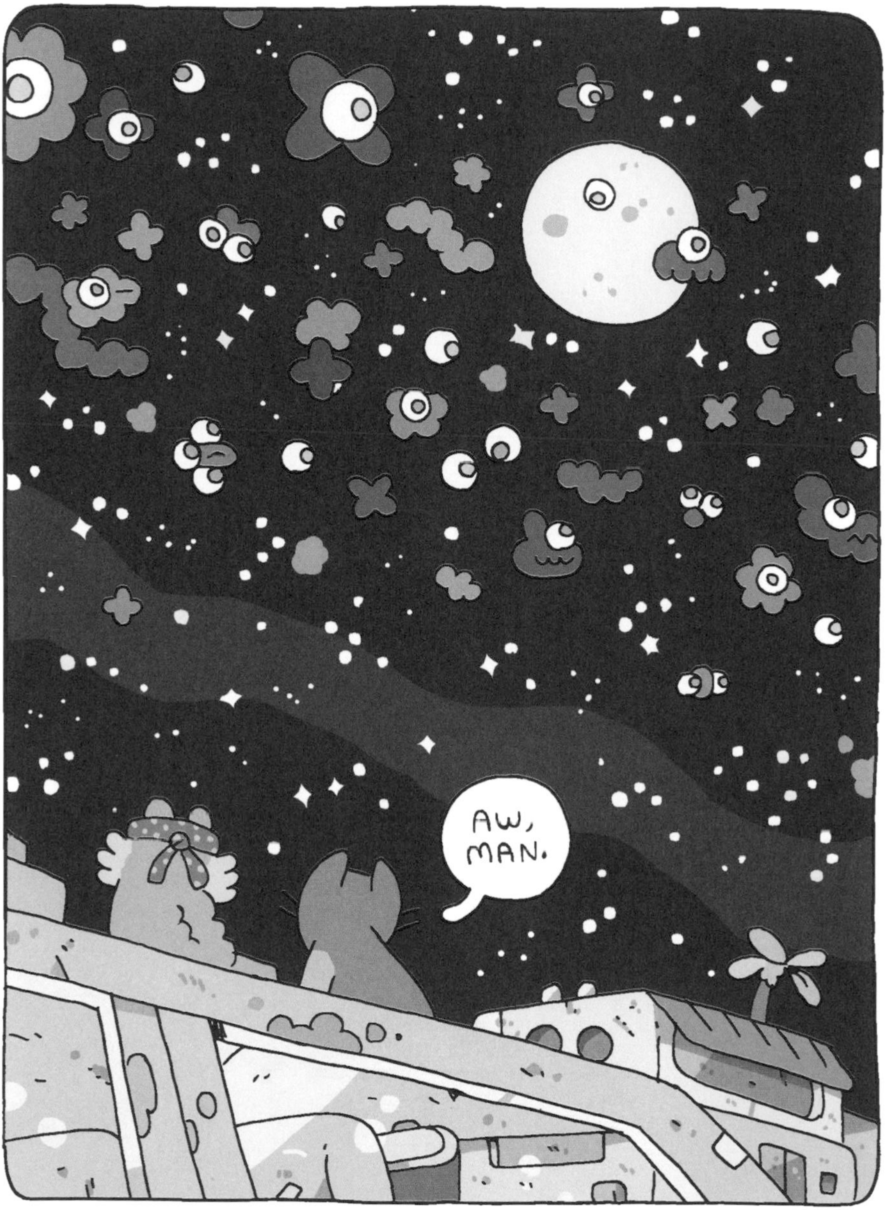
AW, MAN.

MORE HOUSECAT ADVENTURES COMING SOON!

Mason Dickerson lives in North Carolina. He has been drawing and making up stories since he was very young. He has no formal art training except for one class he took during high school, in which he received a low B. This is his first published graphic novel, and he would like to think that kid Mason would be very excited to read it. He enjoys running, making music, petting cats, petting dogs, watching movies, drinking tea, and reading.

@ @_masondickerson

1467